Sophia Karlson writes spicy, heartfelt contemporary romance—often with a dash of sass. When she's not writing, she's binge-watching the latest TV series, being walked by her beagle, planning her family's next adventure. She lives in Vancouver with her husband and children. She loves hearing from readers, and can be reached at:

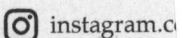 instagram.com/
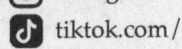 tiktok.com/

RULES DON'T APPLY IN PARADISE

SOPHIA KARLSON

One More Chapter
a division of HarperCollins*Publishers* Ltd
1 London Bridge Street
London SE1 9GF
www.harpercollins.co.uk
HarperCollins*Publishers*
Macken House, 39/40 Mayor Street Upper,
Dublin 1, D01 C9W8 Ireland

This paperback edition 2026

1

First published in Great Britain in ebook format
by HarperCollins*Publishers* 2026
Copyright © Sophia Karlson 2026
Sophia Karlson asserts the moral right to be identified
as the author of this work

A catalogue record of this book is available from the British Library
ISBN: 978-0-00-873368-1

This novel is entirely a work of fiction. The names, characters and incidents portrayed in it are the work of the author's imagination. Any resemblance to actual persons, living or dead, events or localities is entirely coincidental.

Printed and bound in the UK using 100% Renewable Electricity
by CPI Group (UK) Ltd

All rights reserved. No part of this publication may be reproduced, stored in a retrieval system, or transmitted, in any form or by any means, electronic, mechanical, photocopying, recording or otherwise, without the prior permission of the publishers.

Without limiting the exclusive rights of any author, contributor or the publisher of this publication, any unauthorised use of this publication to train generative artificial intelligence (AI) technologies is expressly prohibited. HarperCollins also exercise their rights under Article 4(3) of the Digital Single Market Directive 2019/790 and expressly reserve this publication from the text and data mining exception.

To Richard and all those Ridiculous Fridays in Dar es Salaam.

Chapter One

LEXI

I've imagined the worst thing that could happen.

I've watched it unfold in my mind's eye, sat back and played out every last possible outcome. Doing this exercise with every spin-off scenario in my head makes all of them much less likely to happen. Or so I thought. The meeting invitation currently in my inbox tells me I'm about to fly headfirst into an unforeseen shitstorm.

Unforeseen? Not quite. *Oh Dad. Is this what it felt like?* My heart seems to beat in my temple, way out of place.

There's no doubt that this is about the security video—the one where I walk in on a certain celebrity being serviced by a man whose face is buried so deep between her legs, he's basically unrecognizable.

My whole body has been in a chokehold these past two weeks, but now, somehow, I clench even more. I pull a breath in and try to exhale as the words on the screen blur. A few fast blinks at my useless tears and I refocus and read. The last thing I should do is walk around the hotel with red-rimmed eyes.

At least the head of HR is also invited to this meeting with the GM and my section head, Sheila Foster, the rooms manager. They're the whole ladder of the career I've envisioned for myself at St Chalamet Hotels and Resorts.

As rooms-manager-in-training, my office is situated underground, down with the laundry, deliveries, and all the out-of-sight hustle at a six-star hotel in the heart of Manhattan's Upper East Side. The meeting is in ten minutes in the GM's boardroom, which is on the third floor.

My desk phone rings, and I jump. It's the PA to the general manager. *Holy Mother of God...* One deep breath, and I reach for the phone with a trembling hand. "Good morning. How can I help you today?"

"Alexandra O'Reilly?"

"Yes." She knows my name; I'm in the hotel directory. Nobody else should pick up this phone. I bet she can pick me out of a prison lineup, too, being the GM's assistant. That video wouldn't have skipped *her* inbox. "Yes, it's Lexi."

"Oh, okay. Lexi. There's a meeting in seven minutes in Mr. McIntyre's boardroom. You haven't responded?"

I stare at the three options on my meeting invite. Yes. Maybe. No. *None of the above* isn't a choice. Neither is being sucked into a vacuum and hurled into outer space right now. "I'll be there."

"Good. Don't be late."

I lower the phone to its hook and take a deep breath. *The writing isn't on the wall yet.*

After another shaky breath, I stand and straighten my uniform: a tight pencil skirt and sharp suit jacket in the best quality wool, midnight blue, with two gold buttons. I close them to cover most of my white silk shirt and the *"lure of my breasts,*" as the St Chalamet staff dress code calls it—not in so many words, but I get the subtext. My fingers quiver as I smooth my shirt's collar over the jacket's and make sure the hotel's golden crest sits straight above my name pin.

I gather my wits. This situation won't—can't—get the better of me.

There's a full-length mirror behind my open office door, and for a moment, I close it to give myself the once-over. At St Chalamet, every employee must look put together, as if they might at any moment serve royalty. Today my blonde waves are captured in an elegant French roll—my secret salute to the luxury hotel chain's origins. *Perfect.* The red flush on my pale cheeks is the only thing giving away the riot in my chest.

As for the rest, I look the complete package, everything St Chalamet stands for: exclusive luxury, prestige, money, and class. I've come a long way since my first summer job as a restaurant runner when I was only fourteen, but one thing drills a hole in my head right now: I'm just an employee—one with a background that doesn't reflect any of the above.

With a shrug that does nothing to shake off my foreboding, I grab my cell phone from my desk and stride out of my office. The scent of St Chalamet's signature bergamot-and-lime detergent hangs thick down here. It's subtle, and usually I love it, but today it's as invasive as sulphur.

As I walk down the well-lit corridor to the elevators, I chant in my head, *fake it till you make it.* Or rather, *work until nobody questions your commitment or competency.* This has been my motto all my life, and so far, it's worked. I'm going to fake it for this thirty-minute meeting, too. Nothing about my exterior can show what's going on in my stomach, my head, my heart.

The elevator pings open and I step inside, relieved that I

can take the service car and avoid guests. I force my hands to still their trembling, taking one deep breath after the other.

By the time I approach the GM's boardroom, I'm outwardly calm. Yet as soon as I walk inside and three faces turn in my direction, I tighten like an animal that's stepped on a leg-hold trap.

Mr. McIntyre, the general manager, looks grayer than he did two weeks ago. In fact, everybody around the table looks as if they've had weeks of sleepless nights. I'm in good company, then.

"Lexi," Sheila says. "Take a seat."

I sink into the chair, my gaze flicking from the HR director to Sheila's downcast eyes. *Oh, God.* My stomach wants to bottom out just as nausea stirs and threatens to surge up. This is a termination meeting. It's bad—I mean I've known it's bad for days now—but they have nothing. Not really.

"Okay, Lexi. This is where we stand," Mr. McIntyre starts. He pauses, takes a deep breath and sighs. "It's been a rough two weeks. First the incident with Mia Reed and the unfortunate luck you had to walk in on her during that intimate moment—"

"As a guest, she wasn't supposed to be in that area," I interject. And luck had nothing to do with it. I'm going to fight for every inch of ground here.

"We know. Banquet halls, small or large, are off-limits to guests unless there's an event or a site visit," Mr. McIntyre says.

"And I was just doing my job." *Liar, liar, pants on fire.*

"We know." Mr. McIntyre drops his gaze, signaling he isn't buying any of my bullshit. "But you should have reported it sooner. Per company policy. We appreciate your integrity, but when it comes to this type of thing, we require full disclosure as soon as possible."

I close my eyes and bite my lip for the two seconds it takes to get a grip on the balloon blowing up in my throat. There's a reason I didn't report the incident until five days after the fact—after the hotel's security and IT systems had been breached by hackers. Even now, as I sense things are going seriously south, I can't open up and tell them *everything*.

"It would have given us a chance to wipe the security footage." Mr. McIntyre's tone is softer, and around the table, the other managers shift in their seats. "Now we have a situation."

A situation. Shit. This doesn't sound like a "clean-up on aisle four" where a bucket and mop will do the trick.

"What's the situation?" I ask, my voice uneven.

"When we were breached," Mr. McIntyre continues, "we thought the hackers were only after credit cards and guests' personal information. Now Mia Reed's agent has contacted us, saying the video footage of her and whoever, with you walking in on them, is being used for extortion."

What the actual—"You've got to be kidding me."

"I wish I were," Mr. McIntyre says on a sigh. "Our head office and IT security have been all over us this past week, trying to keep this hacking disaster out of the news. But this? This mess takes the situation to a whole new level. Who would ever trust a St Chalamet hotel again? Our integrity, our reputation, *everything* is on the line."

Yours and mine both, buddy.

I'm shaking as if I were made of Jell-O and someone was

poking and prodding at me. I always do my work with the utmost integrity, and this first mistake cuts deep. "What do you want me to do?" I can't do anything, which is killing me. I'm mid-tier management-in-training. Never mind that this is way above my pay grade, I have to stand by and watch my carefully crafted life spin out of control because of one little but very major misstep.

The HR director folds her hands together, slowly, every movement careful and somewhat rehearsed. "Alexandra..." she starts.

Ah, fuck. The way she says my name sounds like Nan when she's ticked off. Here it comes. "Are you firing me?" I say on a gulp, my mouth chalk. Everything is coming to a head, but now I realize I've watched the hurricane slowly gather and twist into full speed over the past two weeks.

"No." The HR director shakes her head. "We're asking you to resign."

"Why? The hacking disaster isn't my fault."

Mr. McIntyre leans back, and Sheila drops her gaze to the gleaming, polished wood.

"Miss O'Reilly," Mr. McIntyre says, and I shrink at the cold tone in his voice. In mere minutes he's gone from Lexi to my surname, and it's as if he's done sharpening the guillotine's blade. "For decades, St Chalamet Manhattan has been the first choice of billionaires, movie stars, celebrities, anybody really who doesn't have a place of their own in this city. This situation threatens our very existence in that almost unattainable realm of luxury." He draws in a slow, deep breath. "We are only as strong as our weakest link, and this video, your appearance in it, irrespective of your role, is currently our weakest link."

There's a weighted pause in the room as his words sink in...and sink and sink and sink.

I drag in a breath, trying not to drown in the tension in the room. I'm not only being fired because of the hacking. I'm being fired because, even though nobody would question or say a word about it, that video casts doubt over me, my integrity, and what I was really doing up in that banquet hall at eleven o'clock at night on a random Wednesday evening. My person, a mere puppet caught on video, has become the physical representation of a whole hotel group. I see it now. *If staff can walk in on a celebrity having sex, what else happens at St Chalamet?*

"Usually, we can overlook one breach of our policies with a disciplinary hearing," the HR director says, her voice cutting into the silence. "Failing to report the Mia Reed incident is your first infringement at St Chalamet."

I bite my lip, refusing to let it tremble. I knew it, of course. Every single training session, every single rulebook, every single one-on-one training with my superiors has always stressed: stick to the rules. Keep your side clean. But at the first speck of dust, I'm found out and *forced to resign*. If I told them the whole truth, I'd sweep my side clean, but my reputation would be in tatters. And I don't want to be associated with *him*. With The Head. Between Mia Reed's legs. If I had the guts and means to live without a salary, or had a new job lined up, I would have resigned to save face, but I don't, so I didn't.

"After consultation with the head office in France and our lawyers," the HR director continues, "we've decided that you may resign with a good reference from us. I'll sign off on your training, so you'll have that on your résumé as well, even though you have two months left."

What a magnanimous olive branch. Could have been worse. But they don't get it—being out of a job is the last thing I can be. I have a student loan to pay. And my best friend and roommate is heading to LA for a role she finally landed after years of auditions. Just the idea of rent makes me want to hurl. Tessa only heard she got the role two days ago. Filming starts in the new year. She'll be off to LA in two days to get settled there, and we're scrambling to make a plan with the apartment and the crazy city rent I can't afford on my own.

"I don't want to resign." I sound stubborn and somewhat childish, but there's a party of three in that video—me, Mia Reed, and the dickhead with his mouth suctioned between her thighs—and it's the women who are going pay the price.

At least Mia Reed got an orgasm out of it. I hope. I might have walked in on them, but I retreated as soon as the visual of them winded me. They didn't even notice I was there, they were so into each other. *That* hadn't been their first time. I should have known The Head would have women lined up like meat on a skewer. I know I was in the wrong, but nothing happened on video. *Nothing.* They've no proof. Maybe that's what Dad thought, and then, once the authorities started digging, there was so much of it, they had him cornered. The last thing I want is for anybody to dig into my life, least of all these people.

Maybe it's deserved, but the only thing I'm getting out of this is a boot up my ass. "I've been with St Chalamet for ten years," I say, anger sprouting. "Since my first summer job in Miami when I was fourteen. I've worked hard, every single department. I—"

"It's with immediate effect." The HR director's pointed stare challenges me to dare counterattack. "And due to the nature of the incident, we can't offer you another position within the group."

And that's the crux of the matter. The *nature of the incident* is what cuts me off at the knees. A cold chill seems to empty my blood and drain it straight to the floor. When it comes to St Chalamet, *I'm done?*

"To be honest, Lexi," the HR director says, "there's no knowing whether Mia Reed will pay to keep the video from leaking on the internet. Either way, as the only employee possibly recognizable in that video, we can't afford to have someone identify you and link you to St Chalamet. Right now, nobody can guess that the video is security footage from the Manhattan St Chalamet. We need to keep it that way for our reputation's sake." She pushes a white, letter-sized envelope in my direction, the hotel's crest embossed in gold foil in one corner. "Here's some paperwork you need to sign. Please go through it and have it back to me by tomorrow."

Mr. McIntyre stands, and the others follow suit. "Thank you."

"Sheila will see you to your office to pack up," the HR director says. "IT has blocked you from all our systems during this meeting, so you won't have access to anything anymore. Sheila will make sure you leave your badge and see you out. Please...don't make us ask for a security escort."

The GM and HR director file out of the room, leaving me glued to my chair, Sheila kneading the backrest of her own.

"What the hell? Sheila?" Tears sting my eyes.

"I can't talk to you." Her eyes flick to the ever-present security camera in the corner of the boardroom. "I'm so sorry. Let me see you out."

My gaze holds hers in awe. "This is such a joke." Sheila

might be my direct manager, but after countless coffees and chats, I consider her a friend. We're never going to talk about what really happened. This is it.

Sheila sucks her lip and shakes her head. "Company policy."

I stand so abruptly that my chair topples as I grab the stupid envelope. Sheila catches the chair before it can clang to the hardwood floor. Her fingers tremble as much as my own.

My last shred of dignity is the only thing that convinces me to put one foot in front of the other, leading the way back to the elevators with my back ramrod straight. By the time we reach my office, Sheila is huffing and puffing to keep up with me. I'm basically running in my heels to keep my emotions in check.

"Lexi." Sheila's hand finds my arm as we enter my office. I watch her gaze flick to the corners where security cameras usually keep an eye on things, but there are none in my dungeon. There was only one in the small banquet hall, but it got Mia's face, her spread legs, and The Head in a perfect angled view. And me. *All* of me in my idiotic glory, stripping my jacket, my one hand heading for the top button of my blouse. Sheila swallows hard. "I know this is horrible. Honestly—"

"What am I going to do?" This is wrongful dismissal, isn't it? I can fight it, but I know I won't. The situation is too embarrassing. Too personal. My case too thin. "St Chalamet has been my whole career. You know I have my student loan to pay—"

"I believe they've provided a three-month bonus payout. It's all in there." She points to the envelope in my hand. "It will buy you some time. The only advice I have is to get out. Get away. When the shit hits the fan, you're not going to want to be here. Not in Manhattan, not in the state. Maybe not even in the US."

I chuckle, but it's laced with a sob that threatens to crack my chest open. "What do you suggest? That I apply for a job at St Chalamet Seychelles? Or should I aim for Bali?" I swallow as she drops her gaze. *That's never going to happen,* her stance says. Both those resorts were on my work-goals bucket list, but I'm never going to work for St Chalamet again.

With determined strides, I move behind my desk. My PC and laptop are gone. They weren't messing around. I open the desk drawers and gather my neatly arranged personal things. Sheila's gaze follows my every move, until I have placed everything in a St Chalamet laundry bag I have on hand.

I hook my purse over my shoulder. My work phone vibrates in my jacket pocket, and we both still.

"I'll have to take that call," Sheila says, holding out her hand.

I pass my phone to her, not bothering to check the screen.

"You've got your personal phone? Do you need any numbers from this one?"

"That wouldn't be allowed now, would it?" The snark in my voice cuts through the tension in the room. "I have my personal phone."

"Good." Sheila meets my gaze, the phone still buzzing. "I'll keep you posted."

We're more than colleagues. We're *friends*.

"Don't bother. I'll see myself out." I hold my hotel security badge out to her as I grab my coat from the hook on the wall.

I battle to put it on with the laundry bag and my purse swinging everywhere.

I'm halfway down the corridor when Sheila's footsteps fall in behind me. We ride the elevator in silence and stop on the first floor, which has the back entrance for staff. This is so embarrassing. Never in my life did I think my perfect career at St Chalamet would end like *this*. I was supposed to travel the world with them, work my way up and *be* something. Something bigger, something *more*. Worst of all is, deep down I know I can only blame myself.

Sheila escorts me all the way to the exit. "What are you going to do now?" she asks.

"I don't know. Digest? Drink myself into a coma? Leave the city? Go home to Miami? Somewhere where rent and ramen don't eat through my three months' thank-you-for-fucking-off money?"

"Oh, God. Lexi."

No more *Oh, Gods*. I rush out into the late-November gray and speed all the way to Fifth Avenue, strangling my emotions one by one. This isn't going to mess with my head. By the time I've crossed into Central Park, I'm flushed with all the brainwork my head's been doing to distract me.

Numbers. Mine aren't looking good. I can hardly afford rent as it is; without a job, Manhattan is a big no-no. There will be seasonal jobs available, what with December and Christmas upon us, but I don't want to be Santa's little helper. I'm not in the mood.

I slump down on a bench and dig my phone out of my purse. I only hesitate for five seconds before I press Evan's number.

My brother answers in two rings. "Hey, Pickle, if this is

about Mom's Christmas gift, I still haven't made up my mind. I know you said you can't spend more than fifty bucks, but I can chip in more. You know I can."

I love my brother to bits, but his nickname for me is so on point that tears finally spill over. "Dammit, Evan. I'm in a pickle. For real this time."

Chapter Two

LEXI

"Sounds like wrongful dismissal to me, surely?" Evan says after I've explained in broad strokes that I've been politely forced to resign.

I spared him most of the details—no, I spared myself. I skipped the parts about Mia Reed and the extortion. The less the word gets out, the better, and I have an NDA with the hotel group that would still stand, employee or not. That NDA covers my appearance in that video too, and to be honest, I want to keep it under wraps. "Please don't push for me to get a lawyer and yada yada yada."

"Why not?"

"I just can't." Because I am in the wrong. I crossed a line.

"Ooh-kay..." Evan's voice trails off as he starts typing, his keyboard clacking away. "Whatever. Only you can do it, and I know not to push you. At least it means you can be home for Christmas for a change?"

A silver lining. For some. Christmas is always crazy busy in this industry, and it's all hands on deck. Work is my perfect excuse to avoid a family gathering that will only remind me of what we've lost forever. "Yeah."

"I'm booking you a plane ticket. Tomorrow's good?"

Bless Evan. He makes decisions on the spot with zero fuss. It's hardly lunchtime, and the full impact of my situation has yet to hit me. "The apartment—"

"Tessa's moving out. You complained two days ago about how you need a decent roommate and finding someone would take more time than you can afford. Just give it up. Come stay with me and save on rent until you've figured life out."

Not having the woes of city rent on my plate will make a huge difference. I don't have to be in Manhattan anymore. I sink into the bench, nestling my chin into my coat's collar. I'm getting cold now that I'm sitting still. "I suppose I can do that."

"You suppose you can do that?" Evan teases. "Let me add an incentive: I solemnly promise to have zero dirty socks lying around, and to pick up my towels."

I crack a small smile. He knows me so well. "Fine."

"Cool. Pack your stuff. Put what you need to keep in storage and come take a breather. You haven't had a break in like... How long have you been working for St Chalamet?"

Ten ungrateful years. "Too long."

"Yeah, probably. Only one thing. Tris is going to be here too at some point."

My stomach flips. "Tris?"

"Yeah. You remember Tristan."

"Yes." He's hard to forget. "When?"

"I dunno. When his ship sails in. Literally." Evan is typing again. "He usually gives me a heads up a day before. I'm not sure how long he'll stay this time. It all depends on his filming schedule."

Oh, Holy Mother of God and all the saints in a row. "Okay." The perfect solution just got a skid mark.

Plus, this is all so vague and out of my comfort zone. I like my life organized. Controlled routine. Clean bedlinen twice a week. Things in their place. Tristan Martinelli will mess with any peace I can rake together at Evan's place. Best I be gone before he walks into Evan's house. If he stays only for a couple of days, I can fake going to see Dad over that time.

Though nobody is going to buy *that*. Now if only I had the funds, I'd fly to Alaska and stay with Mom. "I'll come visit, but beyond that, I'll have to think everything through. Can I call you later?"

"Sure, Pickle. This is a bump in your road. You'll see. I'd love to have you over for as long as you need."

"Thanks, Ev." I kill the call and stare at the screen for a long moment, my fingertips white with cold. A wave of relief crashes over me. I have a plan—for now.

When his ship sails in. Tristan Martinelli. My teenage crush who crushed me.

I shouldn't. Not today of all days.

Be strong, Lexi. I bite my lip, nostrils flaring as I try to contain the urge to snoop.

The lure is too strong. I'm a sucker for punishment and addicted to my phone as much as the next person. I swipe to open Instagram and swap my private Lexi O'Reilly profile for my incognito user1234sqwerty one.

User1234sqwerty has no posts, zero followers, and follows only one person. Tristan Martinelli. Marine biologist. Ocean photographer. He has over half a million followers, and I am officially his online stalker. Probably not the only one.

Not that he would know. Or care. I glance over his grid.

The past two weeks have been too hectic for me to check in. And for two months before that, I was seeing someone, sooo... I haven't been here for a while.

There are new posts, but essentially nothing has changed. Tristan is standing by a boat railing, the deep blue sea in the background, a beer in hand, his wetsuit stripped to his hips. Lording over a six-pack. Broad, muscled shoulders. Biceps. Pecs. Dark wavy hair still wet from the sea and brushed back from his high forehead. He smiles, revealing perfect teeth between those lickable lips set off by a golden Caribbean tan.

Next to him, the ever-present bikini babe. All thin straps, boobs, and bronzed skin. Highlights in her hair. Basically, woman on Instaroids. Her wetsuit is down to her curvy hips too, and they are raising their drinks in a toast. She, of course, is having water or a spritzer or a zero-calorie cooler. Whatever is girly.

There aren't many photos of him. Most are underwater photography shots and reels, depicting schools of fish and whales and magic. But when you go to where people have tagged him in their posts, every single one features a female by his side.

Enough torture for one day. I close the app and stand, gathering my stuff. Time to go home and break the news to Tessa. She'll be there, packing.

By the time I take the stairs to our third-floor shoebox, I'm on the verge of a meltdown. I'm not a fan of change, especially not when it's forced on me. I've been through that too many times. Now, my life in the city has been upended in two short weeks.

I unlock the door and toss my stuff to the floor as soon as I'm inside.

"Lexi?" Tessa's voice sounds from her room, uncertain and cautious.

"It's me."

Tessa appears in her bedroom doorway, eyes wide. "What're you doing here?"

"I got fired."

"What?" Her voice spikes in disbelief and she rushes toward me, her long, ink-black hair bobbing on her head in a messy bun. "Fired for what?"

"The video."

"Oh. My. God."

"Yeah. Turns out the hackers got hold of the clip and are trying to extort money out of Mia Reed." I've already said too much, but this is Tessa, my bestie since our first stint that summer when we both were only fourteen and worked as runners at the breakfast buffet, clearing and setting tables at the St Chalamet in Miami.

Tessa claps her hands to her mouth, her eyes saucers. "What? Oh my gawd!"

"I know. My timing always sucks." But this time, the universe went that extra mile. I hold out the letter-sized envelope to her, now a bit wrinkled where my anxious grip has dented the paper. "The details are all in here."

Tessa shakes her head as she leads me to our worn sofa. "Come sit. I'll make us tea."

I don't sit down. Everything is suddenly too tight. "I'm going to take my uniform off."

"Yes. Do that. Those assholes."

In my bedroom, I glance over the life I've patched together in the two years I've been in New York. It's sparse, but neat and clean. It won't take long to box up everything, and I'm happy for Tessa to have our shared belongings, as it's mostly kitchen stuff we bought together. Living costs in LA are cheaper than in New York, but she's going to have to find her feet. As for the bigger pieces of furniture, some of them came with the apartment, and most of it we could let go.

I unclasp my hotel pin and name badge and, as habit dictates, put them in the little bowl on my bedside table. Relics of wasted dreams. Note to self: never sell your soul to a company again. They don't fucking care. I strip and hang up my uniform, which I normally would have left at the hotel. Old habits die hard, and the St Chalamet management uniforms may only be dry cleaned, a service the hotel offers its staff because pay in the industry isn't exactly fabulous.

I put on some sweatpants and a tank top and push my feet into the ridiculous monster Minion slippers Tessa got me for Christmas two years ago. Now they only remind me that I'm a cog in someone else's machine and got spat out for being caught on camera walking in on my ex making a meal of a celebrity's pussy.

I don't think I've ever felt that insignificant before. Maybe once, that night on the roof... I fist my hands, my nails cutting into my palms. I can't let this get to me.

Brush it off, Lexi. I'm Miss Sunshine on most days. For all I know, this is the beginning of something bigger and better.

Right.

Tears are streaming down my cheeks by the time I drop onto the sofa and rip open the St Chalamet envelope. I pull out the stack of papers as Tessa comes into the living room from our small kitchen, the perfume of jasmine tea scenting the air.

"Here." She puts down the tray and sits next to me with a soft squeeze to my shoulder. "What does it say?"

I'm glancing through the pages but can't make sense of it, as my mind is all over the place. "I dunno." I hand her the stack and reach for a cup of tea. I slouch back with a sigh and sip quietly.

Tessa scans the pages. "This is more like a restructuring package. There's a three-month payout, and they're not stopping your health benefits either."

"Thank God for small mercies."

"And here's a non-disclosure agreement. Mia Reed... extortion...blah-blah-blah, privacy... *Pfft*," Tessa says on a huff. "They should have forced you to sign it this morning. Just shows they're a bunch of idiots."

I sit straighter. "I already have a non-disclosure agreement with them in place." One I've breached a few times with Tessa. Sometimes the gossip is too juicy to revel in alone, but I trust my roomie. Nothing will go beyond these four walls.

"This one is specific to the video incident," Tessa says. "There might be a few new clauses."

"Ugh."

She tosses the papers onto the coffee table. "You've got to tell him, Lexi."

"No." I sound so resolute, my voice rattles me a bit. Tessa is the only one who knows I recognized The Head.

"It's your *job*! You got fired or restructured or whatever the heck this is because of *his* actions. He's getting away with proverbial murder here."

"What would it even help?" In my mind, snitching will only tarnish *me*.

We have a staring contest for a moment, but I'm the one to look away first.

"Who knows how it would help, Lexi. Stop being such a pushover."

Her words hit several nerves, riling me up. "We didn't have the talk about being exclusive." *Firstly. Secondly, he blindsided me so hard—*

"What the hell, Lexi? There's *having the talk about being exclusive* and then there's sucking off a celebrity guest at work and being caught on camera. If he were still at St Chalamet, he'd be on his knees begging you to keep quiet."

She's right. And I'm an idiot. A few weeks ago, I was still in the throes of a crush on Brent Fisherman, late thirties, hot as all fuck, and so sure of himself as the second in command to the general manager. Staff at St Chalamet isn't supposed to fraternize or date, for obvious reasons. How many would sneak off and have sex in empty rooms or other corners of the hotel if it were par for the course? Enough that the hotel would malfunction.

What Brent knew, and I didn't, was that he was being headhunted by a Chinese five-star hotel group and had been negotiating his flamboyant exit for months. During his last weeks at St Chalamet, he toyed with me—after hours and never at St Chalamet. At work, our interactions—to my infatuation-frazzled mind—were super cute and flirty when out of earshot, but utterly professional everywhere else. I can see the game he played now, but at the time I was too flattered to be the center of his attention, to *mean so much to him* and to be the *perfect girl* and know he'd *never dated someone this hot*. God. He'd sussed out my every insecurity, and I'd fed into it as if I were starving. He was gone the day after I walked in on Mia Reed. Not only because Brent Fisherman is a dick, but he's also the owner of The Head between Mia Reed's thighs.

If someone's head should roll...

What game were they playing? I mean, it's almost as if they wanted to get caught on camera. For the two months I was Brent's secret seasonal flavor—his pumpkin spice latte, to be exact—I didn't pick up on any exhibitionist vibes. But he knew the ins and outs of the security system at the hotel, and they should have been able to skirt them all, playing hide-and-go-seek.

I was the idiot who took him up on his first and only invitation to meet him in that banquet room, late at night, after the press and other influencers who came to interview Mia Reed, had left.

It's one thing to have something going with another staff member off site. To have the blind infatuation to think Brent Fisherman called me up to the banquet room for a little tryst because he couldn't keep his hands off me after a long day of subtle teasing and not-so-subtle innuendo was pure, undiluted idiocy.

Me, men, and idiocy. The perfect trifecta of shame.

I close my eyes with a groan. "No. Brent's gone to Beijing. There's no point." Nobody there is going to care what happened at a hotel on this side of the planet. I was an idiot for falling for him in the first place. Pointing out that he was involved with Mia Reed would only unearth my secret affair with him and put me in a terrible light. I can't have that blight added to my reputation *now*—it's hanging by a thread as it is, and HR would change St Chalamet's squeaky-clean referral if they knew. They might have their suspicions, but they're only suspicions and must stay that way. At that thought, I blurt out, "I'm leaving New York."

Tessa blinks. "To go where?"

"Evan said I can stay with him until I've sorted myself out with a new job."

"Okay." She nods in thought. "Honestly, it's for the best. Can you imagine the circus if Mia Reed doesn't pay them and that video hits social media?" Tessa shakes her head as a pit opens deep in my gut. *That* is literally the last thing I need, and at the thought a cold fever spreads over my skin. "You have to admit, she has a bit of an unconventional approach to self-marketing, and right now, this could find the mark perfectly for her."

Don't I know it. Mia Reed is famous for two things: being a brilliant actress—rumor has it she'll be nominated for an Oscar again next year, for a remake of *Dangerous Liaisons* no less—and for a sexting scandal when she hit her first Hollywood high three years ago in another steamy role.

I suck on my lip. Chances are slim, but they are there, that Mia Reed will decide, *Screw it, let the world have an eyeful of me. It's not as if they haven't seen it before.*

It would be a circus. The video would go viral. *I* would be all over social media. *My face* linked to a nationwide—even worldwide—sex scandal. My jacket slipping from my arm. My hand traveling up to my top button. *Guilty for all to see.*

Dad. Oh God.

I've experienced the media circus that could follow in the aftermath of breaking the rules once before. Yes, it wasn't me, and it wasn't a sex scandal, but once, even indirectly and vaguely similar, is enough to last a lifetime.

"What if I get recognized?" I choke out. I'm already so filled with tension that it has nowhere to go. Suddenly I understand why this whole situation is shaking me to the core: *I can't go through that again.*

Whichever way you choose to interpret my actions in that video, that I'm potential collateral damage wouldn't even come up in Mia Reed's thought process when she considers paying the hackers or not. At least St Chalamet had the guts to cut ties with me before and not after, giving me a clean slate, for what it's worth.

"Girly..." Tessa trails off. "What are the chances?"

I shake my head. Slim to none, to two hundred percent. That's the type of luck I have.

"Honestly, Miami would be good." Tessa reaches for my hand and squeezes hard. "You'll find work easily. Any hospitality company would love to have you."

Her affirmation echoes Sheila's from earlier this morning. *Don't stay in New York; things could become nasty fast.* Finding a job is my biggest concern, as it's difficult to break into the five-star orbit, never mind the most exclusive tier where St Chalamet exists. I crawled my way into it and had planned to stick around until retirement.

"When are you leaving?" Tessa asks. "You're giving up the apartment? It's the logical thing to do."

"It's a mess. We should have given notice." I can't even think anymore. Not with the anxiety that comes from every potential outcome pressing on my chest, nausea roiling in my belly.

"This happens all the time," she assures me. "They have a waiting list for this block. Finding someone is the least of our worries."

We both sigh in relief.

"I'm going to start packing." I finish my tea. I need to deal with the whiplash of my morning in the quiet of my room, preferably starting with vomiting my heart out.

Chapter Three
LEXI

Ten days later, my old life is roadkill that's been picked up by the garbage truck somewhere in the night. Evan is the perfect person for me to hang out with right now—optimistic, ridiculously chilled, and in charge of my *recovery*, as he calls it, which includes lounging by his pool and sipping mojitos most of the time. Now that I've been forced to slow down, I realize how much I needed a break.

Evening is upon us and the sun has set. Evan is heating up his barbecue for burgers. I'm on his laptop, scouring the internet for a job—any job. We've spruced up my résumé, so I'm ready to rock and roll.

So far nothing more has happened with the Mia Reed video and being away from the St Chalamet environment makes me believe it was all just a horrible nightmare. The shock has ebbed. I always knew I was easy to replace. Even my ever-present anxiety has taken a partial hike. And yet my eyes stray ever farther from jobs in the USA. I've started looking at

Europe, Southeast Asia, and even Australia. How far and incognito can I really get?

When moments of panic strike, which they do in sudden surges out of nowhere, the other side of the planet looks very enticing. It won't be forever, and I'd always planned to go places through my work. Maybe this whole situation is the catalyst to kick me out of my comfort zone.

Evan comes to sit on the deck chair next to mine and reaches for his beer. "You finding anything?"

"My dream job." I pass him the laptop and lean back with a sigh, picking up my finished mojito and rattling the ice to coax one last sip out of it.

"An island off an island off the coast of East Africa?" Evan shoots me a glance. "Sounds like a schlep. You can get the same thing in the Caribbean."

Not exactly. This ticks other boxes for me. It's very far away, WiFi is dubious, and it's in a different time zone. The shit could hit the fan, and I would only know about it later, *if* I cared to look.

I know the exact moment when Evan opens the resort's website because he draws in a sharp breath. "Wow. Exclusive much?"

"Oh yeah. Ne'emba Island is a Beaumont property. They're on par with St Chalamet, if not more exclusive. The hotel group isn't in the US, but it has boutique hotels and resorts all over the rest of the world."

"This looks like something else." He keeps scrolling, and I lean over to see what he's looking at on the screen. "Paradise redefined."

"Basically. It's barefoot and relaxed." This is nothing like the extremes of the massive St Chalamet resorts of the

Caribbean. The bungalows at Ne'emba have palm leaves as part of the walls.

"Would be a bit of a mind shift—"

"I can do with that right now." In fact, over the past few days, I've become like a black crayon who's discovered there are other colors in the box. Imagine not having to work in high heels! I secretly hyperventilate a little, but they say change is as good as a holiday, and since I've been flung on this path of *rediscovery*, I might as well go all out. With ten years' experience, I have options.

"Ooh-kay. Here it is," Evan says. "The coral reefs around the island are designated as a World Heritage Site. Only topped by the Great Barrier Reef. Jeez. I didn't know that, and I thought I knew all that stuff."

"It has to be recent."

"And they're the only property with diving rights around these atolls?" Evan smirks. "I'd love to know how that works."

He's on the page now with underwater photos. Each one in there reminds me of Tristan, the snag in my time here that's yet to materialize. I've stopped holding my breath. "It's only a three-month contract though," I say. "They close the resort for two months over April and May as it's the rainy season." Good thing too. I'm not one for cyclones and hurricanes. I've already had my fill, and even a strong wind can reduce my stomach to a pulsing ulcer of anxiety. "It looks like they're looking for a stopgap. Or it's a probation period, but…"

"But?"

"The position is for a managerial couple. The gig isn't geared for singles." Which is too bad. It would have been the perfect solution to my problem and the perfect escape.

Especially since the contract runs until early April—way past the Oscars and any rogue Mia Reed promotional stunts.

It would give me time to look for something else while I hunker down on an island in the middle of nowhere, but the biggest lure for me? It could give me a foot in the door at Beaumont Hotels. I've been on and off on the Beaumont website all day, and it's like dipping in and out of a fairytale with all the gorgeous chateaux they own in Europe. St Chalamet is American classy, like Jackie Kennedy. Beaumont is the original Coco Chanel.

"Come on, Lexi, this looks fantastic. Don't let a minor detail put you off. Where's the job description?" Evan asks, pulling me from my thoughts. "With your work experience, you can easily manage an über-exclusive twelve-room resort without an extra pair of hands."

I laugh at his tone and point at the webpage. "It's there." For a moment, I lean back and stare at the stars shining through the Miami haze, dipping into the dream of going to Ne'emba Island. Crickets start up their nightly song. I'm still getting used to the nature noises and relative quiet of this suburb. Imagine falling asleep at night to the caressing rise and retreat of ocean waves...

Evan is quiet, and I loll my head to the side to watch him. He closes the laptop, seeming deep in thought.

"What is it?" I ask.

"They're looking for a managerial couple because one half runs the hotel, and the other half runs the dive center. Apparently three dives a day are included in their all-inclusive package. Two daytime dives and an optional night dive for overeager folks."

Hmm... I saw that. Literally glanced over it and zoned out. "Yep. There's no chance in hell. I'll keep looking tomorrow."

"Lexi." Evan clears his throat. "Hear me out."

"What?"

"Tristan would give a kidney to spend three months on that island. Trust me."

"What?" I chuckle as I sit straighter. "A kidney?" I might have wanted Tristan's cock at some point, but his kidneys he can keep.

"Oh yes." Evan studies my face. "You know he's a marine biologist, right? He got his doctorate a couple of years ago."

It's *Dr.* Tristan Martinelli now? That's news, but I'm not sure why I'm surprised. The last time I saw him he'd been wrapping up his master's degree. He didn't blast his doctorate all over the internet, and it's not as if I'd google him. His Instagram account is all I need to get my fix.

Evan leaves the comment hanging for me to probe further.

"Good for him." I stand, refusing to take the bait. I don't want to dig deeper into why Tristan would give up a kidney on a whim. "Isn't your grill ready?"

I walk through the sliding doors to the kitchen and pour myself a glass of water, which I guzzle down. I pluck the salad ingredients from the fridge and throw stuff together, listening to Evan move around and lift the grill's hood. Seconds later, raw meat sizzles.

"When did you last see Tristan?" he calls from the veranda.

Five years. Two months. Give or take a few days. I'd just turned nineteen. "I dunno!"

Evan walks into the kitchen, picks a cherry tomato out of the salad and pops it in his mouth.

"Oi! Fingers out of my salad!"

"It must be years?" Evan says around the tomato. "You know, he's still exactly the same."

Which means he's a total dick.

"You two used to get along so well. Sometimes I thought he hung out with me because of you."

"Dream on, Ev. Tristan hung out with you because he didn't want to be at home. I came with the house."

Evan laughs as he opens the fridge and takes out another beer. "And here I thought you were crushing on him like a lovesick teenager."

Ugh. Gag. Uggggh. Why was I so easy to read back then? I might have been nineteen the last time I'd seen Tristan, but I've known him since we moved to Miami and he became best friends with Evan.

Evan winks at me as he strolls back to the grill and flips the burgers.

"He was hot," I call. "I crushed like every other girl who laid eyes on him." No need to deny it. Hormones are a fact of life. And Tristan is *still* hot. Another fact of life.

For a moment it's quiet as Evan focuses on the grill and I finish the salad. I put the bowl and everything else we need on a tray and head for the outdoor table. Best I steer this conversation back to safer waters. "Why would Dr. Tristan Martinelli, marine biologist—who probably spends so much time in salt water he's basically cured meat—give a kidney to spend three months running a dive center in the middle of butt-crack nowhere?"

Evan's mouth splits into a wide grin, and he laughs—the hearty, full-belly laugh of someone who's enjoying the moment way too much. "Because he's in a pickle."

"Ah, buzz off." I claim propriety rights to that nickname,

situation, and *no*—I don't do pickles on my burger. I'm one of those people who tells them *no pickles, please* at the McDonald's drive-thru.

"Nope, he's in a tight spot."

Freaking Evan. He's toying with me, reeling me in like little Nemo on a hook. I cave. "Why?"

"He's been working for years on a TV series about ocean life—a David Attenborough type of thing, but not *grandiose*. It focuses on symbiosis in the oceans, the break in the chain due to pollution and the oceans warming up. You know, that kind of thing."

I don't know, but my interest is piqued. "And?"

"He's running out of time and money."

I snort. "And how is this my problem?"

"This job could give him the break he needs. Imagine three months in a marine reserve where he'd be able to film and dive, all expenses paid? I can imagine that as a World Heritage Site those coral reefs must be untouched, in perfect condition, still supporting life and biodiversity."

I stare at him. The passion in his voice catches me off guard. "Why do you care so much?"

"Because I want him to succeed. He's pumped everything he has into this over the past five years. He's on an environmental trailblazing mission and doing something selfless." Evan takes a drink of his beer. "And I've seen his first few completed episodes. They're fantastic."

Okay. Maybe I've seen some of the footage on Tristan's reels. They're breathtaking, to say the least. "Why's he running out of time?"

Evan exhales. "He sold his series to a streaming service

based on the first two completed episodes. He needs to deliver the rest next year or the deal will fall through."

I hitch a brow. "And?"

"Mother Nature hasn't been playing along, and he's running behind, with no options going forward." He reaches for an empty plate and flips the burgers again. "Three months —imagine all the images and footage he'd be able to take."

"Technically he'd be working. Running a dive center? Making sure guests who pay thousands of dollars a night are happy?" I'm talking as if this could be a reality right now, in full visualization mode. "He won't be able to spend all his time underwater taking photos and whatnot."

Evan smiles. "But he'll make the most of it."

That he will. I take a deep breath and huff it out. "Wow, just look at you, fabricating a whole scenario here. You forget that Tristan needs a better half to get this gig, a better half who knows how to run a hotel, and that isn't going to be me."

"And there I thought you said Ne'emba Island was your *dream job*," he deadpans, eyebrows hitched.

Our gazes lock, and I clench my teeth. I'm not sure Evan understands what he's suggesting we do to get this job. Being coupled didn't seem like a suggestion on the website. It seemed like a requirement. And after the St Chalamet disaster, mixing men with work sounds like a terrible idea. In fact, Lexi O'Reilly's rule #1 for any new job should be *male co-workers are off the menu. Permanently.* "I think the burgers are ready."

With a shrug, Evan plates the meat and closes the grill. We settle at the table, my throat suddenly parched for a very strong drink.

"When's Tristan coming?" I ask, breaking the silence.

Evan looks down at his plate as he squirts ketchup on his burger. "I don't know."

"Before Christmas?"

"That was the plan."

I still have time.

We eat in silence. I peck at my salad, trying to ignore the seed that Evan's planted in my head. *Nope, nope, nope. Not going there. Even though it's perfect. So freaking perfect.*

"It won't be for forever, you know," Evan says between bites. "Just three months. And afterwards you'll have the experience on your résumé and a foot in the door with Beaumont Hotels."

"Whatever. It's such a long shot, and the position is probably filled already. It's for January."

"And yet they're still advertising it on the biggest hotel-industry recruitment site."

"What are you suggesting, Ev?" It's madness. Must I attach myself to Tristan—fake being a couple, married, engaged, whatever—to get a job? My dream job? To Dr. Tristan Martinelli?

Hell no.

"Sleep on it. That's all."

What a joke. I won't sleep at all tonight.

Chapter Four

TRISTAN

I coast my rental the last twenty yards to Evan's house. It's early morning, hardly light, but I know I'll catch him as he heads out for his morning run. I park and lean back in my seat, tired as fuck. Evan knows I'm coming today, but he expects me later. I should have spent the night on the boat, but instead I packed up and headed here. After a month out at sea, I need a decent shower and coffee that doesn't taste like mold.

I drag my hand over my face, where five days of stubble is finally beyond the itch phase. Still, it's got to go. *Now*. I look at his front door, which opens as if on cue. Evan steps out in his running gear, setting his exercise watch. I pop the car door open, and he glances up.

"Bro!" He jogs down the stairs as I get out of the car.

"We came in last night. I reek."

"You do." He chuckles but pulls me in for a bro-hug.

"I know I'm early—"

"It's awesome. Welcome home. Good trip?"

His laidback attitude is just what I need right now. "Yeah, mostly."

"Help you carry?"

"Sure, thanks." Every seat in my rental is covered with boxed equipment—seriously expensive stuff that I can't leave out on the street, even if this neighborhood has zero problems in that department.

Between us we make quick work of the plastic containers and other bags with my cameras and cases, my wetsuits and diving kit, and the duffel bag with my clothes.

"I'll grab us some croissants on my way back," Evan says as we hover at the door. "There are eggs and bacon in the fridge, if you can't wait."

"Thanks." I drag a hand through my hair. It needs a cut, too. "Thanks for letting me camp out here for a while." *Again*.

"You're welcome any time. Stay as long as you like."

Evan has always been the one person in my life I can count on. "Thanks."

"Eh...one thing," Evan says. "You'll be in the smaller room for now—the one with the single bed." He's busy with his watch again, not looking me in the eye. "Lexi's here, and she's sleeping in the main guest room."

My pulse stutters. *Lexi? Crap.* "Okay, cool." Good to know. Minutes ago I was planning to shower and collapse in the double bed where she must be sleeping.

"I had the foresight to move your stuff before she came."

"Cool. Thanks." Evan's place has been my base for the past year, ever since I gave up my apartment to spend more time at sea. Financially and logistically, it made more sense. Plus, I didn't have the bandwidth to keep up an apartment I hardly ever spent time in.

"Make yourself at home. I'll see you in a minute."

More like an hour. "Enjoy. I'll come with you tomorrow morning." My body could do with the freedom of a road run after weeks in a contained space.

I have keys to his house, but the door is still open since we parked everything in the foyer. I close it and lean back, taking a deep, slow inhale and exhale as I groan at the equipment I keep hauling around. I'm so close, yet the past twelve months have felt like trying to shoot a target that's racing away in the opposite direction. I was supposed to be done by now, only focusing on the post-production stages of my last episodes, but instead I'm scrambling.

Our biggest setback came in July, when our sponsor's boat capsized in a storm and I lost three months of footage in the process. Nobody got hurt, which is a lot to be thankful for, but I'm feeling the pressure. Morale is at an all-time low. With my own funds depleted, I have no clue how I'm going to wrap this project up without begging.

I haven't begged for years.

I peel myself off the front door, find my duffel bag with my clothes, and soft-foot it to the room Evan told me to use. It shares a bathroom with my usual bedroom, which is the last room in the corridor. Lexi's room for now. What is she even doing here? She's a big-city, career-focused woman, and I haven't seen her in years. She's been climbing that corporate ladder with a determination that would give most people vertigo, and working hours other teenagers and students would scoff at.

Jesus Christ, that's going to be an awkward reunion—one I've always kind of avoided. It was easier. On her. On me. On how fucking crap I still feel years down the line.

I close my bedroom door softly and head straight for the closet and my clothes. I pick a clean T-shirt from the neat pile Evan's housekeeper—no doubts there—has stacked them in and press it to my nose. Nothing screams land to me more than the scent of fabric softener. I know. Deep down I'm a baby, but it's the small things that make me feel at home. My toiletries are in a plastic bag, and I reach for them as I look over at the closet's hanging space, eyeing my suits and business shirts, which have been ironed to perfection. *Begging clothes.*

It's going to have to happen before Christmas or else I'm totally fucked. Everything in me revolts at the idea. With a groan I reach for a pair of worn jeans. I might take a day off first. Eat some fresh salad and healthy shit. And steak. A Tomahawk should do the trick. Catch an actual nap in a bed that doesn't sway with the waves. Not that I'll fall asleep easily; there are always a few days of adjustment.

I slip into the bathroom and close the door softly. Signs of Lexi are everywhere. A row of beauty products on the vanity shelf, a pink toothbrush, a hairbrush with a tangle of blonde strands. A purple bikini hung to drip-dry in the shower. It's still wet, so I hang it over the bath's faucet.

Nothing about this is new, strange, or abnormal. Only...this stuff is *hers.*

I turn on the shower, giving it a moment to start steaming before I strip. I aim to toss my clothes in the laundry basket, only to hold back at the last millisecond because it's almost full. A pair of dark blue lace panties clings to life on the edge, half in, half out. A matching bra is hooked over the rim, one boob in, one boob out.

Things I don't need to see. A reaction my body isn't supposed to have. *Fuck it.* I suppress a groan and step under the shower, relishing the sting of the heat on my skin, the way it almost scalds and zaps the inappropriate thoughts of Lexi straight from my head.

Except the message doesn't make it all the way south. It's been too long.

I palm my erection. I was looking forward to this—a moment without an audience at such close quarters you can smell each other. Sometimes a guy just wants to savor the release, but it isn't going to be today. I'm done in record time and brace against the tiled wall, letting the hot water wash away the evidence.

All showered, I wrap a towel around my hips and swipe at the steamed-up mirror with my palm. I get busy shaving, but it's slow. My beard is thick, and I'm busy rinsing the blade under the faucet when the bathroom door swooshes open.

I freeze and glance at the door.

Lexi, eyes still half-shut in sleep, bedhead galore, moans. "Evan, jeez, I thought you'd left the faucet running. I've got to pee. Are you done yet?"

She looks up at me, and it's as if the gears in her head click over one at a time, speeding up in alarm as she realizes her mistake.

"Hey, Lexi. Long time no see."

"Oh, holy hell." She wipes at the sleep in her eyes, then scrunches them closed as a blush blooms on her cheeks. She takes a deep breath and schools her face. "No worries, Tristan. Take your time."

"I'm done." I keep my voice steady as I force my gaze away. Her light-blue silk cami-and-shorts get-up needs a robe. "It's all yours."

I put the razor down, rinse the basin and my face. Still

dripping wet but making do, I take my clothes and walk out of the bathroom, having to twist sideways as she's sort of still blocking the door in surprise, and there's no way I'm touching her if I can help it.

Her eyes, big and blue, are wide open now as she stares at me. I could sink into them, like the bottom of the deepest ocean. But Lexi is one hundred percent awake now, her gaze arctic cold and calculating, and her full lips pressed in a line.

"Thanks," she says once I'm out of the way, following it up with words I'm not supposed to hear. "I'm going to kill Evan O'Reilly."

The bathroom door closes with a bit of a bang, and I shrug as I walk into my room. Whatever beef Lexi has with Evan, I'm not getting involved. By the look of it, we're both his guests. I have no clue how long Lexi will be here, but her presence might put a cap on my own stay.

Fuck. As if things aren't dire enough.

In my room I dry and dress, trying to block the visual of Lexi dressed in something so adult, so unexpected and sexy. Our five-year age gap has gone up in a puff of smoke, like a magic trick. None of that matters. She's still Evan's sister. There's one friendship I won't fuck up.

Dammit. Light blue is a problematic color. Especially in silk. Nipples were hinted at. So were the contours of her breasts. Her wavy blonde hair is long and unruly, but it didn't cover anything up, and like any normal man stepping out of the cave of self-deprivation, I was able to take in the whole lot with one glance. And right there lies the problem: she revealed nothing, yet just enough to push my imagination into overdrive. Blocking her image doesn't help, so I file it in the wank bank as a temporary solution.

Jesus Christ. I drag my fingers through my wet hair, glad I got off when I did.

Those cold eyes told me everything. She definitely held a grudge against me five years ago—I mean, she's been avoiding me like the plague—but time doesn't heal all wounds. Sometimes it takes a simple cut and makes it fester, until what's left is a nasty scar, always there to remind you how things ended.

I've always suspected, but now it's confirmed: Alexandra O'Reilly hates me.

And things are about to get really awkward.

Chapter Five

LEXI

I open the bathroom door half an inch and peek out. No sign of Tristan. I pad down the short corridor to my room, pulse wild, wanting to strangle my brother. He knew. I asked him point blank last night when Tristan would be here, and he said he didn't know!

When I opened the bathroom door, I was expecting Evan. He's so sweaty after his run that he takes a quick shower in this bathroom before he dives into the pool, and he usually only strips off his shirt. Those triathlon shorts he wears are made for swimming and he keeps them on in the shower. Not for a second did I think I'll bust in there and catch my brother naked.

I honestly thought Evan had left the faucet running when the slow dribble of water didn't stop. At least Tristan was only shaving and mostly covered. It could have been worse. *Oh God.* I groan. So. Much. Worse.

But Holy Mother of God, the visual of Tristan in a towel was enough to rip me out of my sleepy haze. In the years I haven't seen him, he has matured. I sensed it from his Instagram photos, but I didn't truly see it, not like now. A picture may be worth a thousand words. The real thing, on the other hand... I snatch a breath as I close my bedroom door and crawl under the covers. I want to hide. That stupid blush was so uncalled for. It took me right back to—

Ah, buzz off. I push the memories away and reach for my phone to distract my mind.

There are several notifications. Some are messages from Tessa. Now that she's in LA, she sends them late at night when I'm already in bed. I smile as I scroll. She's hooked up with old friends from New York and seems to have landed on her feet. At least one of us has.

A new message pops up. It's from Sheila. She's checked in several times since I left New York and has kept me quietly informed on developments at St Chalamet. So far, there've been none.

> **SHEILA**
> We have a new problem.

She continues typing, those three dots dancing their jig as my heart sinks.

Shit.

> **ME**
> What now?

> **SHEILA**
> Are you up yet? Better to chat.

No. This sounds even worse. My heartbeat rockets as if on a mission to Mars.

> **ME**
> Yes.

My phone vibrates seconds later, and I answer. "Hey, why does this sound so—"

"Shit, Lexi. We would've let you know yesterday, but we had to make sure—"

"What?" I sit up and toss the covers to the side, suddenly too hot.

"The hackers have figured out your identity from the video."

"What?" The words hang like arrows in the air, paused midflight, giving their target a moment to register Sheila's meaning before they hit. "How?" A fresh chill cruises down my spine to settle in the pit of my stomach, where it seems to morph into bile.

I've seen the clip. Several times. It lives rent-free in my mind. Once I told management about walking in on Mia Reed, the security team scoured all video footage around the date and time for proof, because you know, it's a St Chalamet hotel. And it's Mia Reed. And they've been hacked. Up until my confession, nobody knew, or suspected, that there was a hackers' gold mine in old security footage from a small banquet room at the back end of the hotel's fortieth floor.

The video shows me full length as I open the door, step in, sliding my jacket off one arm as my hand reaches to my chest —to my blouse's top button to get a head start on the business of stripping—then I freeze for two solid seconds midstride, my face *a picture*. Then I slowly, quietly back out of the banquet room, not blinking once, my hands held up in defense. By pure luck, taking off my jacket had hidden my name badge and the hotel's crest. Not that it helped much, as they've still managed to figure out who I am.

"We don't know, probably from employee photos," Sheila says, distress clear in her voice. "It could be anything. Face recognition, AI, who knows. The hackers have all the advantage here, Lexi."

I keep my emotions in check with pure brutal force by digging my teeth into my bottom lip. "How do you know?" I ask when Sheila says nothing more. "How can you be sure?"

"Because they're demanding a million dollars from the hotel group to keep your name—consequently St Chalamet's name—out of it."

I slip off the mattress to the floor and hug my legs to my chest. This is how it starts. This is how it feels to lose control of a situation. Nothing screams career-ending move like your name plastered all over a sex tape on the internet. This type of stunt might work for some, but not for me and the industry I'm in.

My name linked to a scandal. Again. How many iterations of Alexandra am I going to go through in life? I drop my face to my palm to stifle a sob.

"Lexi? You're still there?"

I breathe out a shaky breath. "Yes." But the Earth can spew me out to space, and I'd be glad to wave goodbye.

"Any chance they've reached out to you? The hackers, that is? Mr. McIntyre asked me to phone you to find out."

"I don't know. How would they reach out?"

"Social media? Phone? Your personal email? Anything really. They'll have the information we had for you in our system, so whatever you used when you filled in the employee forms ages ago plus the New York updates. I can send you what we have? You can check."

I'm hot and cold and feel utterly helpless. The only thing left to rise in me is anger. "Are they going to pay?" I ask. "Is St Chalamet going to pay to keep my name out of their security scandal? They've already gotten rid of me with a wrongful dismissal, which I could sue them for—" I break off. I shouldn't say anything more. Not without a lawyer. For all I know, this call is being recorded. "I've got to go." I kill the call and switch my phone off, certain I don't want to see what's going on in my email or social media notifications.

I drop my head back against the bed and go limp. It's way too early in the morning to deal with this level of drama. To feel this drained. I haven't even had a cup of coffee yet. It's hardly eight o'clock in the morning, for God's sake.

The temptation to curl into a ball and stay right here on the floor is big, but I'm better than this. My name is worth at least a million dollars. And St Chalamet will pay if I have any say in it. I'll do anything to keep my face from being plastered all over the news. Ultimately, it's their reputation to protect. If they expose me, I'll expose them. For a long moment, I let the consequences play out in my head. My anxiety pops right back like a jack-in-the-box—as if I could ever really contain it.

This is a freaking nightmare. And I don't want to deal. Not with St Chalamet, which is about to show its true colors, and not with lawyers who might not be able to fight a big corporation once all the details come out in court. I was in the wrong by not reporting the Mia Reed incident immediately. I was also in the wrong by having an offsite sex fest with Brent Fisherman, which, if it came out, would char my reputation black. Bottom line: company policy will serve my ass on a platter.

Rule #2 in the Lexi O'Reilly rulebook for staying happily employed and avoiding nasty lawsuits: *stick to company policy and obey the rules.*

Fuck it. That should probably be rule number one.

But a lawsuit is a different ballgame altogether. Once The Head gets a name—which it will if this ends up in court—I'll just become the poor girl nobody cares to protect, barely good enough for Brent Fisherman to use as a final up-yours to St Chalamet before he made his exit for a GM position at another hotel group. He gave up on being promoted to GM at St Chalamet. I can see it now. Nobody is going to spend a sleepless night worrying about me, that's for sure. Worst of all is, anybody who watches that video would only smirk and think *who would want* that *if Mia Reed is spreading her legs.*

I wipe my cheeks as kitchen noises come through my bedroom door.

Tristan.

I close my eyes and draw in a haggard breath. He's making coffee. The life source. I need some of that. Preferably with a double shot of brandy.

Dealing with my first me-men-idiocy trifecta and teenage disappointment seems like a joke now that this other tsunami is rolling in. I heave myself off the floor and reach for a T-shirt to pull over my head. This silk cami leaves just enough to the imagination—to think I bought it to impress Brent Fucking Fisherman. I hope he grows fin rot on his junk.

I drag a brush through my hair, eye my phone, and leave it right there on the floor like an amputated limb. Evan is going to have to help here. My brain is too messy to make any decisions, but I'm going to have to, and soon.

With my head held high, I pad out of my bedroom. Faking it all the way. As soon as I step out of the short hallway into the open-concept living space, my gaze connects with Tristan's.

His mug is halfway to his lips, but he stops as he takes me in. "I think you need this more than I do," he says as I clamber onto a barstool by the kitchen island. His eyes are on me, chestnut brown, with lighter flecks of amber shining like rays from his irises. "You still like it with double cream and one sugar? This one's close enough."

That he can recall this detail years down the line is enough to make me ache. "Yes." I groan as I reach for the mug he's pushing in my direction. "Thank you."

"What's wrong, Lexi? If it's about earlier—"

"God," I cut him off. *Earlier like in-the-bathroom earlier or like five-years-ago earlier?* We're going to have that conversation at some point. I feel it in my gut. But not today. Please. "No. I spoke to a colleague—an ex-colleague." I cup the mug between my hands and lift it to my nose for a slow inhale. I take a sip. *Ugh*. Tristan still makes the best coffee—something he does with the mix of evaporated milk and condensed milk that's on the counter. "I am so fucked I don't know if I'm coming or going." Well, I'm not coming. And going somewhere seems like the only solution right now. Going somewhere very, very far away.

"Okay." He pops another pod into the coffee machine and puts a mug under the spout. "Care to share more details?"

I glare at him over the rim of the mug, and he smiles that smile that always melted me on the spot.

"No worries," he says on a chuckle. "Have your coffee first."

It falls quiet between us—not uncomfortably quiet, thank God.

Five years is a long time to cradle a broken heart. Thank the universe that we all get to grow up. For years I used to be crazy, madly, blindly in love with Tristan. Just look at him, for starters. As if the bathroom scene wasn't enough, dressed Tristan somehow seems even sexier. Nobody looks like that in a white T-shirt. His tan. His hair, now a dry crop of tangled curls. The cut of his clean-shaven jaw. The fit of his shirt over his broad shoulders and the way his biceps fill the sleeves without wanting to show off—

I groan inwardly. Obviously, there was more to my teenage infatuation than his looks, but it didn't matter. In the end, I meant nothing to him.

As he studies me with an equally intense gaze, I swallow and look away. The coffee machine gurgles and does its thing. Tristan's kidney pops back in my mind, and Evan's opinion that he'd give one to go to Ne'emba Island. I dismissed the whole notion as ludicrous last night, but the idea brews afresh. I even dreamed of white sandy beaches last night between snippets of Mia Reed walking the red carpet with a suckerfish between her legs.

Getting a foot in the door with Beaumont—before this whole St Chalamet disaster explodes—could be my saving grace. If I have a job lined up before the Mia Reed scandal hits the internet, I could be gone and gainfully employed before anyone is the wiser. I could sit out the worst in a place where guests wouldn't even take stock of me as a human. How many people could stay on an island with twelve rooms over a period of three months? Most of them would have serious money to be able to afford such an exclusive vacation. It's not as if I'll be hosting all of *People* magazine's subscribers in one sitting.

Scandals come and go at such speed, the worst will be over in weeks. Eight weeks, max? For now, my reputation is squeaky clean. But for all I know, anybody who googles Alexandra O'Reilly a month from now will find a gazillion hits linking me to a porn-gone-wrong viral video. I can see the headlines already, and puke stirs in my gut.

I take a deep pull on my coffee, but it has a hard time going down past the tight panic in my throat. "What are your plans?" I ask once I've managed to swallow. I need to get my head out of this tailspin. "I hear from Evan that you're working on a TV series or something?"

"For that, I need my coffee." A smile tugs at the corners of his lips, but it doesn't reach his eyes. "To sum up, let's just say I'm currently so fucked, I don't know if I'm coming or going."

I laugh. This is the Tristan I fell in love with: playful, sweet, and honest. "Care to share?"

He chuckles. "I'll share mine if you share yours."

"Ha!"

"Maybe not on an empty stomach." Tristan reaches for the eggs and bacon on the counter. "Want some?"

"Yes, please."

The front door opens and Evan walks in, sweat-drenched, with a pastry box. I have no idea how fast or far he runs, but he's training for the Texas Iron Man in April. His gaze jumps between me and Tristan, and a smile spreads over his face as he comes towards us. "Excellent. I see you two reconnected."

I shoot him a killer glare. It's too late now; Tristan's here, and I can't run. I don't have the energy in any case. I have much bigger problems on my hands. "Yep. Thanks for the heads-up, asshole."

"You're welcome, Pick—"

I lift a finger to stop him midstream. "Yeah, the pickle business stops right now. I hate that freaking nickname." It only seems to jinx me, and to be honest, my future isn't something I want to mess up. Going forward, I'm going to call the shots, play by the rules, and be a good girl. "We need to talk. And I need a lawyer. Do you know someone cheap?"

Chapter Six

TRISTAN

Lexi needs a lawyer? My favorite type of person—*not*. I can only stare, and for a second you could hear a pin drop as Evan also searches Lexi's face.

"What's happened?" Evan asks as he puts the pastry box on the kitchen counter.

Lexi clutches her coffee cup as if it were a life buoy. "The hackers are threatening to release my name with the video if the hotel group doesn't pay up."

Wowowowow. What?

"Shit." Evan drags a hand through his sweaty hair and groans. "Bring Tristan up to speed. I'm going to shower. Gimme five."

Lexi's eyes meet mine, but then she looks away.

"You don't have to tell me anything," I say. "If you need to talk to Evan privately, I'll make myself scarce."

She shakes her head as a tear cruises down her cheek.

My heart squeezes. "Lexi... What can I do to help?"

51

"Stick around," she says on a broken chuckle. "You might come in handy."

"Okay. I'll do anything, you know that, right?" The words are out before they register in my mind, but they're true. At one point, Lexi was one of my best friends. Between her and Evan and their mom, I found an unexpected haven as my own family life disintegrated. I'd do anything for any of them. Plus, I have lawyer connections aplenty.

"Would you? Be careful what you commit to here. What if I asked you to off someone for me?"

I laugh. "You? Offing someone? Never." Lexi wouldn't hurt a fly, but her face is serious. "Feeling murderous much?"

At this she buries her face in her hands to cover a sob. *Oof.* I made it worse. I go around the kitchen island to comfort her, but at the last second, I pull back. The last time I saw her like this, it was my fault. The best I can hope for is that we can be friendly for the time we're in Evan's house, and this isn't the way to go about it.

"I'll make breakfast." I don't touch her, and she isn't aware that I wanted to. I move back to the other side of the counter and find two frying pans. I put strips of bacon in one, turn on the gas, and find a bowl to scramble some eggs in.

When she looks up with a sniff and wipes her face, I pause.

"So, long story short," she says with a woebegone smile, "I got fired because of a security video at work. I walked in on someone, uh, having sex. I didn't report it as I should have, and the hotel's systems got hacked a few days later. Now the hackers are using the footage to extort the celebrity who was caught on video."

I hitch my eyebrows. "What? A celebrity?"

"Yep. And now the hackers have figured out who *I* am and are using me to blackmail the hotel."

"Son of a bitch."

Evan comes down the stairs. The worry on his face is real, but he schools his expression before he comes to stand next to his sister. "What are the hackers asking for? Do you know?"

"A million dollars."

My jaw drops. *Jesus Christ. They're not messing around.*

"And they've contacted you?" Evan asks.

"I don't know. I don't have the guts to check my phone."

"Where is it?" Evan asks.

"On the floor in my room."

Evan walks away, shaking his head. Lexi sits frozen in her seat, hands clenched. I wish she didn't feel like she needed to save face in front of me.

Evan is back in seconds and holds out her phone to her. "Unlock it."

She does and hands it back to him. "I don't want to look."

"I'll do it." Evan perches on the barstool next to her, and we all seem to hold a communal breath. "Email. Nothing. Messenger, nothing. WhatsApp's all good too. Instagram—" He breaks off, glances at Lexi who is staring at her mug as if it were a portal to another world and she couldn't figure out how it works, then shoots me a glance with a cocked brow, then says, "Nothing in Insta either." He carries on, going through other social media apps. "There's nothing dodgy here." Evan pulls her in for a side hug. "So far so good."

"Okay." Her voice is small as Evan lets her go. "What do I do now? I have no clue what to do."

"Shut down all your profiles," I tell her. "Make it impossible for someone to reach you. This is the hotel's problem, and they have the resources and know-how to deal with this."

She looks up at me. "Okay. Can you do that, Ev?"

"Consider it done."

Heavy silence hangs over the table as Evan deals with the IT, and I deal with the eggs, my mind racing. "I'll give my dad a call about the lawyer. Someone at his firm would be able to help with this."

"Will you?" Lexi's sea-blue eyes flood with tears, ready to overflow.

The hope in her voice stills my heart. Here's something I can do to take those tears away. "Sure, no problem." I flip open the pastry box and eye the six croissants. "Bacon and egg croissant, anybody?"

Evan looks up. "Yeah, sure."

Lexi shakes her head. "I can't eat."

"But you should, if only one bite." The distress in her eyes, the strain in her posture is contagious. My shoulders are as tense as a rod.

"Thanks for the offer to call your dad," Evan says as he puts her phone down. "Do you still think my idea is so ludicrous, Lexi?"

She meets his gaze and something passes between them—a memory of what it's like when your world spins out of control. I wasn't there when that shit went down, but by the look in Evan's eyes, he would stop the world from spinning now with his bare hands, if he could. "Have you told Tristan about the job?" he asks.

"No," Lexi says, a flash of fire in her eyes. "And it isn't ludicrous anymore, only crazy. And perfect. Dammit. It's so crazy perfect." She looks up at me and shakes her head. "And no, I haven't told Tristan anything. If you hadn't noticed, I'm kind of dealing with a shitfest right now."

Evan squeezes her hand. "Let me get my laptop, and we'll show him."

I watch Evan go up the stairs, my interest piqued. "Are you sure the hackers will drop the video and things will blow up?"

"All I know is that if they *do* drop the video, it will blow up." Lexi bites her lip and hitches her shoulders. "And I don't want to be here when it does." She sighs, the breath seeming to come from deep within her. "I've shared mine. Now you have to share yours. Let's see if your 'so fucked you don't know if you're coming or going' is worse than mine."

"Nobody can top yours, Lexi. I won't even try." I shoot her a smile. "I've only run out of time and money."

She shifts in her seat. "Time, I get, but money? Don't you have like thousands of followers? And a trust fund?"

Sometimes I forget that the O'Reillys know more about me than the average person who's come into my life over the past twenty years. "I'm not touching the trust fund," I tell her. *Ever*. "I'm doing this on my own steam. As for the thousands of followers, any money I make on social media goes to non-profits."

"Like what?" Her tone says it all. I'm crazy.

"Cleaning the oceans of plastic for one? Money doesn't make me happy, Lexi. Going for a dive and not finding a single piece of plastic while I'm at it makes me happy." And I'm committed now. As much as I would love to divert my social media funds to my project, I can't leave those NGOs in the lurch. What they are doing is more important than my TV series. One day, everything will cross-pollinate, but my work means nothing if the oceans aren't cleaned up.

I can feel her gaze on me as I cut open the croissants and fill them with bacon and scrambled eggs. I put one on a plate for her and push it over.

"Thanks." Instead of taking a bite, she chews on her bottom lip.

Evan returns with his laptop and places it on the kitchen counter. "Read this and then look at this website."

Lexi gets up and walks away, leaving her croissant untouched, shaking her head as she disappears down the hall.

"Should you—" I start. *Should I? Follow her? Make sure she's okay?*

"Nope. She just needs a moment." Evan turns the laptop in my direction.

I wipe my hands on a dishcloth and lean against the counter to read. It's a job description. Ne'emba Private Island. Luxury resort. Diving. That gets my attention. "What's this?"

"Lexi's dream job. She's been talking about working at a place like this for years, and I think she needs to get away right now."

Damn skippy. I take the laptop and read on, not making much sense of it.

"You should check out their website."

"Right." I hop to the next open webpage, and my pulse skips a beat. Of course. It's *Ne'emba Island*. One island in a chain of atolls that link one of the biggest reefs off the east coast of Africa. It's one of the places I haven't been to, money and distance being the biggest impediment. I haven't connected the dots, but these images…they're what dreams are made of. The resort's website doesn't need to do much to sell itself. It's picture-perfect paradise. There's a whole section on the diving alone, and I close my eyes. Fields of lettuce leaf corals. Bouquets of gorgonian sea fans that stretch to the light from the ocean bed. *This.* This is what I live for. This is what I need to wrap up my series. It starts off big with the ocean mammals; it needs to close small with the tiniest of sea slugs.

"Why're you showing me this?"

"It's a managerial couple position. One person runs the hotel. The other person runs the dive center." Evan holds my gaze. "I thought you two could kill two birds with one stone and give it a shot."

"What? How?" I'm not getting the gist here.

"I know you've been putting off filming the smaller things. You focused on animals that always get sponsorships first."

This is true. I started off big because whales get way more attention in the media than sea cucumbers. And now that I'm getting to the small things, I've a deadline hurtling in my direction. Plus, I'm so broke that I'm on the brink of asking for help from the last person on the planet I want to: my dad.

"You and Lexi should apply," Evan says. "She gets to hide out on a remote island where nobody can harass her. You get to run the dive center. It's max three dives a day, so you'll have ample free time. With those reefs on your doorstep for three months—just imagine. It's essentially all-expenses paid. Plus your salary."

I drag a hand down my face, digesting the picture Evan is painting. It sounds too good to be true. There must be a catch.

"Let me get a better understanding of what's going on here."

I take the laptop and my croissant and go sit in the living room. It takes me twenty minutes to read through the job description again and study their website in more detail, and as I do, somewhere within me a bean of hope sprouts. It's only until April next year. The timing is spot on. A dive center would be a breeze to run. I have the highest level of diving qualification and am a certified rescue diver and trainer. Even if the pay sucks, I'll have access to some of the most beautiful reefs in the world. It's more than I could ever hope for, but—

"This will never work," I say.

"Why not?" Evan has made us fresh coffee and puts my mug down on the coffee table.

"They're looking for a management couple? We're not a couple."

"So?"

I chuckle, a bit incredulous. I glance at the hallway that leads to our respective bedrooms. By the sound of it, Lexi's taking a shower. "We haven't seen each other in years, and we didn't exactly part on good terms when I left for Hawaii."

"Yeah? And why was that?" Evan asks, eyebrow cocked. "She was totally depressed for months, you know. She missed you."

My chest tightens, but I know now, just as I knew then, that it was for the best. If Evan hasn't figured it out yet, I'm sure as shit not spelling it out for him. "I missed you all, too."

I look at the screen again, clamping down on the hope that glimmers. Nobody would be stupid enough to do this, would they?

"I think it's worth a shot," Evan says. "You should each submit your résumé and see what happens. You've got nothing to lose."

It's quiet for a long time as Evan putters in the kitchen, giving me time to digest and dip into a crazy daydream of getting my project off the ground again and finally wrapping it up.

When footsteps fall, I look up and watch Lexi as she comes into the living room. The fresh scent of her shower gel, soft and flowery, drifts over, and I can't help but take in her ass in those butt-hugging shorts as she scoots past me. She slumps down in the corner of the sofa and hugs a throw pillow to her chest.

"I see Evan's shown you his devious plan," she says, her tone laced with snark.

"*Your* devious plan," Evan says, his gaze volleying between the two of us.

"It's crazy," I say with a smirk.

"That depends," Lexi says. "How desperate are you, Tristan?"

I search her eyes. It's as if all barriers have come down. She's freaking serious.

"Um…what I don't get is the couple part. What level of *couple* are we talking here?" I ask, then swallow hard. "Married couples?"

"Usually." Lexi stares at me, unflinching.

"Okay." I don't know what more to say except that marriage is a farce. "No one is going to buy us being married."

"Nope." She snickers. "But if it isn't beneath you to fake an engagement with me for the sake of the TV documentary you're so desperate to wrap up, we might get a pass."

"Fake an engagement?" I repeat.

"Forget it." Lexi stands and steps away, but I reach for her hand.

Touching her almost burns; it feels so wrong and yet so right at the same time. "Just—" I start.

She removes her hand but doesn't walk away, and her leg brushes mine, her body so close I can feel the heat radiating off her. I'm trying my hardest to keep our gazes locked, because the only thing I want to do is look down at her breasts.

"Let's just work with this concept for a minute—"

"It'll never work," Lexi cuts me off. "We have zero history, and anybody who goes on your Instagram account will see that you're not the committed-relationship type."

What the actual fuck? *Zero history?* "My Instagram account?" I deflect. "I just told you what I use it for. It's purely business oriented. I don't post anything private on my Instagram account."

"Really?"

That's a rhetorical question. I might not post about my private life on social media, but I'm not exactly a saint and I don't do long-term relationships. I don't see the point. My life is uncomplicated, and I like it that way. As for posts other people tag me in… Well, only friends or colleagues can tag me. It's all business and exposure for me, and ultimately it drives money to the NGOs that need it most.

"Can you sit down?" One more second of her this close— "Please?"

Lexi groans but falls into her seat. We glare at each other as her words ricochet back to me in slow motion. *Beneath me? To fake an engagement with her?* Is this how she views what happened five years ago? That I thought she wasn't good enough? *Fuck.* It was more like the inverse—I wasn't good enough for *her* and never would be. That being with me would only destroy what we had. At the time I thought it was obvious to her.

"If you think about it—" Evan's voice cuts through the tense air "—you'll both be working. Nobody at the resort is going to know you aren't really engaged. PDA is frowned upon in the workplace, even between married couples. It's unprofessional. Plus, you'll probably be so busy, you'll hardly have time to share a cuppa with each other in the morning."

A weighty silence follows, during which Lexi grinds her jaw.

"You know what? Evan's right," she says eventually, breaking the impasse. "You'll be in the water most of the time, taking guests for dives and doing your thing. I'll be running everything else. So, if you're open to it, Tristan, let's submit our résumés." She stands and this time takes the longer way around the coffee table to escape, giving me a wide berth. "The only thing that could top the past few weeks' mindfuck is us actually getting an interview and having to fake being engaged."

Chapter Seven
LEXI

"I blame Evan for this," I groan into the phone. My streak of melodrama seems to be skiing down a very steep hill, on the verge of losing all control. We all know how that ends: a wreck.

"Evan's just looking out for you, Lex," Tessa says. "And it isn't a done deal by far."

"Evan ran with it because he had my résumé on his laptop, and now I've got an interview!" I close my eyes, frustrated because I technically gave him the green light in a moment of snark.

"But that's awesome!" Tessa sounds delighted. "Isn't this what you wanted?"

"Yes, but—"

"How is it that only you have an interview?" Tessa asks. "Isn't the job for a managerial couple? What about the dude? *Tristan*?"

The dude. Ha! She wouldn't call him that if she saw him in person. "I don't know. He's hardly been around, and I haven't checked with him." It's not as if I have his number. The last time I saw Tristan, he was passed out on the sofa looking almost angelic in sleep. I could've stared at him the whole day, but I had errands to run. After that morning, I lost track of his whereabouts. He hasn't been at home by the time I go to bed for several nights in a row now, and he's gone early in the mornings. Part of me whispers that I could probably fake being his fiancée quite easily if he was never around like this.

"You should check with him, but for all you know, they want to interview you for a different position—one where he doesn't need to be your plus one."

This has crossed my mind a thousand times since I got the interview invitation. One half of me wants to strangle Evan, the other half admires his go-getter attitude, because it's gotten me this far. I worked hard to get my promotions at St Chalamet, and I can't let this opportunity slip through my fingers. My experience and dedication have to count for something. Beaumont could have other suitable positions to fill, and I can't blow all my chances because of Ne'emba Island's small stipulation.

"I'm doing it, if only for the experience." I've never been interviewed for a job outside of St Chalamet, and I'm nervous. It's a hurdle I need to leap over.

"You're going to be fantastic. It's over Zoom?"

"Yes, first thing tomorrow morning, with someone from the headquarters in Paris."

"La-dee-da. Wanna do a test run? I'll put on an accent and all."

Thank God for BFFs. By dinnertime Tessa has asked every hard question ten times over. I'm brain-drained but floating on a cloud of optimism as I walk out to the veranda.

Evan sits on a deck chair, a beer dangling from his hand, deep in conversation on his phone. He glances up at me, and the corner of his mouth forms a half-smile. "Yes, I understand. I'll get her to sign the paperwork, and we'll take it from there."

My heart drops. What a mood-killer. I sit down and wait for him to finish. "Who was that?" I ask when he hangs up.

"Tristan. He's got a lawyer from his dad's firm to help out."

"Oh. He didn't run it past me."

"He didn't have your number."

For fuck's sake. That's how in tune we are, and Evan wants us to fake an engagement?

"Okay. What's the verdict?" There's been no more word from St Chalamet, and not a peep from the hackers. Not that I've checked. For all intents and purposes, I've been wiped off the internet. A few horror shots from my teens still float around on other people's accounts, but ever since I started working for St Chalamet, I've kept my accounts private and gossip fodder to a minimum. Company policy. Makes sense now and thank God for that.

"It's a waiting game. And it could drag on forever." Evan drinks deeply. "Bottom line, the hotel must pay to protect your identity since you were working for them at the time of the security footage. They, in turn, can demand that you not expose them. So basically, both of you are between a rock and a hard place. It all depends on Mia Reed and what she's going to do next. We don't have any of that information, and no right to it either."

I've never felt this helpless in my life. "What do you need me to sign?"

"He'll email us the retainer."

Hot panic flushes over my body. "I'm not sure how I'm going to pay him."

"It's standard practice, so don't freak out. So far there's nothing to pay, and it might never come to that," Evan says with a squeeze of my hand. "We're just lining everything up in case. It's highly probable that the hotel group will have to pay your legal fees too. It's not your fault they got hacked, and your group cover included personal liability insurance. So, technically, the money is there."

"Okay." I'm not getting out of it, and I don't have the know-how to deal with this situation on my own. "Where *is* Tristan?"

"He's been going to Rosenstiel to wrap up some research he's working on with two other PhDs. He technically works for them too."

Busy guy. Running around the University of Miami's Marine Sciences department. And he found time to chat with his dad and get me help. I swallow the pebble in my throat. He said he'd do anything… "Do you know if he got an interview for Ne'emba Island?"

"Nope. We didn't talk about any of that." Evan gives me a hard stare. "And I wouldn't put my one chance on the line because of him, if I were you."

"I know. I'm doing the interview to see what happens."

"Good."

"Best you give me Tristan's number," I tell Evan. "I need to know where we stand before tomorrow morning." And I need to thank him for helping out on the lawyer front.

With Tristan's number saved in my phone, I retreat to my bedroom and send him a message.

> **ME**
>
> This is Lexi. I have an interview tomorrow morning at nine for Ne'emba Island. Have you been contacted too?

I press send and wait. I'm in bed by the time he replies.

> **TRISTAN**
>
> Got a call today and took it on the fly. The guy wanted to check if I know what I'm talking about so I walked him through my pedigree and showed him my socials.

Pedigree? Probably means his string of degrees.

> **ME**
>
> Who interviewed you?

> **TRISTAN**
>
> Didn't catch his name. Sorry, was rushed. He's a Brit. It was a solid interview. Guy knew his diving, that's for sure.

He keeps typing.

> **TRISTAN**
>
> Nathan Bauman or Baumont or something?

With that, my heart sputters and dies. Nathan Beaumont. I dug deep on that Beaumont website. I've drilled down all the layers.

> **ME**
>
> FUCK, TRISTAN! That's just the freaking CEO of Beaumont Hotels. Like in BEAUMONT hotels!!!!!!!!!!

Those three dots dance their jig.

TRISTAN

> Well shit. It went fine. Don't get those panties wedged up there, Lexi.

My hands are shaking so much, I can't respond.

TRISTAN

> Good luck with your interview. Let's catch up tomorrow. Sleep tight.

I toss my phone away and drop back in despair. Tristan dismissed me. I've no idea how he can be so freaking chill about the whole situation. He just skipped the line straight to Beaumont executive management and took it in stride.

At ten to nine the next morning, I sign in on the link to the interview. I haven't had time to talk to Tristan. His bedroom door is closed, and I'm not sure if he's in there. For all I know, he's sleeping somewhere else. Not that I care.

On the hour, the recruiter dials in. She smiles with her lips only, and we start with the usual pleasantries. It takes me a minute to get used to her French accent, but somehow it helps that this isn't in person. Five minutes into the call, someone else logs in but doesn't switch on their camera or microphone.

"It's Nathan Beaumont," the recruiter says as she lets him into the meeting. "He'll listen in but probably won't ask any questions."

Holy Mother of God.

"Usually we have a longer procedure for recruiting," the

recruiter continues. "But because Ne'emba Island is our flagship tropical resort, and the position needs to be filled soon, we've streamlined the process a bit."

"Right," I say with a nod. For the next half an hour, we cover all my work experience at St Chalamet. Soon I'm at ease. I do, after all, know what I'm talking about.

"We followed up on your references with St Chalamet," the recruiter says. "St Chalamet Manhattan hotel had only the best to say about you, so I have only one last question." She pauses and lets the statement hang. My heartbeat speeds up again, jerked out of the lull of reassurance. "Why did you leave St Chalamet?"

I swallow, keeping my face straight. Tessa drilled me on this one, but every answer we concocted sat poorly with me. Twisting the truth is just a gentle way of lying, but I can't tell the truth here. I have an NDA—not that it helps my conscience. It hits me that the easiest lie would be one that doesn't involve the hotel at all. "To be with Tristan," I blurt out. *Shit*.

"Ah. Very good." She smiles. "You've been together a long time?"

"I've known Tristan since I was ten years old," I say, not hesitating at all. "And, well, then we just sort of...happened." It's not a lie, but it's not the truth either. I don't know what it is. We haven't *happened*, but the recruiter can fill the gaps with whatever she wants.

"So sweet," she says. "Couples who know each other well and who've been together for some time usually settle best in a location like Ne'emba. As I'm sure you understand, having worked in this industry, we only employ couples at our small, off-grid establishments."

I don't understand at all, but I feel too stupid to ask why. I've spent ten years at St Chalamet and just sold myself as knowing *everything*. I manage a smile that I hope doesn't look like a grimace.

"Do you have any questions, Mr. Beaumont?" the recruiter says.

My palms burst out in sweat.

A second frame opens, and Nathan Beaumont appears on the screen. I recognize him from the board photos on the Beaumont website, but here he looks younger—mid-thirties max—and blindingly handsome.

"We're not in the habit of poaching staff from St Chalamet," he says with a smile. "They're our competition, but we work with the utmost respect for each other." *Holy Mother*...that British accent is swoon-worthy. "Your American experience is interesting," he continues. "We're building a portfolio in that market, and we have very few Americans on our team at the moment."

"Are you planning to open hotels in the States?" This is news to me, and I'm latching on to it as if this were the last bus passing this stop forever.

"We've started building our first project in Massachusetts and are looking to expand. We have an in-house recruitment policy wherever possible, and with several new hotels opening in the States, it would be nice to have some experience in-house already. We'll be recruiting a lot of staff."

My heart is in my throat. I can't miss this chance. Getting a foothold within Beaumont when they're starting out in the US would be a game-changer.

"Do you have questions for us, Alexandra?" the recruiter asks.

"Um, the position in Ne'emba Island is only for three months? Why is that?"

An awkward silence hangs as the recruiter stalls and Nathan blinks at the screen. Their hesitation is just that moment too long. For once the recruiter has been caught off guard by a question. It always amazes me how much can be said in a few seconds of silence.

I shift in my chair. Something's off here, but I can't figure out where it comes from or identify the smell yet.

Nathan clears his throat.

"Of course you'd want to know," the recruiter says. "The couple who were managing the resort had a family crisis, so they had to cut their contract short. We'll be recruiting for someone for a long-term contract over the next few months."

"I see." A tiny red flag. That's what I see. "And who's managing the resort now?"

"We occasionally get into this type of situation, but Ne'emba runs itself with our permanent staff on the island. Jem and Mike Shabani, who manage the admin and activities, have been there for thirty years," Nathan says as he leans back in his chair, giving me a glimpse of a mahogany bookcase filled with leatherbound books. "As for the face of Beaumont management, we have a loyal employee base and can ask our experienced couples to come out of retirement to help us. We have a couple there now who've been with Beaumont for over forty years."

I nod, seeing my future unfold again like I'd always envisioned it with St Chalamet.

"I see you have ample event experience," Nathan continues as he glances down at something. Must be my résumé. "We have a couple of high-profile guests staying at Ne'emba in the first quarter next year, plus six weddings. The weddings are high maintenance."

"I bet." I chuckle.

"And usually not because of the event itself. The guests are the factor we have limited control over, and they tend to be a mixed bag."

Don't I know it. "I'm sure there's nothing I haven't come across already."

Nathan laughs, and it's rich and velvety. "You'll let us know. With your experience at St Chalamet Manhattan and their usual guest profile, I'm not worried about those events. Finding a manager for the resort isn't our challenge. It's the dive center that needs more attention right now. The type of diver who comes to Ne'emba usually wants to see and experience more than pretty fish. So the fact that Tristan is a marine biologist is a big plus for us."

And there lies the crux of the matter. I'm not the important half. I only get in by piggybacking on Tristan's credentials. I nod, wanting to sink into my chair as if it could swallow me whole. The interview has been thorough—too thorough for a first round. They're dotting the i's and crossing the t's here. And not because of my skillset, but because of Tristan's. Worst of all, I will never know what was said in *his* interview.

"At Beaumont, we hold our employees to the same standards as St Chalamet, if not higher. For us, our integrity, dedication, and pride in our work is what makes Beaumont stand above the rest," Nathan continues. "Your résumé is impressive, and I think you are an excellent fit, Ms. O'Reilly. See this time at Ne'emba Island as a type of probation. If it all works out, we'd consider having you on board when we open our first hotel in Massachusetts." Nathan smiles, and it's so genuine it only makes mine feel fake. "Not to worry, though, we're looking at Miami too, and I suspect long term that is where you'd want to be."

Oh God. He's referencing Tristan and his work. What did he say about us?

"That's it from our side," the recruiter says. "Any more questions?"

So many. But my head is a scramble of brain best served hot —the staff accommodations, how many staff are on the island permanently... God, the list is endless, but Nathan Beaumont is staring directly at me from the screen, his mouth in a half-smile. "No. No, thank you. I'm good." I have to get off this call before I blurt everything out and screw myself over. I have to think this through.

We wrap up with final goodbyes, and I exit the meeting, then promptly plonk my head down on my desk.

Everything I want and desperately need might be coming my way, tied with a pretty bow and all, but it's thanks to Tristan Martinelli.

And a fake engagement.

For a long moment, I break down the concept and what it would entail. Shared accommodations at Ne'emba? Probably. I don't even want to go there. There's no reason to dig too deep. It's not a done deal, and bottom line, if nobody knows or finds out, we could get away with it. After all, faking an engagement is just another way of bending the rules to get what I want.

But then a helpful voice in my head chimes in...

Just like I bent them with Brent Fisherman, convincing myself that having a relationship offsite was okay. What a fail.

I bent them again when I reported the Mia Reed incident

five days after the fact. In my head, I was still reporting it, if a tad late in an attempt to save my own skin. Another fail.

And now, a fake engagement to Tristan Martinelli? Do I really believe the third time's the charm?

We haven't bagged this job yet, and probably never will, but I'm penciling in rule #3 in the Lexi O'Reilly rulebook for happy employment: bend rules with caution, it's the breaking part that comes with hazards.

Chapter Eight

TRISTAN

I startle awake at the sharp ring of my phone under my pillow. I feel for it and blink at the screen. *Freaking hell.* Eight in the morning. I'm on land, for fuck's sake. But it's Dad, and I have to take it; he's doing me a helluva favor.

"Yep. Dad," I answer as I rub my eyes.

"We got the retainer from Alexandra last night, so we're good to go," he begins. "The one thing we never discussed yesterday is our fees."

"Yep." Still don't know how I side-stepped that conversation, and it's a bit early in the morning—

"Because we don't do this type of shit for free."

"Yep. I know." There's a short pause, and I haul myself into a sitting position.

"How's filming going?" Dad asks.

We didn't discuss that yesterday either. Dad's always short on time—less so on money—but everything has a price tag, and everybody has their price. "It's going." I'm not begging until I've exhausted every other viable option, which currently is Ne'emba Island.

"Run out of money yet?" Dad prods.

How the hell does he know? It's as if he's waiting for me to tell him I've failed, and I'm not going there right now. Best I steer the call back to business. "I'm okay," I say. "Lexi must have personal liability insurance of sorts, and the hotel will be covered for every eventuality, so I'm not worried." And thank you Matthew Simmons—a junior at Dad's firm who is on a mission to impress me in the hope that I'll sing his praises to my dad—for that information. "Even if things go totally pear-shaped, I'll take care of it."

"Yeah? Pear-shaped, you say? Let's make sure we understand each other. *You* will stand surety to cover *our* legal fees?" Dad gives a dry chuckle. "This case involves a celebrity, Tristan, and St Chalamet is no small fry. I'd think twice if I were you."

"Yep." *Fuck.* He knows how to wind me up. "It's fine." It's Lexi. I'll figure it out.

"Still think going into fish was the right choice, Tristan?"

Now I have a pulsing vein in my temple, ready to pop. "Yes, Dad. I'll use my trust fund, if it comes to that. Seems like a fair exchange. Listen, I've got to go. I have fish to feed. Catch you later."

I cut the call before he can make any more comments about my career choices and fall back on my pillow. Tossing his trust fund back at him for his own legal fees will be fine retribution, and I'll do it with a smile if it helps Lexi.

Lexi. I owe her proper face time. She must be on pins and needles. Since I got back to Miami, things have been intense at the university lab, but at least we're done now. I crawled into bed at four this morning, feeling like roadkill. And then I couldn't sleep. Yesterday, on top of everything else, I got a call from my agent, Nick Mallett, reminding me that my deadline for submitting the rest of my documentary is coming up fast and wondering if I have new work for him to look at? *"Where are you, exactly?"* he asked.

"I'm at the corner of Fucked and Fuck Off," I'd wanted to reply. *"So pick me up on your way to We're Screwedville."*

I managed to stall him with a short story of time-sensitive experiments and told him I'd call back later. And then the interview call came in and, I don't know, there was hope?

I've yet to call Nick back.

"Tristan?"

A knock on my door follows, and I stifle a groan in my pillow.

"Tristan?" Lexi asks again. "Are you awake? I heard you talking."

"Yep. Just gimme a minute." I get up, pull on a T-shirt and some sweatpants, and drag my fingers through my bedhead. Ideally, I would like to shower and all that before I see anybody in the morning, but life on a boat at close quarters makes you forgo formalities rather quickly. I've been in that zone for years now.

I find her in the kitchen, making coffee. *Oof...* She looks hot in that business suit with its pencil skirt, form-fitting jacket, and white button-down shirt. Her hair falls in waves over her shoulders, and as she glances up, I do a double take. This isn't the Lexi I have burned into my mind. She looks professional and in charge. And older. Thank God for that.

"You had your interview?" I step up to the kitchen island and settle on a barstool. "How did it go?"

"It was good," she says as she takes the half-and-half from the fridge. "Nathan Beaumont was there as well."

"Uh-huh." Lexi will clearly lick this guy's ass if he offered it.

"Tristan! He's the oldest great-grandson of Louis Beaumont, who started Beaumont Hotels between the wars. He's the next-generation CEO and is expanding their business into the States!"

I hitch my eyebrows. "Making friends in high places?"

"Ha, I plan to," Lexi says as she offers me a mug of coffee. "This is my one chance to impress."

"I'll hold your hand all the way, Lexi."

She chuckles. "You might have to. Did he ask about us? About being employed as a couple? Whether we're engaged?"

"Nope." We stare at each other. The tension in the room twists tighter. "Somehow I don't think that's the deciding factor. Do you think they'll offer us the position?"

"I'm not sure that's true, but my position is easy to fill. I'm replaceable—"

"Don't say that, Lexi." Her revelation the other night about how she felt when I left still eats at me. How could this girl—this woman—who meant so much to me, think she's beneath me and *replaceable*?

"It's true. If we get an offer, it will be because of your skills, not mine. That was clear in my interview."

"But they'll want us both. The question is whether *you* want to do this." I run my tongue over my bottom lip. "I'm feeling the pressure, Lexi. I *need* this."

"You can solve your problem so easily. Just ask your dad—"

"No." The word comes out snappy, and I immediately

regret my tone. I'm too tired to have this conversation. My head's hardly out of its sleepy bog, and to ask Dad for money after *that* phone call? "Sorry, I..." Residual anger sits on my chest, and I shake my head, not knowing how to make her understand.

"I see," she says softly. "You're trying to prove something to him? And taking his money would be like—"

"Failure. Yeah." I rub a hand down my face. "He never wanted me to go into marine sciences. He wanted me to go into law and join his firm. He doesn't get my love for the ocean —or for conservation, for that matter."

Lexi's eyes are on me, weighing every word. "You mean getting a doctorate wasn't enough for him?"

No. Nothing is ever enough. I avoid answering her question by taking a sip of coffee for courage, but don't break eye contact with her over the rim of my mug. If we're going to do this, I need to be honest with her.

"This documentary, Lexi," I start, trying to find the right words. "It's about capturing something that's stood the test of time, something that's bigger than all of us. It's about a world we need to nurture and care for, instead of slowly asphyxiating it as we're doing now."

She doesn't respond, and I might have revealed too much, but it's too late now.

"Okay. I can totally get on board with that." Lexi smiles, warm and encouraging. "I want that too. I want all of it. Only my angle isn't so...unselfish."

"Some people think what I do is very selfish. The lifestyle does have collateral damage."

"Hmm...except this time you'll be engaged," she says, making quotation marks at the word "engaged."

I smirk. "What could go wrong, really?"

She laughs. "We could be found out?"

"And then?"

"I don't know? I honestly don't know." She shakes her head. "I can't help feeling that this is the moment where I face the same choices my dad faced, and look where he ended up."

That would be prison.

"Lexi, being engaged is personal. It's between two people, and what goes on in anybody's relationship is nobody else's business." Jeez, just listen to me sounding like a relationship guru. "Faking an engagement for three months is hardly defrauding a charity of millions of dollars." Then being caught and landing on the national news for weeks as the criminal case dragged. The consequences basically destroyed her family. No wonder Lexi is freaked out about this whole Mia Reed situation. She sees herself living through all that again, but this time, in the starring role. "And trust me, no one would come to arrest you at home for faking an engagement."

She pales. *Oof.* I did it again. Put my foot right in it.

"No, but it still feels wrong."

"What would it take to make it feel right?" The question is so layered that even I have a hard time getting through all of them.

After a long moment she chuckles. "Let's see if we bag it first."

My phone rings in my room, and I get up to fetch it. I hope it isn't Nick Mallett with his complimentary follow-up call. The number isn't one stored in my contacts, but it is from Europe, given the area code. I answer before thinking too far ahead.

"Tristan Martinelli?" a woman with a French accent says.

"Speaking."

"I'm calling to let you know we'll be offering you and your fiancée the position at Ne'emba Island. We wrapped up the interview with Alexandra minutes ago. We hope to have you both on board soon."

I hesitate, heart pumping wildly. "Okay." I've never worked for a hotel before and have no clue about the protocol here. I need Lexi. "Thank you." I walk out of my room and wave to catch her attention.

"I'll be sending you the contract, and then we can start your onboarding as soon as possible," the woman says. "First there's the medicals and then we have mandatory training you'll both need to complete, all online, before you transfer to the island. What I need from you right now are the details of how soon you could start. The position is for the seventh of January, but ideally we will have a handover period of a couple days, where the current management team will be onsite to help out." She pauses for a moment. "You're still there?"

"Yes. Still here. I'm putting you on speakerphone," I say as I do so. "Lexi—Alexandra—is here with me, and I want her to listen in."

"Lexi? Cute." There's a smile in her voice. "It would be great to speak to you both at the same time."

I place the phone on the kitchen counter. Lexi, eyes like saucers, looks like she's seeing multiple ghosts.

"I spoke to her fifteen minutes ago," Lexi mouths at me, pointing at the phone.

"We're both here now," I say as I throw my hands up in an I-don't-know gesture.

"Excellent. So, I was hoping to book flights for you to Ne'emba Island on the first of January. That means you'll arrive on the island on the third, giving us at least three days of handover with the current management there. Would that suit you? We need to get the ball rolling because there are the work permits on that side that our agent will sort out. If you are agreeable on the dates, I'd like to get started."

I stare at Lexi, watching an array of emotions and hesitation play out on her face. She's torn between this perfect solution and being Little Miss Perfect who never does anything remotely questionable. Her anxiety is palpable. But I'm not making the decision for her, and if there's a time to speak up, it's now.

"Yes," Lexi says and clears her throat. "The first of January is fine with us, isn't it, Tristan?"

I lift my eyebrows at her, hoping she gets my question here. *Are you sure? Last moment to pull out?* Lexi raises her hands in defeat and shakes her head. She has nothing more to say? I give her two more seconds. "Yes," I say. "That should work."

"Wonderful. You'll have everything from me via email. If you have any questions, please don't hesitate to ask."

"We will, thank you."

The recruiter disconnects, and I clutch my phone in my hand. "You know what you just signed up for, right?"

"A small moral conundrum? One that's going to give me sleepless nights?" she says.

"Hopefully the idea of being engaged to me doesn't give you sleepless nights." Of *that* sort. *Fucking gutterhead.* I blame it on that prim and proper corporate suit she's wearing.

"Ugh," she groans and rolls her eyes. "It's only three months, and we're in this together. Nathan Beaumont said it's a probation period. If all goes well, he could have a job for me in Massachusetts next year, but I'd go anywhere with them."

She slips off her jacket, tosses it on the sofa, and fans herself with her hands. "That's all I want, Tristan—a job with Beaumont at the end of this—so let's not mess this up."

"Three months will fly by. You'll see." As for messing this up, that's one thing neither of us can afford. At least I have a plan now when I call Nick back. And I can send Dad his fuck-off notice in the post.

Evan comes down the stairs, yawning. He has a dress shirt and tie on but is still in sleeping shorts and barefoot. Ah, the luxury of Zoom meetings. "What can't you mess up?" he asks.

Lexi shoots me a look. "We just committed to the crazy," she says.

"You did?" Evan's face splits into a grin that could shred a pair of panties. That's my bro. Naughty little fuck. He's been rooting for this from day one. Makes me wonder what's really going on in his head.

"Fantastic. Lexi, you're employed and can now flip off St Chalamet in style. Check. Tris, you've got three months of endless diving and will meet your deadline. Check." Evan looks like he wants to pat himself on the shoulder. "When are you leaving?"

The way he says it sounds as if we've overstayed our welcome. "We've been cramping your style, have we?" I ask with a dry chuckle.

"Nah, for real."

"First of January," Lexi pipes up, her voice small. "I can't believe I signed up for it. I'm a good girl!"

"That you are," Evan says with a tease, but his eyes are serious. "Just for the record, I wouldn't let you do crazy shit like this with anyone but Tristan."

"What?" Lexi sounds somewhat offended.

"I wouldn't let you go to some random island in the middle of the Indian Ocean with just any guy. I know Tristan will look after you, so I don't need to freak out when there's no internet and I can't get ahold of you." Evan's gaze meets mine. That grin is still spread on his face, but his eyes tell me everything he isn't saying. *Don't break her heart twice.* "I trust Tristan to take care of you."

"I can take care of myself, thank you very much."

Fuuuuck, Lexi. This whole situation has taken on a sexual edge, which she seems totally unaware of. *I bet you take good care of yourself, babes, but I promise you, I can do it better.* "I'm going to take a shower."

Preferably a cold one. I've signed up to be Lexi's fiancé for three months, and we haven't discussed or thought about any of the logistics this is going to entail.

Chapter Nine

TRISTAN

"Oh, this is so wonderful," Anita says as she pulls me into a side hug. Her other arm is around her daughter, so we're basically making an Anita O'Reilly sandwich.

Lexi and Evan's mom arrived from Alaska late last night, just in time for Christmas. She's been teaching in a small town an hour's drive from Anchorage for the past two years. Once her kids were out of the house and on their own career paths, Anita tackled her bucket list. Over the past six years she's taught in three different states, exploring the country on her own terms.

"To think I don't need to go to New York to see Lexi for the holidays. It makes for a nice change." Anita gives me a last squeeze before she lets go. "Are you going to New York to see your dad, Tris?"

I reach for a beer as I gear up for the annual Anita O'Reilly Christmas update. "No, he's spending the holidays in Europe." With wife number three who is younger than me. I raise my beer in a mock toast. I didn't ask what ex-wife number one and my two half-brothers are doing this holiday season. I'm Dad's third child, from ex-wife number two. "Can I top off your wine, Anita?"

"Thank you." She picks up her glass from the table and holds it out for me. "And your mom?"

"I went to see Mom over the weekend. They're taking the girls skiing as usual," I say as I pour pinot grigio. "The triplets are seventeen now, and my mom's eager for them to all be together one last time. Next year it will be a different story."

"Oh, nice. Funny that as much as things change, they stay the same." Anita sips her wine and studies me over the rim of her glass.

Yep. I haven't been included in either my dad's or mom's respective holiday plans and have no family to go to for Christmas. It doesn't matter. I've spent less and less time with my blood relations over the years as navigating composite family holidays only left a sour taste in my mouth. When the triplets were born, Mom had zero time for me. I was hardly ten when she divorced my dad, remarried, and we moved to Miami. Soon I was only an inconvenience and a reminder of Mom's first marriage's bitter ending. The number of weekends I spent in New York—flying up so Dad could have his fair share of custody—earned me enough air miles to fly around the world first class.

Anita's comment echoes in my mind. *Funny how things don't change that much.* Lexi is by her mom's side, looking nervous. Over the past few weeks, I've gotten accustomed to all her little signals again. She's shifting from one foot to the other and forever trying to find a stray hair to sweep from her temple and tuck behind her ear. She isn't used to keeping secrets from her mom, and right now she has a bag full of them.

We aren't telling Anita about our communal job and fake engagement. The fewer people who know about it, the better. And then there's the Mia Reed mess. To my knowledge, it's only me, Evan, and her friend Tessa who know why she was released by St Chalamet. Anita is under the impression that Lexi left St Chalamet of her own accord for a promotion with Beaumont.

"Things do change, Mom," Evan says as he points his barbecue tongs at his sister. "Lexi has finally moved on from St Chalamet."

"Yes! How exciting! A private island in the Indian Ocean sounds totally dreamy." Anita raises her glass and clinks it with Lexi's. "I wonder if I'd be able to sneak in a visit."

"It's only for three months, Mom. Plus, it's my probation period," Lexi croaks. "And surely you don't want to travel all that way for your spring break?"

"Maybe. Do you think they'll give you a family discount?"

"*Pfft.*" Evan chuckles as he directs his attention to the grill. Vegetable skewers and strip loin are sizzling away, and the scent of a summer barbecue hangs heavy in the air. "That place is more than three thousand dollars per person per night, Mom. What level of discount do you have in mind?"

Anita's eyes go wide. "What? That's ridiculous. It certainly sounds like a step up from St Chalamet. Maybe I can share your staff room?"

Lexi's gaze catches mine as a blush colors her cheeks. Yep, we've gone through all the mandatory training and that's one mystery we haven't solved yet: where exactly will we be staying?

"I don't want to rock the boat, Mom. Once I'm a permanent

employee, I'm sure I'll be able to figure out how to let family stay on the cheap at Beaumont hotels."

Time to rescue Lexi before her mom digs deeper and finds treasure. "Anita, come see what I've been working on." I take her by the elbow and nudge her in the direction of the house. If I can keep her busy until lunchtime, we can then get her talking about her fourth-grade class and plans for the summer. That should keep her going until the pinot grigio demands she takes a nap.

Lexi and her mom are sharing the bigger guest room for Anita's four-night stay. After Miami, Anita is going to visit her sister who still lives in New Orleans, and we'll be off the hook.

I've squeezed a desk into my small room, and my two monitors take over most of the space. We've packed all my diving and photographic equipment in the garage, except for my most expensive cameras and lenses, which are in crates stacked against the wall. It's cramped.

"Heavens, Tristan, a man your size needs more space," Anita says as I hold the door for her.

"I'm used to it. Here," I say as I pull out the chair for her.

"If this is anything like your first two episodes, it's going to be epic!" She sits with a grin, and I shake the mouse to bring the screen back to life.

"I present to you, episode three. I've been wrapping this up with the postproduction team over the past few weeks. Episodes three and four are almost done." I lean over to close the blackout blinds and raise the volume. With the room pitch black, the only light comes from the screen.

Atmospheric sounds of the deep ocean fill the room with the opening credits. Whale songs. They're eerie until you realize what you're listening to. The song morphs into dolphin sounds and a lighter whisper of waves rolling out on the sand, and the opening scene... It stills everything in me. I'm in awe that we were able to catch this with both the drone and in the waves. A school of dolphins slice through the water, cresting and jumping, their bodies etched against the sun-filtered electric blue of the water.

"Oh wow," Anita murmurs. "It's giving me chills."

I smile. *This.* This is what I need to hear. "These two episodes are about dolphins and sharks and their prey. For episodes five and six, we're going smaller. By seven and eight we're down to the tiniest of sea creatures. We'll wrap up with plankton, bringing it full circle with the whales from episode one." There's movement behind me, and I glance at the door. Lexi is leaning against the jamb, quiet so she doesn't distract her mom. "I'll be focusing on filming that for the first quarter of next year."

"This is still all your own footage?" Anita asks, not looking away from the screen.

"Yep. I've been at it for years. Lots of hours, but it's tricky to get enough footage to make an engaging forty-minute episode."

She nods as the narrator adds the commentary I've pored over late at night. My fantastic sound team brings the patchwork of clips together and makes it whole. This is definitely a case of teamwork making the dream work, as I have no expertise in these other areas.

Lexi inches closer. "I haven't seen any of this."

"No?" Anita shoots her a glance. "Tristan showed me his first episodes over Easter. They're amazing."

"The footage is breathtaking." Lexi steps up, and now she's inches from my back, looking past my shoulder at the screen.

I step aside to make space for her, and she brushes against me. It's a tight fit in the room, and my arm touches hers all the way from shoulder to wrist, making my skin tingle.

"You set out to do this and then actually did it." Anita shakes her head as she looks up and gives me a smile that looks just like Lexi's.

"Technically I'm still doing it," I say with a dry chuckle.

"Yes, but getting this done between your other research work and the teaching you do—you've made me so proud, you know." Anita turns to the screen again. "When you came in that first afternoon with Evan from school to hang out and told me with such passion how you'd gone diving that weekend, I knew you were going to do great things, Tris. Bigger things than all of us put together."

I bite the inside of my cheek, trying to ignore Lexi's body heat and manage my joy at the praise from the woman I've secretly adopted as a substitute mom. That Anita's home was a welcome haven for me in my teens was probably what saved me. As a kid, I tried to ignore the bickering at my house, but if you're the only kid and your parents are at it like adolescent siblings, it's hard to hear anything else.

I look over to where Lexi is staring at the screen. I can recite the narrator's script word for word; I know the clip that's showing with each new scene. So it's more fascinating to watch Lexi as she takes it all in. She blinks, and I realize there are tears in her eyes. She's unaware that I'm studying her, and *this*, seeing her so open and unchecked—it twists my throat into a pretzel.

I brush my thumb along the top of her hand, and when she hooks a finger with mine, I don't draw back. She looks into my eyes for a moment, bites her lip, and then tugs at my hand, indicating with her head that I should follow. I turn, but she stops, and we stand toe to toe, my body screening her from Anita's view.

Lexi drops her head to my chest, and the gesture catches me so off guard that I let go of her hand to squeeze her shoulders. "What's wrong?" I whisper.

Behind us on the computer screen, urgent and frenzied music plays, accompanying the footage of a school of fish that swarmed into a ball during a dolphin hunt. It's loud.

She leans up to my ear and whispers, her breath warm, her body soft against mine, "I didn't realize the stakes were so high for you. What you're doing is amazing, and you must finish it."

Her cheek brushes mine as she pulls back, and for a moment our faces are inches apart in the darkened room, lit only by blue flashes from the computer screen.

I rest my hands on her hips, burning to pull her into my arms, and she doesn't move away. "Thank you." I smile. I've been so busy, so into this production with my heart and soul that I've never stepped back to look at it with fresh eyes. I lean closer to make sure Anita doesn't hear. "Thanks to you, I'll get to finish it."

"*Tristan*," she mouths as she shakes her head. "You don't understand. I... I just have a job, a totally insignificant job a million people can do. This—*this*—" She breaks off and swallows. "Only *you* can do this."

"Lexi—"

"No. For the first time, I'm bending the rules *with* someone, and if this goes belly up, *you* stand to lose so much more than me."

She steps away and wipes at tears. Frustration, in every possible form, balloons in me.

She's always talking herself down, and now Anita's presence here has unearthed every doubt in her. Anita O'Reilly is probably one of the nicest, kindest women to ever walk this Earth, and Lexi has always wanted to be Little Miss Perfect in her mom's eyes—a side-effect of having a fourth-grade teacher for a mom—except Lexi has grown into a woman who likes to test boundaries, question rules and bend them. Since Anita's arrived, she's been staving off a mini-meltdown and trying her best to hide it.

No, we aren't telling the full story, but Lexi is an adult, and her mom doesn't need to know everything that's happening in her life. Hiding our fake, temporary engagement from her mom is the most logical thing to do. Plus, we're leaving in a week, and there's no turning back. Pulling out now would be worse than faking our relationship.

"Nothing's going belly up." I widen the gap to have her at arm's length, tamping down on the desire to touch her more than I already am.

"What's that?" Anita asks.

I close my eyes for a second, trying to get a grip. "I forgot about the pork belly I bought yesterday," I say, glad such a logical response is at hand. "We still wanted to grill some."

"I'll go see to the rest of the food," Lexi says as she steps out of the room, her eyes no longer meeting mine. "I'll call you when it's ready."

"Sure, thanks." Behind me, Anita is hopefully transfixed by the sardine hunt on the screen, clinging to her glass of wine, oblivious to our interaction.

I turn back to the screen, but I'm staring blindly. *What the hell was that?* Not that I object but…

Over the past few weeks, busy as I've been, Lexi and I have spent a lot of time together as we got through the training and prepared for our trip. We've grown closer. So close that we both know neither of us has gonorrhea.

Despite the time doing the training, paperwork, and medicals with all its high-five moments, I've not let my guard down around her at all. In fact, I've done my best to build a virtual Fort Knox around Lexi to contain her and keep her where she belongs. *Far away from me.*

If she's going to open herself up, touch me even innocently like she just did… I can't even go there in my head. Not with her.

When I arrived that day in early December, I knew Lexi and I had baggage. We haven't examined it yet, opting instead for a temporary truce. And now a temporary fake engagement. I don't know what we were thinking, but it's too late now. We just need to get through these three months and walk away from Ne'emba Island and each other with our goals met—nothing else.

Nothing else.

Fuck.

Chapter Ten

LEXI

My phone vibrates with a message. *Tessa*. Finally. I swipe it open.

> **TESSA**
> Best New Year's ever.

I smile and reply.

> **ME**
> I got worried. No word from you in like years!

She types, and I spot Tristan coming back from taking a shower in the airport lounge's facilities. He's dressed in a white shirt, a pair of cropped chinos, and brown boat shoes, with a dark blue sweater tossed over his shoulder. He looks like a preppy yacht boy—like the type who would stay at St Chalamet.

> **TESSA**
> Where are you now?

Tessa's message drags my gaze away from Tristan.

> **ME**
> Business class lounge in Heathrow. It's chef's kiss. Only one more long haul and then we're almost there.

> **TESSA**
> How're you feeling about the job?

My fingers hover above my phone. *Honestly? Nervous as all shit and somewhat exhilarated and excited and crazy.*

Tristan sinks into the chair next to mine with a smile. "You should grab a shower. The bathrooms are spotless." He leans closer, sending a waft of intoxicating clean man in my direction, and whispers conspiratorially, "For all you know, this is the last good shower you're going to have for a while."

"You're probably right." I check the time on my phone. Maybe I should take his advice. After all, half of our Beaumont training was about how to manage, troubleshoot, and make do in case there's a malfunction of the high-tech green solutions on the island, from the solar panels to the water desalination plant and septic tank systems. Scientifically, I've now gone places I'd never been before. Tristan breezed through those. But science of any sort has never been my thing. Who knows what the shower water is like on Ne'emba?

I reply to Tessa's last message about how I'm feeling.

> **ME**
> Nervous.

For all the right reasons and possibly for a few new ones that hadn't been on my radar when we made a play for this gig. I mean, what was I thinking that day in Tristan's room with Mom? Touching him like I did while she was watching his latest edits. I need to keep myself in check. Tristan is hot, but he's *Tristan*. It's just that after seeing the magnitude and importance of his project, I realized failure wasn't an option and I couldn't be the reason he didn't spend time on Ne'emba Island. I was moved by the work he's doing. I meant what I said about it being important. So I've since been turning a blind eye to my small moral conundrum, ignoring any inner voices that whisper to me that, just like Dad, I'm a fool to think I'll get away with this.

"We still have another hour before we board," Tristan says as he swipes away on his phone. "Can I get you anything?"

A bout of amnesia? Covering the last month and the next three to come? I clear my throat and glance at the small plate of snacks and half a flute of Prosecco still on standby. "I'm good. I'll go shower in a minute."

"Mind if I go shop quickly?" he asks.

"No, go for it. For all you know it's the last good shopping you're going to get in for a while."

He chuckles as he gets up and gathers his things. "I'll meet you back here."

"Sure."

Tristan walks off with his carry-on luggage in tow, and I'm glad I don't need to keep watch over any of his things. It's as if his life-support system is in that bag—his Mac laptop and some of his most expensive camera equipment made the carry-on cut. As for his scuba diving and oceanography stuff, the packing was interesting. Luckily, we're flying business class and have a larger weight allowance, but he still had to pay for overweight baggage.

My phone vibrates in my hand, and I glance down at the screen.

TESSA
Why are you nervous? You've come this far; you should let all those feelings of being a fraud and faking it go. Hell, most people are faking something nowadays.

Yes, I've come this far, but I'm nervous because I can't ignore the very real feeling in my stomach I get whenever Tristan looks at me. Since that day in his room—no, let's be honest here, since that morning I walked in on him in the bathroom—it's like something old has been stirring, waking up slowly.

TESSA
Is it the fake engagement still eating you? Or is it the man himself?

My gaze finds Tristan as he makes his way to the business lounge's exit. *Damn. That ass.* Faking anything will always eat at me, even faking a smile for guests. But Tristan nibbling me? I'd take that any day. The mere idea sparks a trail of pleasure down my spine. He's been nothing but a gentleman and incredibly sweet in his efforts to nail his training. We're a team and in this together. Problem is, I've always been a sucker for tall, dark, and handsome guys. And Tristan was the first, the prototype on which all my other romantic expectations were built.

My teenage infatuation never came to anything—pretty much the opposite of that—so it's a bit much to realize that, five years on, I have the same nervous flutter in my stomach when Tristan looks my way. I have miles on me now and should know better than to let that intense gaze and sincere smile, that six-pack and pair of pecs turn me into a pile of mush. Never mind his arms and hands... *Ugh*. As long as we don't touch, I can keep myself in check. But on the last flight, I fell asleep with my head on his shoulder. Bad start to a business that's already tainted.

ME

> Nothing's eating at me. I need to get there already. We get along and won't be in each other's way much. We don't have time off during the contract. It's full-on for twelve weeks. I have no clue how booked the hotel is. Maybe there'll be a night or two with no guests. I hope so!

TESSA

> Keep your eye on the goal, bestie, and you won't cock up.

Wise words. What Tessa means by "cock up" is left open, though, and I can't let my imagination go there. With a sigh I text that I'm off to have a shower. Then I head for the private bathrooms and sign in with the hostess. Half an hour later, I'm done and feel ready for the next leg of our trip. As I return to the lounge, I spot Tristan. He's sitting in another set of twin seats, in the vicinity of where we sat before.

"You were right," I say as I park my bag next to his. "Best shower ever." I've never traveled in style like this before, but Tristan has for sure.

As I sit down, I glance at the two fresh glasses of Prosecco on the small circular table between the two seats. "Is one for me?"

"Yes." His eyes bore into to mine, but then he looks away, sweeping his gaze over the room. A smile hovers on his lips. "I have something for you." This time he pins me with those warm brown eyes I could practically melt into, leans forward, and takes my hand.

"What?" My gut tells me something is about to happen that I'm not prepared for. And didn't I just decide things would be easier if Tristan didn't touch me, and I didn't touch him?

He slips his free hand into his pants pocket, pulls out a small, robin's-egg blue box, and flicks it open with his thumb. "We still have time to change it if the size isn't right." He drags his teeth over his bottom lip. "Or if you totally hate it, of course."

I tense as a hot blush spreads like wildfire over my face. My heart is all over the place, but mostly it's hammering in my throat. "What did you buy?"

But I already know what he bought. He holds out the open box and a small but dazzling solitaire sparkles up at me.

An *engagement* ring. *Holy Mother of God and all the saints in a row.*

"I know we're doing this for the show, and after the time at Ne'emba we'll go our separate ways, but I don't want you to feel—" He breaks off and blinks, looking shy. Our hands quiver. "Lexi, I know we never plan to say vows or anything, and I'm the last guy to put a ring on a woman's finger, but I can't go in pretending without you having this."

Oh my God. "I..." Words are trapped in my throat, unable to get past the rapid beating of my heart.

He brushes the pad of his thumb over my knuckles, and the tender touch makes my knees go weak as he waits for me to say something.

"The ring isn't a fake," he says softly. "I know how you feel about doing this, and getting you a real ring is the least I can do." He gives a deprecating chuckle as his gaze jumps between my eyes and our hands. "Crap. This could make you feel worse, not better. I seem to be good at doing that..." When I still say nothing, he lets go of my hand and takes the ring out of its box. "Here, let's at least check it for size."

The moment is surreal. Tristan's skin is warm and rough against mine. He slips the ring on my finger, and a rather sensual tingle spreads through my body. Because his touch is intimate—slow and deliberate.

"There." He releases my hand, and suddenly my palms are all sweaty.

"You shouldn't have," I finally manage as I meet his gaze. "At the airport, of all places."

"I didn't have time before, and it bugged me. This is our last chance." He smiles. "Do you like it?"

What a question. This is no ordinary engagement ring. It's a *Tiffany*. "You're crazy," I murmur. "But God, I love your type of crazy."

He laughs. "You like it then."

"I love it." I touch the ring and feel it for fit, and it sits just right, as if he knows my fingers, my hand, my body. "It's perfect."

"Good." He reaches for the glasses of Prosecco and hands me one. "To us."

I raise my glass and return his toast as I scramble for words that will make me sound unaffected. "To our partnership and mutual success."

We sip, and the bubbles burn as soon as they hit my tongue. I choke up and barely manage to swallow. Tristan caught me off guard. This engagement ring is the most unexpected and romantic gesture ever, and in the same breath, it is possibly the most unromantic engagement moment ever—not that he popped the question or went down on one knee, but that goes without saying.

I herd my scattered thoughts and rogue emotions into a corner and glance down at the ring as it catches the light and sparkles. This must have cost him a fortune. *Who the hell shops for engagement rings at the airport terminal?* Now I know who. "This must have been seriously expensive, and I thought you were broke."

"I'm now, flat out," he says with a dry chuckle as he leans closer. "Listen, I'm selectively broke. I choose where to spend my money and in the next three months I'm still going to pull my university salary, get some funds from my social media stuff, and I'm not going to spend a single cent while at Ne'emba. Plus it was tax free."

"What a bargain." I take another sip and shift in my seat. I would have been happy with a bottle cap ring. "You should keep the receipt and take it back once we're done. Pump the money back into cleaning the oceans."

"Lexi—" Tristan starts, but someone approaches our two-seater enclave.

We both look up in unison. It's a woman with her phone in her hand, beaming. "Aww, that was so cute. I got it all on camera. Can I share it with you? And let me see the ring up close!"

Oh help. I swallow and hold out my trembling hand.

"It's so *gorge*! You are such a cute couple! Can I Airdrop?"

"Eh, sure." Tristan reaches for his phone, a weary smile on his lips. "Thank you."

For a moment there's a reprieve as the woman who's witnessed our whole unromantic engagement sends the photos to Tristan's phone.

Ever since that day I walked in on Mia Reed and The Head, I've been camera cautious. And now I've been recorded getting fake-engaged in Heathrow Terminal Five. I'm not superstitious, but this has black cats and broken mirrors all over it.

"You two haven't kissed yet," the woman says as she readies her camera for more shots. "I'm waiting for that moment—"

I stand and reach for my bag. "Tristan, I bet they're boarding our flight already, and we're running late."

"Yes. Yes, we are. Got a bit distracted there." Tristan is up and grabs his things.

I shoot the woman my fakest happy-guest smile and make a beeline for our gate.

Chapter Eleven

TRISTAN

It's just past two in the afternoon, and after a stop in Dar es Salaam, on the coast of Tanzania, we're finally stepping out of the airplane at Pemba Island's tiny airport. A trickle of sweat ambles down my temple—this heat is next level—as I look at Lexi. She's showing the signs of two days' nonstop travel: dark circles under her eyes, clothes a sticky, creased mess, and an itch of irritation as she breathes in the heat. Yep. Traveling in jeans to the tropics is never a good idea.

"Here." I reach for her hand and offer an encouraging squeeze. She wants to pull free, but first impressions and all that. Best not fail off the bat at this fake-engagement business. "That's us." I hold on tighter and tug her toward the man holding a board with our names on it. He's dressed in a white cotton shirt and stone-colored shorts and smiles widely as I make eye contact. "This is it." I let go of her hand so we can both steer the carts with our luggage. "You good there?" I ask.

She audibly swallows. "Oh God. I think I'm going to expire."

The closer we come to our final destination, the more tense Lexi grows. During the overnight flight she was fidgety as all hell, and neither of us got proper shut-eye. At one point I threatened to squeeze into her chair and wrap myself around her like a straitjacket. *That* froze her for a second, and then she exhaled a long, hard sigh. She finally relaxed enough to fall asleep. The idea of faking an engagement was one thing, putting our ruse into action is stressing her even more.

"Relax," I mutter under my breath. "Nobody here knows you from a bar of soap."

"Can I remind you that my career is on the line, and you have a crazy deadline?" she huffs.

"Yes, but Nathan Beaumont isn't meeting us off this plane, so we're good." I hold my hand out and look our African meet-and-greet straight in the eye. "Hi, Tristan Martinelli. My fiancée, Lexi O'Reilly."

"Welcome! I'm Mike Shabani, your captain. Welcome to Beaumont Hotels." Mike pumps my hand and then his gaze jumps to Lexi's face before settling on her hand with the ring on her finger. "Lexi. Short for Alexandra? Welcome!"

"Hi," Lexi says with a smile, finally deflating. "I look forward to working with you."

"Yes! Me too!" Mike's enthusiasm seems entirely honest and sincere, and he's all smiles. "Let me help you with that." He takes hold of Lexi's luggage cart, which is stacked with my things. "You don't travel light, huh?" He laughs.

I chuckle. "I'm the guilty one, not Lexi. Those crates are full of diving equipment."

"Ah, good. Good. Very good." Mike nods toward the exit. "Just a short ride to the port and then the last stretch by boat."

Soon we're making our way from the small airport through

a rural landscape. Eventually we pass a scatter of dwellings packed tighter and tighter as we head into the small port town.

Mike points out a few things along the way, but both he and the driver seem to be equally happy to drive in silence. They must be used to people arriving exhausted and ready for the ultimate beach vacation. The minibus's air conditioning is on, and as the minutes pass, Lexi seems to perk up like a wilted flower finally getting a drink of water.

"Eeek! This is so exciting." She leans closer to me. "It's so different from everything I'm used to."

"We're very far from New York now, babes."

"Babes?" she murmurs, and I get an elbow in the ribs. I suppress an *oof* with a smile.

"Yes, *babes*."

She's grinning, and not for the first time, I want to squeeze some part of her, even just her arm. Putting that ring on her finger yesterday at the airport got my wires all twisted up. If I'm honest, though, there've been parts of me short-circuiting for a few weeks now. Actually, since the moment she barged in on me in that sex-goddess cami set. *Fuck*. What if she's packed that little number?

We've circled around without getting into the logistics here for weeks now. Lexi hasn't done this type of gig before, and I bet she's as clueless as I am about what to expect. Google Earth didn't share any secrets when I studied the island in detail. All you can see from the air are glimpses of grey rooftops through densely packed tropical foliage.

There's no deciphering where guests stay and where staff stay, but I can only assume that Lexi and I will share staff accommodations. She hasn't brought it up, and I'm not too worried. I'm used to boat life. Small spaces. Narrow beds. I can manage. Hopefully it's just spacious enough that we can keep out of each other's hair.

Not that I want out of her hair. Lately my fingers want to burrow into those blond waves and tilt her head to the side so I can tease my lips over that spot where her pulse gives every emotion away. With her ready blush, I can read Lexi like a book.

Right now, she's nervously excited and obviously not thinking about where we're going to sleep tonight. I can't think of anything else—not since I slipped that ring on her finger and felt her hand quivering in mine. For a guy who's sworn off the whole marriage farce, this reaction is weird and unwanted. Who knew putting a ring on a woman's finger would awaken some caveman beast with a Flintstone-style club in me? And that's not the only hard piece of wood I'm worried about.

At the end of the day, I'm a man. A man who's been wondering for five years *what if*—

"Here we are," says Mike as we reach the small marina.

A young man in Beaumont uniform is waiting for us at a Beaumont-branded bowrider.

"My sidekick," Mike says. "Roger Magombo."

I smile as we all shake hands. "As in 'Roger, Captain?'"

Roger shrugs. Either he doesn't get my joke or doesn't care for it.

"Excellent," Mike says, not looking me in the eye. "Let's get going. This isn't the best of places to stand around idle."

I glance around and catch his meaning. Too many dudes loitering around on corners, watching. Waiting.

The men quickly load our luggage as I help Lexi onto the boat. I squeeze her hand. "You're good?"

"Just nervous...and hot." Her clammy hair clings to her face and droplets of sweat rest on her upper lip.

"There'll be a breeze on the water," I say, wanting to pull free, but she clings to my hand. "Once we're at the island, you'll see that everything's going to be fine. Stop stressing."

"Yeah..." Her voice is quaking now. "It isn't that."

I read her face, and the look in her eyes hits me in the chest. "I'm here, Lexi. I'm not leaving."

"I know." She takes in a shaky breath, turning into me. "It's funny how a bit of water can bring back a swath of abandonment issues."

"It's not exactly *a bit* of water," I tease gently. Neither was Hurricane Katrina.

"I didn't even think about this part... God. This is how much Mia Reed and this *situation* have messed with my head."

"Well, if it gets you to the other side without freaking out, keep on thinking about Mia Reed and don't peep a word about our *situation*." The last thing I need is Lexi blurting out point blank that we are faking our engagement.

She nods, but her eyes glaze over.

We both hold on as Mike ups the speed of the bowrider, hitting the waves. Roger still hasn't cracked a smile, just stares at us as if we're aliens.

"Is this the only way to get to the island?" Lexi asks Mike once we're hitting bigger waves.

"Ah, no." He shakes his head. "Guests fly in with the floatplane because it's quicker. Staff we bring in with the boat because we know you have too much stuff."

"Nice." I glance at Lexi. She had a red heat glow on her face minutes ago, but she's now gone pale. I rub her back in slow circles as she leans in to me.

"I remember that floatplane bit now. It was in the training." She shakes her head, and the wind whips through her hair. "It's all been a bit of a whirlwind."

"We'll catch on quickly once we're on the job."

"Yes. But I suspect this isn't going to be a soft landing."

We turn quiet, too tired to talk over the loud hum of the boat's engine. We pass the Tanzanian coastguard, and they wave at us. We wave back, our smaller boat rocking in their wake.

Fifty minutes later, we're still at the railing, Lexi green around the gills. I'm grateful that the island is finally on the horizon. "Next time, you need to take something for the nausea before we head out."

"Next time I'm taking the plane," she mutters under her breath. "Don't know what I was thinking."

We weren't thinking, babes.

Mike slows the boat, and I stand at the rail to look into the water. It's deep here and a dark azure blue, but crystal clear. I lean over, sinking my gaze into the abyss. *Right there.* A school of fish with the sunlight blinking on their silver skins. The visibility here is going to be phenomenal, and I can't wait to get my gear on and go for a dive.

Soon corals come into view in the ever-shallower water, dark flecks on the ocean floor that stretch like black tiger stripes over the white sand. I look up, wanting to gauge how close we are. Still at least two hundred yards to go before the island, but here I can see the bottom of the ocean, and that must be at least a hundred feet down. I'm starting to feel like a kid in a candy store. I haven't been in the sea since arriving at Evan's house in December, and I'm having withdrawal.

Lexi comes to stand next to me. "Oh my God."

"Finally going to feed the fishes, are you?"

"This close," she murmurs, holding her thumb and forefinger half an inch apart.

"Just look at them." I nod toward the water. "There are so many, not a bit of vomit would be wasted."

"Eww, Tristan, that hardly helps." She groans. "What are you staring at?"

I point at the water. "Look carefully. You can see the bigger fish swimming around the coral."

Lexi stares and stares. "For real," she whispers as she finally sees what I see.

"Yep. This is paradise."

She smiles up at me and pushes a strand of windswept hair away from her brow. "All yours to explore and capture on film."

I want to hug her, so I do, giving her a tight side squeeze. "Thanks to you."

"Look that way." Lexi pushes herself awkwardly from my chest. *Too much*, I note. "My perfect escape, thanks to you."

I look up as I drop my arm. The island is a breathtaking swath of green, seeming to float in a custard of creamy white sand. Palm tree tufts rise above the lush tropical forest and bow to the water. Nobody is going to come get her here. "Now you can finally relax about the whole Mia Reed mess."

"Yes. This feels like the end of the Earth, in a good way."

Buoys line the route the skipper needs to take to avoid hitting the coral, and soon we cross over into idyllic turquoise blue, where there's only soft sand under the water. On the beach, two people are waiting in the shade next to a sign that says *Welcome to Ne'emba Island*.

"Best you roll up your jeans," Mike says as he switches off the engine. "You're about to get wet."

"Who's waiting for us?" Lexi asks as she toes off her sneakers, stuffs her socks in them, and rolls up her jeans.

"That is Miriam and Don, the current management couple."

Roger drops the anchor to keep the boat floating close to shore, then lowers a small ladder, jumps barefoot out of the boat, and Mike indicates to Lexi that she should come down first with Roger's helping hand.

"We'll get your luggage to your cottage in no time," Mike says. "With all the travel and this heat, you'll probably want to catch up on some sleep."

"Yes, thank you," I say. "I'll see you around?"

"Every day. I'm in charge of the fleet and the other activities," Mike says. "Roger is your skipper for the diving."

Awesome. *Or not.* "Small world," I say, just to say something.

At this, Mike laughs. "Small island."

I make sure Lexi is secure on the ladder, and Roger smiles for the first time as he helps her down. I'm going to ignore that. I jump down, and my feet sink into the soft sand, the water up to my knees. It feels like coming home.

Lexi wades to the shore, wet up to her crotch and jeans clinging, sneakers and purse held high. I bet none of that is coming out of the closet again. I catch up with her, fingers brushing her elbow. "Not so fast, babes."

"You don't have to say that when we're out of earshot, you know."

"Just method acting."

She pauses, hand outstretched, eyes rolling. "Don't get used to it."

I chuckle as we walk up onto the beach hand in hand, and Miriam and Don head our way. They're an older couple, probably late sixties, but looking fit as fiddles.

"Welcome to Ne'emba Island," they say in unison. Handshakes and pleasantries about our flights and jet lag follow.

"Let's show you your place," Miriam says. "We have no plans for today except to get you settled in." She leads the way from the beach to a sandy trail hacked out of the tropical thicket. "We've vacated the management cottage for you. We're in the last available room in the staff quarters since the hotel is full."

"Oh wow." Lexi lets go of my hand since there isn't enough space to stay abreast. "You didn't need to do that. Surely we—"

"Oh, it's only for three nights, and before coming to fill this gap, we were RV-ing through the US," Don says. "It's perfect practice for us to get used to small spaces again. We'll be picking up our travels where we left off two months ago." He pauses at a split in the trail. "This path goes to the lodge and this one goes to your cottage."

A small sign that says *Private* is the only indication that something hides in the thicker tropical forest.

"This is a young couple's gig, not something for retired folks. By the look of that ring, your engagement is recent?" Miriam's gaze homes in on Lexi's hand, where the diamond winks in a drop of sunlight that penetrates the foliage.

That ring had me so torn, but it was the right thing to do if management notices it like this. After walking all the shops in the terminal building, I ignored the expense. My only conclusion was this: Lexi deserves nothing but the best. She's putting everything on the line here for me, and this was the least I could do. I wanted to get her that eye-popper and half of me cursed. Somewhere in me there is a boy that still wants to be just like his dad and fling money around and buy expensive things for the woman in his life.

Lexi giggles—that little laugh she has when she's uncomfortable and called out—as she brushes at a rogue strand of hair. "Very recent. How do you know?"

"We get a lot of honeymooners. No wear and tear on their rings, just like yours."

"Ah." Lexi's gaze catches mine, and maybe it's my imagination, but I'd swear that's a spot of panic in her eyes.

"Your job descriptions always say *pay attention to detail*, babes." I reach for her hand and get in a squeeze before she can pull away. We're under a magnifying glass right now.

"All you need here is a bed and some space away from guests for your own privacy." Miriam indicates for us to continue on the path. "The management cottage is perfect for that, and probably the most romantic cottage of them all, if you ask me."

Don leads the way until the forest opens up to what must be our *cottage*.

"Oh…" Lexi breaks off.

I blink in confusion. It's massive.

"This is it," Don says. "We'll run you through the basics and then give you some space."

We stroll up to the entrance of an A-frame wood-and-woven-palm-leaf structure. This is what I could see on Google Earth—the pointy rectangles that got so pixelated as I zoomed in that I couldn't figure out much except that they all had solar panels. The frame is tall and wide but has no walls as such, and it covers the verandah and interior of the space. Under this "roof," the room is another wooden frame with big glassless windows. It gives open concept a new meaning. Woven grass "curtains" have been rolled and pinned up so you can see straight through to the massive king-size bed, which has mosquito net hanging like a veil around it, suspended from a wooden frame up above. It's a snug fit but leaves about two feet of space open around the bed to move around.

I swallow, refusing to meet Lexi's gaze. *This is...* I clear my throat. Expectedly unexpected.

"So, this is pretty much what the guest rooms look like," Don says. "This is bigger, though, as you have this extra sitting room to the side, over and above your outside living area." He pauses to take off his flip-flops and wash his feet in a foot basin at the door. "For the sand, you know." He leads the way into the room, and we all dip our feet and trail behind him through the covered outdoor seating area. "Here's the kitchenette for coffee and so on, but meals stay in the staff canteen to keep it contained. We don't want to develop a cockroach problem."

"Cockroach problem?" Lexi croaks, her tired eyes blinking.

"It's common in the tropics. Just don't tempt them with food," Miriam says. "This way to the bathroom."

We follow into the open space behind the dividing wall. "The toilet is separate, but here you have the bathtub and outdoor shower," she says. "Twin basins, and a walk-in closet with a safe and a door you can lock."

"Perfect. Exactly what we need. Very spacious." I'm rambling now, but Lexi hasn't peeped a word. She's staring at the massive bathtub, set in an alcove on a raised dais. Next to it are the only glass windows I've spotted in the whole place, offering a view of the thick tropical forest. Candles line the windowsill. *Fucking. Candles. Line. The. Windowsill.*

"All good?" Don walks out of the bathroom back into the bedroom. "We were very comfortable here. Housekeeping looks after everything, of course. And you look after housekeeping." He gives Lexi a smile, and her lips twitch up at the corners.

Oh babes, not the fake smile. She's been stunned speechless.

"It's fantastic," I say as I try to guide everybody to the front of the cottage. We need alone time. As a last resort, I pull Lexi to my side in another awkward hug. I plant a kiss on her forehead. "We made it, babes."

"We sure did," she says, stiff as a plank as she pats my chest.

"And here's your luggage. Perfect timing." Miriam's all-consuming gaze locks on the porters as they stack our luggage in one corner. "We'll meet again at the general guest area in three hours? Dinner is served starting at seven, so if we meet at six, it will give you some time to take a rest."

"Sure. Thank you," I tell them. "We'll find our way."

Don laughs. "You will. Can't get lost here. Just follow the walkway."

As soon as Miriam and Don's backs are turned, Lexi twists out of my embrace. With a suppressed groan, I watch everybody walk off. Finally we're alone, with only the piercing sound of a million cicadas and the gentle kiss of the waves on white sands coming through the few palm trees that separate our cottage from the beach.

I turn to Lexi, only to find her standing frozen, her face buried in her hands.

"You knew there was going to be a catch, didn't you? Surely." I wait for her to move, to peel her hands from her face, but she doesn't. "Well, this is it," I say as I wave at the most romantic hotel room I've ever seen. *"This* is the catch."

Chapter Twelve

LEXI

The catch.
Shit.

The worst thing is, in the back of my head I knew this was coming our way. Here I am, with Tristan Martinelli, ensconced in what can only be labeled *honeymoon bliss*. What a joke. But this is what I get for lying about being engaged. Serves me so goddamned right.

A shuffle sounds over the polished cement floor, which is cool under my bare feet. Warm fingers touch my own and slowly pull my hands from my face.

"You're going to have to keep it together, babes. Otherwise we're screwed."

I stare up at Tristan, his dark eyes serious in the ill-lit interior of our... What the actual fuck do you call this? It has a roof, but it isn't attached to the walls. Through all the open spaces, the ocean breeze shifts the air, and the quiet *chomp-chomp* of a fan that's suspended over the bed is almost hypnotic. In this climate, the structure makes sense, as it's cool and comfortable inside even though the sun is blazingly hot outside.

"Just say something, Lexi, anything."

I pull in a sharp breath. "Don't call me babes." I shake my hands away from his firm hold. As much as his touch is comforting, it's also dangerous.

He lets go and raises his hands in defense. "Right. What do you prefer? Baby? Baby *girl*? Doll face? Ma petite puce?" The last one he laces with a French accent. *My little flea.* "That should have the golden seal of Beaumont approval."

"Ugh." We are clearly both hot and bothered and winded by this only-one-bed-in-the-world's-most-romantic-haven curve ball. I had one thought about this situation after my interview. Ever since, I've been suppressing the knowledge that bed-sharing might be coming our way, convinced I'd just handle it on the fly. That we'd wing it somehow. I brought this on myself, but winging things like *this* is dangerous. I mean, honestly, does the bed need to look like *this*? "This was such an idiotic idea—"

"Yes, but we're here now, and there's no easy out—*literally*—so we're going to have to stick it out, whether you like it or not."

There's no way off this island without a boat or a floatplane. And even then—"I need to shower." I need to get away from Tristan and have a moment to adjust to this new reality.

"Go for it."

Tristan walks to our stacked luggage as I dig for my phone in my purse. The last time I sent Evan and Tessa messages was in Dar es Salaam. I'd like to let them know we've arrived in one piece, even if things between Tristan and me are falling apart. That funny truce of the last weeks? It's now trying hard to keep its balance on a cliff's edge.

Phone in hand, I lean against the bedpost. There is zero reception here. Nada. Zilch. "Do you have any connection on your phone with your network?" I ask.

"Nope. No chance in hell there's anything here." Tristan doesn't bother to look up. I haven't seen him with his phone since... I don't know anymore.

"Hopefully at the main reception areas." I toss my phone on the bed.

Tristan tilts his head and gives me a long, hard stare. "I thought we were here so you could stop hyperventilating as you search the internet a thousand times a day, waiting for that bomb to drop."

I glare at him. He can fuck right off. Except that he can't. He hasn't seen the video—thank God—and can't begin to understand...*argh*. Hopefully Tristan will *never* see that godforsaken Mia Reed video.

This is us for the next three months. We are firmly ensconced in the crack of butt-fuck nowhere because *I* wanted to be here. And I want him to be here too. He needs to finish his project. I close my eyes and bite down hard on my lip. This is the opportunity I desperately wanted and needed. This is the opportunity that got handed to me because of *him*. There's no way I'm messing this up, even if Tristan and I are going to be in each other's space like this.

"I'm going to check whether my equipment survived the flight." He picks my suitcase out of the pile and heaves it onto the bed. "Make yourself at home."

He turns his back, and I fight the irrational burn of tears.

I swallow hard, forcing myself to focus. My wet jeans are itchy and so uncomfortable, and all I want is to strip them off, but I am going to address the elephant in the room first. "What are we going to do about the sleeping arrangements?"

Tristan glances over, then gets busy opening a lock on one of his crates. "You take the bed. I'll figure something out."

"Fine." I swivel around, only to stare at the king-size bed. It's extra long, too. What a waste. There's more than ample space…but—a giant fucking *BUT*.

"I'm more worried about a space to set up my computer for the work I have to do," Tristan says. "I'll have to rearrange a few things to make a workable office."

"Whatever you need." *Just keep busy and keep to your side of the room.* I unlock and unzip my suitcase and start digging for a sundress. I'm so tense that despite my exhaustion, there's no way I'm going to take a nap. Or lie down on this bed with Tristan right there. That feels too much like an invitation.

With my toiletry bag in hand, dress and fresh underwear gathered, I slip behind the wall that divides the sleeping and living areas from the bathroom. The jeans go first, scratchy and horrible as I peel them off my legs. As soon as I'm down to my panties, I still. Tristan won't come in while I'm in here—that's a given, right?

Shit.

I tug at the ludicrously expensive engagement ring, but my fingers are so swollen from the heat and the travel that it won't budge.

Cursing sounds from the bedroom, and I swear he read my mind.

"What?" I call.

"Freaking cornstarch uncapped. It's everywhere."

I roll my eyes. Diver problems. What does he use cornstarch for? I don't even care.

With the reminder of the fake deal we've got going stuck on my hand, I get naked and step into the outdoor shower. It has a half-circle stone wall and a glacier-blue beaded glass curtain that provides more privacy than I expected. Thank God. I open the faucet and shudder as cold water hits my skin. It's wonderful and strips the sticky heat right off. How do they have such cool water on tap? The water pressure is perfect, the rainfall shower pure heaven, and the Beaumont toiletries smell like expensive perfume.

"Lexi?"

I freeze at Tristan's voice, my fingers pausing as I massage shampoo into my scalp. My skin pebbles with a rush of goosebumps, and my nipples harden. He's *right there*. I cross my arms over my chest. "I'm naked! In the shower!"

"I'd hope so—would be kinda weird otherwise." He chuckles, then sighs, and it's as if the exhale held a thousand apologies. "Can I pour you a stiff drink? Gin and tonic? Rum and Coke? This bar is well stocked. Lemons, limes, sugar syrup, the works."

Damn. He's still in the bedroom, but there are zero sound barriers here. Even when I can't see him, he's going to be there. There's no escape. The tears I've been warding off reach saturation point, and now they're flowing down my cheeks. I clear my throat. "A gin and tonic, please. Just a single," I manage before I lean against the wall, pressing my fists to my stomach to quiet my sobs.

"Don't run that water tank empty, Lexi," comes Tristan's

voice again. "Desalination takes time, and I need to shower too. Probably a couple of times a day going forward."

God. Can he stop being so annoying? Can he give me a moment's peace to deal with the umpteenth mindfuck I've had to manage since I walked in on Mia Reed and The Head?

Worst of all, The Head is so much history now, he might as well have been medieval. Over the past few weeks Tristan has crept back to centerstage, and there's nothing I can do to boot him out of the fantasy that plays on repeat in my head. A fantasy where several aspects were real once. His hands on my skin, grazing the soft curves of my hips, his lips on mine, my hands inching underneath his shirt—

I drag in a ragged breath, trying to get a grip, but I can't. Now that we're here, it's as if all the other characters have stepped away, leaving the spotlight only on Tristan: the guy who refused to have sex with me when I was nineteen, still a kid in his eyes, and so in love with him that I was a walking hormonal mess.

I've never recovered from his rejection, and now *this*? Coming here with him was undiluted madness. I wipe my cheeks and tug again at the stupid ring that binds me to him. Still too tight. It's annoyingly symbolic. Can't get this ring off, can't get out of this little deal, and can't get off this island. "I'm almost done," I call as I give up on taking it off and get under the rainfall to rinse my hair.

This is going to be a juggle, but I can't make a fool of myself again with Tristan. I've been made enough of an idiot by men in my life, and Tristan can go fuck himself. As will I. My vibrator sits neatly in that handy suitcase compartment with its charger. This girl has herself sorted.

I run my thumb along the band of the ring, reminding

myself that I will get used to it being there. This ring is the key to making everything here work—nothing more, nothing less. Maybe it's good that I can't get it off. It will keep me focused. I take a deep breath and feel the ground beneath me grow more solid. I can do this.

Chapter Thirteen

TRISTAN

As Lexi comes in from the bathroom, I try not to ogle her. In Miami, she was always in shorts and some nondescript T-shirt. Now she's wearing a yellow dress with pink hibiscus flowers, thin straps, a cupped bra top that gives her hot-as-all-fuck cleavage, and a fitted middle I want to squeeze so badly. And it's short. It's perfect for an island like this.

Jesus Christ. I'm in trouble. "Good shower?"

"Better than Heathrow." She comes to a standstill in the middle of the room with her arms folded over her chest. That move presses her breasts up more, and if I didn't know better, I'd think *babes* was being a cocktease.

I look away. "Thank God. There's hope." This has the potential to get crazy awkward. At Evan's place, we each had our own room and navigated the shared living areas like civil roommates when we bumped into each other. There's going to be none of that space here. I point to the coffee table where her gin and tonic is sweating. "Your drink."

"Thanks."

I'm still unpacking my things but have scouted for electrical sockets and a place to set up shop. There's a small writing desk in the room, but clearly this isn't an office space.

Problem is, I don't want to set this up anywhere else on the island as I'll be working on this project on the side. Nobody at Beaumont knows, and I think I should keep it that way. The project is the primary reason I'm here, not the dive center and keeping guests happy. Not being upfront with Beaumont isn't how I like to operate, but it's too late now. In my enthusiasm, I also failed to consider the legal ramifications of filming at Ne'emba. It's tricky, what with Beaumont having the only diving rights. Thing is, it's underwater footage, and nobody's going to know.

At minimum I should have run it past someone, but this whole shebang happened so quickly, it had spun out of control before I realized what I'd signed up for. *Now I need to deal,* as Lexi would say. Zero options. The only honest thing I can do to keep my integrity intact is look out for Lexi and make sure she gets what she needs out of our time here.

"We could move the kitchenette." Lexi takes a sip of her drink. "I can't see us using it much, and there'd probably be enough space for your computer."

I stand from where I've crouched as I stacked my things in a line along the floor. At least the cornstarch exploded only in one side pocket. It helps with the process of getting into a wetsuit. Now a fine dusting patterns the floor, though I've mostly wiped it away. "Everything's made it in one piece."

"Good." She walks around the room, taking in the space.

It's very different from the luxury places I've been to with my dad or mom. Some seaside resorts are so disconnected from their surroundings, you might as well have stayed in a high-rise hotel on Times Square. Here every detail whispers *island life*. The interior and exterior sofas—sleeping option A and B, respectively—are in sandy creams, but littered with brightly colored throw pillows for a very African feel. The splashes of color are playful and unpretentious. The mosquito netting around the bed gives the room a romantic vibe without even trying. It's a perfect home for an engaged couple thoroughly in love.

"I'm going to check out the beach," Lexi says as she puts down her drink. She's barely had two sips. "Maybe you should wait and see before you set up your office? There could be other desk options available that the hotel isn't using. There might be a separate office you can use—"

"Yep. You're probably right." I drag my fingers through my hair.

"I'll give you space," Lexi says, and before I can stop her, she's disappearing down the path that leads to the beach.

I exhale and roll my shoulders. Shower time. And I'm not going to care about wasting the fresh water. Lexi has, after all, had her turn.

We've had two days of traveling in close quarters, and I need to get her out of my system while she's out of the house. Lexi has always been under my skin, in that *can't-touch-this* way that comes with being my best friend's younger sister.

Problem is, when we did cross that line five years ago, she'd wedged a part of her under my heart. Fuck, it hurt. Still does, like that thumbnail that you banged in the door, still pulsing pain hours later. Now it's as if my whole being has become that bruise, conscious of her every move.

I'm going to have to get a grip. Three months. It's *only* for three months. What with the shit ton of work I have to do, steering clear of her should be a breeze.

When Lexi is still not back an hour later, I push down my annoyance. I'm worried about her. Who knows why, because where's she going to go? But it turns out not having her attached to my hip in a strange place gives me a weird churning in my stomach. I'm dressed in chino shorts and a white button-down with rolled-up sleeves. I don't bother with shoes and head out to where she disappeared toward the sea.

As the path opens to the beach, I pause. It's breathtaking. The sun is dipping low, and with the clouds packed together on the horizon, the sunset is phenomenal. Orange and pink hues beam down on the sea, scattering a reflection of shimmering gold on the water. The wind has picked up, sweeping the afternoon's tropical heat away with it. It's the perfect time to be out on the beach.

I spot Lexi where she's settled on the sand some distance away, her hair now dry and dancing in the breeze. I cross the wide stretch of sand. "Hey."

She looks up with a soft smile. "Hey."

"How're you feeling?"

"I'm exhausted." She looks to the ocean again. "Can't get enough of this view, though. If we get fired tomorrow, it will have been worth it."

"It's spectacular." I sit down next to her. "And nobody's getting fired."

The boat we came in from Pemba is bobbing in the water, and now there are two rubber dinghies floating next to it. Out toward the horizon, I spot a couple of white sails catching the wind. "Those must be locals going out to fish in the night."

"It's a crazy privilege to come work here."

"Yep. For both of us." I glance at her. "Did you explore more?"

"No. I spotted a few couples walking around the island, and they're setting up for dinner on the beach about three hundred yards away, beyond that bend. I didn't want to stalk around. Not yet, anyway."

I chuckle. "It's almost time for us to meet with Miriam and Don."

"Yes." She sighs. "Three months of faking it is going to be tough."

"Unless we make it easy on ourselves."

"How?"

"Dunno. Solely focus on the end goal and what we're both gaining from being here?" I sigh. There's no other way I'm getting through our time here. "Let's make it through tonight and get some decent sleep."

We both stand, and as she shakes the sand from her dress, two people come around the bend. Don and Miriam wave at us.

"Show's on," I say as I reach for her hand.

I feel the hesitation in her grip, but give her fingers a warm squeeze. "In public, this is all we have to do to sell our engagement."

She squeezes my fingers back. "Okay. Nothing more. Ever."

"Yes." It's as if we've covered the whole awkward room situation with these few words, but I know we're still pretending. This situation has stirred up our complicated past like silt, and now I can't see anything else.

Either way, this is it. If we can fool Don and Miriam, we can fool anybody. And these two will be leaving soon enough.

Once our only link to the Beaumont head office is gone, things will be smooth sailing.

As we close in on Don and Miriam, they smile. "Manage to take a nap?" Don asks.

"Nope." I shake my head. "Best to soldier through this jet lag until we can go to bed."

"So true." Miriam is by Lexi's side. "We've set you a table with the rest of the guests. We thought it would be nice for you to have at least one night of the Beaumont Ne'emba Island experience before we hand you your uniforms in the morning."

Lexi smiles. "That sounds dreamy."

"It is," Miriam agrees. "Tomorrow morning, if you're up to it, I'll run you through our basic day here, introduce you to all the staff, get you kitted out in the Beaumont uniform, and then see what you need from there. From what I've seen of your résumé, you'll be quick to catch on."

"You've seen my résumé?" Lexi asks.

"We've seen both of your résumés," Don says with a smile. "You're going to be fantastic additions to the staff. We've had too many dive masters coming and going, and the staff are restless. Guests aren't happy with the service, and it shows in our reviews, so I'm afraid you're going to have your hands full."

"We'll swing it around," I say, as Roger's surly attitude comes to mind. I squeeze Lexi's hand where it's nestled against my palm. Hopefully the problem is mostly with the dive center, not the rest of the staff too.

"Beaumont is lucky to have you here. Even if it's only temporary," Don says.

We round the bend, and I catch my breath. *Wow. Wow. Wow.*

All along the water's edge, tables for two have been set, each some distance apart for privacy. A line of lanterns hanging from poles curve along the water's edge, while white tablecloths stir in the breeze.

"It's stunning," Lexi marvels. "Just beautiful."

"Yes. We try to make it as special as we can here in the last outpost for folks who trust us with their dreams," Miriam says. "Although most of our guests are loaded, for some people coming to Ne'emba, it's a once-in-a-lifetime experience. We don't mess with that."

"And with what Beaumont charges," Don adds, "expectations are high."

"For sure." Lexi looks at me, her eyes wide.

"You've got this," I assure her.

"Can we get you a drink?" Don asks as we make our way up the wide stretch of sand to the general guest area.

This is the first time either of us has seen the lodge, and like our cottage, it's earthy but spectacular. Similar high and overlapping A-frame roofs cover the communal spaces. Several cushioned enclaves create privacy for people to sit in the shade, and there's a fully covered dining area where they can serve meals when it rains. There's a beach bar on hand, but farther in, I spot a bigger bar area with colorful liquor bottles on display.

"What would you recommend? Do you have a house cocktail?" I ask as I let go of Lexi's hand.

Don nods. "That we do. Two of those coming right up."

He walks off to the beach bar, and Miriam indicates for us to follow her to where waiters, dressed in chinos and white shirts, are getting ready for service. "Might as well start introducing you now."

We're dunked in a whirlwind of names and smiling faces with a lot of hand shaking in between. Miriam then takes us to the kitchen where we peer in. One chef, one sous-chef, and two assistants later, my stomach is growling from all the delicious smells.

"You know we'll probably have to redo all these introductions in the morning," Lexi says as we walk out to meet Don, who's holding our cocktails.

"Yeah." My jet-lagged brain screams for a break. "I'm a bit fried."

"Not to worry," Miriam assures us. "At least they know who you are and can help you going forward. The staff here are lovely, except when strangers step in short term like they've done with the dive center. There's been an undercurrent of dissatisfaction for weeks now."

Don and Miriam are painting this too pretty. Miriam's earlier comment about the dive center already sounded a warning bell. For all we know, we've stepped into a ship with a mutiny on our hands. But if there's trouble on the ground, surely we're supposed to know? They could have told us something during the interview process...or not. This sounds like they have a revolving door of people coming and going. This Beaumont gig could have another side to its very shiny coin—one we may not be ready for.

"I'm sure we can figure it out," Lexi says as she takes her drink from Don. "Cheers!"

I raise my cocktail to hers, but as our gazes meet, it's clear Lexi's read between the lines too. I can see worry sitting shallow in her gaze, and those frown lines between her eyebrows etch deep.

When we sit down at our romantic table for two ten minutes later, within a lick of the waves at our feet, she looks up to me with a grimace. "How well do you know your way around boats?" She swallows as she leans closer. "Do you think we could build a raft and row to Pemba if we needed to escape?"

Chapter Fourteen

LEXI

Dinner was amazing. I can't believe the food that came out of that kitchen tonight. If this is the Beaumont standard on a tiny speck of an island in the middle of the ocean, I wonder what the food is like in France, where they have their stronghold.

Tristan and I are walking back to our cottage after saying goodnight to Don and Miriam and the waiters who were cleaning up. Our cottage is in the opposite direction from the guests' accommodations, and this time we take the boarded walkway that starts at the main reception area. At the end of the lit walkway, one sign says *Private* and the other way says *Forest Trail*. At this fork, Tristan lets go of my hand and we step down onto the sand.

We're finally out of sight and earshot, and I stifle a yawn. It's still early, but I'm happy to go to bed. We're both on duty at seven in the morning. There is a daily housekeeping briefing first thing, and obviously, I need to be there.

Tristan's first dive is at around nine thirty, but he told Don he'd be at the dive center early to see what's plotting there. The hints were few and far in between, but I saw the signs. Despite the pleasant smiles and happy island vibes, some of the staff here are disgruntled. The red flag that waved during my interview with Nathan Beaumont now flaps in the wind. Who knows how this is going to manifest in my day-to-day? But that's tomorrow's worry.

I'm too tired to be nervous around Tristan. Our first night alone in this intimate space loomed over me earlier, but he said the bed is mine, and I'm happy to have it, despite feeling crap about it.

"You use the bathroom first," he says as we walk into our cottage.

We both freeze on the spot as we approach the bedroom. There's been a room turndown of sorts. Some windows are now covered with the roll-down grass-woven curtains, but the breeze still moves through the space. The mosquito net has been pulled closed and tied just beyond the bed frame, forming an intimate box of protection. Where we'd shifted a pillow or put anything out of place, things have been rearranged to perfection. Citronella is burning somewhere. A standing light is lit in the living area, and a moth dances in the golden hue.

"Nice," Tristan mutters as we stare at the bed.

Here's something we didn't consider: bugs.

I try not to freak out, now even more aware of how exposed Tristan will be in the open, since there's only one mosquito net.

"Can't be that bad," he says, as if reading my mind. Then he turns away, leaving me standing, indecisive, as he disappears into the night.

My indecisiveness doesn't last long. Not much I can do about the bugs now. I go through my nighttime routine and am very grateful when I finally slip into the safety of the netted bed and switch off my bedside lamp. Everything is weirdly open, but here, ensconced behind a veil, there's a false sense of security.

And yet...this bed is the most dangerous place of them all.

I glance to the side—*Tristan's side*—and then to the light in the living area I've kept on for him. I have no idea when he's going to come back, or what he's going to do, so I roll on my side and look the other way, hoping to be asleep before he returns. It's too warm for anything more than the tank top and sleep shorts I'm wearing, and I don't bother to get under the light covers.

Two minutes later, I turn back to face his side. *Shit*. We haven't made a plan about extra bedding for him to use on the sofa. And it's not as if we can ask for it...

I get up and go in search of some extra linen in the walk-in closet. It's quite spacious and serves as a storage place too. Thank the Pope there's an extra linen set and a blanket on hand. I take it, fold it neatly, and lay it on the sofa that looks the most comfortable, then add a pillow from the bed to the stack. *There*. Housekeeping perfection. I would know; I've worked that branch on weekends and holidays hands-on for four years, from the most standard double room all the way to a St Chalamet penthouse suite.

I clamber back into bed and wait, listening for Tristan's footsteps over the gentle whisper of the waves. If the bugs become too much, there might be a point during the night when he decides to get behind the mosquito net and into bed with me. I turn my back on the light, heart pulsing with the possibilities of that going on long term. *Nope. Nope. Nope.*

My head is still chanting those words when I wake up. The first morning light filters through the dark forest surrounding our cottage, and I sit up and look around, confused. The other side of the bed is untouched, and there's no sign of Tristan. No lights are on, so he must have switched them off last night. I reach for my phone on the nightstand and check the time. It's just after five in the morning.

A soft groan floats over to me, and I sit straighter. "Tris?"

"Hmm?"

That doesn't sound good. "You okay? Slept well?"

"It's been a night of blood donation."

Eh... "What?"

"I might need coffee so my body can have some liquid for hematopoiesis."

I have no clue what he's saying, but I got the coffee part. I get out of bed and wrangle the mosquito net for a second before I find the slit and get out. I go over to where Tristan is lying on the sofa, a flat sheet covering his stomach and thighs but the rest of him naked. He's lazily scratching his chest, eyes closed, dark circles under his eyes.

My heart stills. *Oh hell.* He looks like he has measles.

"You got chowed."

He opens one eye. "You think? Itches like Satan's crotch."

"Don't scratch! You're only going to make it worse."

"*Pfft.*" His fingers move from one bite to the next. "Did you sleep okay?"

"Yes." I slept like a log and wasn't annoyed by a single mosquito. He struggles up, and now I get to see his back. I suck in a breath. *Ouchy ouch ouch, itchy itch itch.*

"You're welcome, babes. Anything for you. *Really.*"

For the first time, I don't protest about him calling me *babes*. "I'll make coffee," I say, guilt nagging at my conscience. "Did you bring Afterbite or anything?"

"Nope."

God. This whole situation pounced on us so quickly, we didn't properly prepare. "Maybe they'll have something in the boutique or in their first-aid kit."

Tristan says nothing, and it's quiet as I make coffee. With two mugs in hand, I find him leaning against one of the supporting poles in a pair of sleep shorts, still scratching. Through the vegetation, the sea is a slate grey brushstroke on the horizon. The ever-present breeze stirs the palm leaves, but the heat of the day is a promise nothing is going to break.

"Here." I hold out Tristan's coffee.

"Thanks." His stubble is thick and about the only place he isn't littered with bites. "Walk with me?" he says as he meets my gaze.

"I'm sorry about all of that." I wave at his body in general, trying not to stare at his naked chest. It's warm, yes, but it would've been harder on those skeeters if he'd worn a T-shirt. And it would be easier on *me* too, not living with his bare chest in my face.

"Not making this easy on ourselves, are we?" With that, he stalks off, leaving it to me to follow him or not.

Of course I don't stay behind, already feeling like total shit about the situation. We walk down to the beach as the sun's first rays shimmer over the sea. A flock of black birds swoops up as we come closer, and with a groan, Tristan sits down. I follow suit, and in silence we watch as the colors change rapidly around us as day dawns.

"I'm sorry about last night. If you want, I can take the sofa tonight," I offer quietly.

Tristan sighs, and thank God it isn't an awkward, unwelcome silence between us. It's one of resignation.

"No. Imagine your skin—won't let anything take a bite out of you, Lexi." He chuckles as his hand comes up to stroke my hair away from my cheek.

His touch is warm and gentle, and my stupid head runs on with the sentence. *Unless of course, it's me.* A tingle idles down my spine, and my skin pops a spread of goosebumps. *Oh my gawd.* He's sitting so close, I can feel his body's warmth. I can smell his intoxicating male scent, the same from that night so long ago, but breathing him in makes it feel like it happened yesterday.

"You're cold?" Tristan asks, but he must know better because his gaze travels over my face where a heady blush blooms at the thought of his lips and teeth on my skin. His hand on my breast. His thumb grazing my nipple.

"No." I suck on my lip, forcing my mind back to neutral.

"Good." He finishes his coffee and lets the mug dangle from his fingers. "Here's what we're going to do. See if you can get an extra mosquito net from housekeeping. I'll make a plan to put it up somehow. I'll dig in the maintenance area for tools."

"Okay."

He stands and holds out his hand to pull me up. I place my hand in his, the ultimate gesture of trust. As I rise, his gaze, which for one long second holds my own, dips down to my breasts in this stupid tank top that leaves little to the imagination. I'm not exactly in a wet T-shirt contest, but you'll have a hard time missing my nipples, which seem to play a dirty game of treason here.

My mind is trying its best to find a way out of this Don't Perve Over Tristan escape room, but my body just wants to stay put and play. *With him.*

Chapter Fifteen

TRISTAN

It's just after seven now, and Lexi has left to meet with Miriam. I didn't mean to be curt to her earlier, but I'm not sure she was even aware of my mood this morning. I'm still exhausted. Long-haul flights, jet lag, and the crowning glory of feeding every last fucking bug on this island last night got the better of me. I might have to work in a nap at some point today to get back to my usual even keel—a nap that preferably happens on the bed and not on an uncomfortable sofa that gives a boat bunkbed a run for its money.

Poor Lexi. She had a hard time hiding her chagrin—it was almost comical. If she thinks I'll serve her up to the mosquitoes, she doesn't really know me. And that thought itches more than all the bug bites combined.

The thought of her and those innocent—*my ass*—girly PJs she slept in only makes me groan. When I came home last night, she was fast asleep. I couldn't stop my gaze from running over every part of her as I got ready for bed, mapping out the parts I touched once. I won't fuck it up like that again.

My temper's short for more than one reason, but today of all days, I can't let it show. There's only one way I'm going to survive these three months—by not looking at her at all, which is impossible. I'm going to figure out a plan B here.

All showered, I'm digging through every last long-lost emergency kit squished in my general diving bag, but the best I have are some antihistamines. They should take the edge off. Dressed in board shorts and a T-shirt, I heave my diving bag over my shoulder and it digs in, rubbing the bite that's been driving me nuts since four this morning. Ugh...*ahhh*. The relief!

I walk over to the general guest area, but there's no sign of Lexi. Only some waiters are milling about, setting up the breakfast buffet. I recognize our waiter from last night, and he smiles at me.

"Don said to point you to the staff canteen first so you can have breakfast," he says, and I follow him to the kitchen and around the back. Quiet chatter comes from a dining area where several uniformed staff are either eating or finishing up their coffees. I spot Don and walk over to him.

"Wow. What happened to you?" he asks as his gaze plots the constellation of bites on my face.

"Fell asleep on the sofa."

"Whoa-whoa-whoa." Don shakes his head. "And Lexi didn't come wake you up to call you to bed?"

"She was out stone cold before me. With the jet lag, it sort of happened before we noticed." At least on a boat if you're grumpy as fuck everybody else is delighted that you're leaving them alone. Here there seems to be no escape.

"You should be careful," he warns. "We don't officially have any malaria or dengue fever on the island..." He lowers his voice. "But that's because everybody who comes here travels via the mainland and can pick it up there. We've never had guests report that they got sick after a stay with us, but don't do something irresponsible like that again, okay? Get under the net at night and stay there."

Right. Between Don's age and word choice, I feel as if I've been reprimanded by the school principal. "I hear you."

"Do you have anything for the bites? Ointment?"

"No, it'll be okay. Nothing like seawater to cure an itch or two."

Don harrumphs. "That fiancée of yours should take better care of you."

Irritation grates through me—to imply that a woman should *mother* me when I've functioned without one since I was *ten*. Fuck. Lexi would spit fire at Don's suggestion.

I hold back an acerbic retort, and luckily, Don is quick to move on with a rush of staff introductions. I nod at everybody. Roger and Mike are here too, and although Mike smiles at me while chewing, Roger gives me that glare. They've listened in on Don's reprimand, and Roger's eyes tell me everything I don't need to know. He thinks I'm an idiot.

I grab a fresh roll and some cold cuts and cheese, stack it all together, down a glass of orange juice, and nod to Don. "Let's go."

"That's all you're eating?" Don asks as I heave my bag over my shoulder again.

"I don't dive on a full stomach."

With a nod, he leads the way to the dive center.

As we approach, I see the big freshwater dipping barrels for cleaning gear after a salty dive, and a neat hanger system for suits to drip dry. The dive center itself is in the first enclosed building I've seen since arrival, and Don actually has to unlock the front door.

"Don't tell me you have security issues here?" I ask as he disarms the alarm.

"No, not really, not of that sort, but the equipment is expensive and has good resale value, as you know." He opens the door wider. "I'll run you through the security system when you lock up tonight."

"That's good." Semi-decent scuba gear can set you back five thousand dollars, and from what I've seen of Beaumont, they won't use a basic brand. I don't give his comment any more thought as Don switches on the lights. I breathe easy. Whoever designed this had a plan. Don walks around and opens the locked window slats one by one, and natural light floods inside with a welcome breeze.

I lower my bag to the floor. A wide counter runs along one wall which hosts a whiteboard with a roster, a list of dive sites, and a few other just-stick-me-up-somewhere notices. There are the usual rails filled with dive suits in all shapes and sizes, the fins, the masks, the buoyancy control devices or BCDs, and regulators. Everything is neat and tidy, exactly as I expected it to be.

"The air compressor and tanks are at the back," Don says as he unlocks another door, leading me to a cage for the oxygen tanks. "There's also a washroom and shower here, but I don't think it gets used much, as guests tend to go back to their rooms."

"Fantastic." I may have stumbled upon my alternate sleeping quarters. Nobody will know if I come bunk here at night to avoid being feasted on. That said, three months is a long time to hide out, and at some point, someone will notice.

The word will spread that Lexi and I have broken up or something equally as ridiculous as our fake engagement. I'm not looking to turn our relationship status into the latest staff gossip.

Don goes behind the counter and points to the roster up on the wall. "These are the guests who signed up for dives today and where they'll be going. Setiawan should be here soon. He's from Indonesia and has kept the show going, but he's leaving tomorrow. So, pardon the pun, we're throwing you in the deep end. Setiawan's wife is pregnant with their first and could give birth at any moment, so he's not sticking around one minute longer than necessary."

"I see." Setiawan will be flying, so that means he can't dive today. Can't be upping his risk of decompression sickness when he's about to become a dad for the first time. *Deep end indeed*. I look over the roster. The Pinnacle and Shark Corner are the two dive sites today. Tonight's optional night dive has no sign-ups. The rest of the week is filled out too, and not one site is repeated. *Excellent*. I knew there'd be variety here.

"Speak of the devil," Don says, and I look up to see a man walking in. "This is Setiawan. I'll leave you to it. I'm going to see how breakfast's going."

"We don't have a lot of time, but you'll catch up quickly, yes?" Setiawan says as we shake hands.

"Haven't much choice, do I?"

He chuckles. "You'll be good. A marine scientist! I'm only a master diver, and to be honest, I don't have the experience to deal with some of the people who come here. Be prepared for some *enthusiasts*." He sighs. "I also have too much on my mind."

"It will be good for you to be back home." Seems

everybody here has gotten the lowdown on Lexi and me. "You're going to stick around today?"

"Yes, I'll go out with you, but I'll stay on the boat. For the rest, you're mostly in Roger's hands, with Mike on standby."

Soon we've covered a lot of ground, from GPS coordinates for dive sites to where all the closest medical facilities are. It strikes me that I'm a man alone here. "What happens when I can't dive? Get a cold or something?"

"Ha. Don't get a cold or something." Setiawan doesn't look up from where we're busy compressing air into the oxygen tanks for the morning's dives.

Okay. I never thought to ask before taking the job—because I had other things on my mind—but a dive center can't run with one dive master alone. "No, seriously? What happens?"

"They boat someone in from Dar es Salaam or Pemba. In general, it's a mess, so make sure you give advance notice for getting sick."

Roger walks in seconds later and nods in our direction as he starts putting equipment together for the ten divers we have on a double dive today.

"What's wrong with him?" I ask under my breath.

"I haven't been here long enough to figure that out," Setiawan mumbles back. "Luckily he's your problem now, and good luck with that."

Chapter Sixteen

LEXI

I have a pounding headache, and if I don't go rinse off the morning's heat soon, I might snarl at someone. At St Chalamet I used to run in heels in a temperature-controlled, five-star-plus environment. This morning has been a rollercoaster ride in a tumble dryer. I'm wrung out, parched, and sick to my stomach after gobbling down my lunch.

Miriam seems to take it all in stride. She's environmentally fit, whereas I'm feeling my New York fall. My time in Miami was a blip of air conditioning and cooling off in Evan's swimming pool with a mojito in my hand. Nothing like this. I didn't appreciate it enough while I had it.

Miriam took me to see the office I'll be working from, and there I found the holy internet I'd been missing like a freshly pulled tooth. She gave me ten minutes to email Evan, Mom, and Tessa, which I did in no time. Then, after spending two minutes searching for *Mia Reed and sex scandal* and only getting old hits, I exhaled, feeling I'd been saved for another day. I didn't have time to linger, though, as Miriam was on a mission this morning to explain how every last thing works. Luckily nothing is new. Things may work differently from St Chalamet, but they're not unfamiliar. The office assistant, Jem Shabani, who's been here since Ne'emba's construction thirty years ago when she started as a nanny, has slowly moved up the ranks and knows everything in and out. It's going to be fine. In fact, everything is so fine, I feel like a lost extra on stage with no real purpose.

After lunch we go over the details of the first wedding party, which arrives in a couple days. This is no simple destination wedding. It's over-the-top luxury. Everything is being flown in from all over, and it's a logistical nightmare. For such a small venue, this place does things with a big bang. Jem holds all the strings, though, and she's not going to drop a single ball.

In the heat of the day, there seems to be a siesta break, so I'm off to our cottage for a second shower. I hate sweating and can't stand the idea of seeing guests in a less-than-pristine uniform. I received several sets, and at least the clothes are practical—a sand-colored mini skirt, Bermuda shorts, or capri pants and sleeveless button-down cotton shirts with light brown leather sandals. Not quite St Chalamet, but it works with the island vibe.

I haven't seen Tristan at all since this morning's coffee, and while half of me misses him, the other half is sighing in relief. The less I see of him, the better. I haven't been able to procure an extra mosquito net, as the question only raised the head housekeeper's eyebrows to her hairline. "Why?" she asked. "Did you rip yours? *Already*?"

The accusatory tone of that question shut me right down. "No, I was just wondering—"

"For guest rooms we'll source during the year if necessary, but for staff, we stitch them. The nets are tailormade in Nairobi. We don't order them and have them delivered the next day, you know? This isn't America."

Okey dokey. I backed right off.

"Tristan?" I call as I approach our cottage to make sure I'm alone. No answer. I kick off my sandals, rinse my feet in the foot basin, and walk inside. Someone has cleaned the room, and the place looks immaculate. Chances of privacy here? Sub-zero. I can be a bit OCD when it comes to clean and neat rooms, but a pair of discarded shoes and a bra hooked over the back of the chair would be welcome right now. Anything to provide that baseline home-comfort look over this feeling of constantly being watched and cleaned up after.

I toss the tube of anti-itch ointment I got from the hotel's boutique onto the sofa, out of habit check my phone where I left it on my nightstand for messages, roll my eyes at the zero-internet situation, and continue to strip all the way to the shower where I open the faucet. The cool water is a soothing balm, and I drop my head back with a moan.

The guest rooms have glass-rimmed infinity plunge pools; we have the ocean and a cold shower. Thank God. And at some point, I'll take a bath in that tub that's made for two. I stand under the spray for too long, and then remind myself, *desalination takes time.* Ugh.

I step out of the shower, feeling loads better, if still woozy and tired with dragging jet lag that won't give up. My headache has eased. It's easy to dehydrate here, but guzzling a liter of water over lunch seems to have sorted me out. I don't bother to dry off, but instead knot a towel above my boobs and walk into the bedroom. The first thing I see is that my trail of clothes has been picked up, and the bits and pieces are hanging neatly over the back of the sofa. Now that's *extra*.

But then I spot long legs stretched out on the bed—long, muscular legs that end in feet I've come to love because they're sexy.

Tristan. A soft groan slips from my lips before I can stop it.

"Babes." He sounds halfway asleep already. He can't see me from where I'm standing in the alcove that leads to the dressing area and bathroom.

"Are you decent?" The last thing I need is to walk in on Tristan naked or getting down to *man business*.

"Yup. Just taking a nap."

"Okay." *So not okay*. My suitcase, still unpacked, is on the floor, the lid closed but with garments spilling out the sides. "Don't mind me."

I tiptoe over to my suitcase, overly conscious that I'm naked underneath the towel. My heart rate ticks up. Tristan has seen me in a bikini, which is technically less than this, but only a towel is different. It's a flailing grip away from being naked.

I don't look in his direction but drop to my haunches to rummage through my clothes. I'm not getting back into a uniform until four when I need to check in with Miriam again. I dig out a swimsuit cover-up, which is the coolest piece I have, plus some fresh underwear. It'll have to do. I get up slowly, making sure the towel covers my butt and is still fitting tight around my boobs. My breathing is slow now—I can feel Tristan's eyes on me.

All I want to do is rush back to the bathroom to get dressed, but I look up to find him staring at me. He might be half asleep, but his eyes are taking in everything. For a moment,

I'm almost hypnotized as his gaze roams over my body, setting my blood on fire. He's looked at me like that once before.

"Is that a blush or a sunburn, babes?"

With a swallow, I glance at my bare shoulders, which were exposed in the sleeveless shirt, only to see lobster-red skin. "Oh God." We spent time walking in the sun, and it's a bitch here.

"Your face is red too," he says softly.

That would be a blush. My moisturizer has an SPF 50 sunscreen. I'll have to spread it everywhere.

"Where else did you burn, hmm?"

Is he daring me to drop the towel so he can have a full inspection of my body?

I suck in a slow breath. "It's okay. I'll put on sunscreen." I reach for the tube of anti-itch stuff on the sofa. "I'm not sure how good this it, but I got it for you at the boutique."

Tristan sits up, and it's as if the cottage shrinks. "Thanks. You'll have to help me on my back. Some of these bites have been driving me nuts with my wetsuit."

"Sure. I'm going to get dressed." I stalk back to the bathroom side of the room and hesitate before dropping the towel to the floor. *Crap.* Why am I fantasizing about Tristan *watching* me? Looking at me with that thirst in his eyes?

I get dressed and feel less exposed as I return to the bedroom. He hasn't moved and is still lying on his back, eyes closed. "Tris?" If he's sleeping, I'm not going to wake him.

"Still here. Barely."

"Okay."

He's tossed the ointment onto my side of the bed, and it's been opened and amply used. I kneel on the bed and reach for it. This is the most intimate situation we've been in. I breathe.

He smells fresh, and his hair is still moist. "Where did you shower?"

"At the dive center. They have an indoor and outdoor shower there."

"Oh." I haven't been to the dive center. "You've put ointment everywhere else?"

"Mmm-hmm." Tristan rolls onto his stomach.

His back looks like a minefield. I'm not sure what we're doing tonight, but I can't subject him to this again.

"Don threatened me with malaria and dengue fever."

My hands still as I squeeze ointment onto a fingertip. "He did?"

"Uh-huh."

Shit. I swallow as I smear ointment over a badly scratched bite. Touching him feels almost sinful, it's so delicious. I have to steer my naughty thoughts away from the muscles on his back, the deep groove of his spine, and the slow, unaffected way his body rises and falls as he breathes, as if this has zero effect on him.

"How was the diving?" I ask, not sure he's even awake anymore.

"Phenomenal."

I smile. "Yeah?"

"This is it for me, Lexi. This is changing the ballgame completely. Now I just need time."

My hand trails up his back, where there are bites he wasn't able to reach. I have to stop myself from making my caresses sexual, because it's so easy to slip into that frame of mind. Worst of all, I *want* to slip into that frame of mind... I want to go there. *Get a grip.* "Good." Three more bites and I pull away. "I'm done."

He groans and mutters something under his breath.

Was that a *don't stop*? Oh God. I wait quietly for more, wanting to touch him again but also wanting to run away. I'm still torn when a soft snore shatters the moment.

Tristan has fallen asleep; whether for real or whether he's faking it, I don't know. But he's saved me from myself, and not for the first time. I sink back against the pillows and stare at the fan that's stirring the heavy, humid air.

I'm fucked. I have been for five years. And not in the way I want to be.

Chapter Seventeen

TRISTAN

When I wake up, it's dark. It takes me a moment to realize the white haze I'm in is the mosquito net draped around the bed. Next to me, Lexi is asleep, her back turned toward me, her hair gathered to keep her neck cool. She's wearing those freaking PJs with the shorts that are too short. With the way she's lying on her side, I can see the lines of her butt cheeks where they curve up from her thighs. Her sweet pussy is right there...

I close my eyes and suppress a groan. So this is how we're going to roll? Not much choice right now. At least if we sleep in relay, we can avoid this thing brewing between us. What I really want is to roll over and pull her against me to spoon, inhaling her scent as I fondle her breast. I drag in a shaky breath and twist away softly to put my feet on the cool, polished cement floor. I find the gap in the folds of the mosquito net and slip out, headed for the toilet. I check the time on my dive watch. Four in the morning! I was out stone cold for hours. I use the bathroom and when I go to wash my hands, I find a Post-it stuck on the mirror. I peel it off and flash my watch's light on the message.

Don't tell the roaches, but I left dinner for you in the minibar fridge. It's only a sandwich. We don't want them to think there are Michelin-star crumbs here :-)

I smile as I move to the minibar fridge and find a plate with a thick ham sandwich and a banana cling-wrapped and ready for me. Sweetest Lexi. I'm freaking ravenous. I don't want to wake her, but I also don't want to be mosquito fodder, so I go hide in the walk-in closet. Here I can switch on a light and not wake her. As I lean against the closed door, I look around the space. We haven't had time to unpack, but there's ample space for the clothes we brought. There are electrical wall sockets too, and if I arrange things with a bit of logic, this will make the perfect office. And if we close the door and spray for bugs, I'll be able to work at night without being munched on. It's the perfect solution.

Two hours later, Lexi is still asleep, and I'm dressed for a run. It's no longer dark at six in the morning, and the birds are up and about. The promise of a beautiful sunrise glows on the horizon. I've no idea how big the island is, but I bet I can run around it at least once in less than an hour. I walk to the beach and stretch, then get going, opting to go toward the lodge first so I don't have to come across guests after I've gone full circle.

The sand is cool and soft, and the waves lick at my feet as I make my way along the beach. No need to kill it here. I'm not as fit as I'd like to be, for which I blame all those months spent at sea. I've been busy with work and stressed out about this deadline dilemma, but with the diving here, I'll have enough footage to wrap up the last episodes in a matter of weeks. For the first time in months—maybe for the first time in a whole year—I'm in the right headspace again for this challenge.

I'm about thirty minutes into my run when I spot someone sitting on the beach. A man and a woman. I slow down as I recognize Roger.

"Hey," I say in greeting as he looks up and sees me.

The woman, who seems to be of Indian descent, bites her lip and averts her eyes. Roger gets up and steps away as if he's been caught with both hands in the cookie jar.

"Nice sunrise," I say to slice through the awkward silence. Whatever he has going on here has nothing to do with me.

"Yes." Roger doesn't hold out his hand to the woman, and she gets up by herself.

It's quickly clear that introductions aren't going to happen. "See you later at the dive center," I tell him.

"Yes."

I start running again without looking back at the couple, and as I glance inland, I see several cottages, built in the same style as ours, lined up along the shore—the other staff accommodations. It's like a tiny village. I know some staff are on rotation, some live on the island, and some come and go at an alarming rate. What I read between the lines as Setiawan and I chatted between the two dives yesterday, is that staff retention and happiness are an issue here.

And to think this is what they call paradise, and Lexi and I are faking an engagement to be here. Maybe by the end of our three months, we'll be ready to escape too. For now, I aim to spend all the time I can underwater and max the filming so I have footage to edit.

I go straight to the staff canteen after my run, and it's clear

I'm not the only early bird around here. A lot of staff seems to like to get things done in the cooler hours of the morning. Inside the kitchen, the chef and his assistants are prepping for the day. Food is already laid out for staff, and I introduce myself to everybody I don't know yet. When Don appears minutes later, I smile.

"You look better rested. Heard from Lexi that you crashed yesterday," he says as he pours himself a coffee.

"Yep, I'll be fine now. The jet lag got the better of me."

"That's okay. We built it into our planning. We've got a lot to go through today, though, so let me know when you're ready to get started."

The next couple of days are beyond bananas. Between two dives a day, several night dives in a row, and a whole rotation of guests—people who leave after the Christmas and New Year's break and those who come in after—it's mayhem.

Or maybe it isn't, but it feels that way to me. Setiawan's gone, and I'm accosted by new guests who walk into the dive center at random to ask questions, and I don't always have the answers. I drag in Mike and Roger to help, but Mike always defers to Roger, which is weird. Mike has been at Ne'emba since the lodge opened, is married to the office assistant, Jem, and lives onsite, but he doesn't seem interested in helping me out. He's quite friendly, until he isn't. And since meeting Roger on my morning jog—which hasn't happened again—he seems even more suspicious of me than before. He knows everything about the dive center, though, so I let him run with the questions and learn as I go.

Now we're standing on the beach, giving Don and Miriam the subdued staff farewell. Mike is taking them to Pemba by boat, and from there they'll travel back to the US.

"Well, thank heavens for that," Lexi murmurs once they're out of earshot. "Now we can breathe."

I look over at her, not sure I heard right. "You're not a fan?"

"Miriam likes to micromanage. She's set in her ways and doesn't bend to what the rule book dictates here, which gets on everybody's nerves. Not that there's much to manage, with Jem at the helm." She shrugs. "You're lucky. Don didn't follow you underwater."

"No, he didn't," I say with a chuckle. "But it's your show now."

"Yep. Time to shine…if Jem will let me."

We turn to walk back to the hotel. "What do you mean?" I watch as Jem heads back in the direction of the offices, huffing with the slight incline of the beach. She's a short, stout woman, her African hair neatly braided. Thirty years is a long time to spend on a small island in the middle of nowhere. She and Mike have no children—or at least it doesn't seem so—and Ne'emba is their whole life.

"This island is Jem's baby, and she's as protective as a mother hen." She sighs. "It'll be fine. How're you holding up?"

We've been like ships in the night. I've set up my closet office and disappear into it as soon as I'm home after the night dives, working on the footage I was able to take that day. Every night I've found a meal of sorts waiting for me, that Lexi's snuck out of the staff canteen. I'm always careful to clean up after eating. If the cockroaches are anything like the mosquitos, I don't want to come face to face with them.

Lexi's asleep by the time I go to bed, and it's with silent

agreement that we've gotten into this habit. I go for a run before she's awake—she might fake still being asleep for all I know—but by the time I'm back for a shower, she's gone. Evan joked that we'd be so busy we'd hardly have time to share a morning coffee, and this is exactly where we are.

"I'm good," I say. "Hanging in there."

I glance toward the dispersing staff. I haven't met everyone since my world revolves around diving and the work I try to get done on the sly.

"Who are the two Indian women? They look like twins." I'm not sure which one I saw with Roger, but it was one of them.

"They're sisters and run the spa," Lexi says. "Organized, solid, and here against their dad's wishes."

"What?" I'm far removed from the gossip, whereas Lexi has plunged straight into its slipstream. "Weird."

"Yes. Long story. Something about running a spa being culturally inappropriate this far away from parental supervision. Their dad doesn't like it one bit, but their mom is rooting for them all the way. They wanted to start their own business and got a short-term contract, just like us, two years ago. They were only meant to fill a three-month gap, but they've been here ever since."

"Good for them."

"Good for us. They do amazing hair and makeup, which is a key part of the Beaumont wedding package included for the bridal party."

"I see." We turn away and walk to our cottage together for the first time. It's just after lunch, and I need to get back to the dive center if I want to sneak in a solo dive on one of the reefs this afternoon.

"How's your project going?" she asks.

"Even better than I thought it would. Do you want to see?"

Lexi smiles, and my heart does this stupid little flip thing I'm so glad no one can see. "Sure. I have time now that I don't have Miriam's laser eyes beaming on me."

I nod, sorry she's been suffering. It's quiet between us as I lead her into the walk-in closet where our clothes are hanging on respective sides. I've set my laptop up against the far wall. With Lexi this close, the space immediately seems to hug itself tight. Being without WiFi has been weirdly gratifying; I'm getting more done that I anticipated, as I can focus on my work without any distractions. At some point I'll need to connect and send things off to the producers, but that I'll be able to do from the office.

I sit down on the hard chair that came with the desk and move my mouse to wake up the screen. I log in with my password, and it opens to a clip I've been working on.

"That's—What *is* that?" Lexi leans in, and her ponytail swings over my shoulder.

"It's a sea slug."

"It's too cute to be a slug. It's all pink and orange and pretty."

"True. Does *Cadlinella ornatissima* sound better?"

She rolls her eyes and perches a hand on the desk, shrinking the space between us further. She leans closer. "Yes, but still, it's so tiny for such a big name."

I smile. "Yes, hardly half of my pinky. Have you ever been snorkeling or diving?"

"No. I—" She breaks off. "Being in the open water... You know it makes me nervous. The boat ride here was enough of a test."

"You did so well, though." I run a finger over hers where our hands rest on the desk, needing to touch and reassure her. "We won't go in deep. You'll be able to stand all the way. And I'll be with you and hold your hand."

Lexi chuckles as she pulls away, just out of reach. "I don't think we'll have time."

I know her. She's so desperate to prove herself to Beaumont that she'd rather work than make time to go snorkeling in a World Heritage Site. Work is always the perfect excuse, and one she's been abusing for years.

"We'll have time. Once you're comfortable in your role, book a spot. The reefs here are something you need to see, and we can do a walk-in snorkel."

For a long minute she's quiet. "Okay." She bites her lip. "It would be nice, but only if you hold my hand as promised."

"I won't let go, babes." I reach for her hair and move it so I can see her face.

She stills as my hand brushes against her neck, and after a few seconds that feel like an eternity, she straightens and steps away. All I want is to hold her here with my hand on her hip. And I don't want to stop there. I want to stroke my palm down that sexy little skirt and trail my hand up the inside of her naked thigh to feel how wet she is. For me. Just like she was that one time all those years ago.

Funny thing? I can smell her and it's driving me freaking nuts. She's so close that her essence is putting my caveman instinct on full alert. *Fuck.*

Stop being such a fucking dick, dude. You had your chance and blew it.

"I've got to go," she murmurs.

No, she doesn't. I can't stop my stupid single-focus male

brain from flitting through these thoughts. It's after lunch. Everybody knows what happens after lunch. I stand, and she takes another step closer to the closet's open door. If simply sleeping next to each other does this to us, what would getting it on be like with her? *As if I haven't been wondering that for five long years.*

"Are you diving tonight?"

I blink, trying to drag my head out of the gutter. "Yeah."

"I'll leave something for you to eat in the fridge."

"Thanks. You know I appreciate that, right?"

"It's the least I can do as your fake fiancée." With a wink, she walks out of the closet, and I follow suit, stopping in the doorway to lean against it with folded arms. She doesn't realize it yet, but I'm watching as she rinses her face in the sink. Yep, she's hot and bothered all right.

Lexi reaches for a towel and pats her face dry. When she notices I'm there, she turns to me with a huff. "What?"

"Nothing." I uncross my arms and reach up with both hands to hang on the door frame. This move hitches up my T-shirt and will show her more than my six-pack if she dares to look lower. I'm playing dirty but loving it. "Since you'll be asleep by the time I get to bed, I just wanted to say…sweet dreams, babes."

Her cheeks turn pink, and her eyes tell me she felt every snap of tension in that closet. Not only that, she wants everything my mind conjured up while she stood next to me—my hand between her legs, sliding closer and closer, until I can finally dip into those panties and circle my finger around her clit.

Now she narrows her eyes, resolve solidifying. I bet she wants to flip me off sooo hard.

"You might be taking your method acting a bit too far, Tris." She stomps past me, and I chuckle to myself, resisting the urge to give her a teasing slap on the butt as she goes on her merry way.

One thing is certain. There's going to be trouble in paradise, and it's been a long time coming.

Chapter Eighteen

LEXI

"Why is it that every permanent employee here is either married or attached in some form?" I ask as I sit down at my desk across from Jem.

This fake engagement with Tristan is turning into a farce, and to keep it up for three months seems nearly impossible.

What was I thinking signing up for this? Everything he does grates on my nerves—also known as libido—and the way things are going, I'm going to need lots of time with the Bob, my battery-operated boyfriend, because I'm not going to let Tristan... *Ugh.* My heart is pulsing—everywhere. If he hadn't been there in our room earlier this morning, I would have taken yet another shower because I'm so *fucking wet.* Sea slugs shouldn't be a turn-on, but I was watching Tristan's hands more than anything. And then he touched me. *God help me.*

"You'll see," Jem's voice bulldozes through my Tristan-sex-fogged mind. "Check out that board. All those single guys coming to 'dive' want some kuma on the side."

"Kuma?" I lean on my elbow, forehead in my palm. *Do I even want to know?* Maybe I'll have basic Swahili down by the time I'm done here.

"Pussy. That's what you call it. You know, they come here and think it's Love Island or the hub of the local sex trade. The disappointment! And having to explain to them that the massages happen out in the sala on the beach where they can't ask for a happy ending? Sheesh." Jem shakes her head. "You have some things to learn, don't you? Lucky for us, we have some regulars who know to pick up their piece in town before they fly over."

Oh hell. Things to learn? I can tell her a story or two. I stand and turn toward the massive whiteboard where four weeks are plotted out with guests coming and going, color-coded with special needs—whether it be dietary requirements, allergies, honeymooners, repeaters, whatnot. Wedding parties have their own line and are blocked out in bright orange. Can't miss that. The board is a relic from the past when there was no internet connection. Some habits die hard, especially since Jem still runs the show here and makes sure it's updated daily.

My eyes travel over every single room booked for the next month, and I groan as I note that they're written in red, with warning bells and all. They're all men. Might it be that women don't feel safe traveling here alone?

"Not everybody who works here is attached or married, but the singletons don't last. We always hire couples when we can because it gives us better staff retention," Jem says. "This isn't a job for young singles anyway. People get lonely. They want to party and hang out, get drunk, do drugs, sleep around, you know how it goes. But that isn't allowed on the island. That's one reason. Now imagine one of the staff getting lonely and trying to get it on with a guest? Hmm?" She shakes her head in disgust. "Beaumont isn't that type of establishment. Therefore, the couples rule."

That's something I hadn't considered. This isn't New York with millions of people. Tensions can run high when there's no outlet in a small community like this, and crossing the line could destroy the hotel's reputation, not to mention being career suicide. But...humans are humans.

"Makes sense. So who are our singles?" I've met all the staff, but I'm still getting who's who sorted in my head. Now that Miriam is gone, I might get more than two words in with everybody I'll be working with.

"Well, Deshni and Sarika are both single. The only reason Beaumont allowed them to run the spa was because they're sisters and could keep an eye out for each other. They're still here, and they're still single." Jem sighs, and it's almost world-weary. "And there's Roger. He's still here too, to my surprise. When he came two years ago, I thought he'd be gone in a month, like so many of them."

I nod, putting it together. "I met Roger when we came here. He works with Tristan."

"Yup. He's a boat boy but wants to be more than that. He almost left—" She clears her throat. "Well, he would have left long ago if it weren't for—" Jem breaks off. "Never mind. This little island...it is what it is."

I glance at Jem, but her eyes are on her computer screen as she types away. I want to dig deeper, but I didn't miss the undercurrent of resignation in her tone. Here's Jem, completely able to run the show by herself, but someone from Beaumont's head office must be peering over her shoulder day and night. Nothing would drive me more nuts than having my competency questioned for thirty-odd years. I'm not really needed here. I shouldn't be in that managers' cottage; it should be Jem and her husband Mike.

I sit down with a sigh, and Jem shoots me a look over the rim of her glasses. "You keep that zirconia on your finger, Lexi. It's the first step in warding off the creeps."

Zirconia? If I had it in me, I'd let her know it's a freaking *Tiffany*. An airport Tiffany, but still. "Tristan's here," I say.

"Uh-huh. You'll see how much he's worth within the next weeks. Nothing tests a relationship like spending time on this little island. A place like this brings out a man's true colors."

Oh, God. If she only knew... *Shit*. What if she knows? Has she figured out our secret fake engagement in less than a week?

Impossible.

I sink down into my seat so I can hide behind my computer screen, ready to put my head in the space that dries up any salacious thoughts about my fake fiancé, his smile, his teasing, his general hotness, or the fact that I know what he looks like when he's asleep. So freaking sexy. I haven't exactly been sleeping through at night, and staring at Tristan on his side of the bed is half the reason for my current frustrations. Because lying there, watching him, breathing in the same air, reminds me so much of how far we went once and how that one night changed—no, *ruined*—everything.

And then he stroked my hand in that closet. It was such a small, gentle gesture, but it reverberated straight to my underbelly where the tension's been mounting.

I need something—anything—to get my mind off my roommate. I open the internet browser to feed my Mia Reed addiction. I log into my email and check that first, telling myself I shouldn't be so desperate for my fix. There are new emails, three of which I care to read: from Tessa, Evan, and Mom.

Tessa's started her filming, and she's loving every minute of it. *Things are so real now I have to pinch myself like a thousand times a day. And guess who's been cast as the male lead...* She goes on for several lines about the cast and finally ends her email with a triumphant *and Mia Reed is lying so fucking low, nobody can find her! Do you know she's ghosted social media???!! She's ghosted the world!!! She's gone, girl, GONE!*

Uh, nope. I didn't notice. But now that she's the topic of discussion, I hastily do the rounds of every social media platform the actress uses. It's all old news—no new posts, reels, video, or anything since New Year's. I was in such a travel tangle and heat haze that I didn't notice this until Tessa pointed it out. What the hell?

I reply quickly, with happiness for her happiness, and then end with *Why would Mia Reed ghost social media? There isn't any news of her being out and about?*

Because she isn't out and about. The notion sends a chill down my spine for a reason I don't understand. I shudder, send the email into the ether, and continue on to Mom's email —school's the same, yada yada yada, how is my new job and so on. I send her a reply, which can basically be translated into ocean waves and smiley face emojis.

Next, Evan's email. *How's life? How's the job? Is Tristan behaving?*

Short and to the point, but to end with *that* question?

I reply: *Life's great. Job will be better now that the old management team has bowed out—feel like I can finally breathe. As for Tristan...*

I lean back to think. Evan said Tristan was the only guy he'd trust with me in this outpost of outposts. What did he mean by that?

I end my email with *Define behaving?* and send it off with a smirk.

Chapter Nineteen

TRISTAN

"That was a crazy sighting," says one of the guests as we make our way back to the dive center.

"I know, right?" I smile. This one should do something for the hotel's ratings. "I can't believe we saw whale sharks at night." And not just one, at least ten of them together. So close to our drop-in dive too. The photos are going to be extraordinary—probably mostly just swaths of black with white spots and stripes, but then those gaping mouths... It was a close encounter, and in the dark. "I'm glad everybody kept their cool."

Chuckles break out, and soon everybody is talking at once. I laugh. This is what I live for. I realize Roger is hauling equipment from the dinghy alone, and I want to help, but a guest corners me when we reach the freshwater tanks to rinse the gear.

"I was wondering if we can focus tomorrow's night dive on eels? They make the best photos," he says.

"Sure. What else would you like to see?" The guest talks

on, and when I next spot Roger, he's bringing in the last of the tanks. "Hold that thought. Just give me a second." I rush over. "You can go home. It's late, and I've got this."

Roger looks around and shrugs. "Fine."

I hope he has time to spend with his girlfriend, because at least for me, things have been nuts. Ever since Don and Miriam left, it's been nonstop. The hotel is at capacity, and I've hardly seen Lexi. Between getting a grip on the work, getting comfortable with the different dive sites, and being the friendly face of Beaumont Ne'emba's dive center, I'm treading water with a boat boy who's giving me lip.

It's almost ten thirty when I set the security alarm and lock up the dive center. Everybody was on a high after that dive, and we chatted for over an hour about everything from conservation to other world-renowned dive sites. After that rush, the main guest area seems almost unnaturally quiet as I walk past the lodge.

When I get to our cottage, Lexi is already asleep as usual. But this evening, something's different. She's put a pillow barrier between us. I'm not sure why that's suddenly necessary, since we've barely managed a decent conversation the last two weeks…

If she thinks this Great Wall of Goose Down is going to stop an invasion, I have news for her. We might be busy and exhausted, but nothing's going to stop the desire pulsing through my veins every time I see her like this. I curse under my breath as a fantasy where she clambers over that wall and lowers herself onto my rock-hard cock zaps through my brain.

And my body reacts right on cue. *Fuck me.*

Work is my only solace. I eat my dinner in my closet office while checking out what I managed to film today. *Wow.* The daytime footage is fantastic, but tonight's whale shark photos are unbelievable. These are once-in-a-lifetime shots, and I'll have to share them with the guests who were on the dive. It's the perfect memento.

Eventually I call it a day and ready myself for the bed of torment. I need sleep, but I've been holding off getting in bed with Lexi. *Fuck.* I could also pound out some of the tension, but with her right there it feels...I don't know, *weird.* Lexi getting into my headspace like this is a catalyst for blue balls. I'm tired and could go another night without, but...I suck in a breath. I'm pushing my limits here.

I weave my way inside the mosquito net and get on top of the covers. Babes is right there, this time in the blue silk cami set from that first day. It seems like years ago now. She wears *this* and expects me to be unaffected? Little cocktease.

It's too hot to sleep underneath even a flat sheet, and for a minute I stare at the fan, trying to still my mind and cock, which doesn't get the message. Lexi turns in her sleep and shifts one leg up as she settles onto her stomach. The movement adjusts her pillow, and something dark rolls out and disappears between the mattress and the headboard. I want to reach for it, but it's gone. I sit up and listen as it drops, as if in slow motion, sliding down and landing with a soft thud on the thick hem of the mosquito net.

Lexi gives a soft moan. Yep, she's a minx. If women only knew what that sound does to the average male brain. Then she's moving again, getting comfy in her sleep. When she's been still for a couple of minutes, I slip off the bed and peer under it to see what dropped to the floor. The bed is a high four-poster, with crawl space underneath. Gives off all the luxury vibes without having much to it. I reach for my dive watch on the nightstand and throw a beam of light along the back of the bed.

Right there. I dip underneath on all fours to reach for it, and as I curl my fingers around the shape, I freeze. *Fuck*. The girth is kind of familiar. I'd like to think of myself as above average, but—

Here I am with my hands on my biggest competition.

I might go so far as to call it the enemy.

Enemies now…might turn into frenemies…might turn into friends. I can roll with that. Careful not to start Lexi's magic wand, I crawl out from under the bed and through the gap in the mosquito net. I stand, slink over to the closet, close the door, switch on the light, and give the purple monster-cock a quick inspection.

Nice. So this is what she gets up to when alone in this bed. I should have known. *Not fair*. I'm literally itching to feel what vibration she likes, but that would be taking things too far.

Instead I shove it into my laptop bag, ignoring the tingle of guilt.

Congratulating myself on a good job, I get back into bed, more alert than I was before this interlude. The fan is swooshing around at its usual pace, and with the far-off waves, it should be the perfect lullaby, but my mind is racing. That monster cock comes with a charger. I can get rid of one or the other, and she'd be screwed. Or not, ha-ha, which is exactly where I want her to be. Let her feel my pain.

A monster cock is hard to hide; a charger, on the other hand, can be so generic-looking. Counting on Lexi being in one of those post-orgasm deep-sleep cycles, I get out of bed again to scour all the electrical sockets. I know where they are, as I hunted them down when I decided where to put my office.

It takes all of a minute to find the charger, and once it's in my hands, it feels like a fucking trophy.

I startle awake and sit up. It's light outside—much lighter than when I usually go out for my morning run. The bed next to me is empty, but somewhere a soft clang sounds with a sigh.

"Lexi?" *Crap*. For all I know I've overslept and housekeeping is scrubbing the room again. I reach for my watch. *Phew*. Ten to seven.

Lexi walks in and pushes the mosquito net to the side, toothbrush working those pearly whites. She's already dressed in her sleeveless shirt and that miniskirt that should be illegal. "You overslept," she says around the toothbrush in her mouth.

The Great Wall of Goose Down comes in handy as I sit up and tilt it toward my crotch. So far I've had the good fortune of not giving her a morning wood full-frontal. "I stayed late at the dive center last night. It was a great dive with some folks who don't chew through their air in thirty minutes."

She shrugs, and then for a split second her eyes go wide and her gaze zaps to her pillow. I fall back, watching her as the puzzle pieces tumble into place. She'd forgotten about her solo session last night, and now... I try my best not to chuckle at the blush that flushes her cheeks, hiding my smile with a yawn.

With an elaborate stretch, I make myself comfortable, toying with my watch as if I'm checking readings, ignoring her and her dilemma. With me there, she can hardly go on all fours and dig under the bed like I did last night.

Lexi turns and stomps off, and the frustrated rinsing and

spitting that sounds from the bathroom almost curls my toes. *Oh, babes. Don't make this too much fun.*

She's back minutes later, her loose blond curls twisted into a bun at the nape of her neck. "I have a meeting at seven."

"I still have time for a quick run. For tonight, I might work in a double dive, so…"

"Good. Good for you. See you whenever."

"Bye, babes."

There's no retort to my endearment, but she gives the bed another surreptitious sweep with her eyes before she saunters off.

As soon as she's gone—and I know she won't be back because that seven o'clock housekeeping meeting is holy, and Lexi is overly work-conscientious—I hop out of bed to grab some tissues in the bathroom. A man's got to do what a man's got to do.

For a moment, I consider my closet office for privacy, but then I have a fuck-it moment because it's so early, and I'm desperate, and my hand is already dick-deep into my underwear. I head for the bathroom and close my eyes, comparing my own familiar weight with the feel of Lexi's wand in my hand. The knowledge of what she did with it, how it must have worked her sweet clit until she moaned that little moan that sets my pulse on fire is enough to make me so hard it's almost painful. This is going to be quick. If she were here, however—with me, under me, on top, bending over the sofa—I would slow down, make sure I lasted until she had triple her fill, but my need and the urgency have only compounded since arriving here.

Fuck. I breathe and clutch the white marble vanity as my

other hand works my cock, trying to delay the inevitable and ride that wave a bit longer, holding back on that moment—

"Oh my—*ohmygodohmygodohmygod.*" As Lexi's voice fills the space, it catches me so off guard that I start to come.

Fuckfuckfuck.

There's no stopping this now. I try to turn away, but my body is in an orgasmic deadlock. Nothing is going to happen until—My eyes want to roll back in pleasure, but instead I manage to look at Lexi, finding her solidified on the spot, transfixed.

Her eyes are on my cock, my hand, my cum that shoots like only cum can onto the vanity mirror. I groan as I fist myself harder, hoping the ripples will ride out faster, allowing my body to move.

"Oh. My. God." She cups her face in her hands, but she isn't budging either.

"Ah fuck, babes," I mutter when I'm eventually able to turn away from her. I could—probably should—be embarrassed, but I'm not. *She* walked in on *me*. I exhale and inhale on a chuckle. Serves me right in some ways. "Don't you have a meeting?"

"Uh-huh." That whimper is too small and too sweet and too pathetic. It almost softens my heart to her conundrum.

Came to look for your toy? And found this one instead? I'm so tempted to tease her, but instead I let go of my cock, which already seems interested in a second round—a round that involves her. I reach for the tissues and wipe up the aftermath.

Why the hell isn't she moving away? "You can go now. Show's over," I tell her, trying to downplay this awkward situation. I kind of want to crack up, because it's fucking funny. And mentally, I want to cling to the past few seconds. This scenario has taken over every spot in my wank bank Top 10.

Lexi doesn't pull her hands from her face, but her fingers split apart so she can peer at me through them. "I came back for a…a…a tampon."

Oh yeah? Nice try. "Right. Give me a minute."

"And you're supposed to be out on a run!" She gulps. "With all this travel and my phone that's not very useful, I've stopped tracking, and now I've been taken by surprise, and now *this*—and I should stop talking right about now."

"Yep. Good plan." I roll my lips together to hide a smile and toss the used tissues in the trash bin under the vanity. Since she's still frozen in shock, I can't walk past her, and she doesn't seem to want to squeeze past me either, so I open the cupboard. This is where she's stashed her things, and, well, it's within arm's reach. "Small, medium, large…or supersize? We all know size matters."

"Tristan!"

Oh, *that* ticked her off, or at least zapped her out of her stupor.

Lexi finally drops her hands. "Do you mind? Now that you're *done*?" She is blushing so hard I want to pull her into my arms, hide her face in my neck, and laugh at the situation together. I'm not half as embarrassed as she seems to be. I mean, shit, jerking off happens. A lot. It would happen even more if she was a regular—and willing—voyeur, for her evident pleasure.

"Who says I'm done?"

"Oh, fuck off." Her hand lands on my chest and she pushes me out of the way. "You need a shower."

"I do." I trap her hand with my own, laughing, letting her feel my heart's frantic beating, if nothing else will get through to her. This seems like an intersection of sorts for us. "Care to join me?"

"Join you?" She gasps as she pushes, but I hold strong. "I have a meeting, my period just started out of nowhere, and... And I just saw my fake fiancé jerk off! And now you want me in the shower?"

"If you want to put it so directly, *yes*. Because I'm not done, and clearly you need to blow off some steam. I can help with that, you know." I bet that's a fake period. Someone's trying to locate a missing toy. Either way, I'm happy to help her out.

The blush is back in full force. "Yes, I need to blow off some steam! Thanks to *you*! But I'm not blowing anything else! And not in the shower! Not with you!"

"Wow. Don't let this get out of hand. I'm just teasing you, babes." Her eyes shoot daggers, and I bite down on my smirk. "God, Lexi, you shouldn't make it so easy to get under your skin." I let go of her, and she shows me her back as she starts digging in the cupboard, muttering curses under her breath. "There's a little storm cloud right there, all right. With lightning bolts and all." I point and circle my finger just above her head as her eyes catch mine in the mirror. Then I lean closer to where my lips should start a rush of goosebumps down her neck to those perky tits I'm so desperate to fondle, and whisper in her ear, "Don't get wet now, babes."

Before she can turn around and give me a well-deserved punch, I stalk off to the closet to get some clothes for the day and protect my treasure. *Finders keepers*. When she stomps past seconds later, her face is a picture of befuddled, frustrated annoyance.

"Miss you already, babes!" I call after her, unable to stop myself. I have officially gone off the rails. This time I'm rewarded with a double flip-off that basically makes my day.

Chapter Twenty

LEXI

The point of coming to Ne'emba was to have fewer problems. Two weeks in, and now I have more than ever before. Not only do I have a magic wand MIA, I've also been stunned by Tristan Martinelli's version of the real deal. I'm still flustered, and it's been four hours since I walked in on him.

The visual of him, bare-chested, all tensed-up muscle as he held himself in check, that tanned hand gripping the vanity, and then...*God*. I bite my lip. Epic lady porn. I've never seen anything like it.

Making a coherent sentence at that point was a tall order, and then he brushed over the whole intimate affair and had the audacity to invite me to shower with him as a joke? I swallow and bite my lip harder, trying not to squirm in my seat. Tristan's invitation to have a fun time was maybe meant to tease me, but his honesty about what he wants took me by surprise.

He hadn't wanted me five years ago, but now... Many a truth is spoken in jest.

Worst part is, if it weren't for my period, I would've stepped right into that shower without thinking twice. The desert-dry weeks and the months we still need to spend together on this island stretch out in front of me. There's no way we're going to hold out at this rate. Human nature is going to be my Achilles heel.

And then he said he *missed me already*. I've never been annoyed with a guy to the point that I want to physically wrestle him. But that's where I am, and it's both a fun and ridiculous idea, because Tristan's tall and built and would let me toy with him for the fun of it. And then he'd flip me over and pin me down in a second with his thigh pressing *right there*. I'm out of breath just thinking of it.

This morning was a flashback to the Tristan I knew long ago—playful and full of jokes, except now they're thick with innuendos, or even worse, including no innuendos whatsoever. For some reason, the way he wanted to make light of the situation riled me up even more, because it put him in that space where I don't need him to be: the space where I fall in love with him again. And again.

I'm staring at my computer screen, wondering how to deal with whatever comes next.

How to look him in the eye after—

My phone beeps with a string of messages and plucks me out of my thoughts. As I reach for it, I meet Jem's gaze where she's studying me. She doesn't say anything, but she doesn't have to. *You're on the clock, honey, and your private life has no place at work.*

She can fuck off already. I'm hardly ever on my phone. Ever

since my responses to friends and family have ground to a halt, what with the time difference and work, people have given up on me. Not Tessa though. It must be really late for her to message me now.

TESSA

> Third day of filming and today I had to shoot the same freaking scene twenty times.
>
> Twenty times!!
>
> Fuckit girl, I sucked sooo bad. I've never felt so dumb in my life. By the end of it, I bet they regret giving me the role.
>
> What if I'm a total dud and this movie is basically the start and end of my career?
>
> At the current rate I might never be cast in anything again!

A rapid fire of crying emojis follow her string of one-liners and I slump in my chair as my heart sinks. My arms itch with the need to pull my bestie in for hug.

Self-doubt runs rampant in the actor circles and so few people actually make it. All I can do is cheer her on. My thumbs hover over the keys to type back, but I'm not sure what to say.

Jem's eyes are still on me, and now she studies my hesitation, so I stand and walk out of the office. I'd love to phone Tessa, but hell, the girl needs to be in bed—

"Lexi?" Jem calls, her voice stern. "Where are you going?"

I drop my head back with a groan and curse. Can she just give me space? Jem has no life and can't bear the thought of anybody having one either.

Still, she's the one who is going to report to Beaumont on every minuscule wrong I commit on this island, so I need to toe the line.

In haste I send Tessa a message:

ME

> You're amazing, gorgeous, a FANTASTIC actress, tomorrow is a new day and I know you will NAIL this. They chose you because you're brilliant. One bad day isn't the precedent, it's a glitch in the Matrix. Go to bed, girl, you need to be fresh for tomorrow. I'll try call you later. xxx

I send it off, feeling crap that I can't do more. Tessa has been there for me through all my ups and downs, and now that she needs me, I'm stuck in the middle of nowhere.

With a sigh I walk back into the office, refrain from giving Jem the finger and sit down again.

"Lexi?"

I look up. Deshni is standing in the door, wringing her hands.

"Yes. Deshni. How can I help?"

Deshni shoots a nervous glance at Jem, and I force myself not to look her way too. The hierarchy here is not exactly in the shape of a pyramid. I'm still trying to figure out how some things work, but something's up here and whatever it is, Deshni isn't going to open up in front of Jem. The problem probably *is* Jem.

"I'm going to get some coffee. Walk with me?" I say as I stand.

"Don't forget Matthias de Foch is flying in and will be landing at lunch time," Jem says, giving me *that* look over her reading glasses. I'm playing truant again in her books. "He's the first to arrive for this wedding and is alone, so he's going to need some TLC."

Tender loving care when it comes to guests means only one thing: he's difficult as fuck. But Matthias de Foch is a regular, and he's footing the bill for his sister's wedding. "No problem. That's plenty of time. I'll have the radio with me, so let me know when he arrives if I'm not here." They still use walkie-talkies here, and I take mine and nod to Deshni. Once we're outside the office, she falls in next to me and we walk abreast.

"So what's up?" I ask. Deshni and Sarika are both sweet, mostly soft-spoken, and flawlessly beautiful with thick black hair that is always neatly braided. But I suspect those are their general spa personas they reserve for their hours as Beaumont staff.

Deshni waits until we're almost at the canteen, and when there's nobody there, she says, "We've been working on some plans for the spa and were hoping you'd allow us to implement them."

I've looked over the spa's offerings and was surprised to find them so stock standard. It's something to keep partners and spouses who don't go out for all those dives or other activities happy, but being on this side of the world, you'd think people would like something more exotic. "I'd love to look at your plans. Sounds exciting."

"It is. We didn't dare propose the changes to Miriam and Don, and Jem..." She shrugs. "You seem to be more open to fresh ideas."

Hmm... Don and Miriam were a bit old school, but as for Jem, I've figured her all out. She's in charge, and I'm just a front for guests. Me finding a way to strut my stuff for Nathan

Beaumont is going to be difficult, if not impossible. "So where's the plan? Do you have it in writing?"

Deshni smiles but blushes profusely at the same time. "Yes. It's at the spa. If you can come over, I'll talk you through it. Sarika is with a guest, so…"

"Sure, let's go right now." I'll do anything to take my mind off what happened this morning. And the fact that my magic wand might be under the bed. Hopefully it's hiding away where nobody else can find it until I have time to crawl around.

We change direction, skipping the warm coffees in favor of water, and head out to the spa. The walkway takes us past the dive center, where everything is quiet. The dive boat is out, which means Tristan is diving right now.

The spa has thick stone walls and a cooling waterfall feature with tropical plants that makes for a relaxing, zen environment in the seating area. There are two treatment rooms for facials and other beauty treatments. For massages, they have the outdoor sala where guests are treated in semi-privacy. Jem so eloquently explained the reason those don't happen behind closed doors here.

The place is spotless, and clearly the women take pride in their work. Deshni goes behind the spa's counter and pulls out a stack of papers. Her eyes are downcast. "You asked for it in writing."

I take the papers from her. They're covered in neat-as-a-pin handwriting.

"Sorry it's like that, but we don't have access to any of the computers or printers here, and it's been put on ice for so long that… Well, we haven't bothered to do anything with it when we go home."

This stack of paper is a life and situation summed up. "It doesn't matter," I assure her. "It's the contents that are important." I nod toward the seating area. "Let's go through it together."

Forty-five minutes later, it's clear that there's treasure here ready to be dug up. The changes Deshni and Sarika are proposing are inspired by their Indian culture and Ne'emba's location on the Spice Route. They would like to supplement the traditional Beaumont spa menu with Ayurvedic treatments. Some massages would require three sessions over three consecutive days, and that's where everybody benefits.

This excites me more than any French manicure ever will, and would probably double the spa's income in a few months. Deshni and Sarika will also be busier, which is probably why they came up with these plans in the first place.

"Do you have training in Ayurveda?" I ask.

"We spent time in India with family, and that's where it all started. We were trained in Ayurveda before we trained as beauticians."

"Fantastic. I'll support you in all of this, but you know I can't authorize anything. It has to go through head office."

"Yes, but if we have someone in management putting our ideas forward, our chances are better."

I nod. "I'm going to type this up and put it together in a proposal template. You can sign off on it, and then we'll take it from there."

Deshni studies me for a long moment, as if she's weighing the situation—no, it's as if she's weighing *me*, considering whether she can hand their plans over or not. For the first time, I realize the amount of trust she has to have in me to surrender their vision.

"There's no need for us to sign off on it. Only...will you claim these as your own ideas?" she asks, a weary edge in her tone.

"God, no. Why—" *Oh.* So this is how it's been going. The staff here don't trust anybody. And now I wonder why they would trust me. Maybe it's because I'm an American, and they've never had an American manager here before. Maybe it's because I'm young too, especially for this position. "Of course I won't. I'll support you all the way."

Deshni heaves out a breath and smiles. "Thank you. We knew you'd be different, so Sarika and I had that it's-now-or-never moment this morning. You seem to have everything so perfectly together, and it would be great to have you on our side, even if it's only until April."

If she knew what a shitshow my life is, she wouldn't be in such awe. As for our time here, we're chipping away at it day after day. "Get your products lined up, and do some practice runs on Sarika. I'll start today so we can get the ball rolling."

"Thank you."

I stand, and she does as well. "What are your long-term goals here?" I ask. "Have you thought them through?"

Deshni hesitates. "This is enough for now. Long term...I don't know. I'm on contract with Sarika, but she won't stay here forever. This is the only way we're allowed to do it. My father is not old-fashioned, and he is kind and want us to have this career, but the expectations are for us to get married too, and soon. It's just..."

Now there are tears in her eyes, and my soul sinks into a puddle, seeing her like this. "Yes?" I touch her shoulder, encouraging her to continue.

"Well, for me... I'll have to see what happens with—" She

breaks off and sighs as a blush spreads on her cheeks and tears finally spill over.

"With?" I prompt when she doesn't continue.

She shakes her head as she wipes her tears with a deprecating chuckle. "It doesn't matter. You're so lucky. To be here with the man you love? To be open and honest about it and have your family's blessing? You're not even married. You're only engaged and can be here, with him. For me, it's not so simple. I'll have to settle for something arranged." She shakes her head again, and this time, I watch her close down.

Oh my God. Deshni just gave my heart a hairline crack. She's in love with someone she can't have. In her future awaits an arranged marriage. The notion is so foreign to me that my world, which has always seemed so big and wide, suddenly seems small and insignificant—so small and insignificant that I can get away with faking an engagement and not thinking how bizarrely *lucky* I am able to transplant myself and flee my problems on a whim. And that Tristan made it possible with our *arrangement*.

As if today hadn't started off rough enough, I'm now a fraud with my staff. This has been my moral conundrum from the start, and now it's personal, with someone who has taken a leap of faith with little old me. "I'm sorry," I tell her as I squeeze her shoulder. *Sorry for so many things I can't talk about.* "If there's anything I can do—"

"This is a good start," Deshni says with a sniff. "That's all I can ask for. Happiness is, after all, a decision, not a choice."

Chapter Twenty-One
TRISTAN

This morning's sizzling fun and games have evaporated. In plain terms, my day has gone to shit before it's even started, thanks to Roger.

The first thing he's done was to change our first dive's location without consulting me. That I could run with. I've now covered all the dives here at least once, but still, getting underwater and not finding what you sold to guests made me feel like a sleazy secondhand car dealer. Then, when we came up after the second dive, he ignored my signal to boat over to where we'd drifted almost hundred yards from where he dropped anchor. We had to swim—*swim*—toward him to catch his attention so he would bring the dinghy over to get divers out of the water.

I couldn't grill him for an explanation in front of guests, and to top it all off, he's been as sour as a pickled prune.

Did he apologize? Nope. Did the guests feel the tension between us? No doubt. Was there an awkward-as-fuck silence on the boat as we came back to shore? Indeed. Even now, as people are stripping out of their wetsuits, the chatter is subdued.

"Let me stamp that for you," I say as I move behind the counter to stamp and sign the paper dive logs some people still keep as mementos.

"Those were two great dives," the guest says, but we exchange an awkward glance.

Fuck Roger. "Tomorrow will be better. I'll have those whale shark photos for you to download." I smile wide, and inwardly I steel myself. The diving is phenomenal here, but Roger's attitude is enough to give us a bad rap anyway. I'm not going to swim against the tide here all the way until April, so something's going to change, and it's going to do so today.

As soon as the guests leave for lunch, I strip off my wetsuit and go to the back where Roger is hanging up gear that's been rinsed in fresh water. I add mine to the production line.

"What happened this morning?" I ask as I start dunking the equipment that still needs to be rinsed.

Roger shrugs. "Nothing."

"Fuck that." I'm not on this island to dance around someone's mood. "Four of our guests are here to specifically photograph Indian Ocean nudibranchs I've already spotted at the Pinnacle, but no, we got dropped down at Shark Alley to find only sand and sea cucumbers. That isn't how I'd like to start my day. Why did you change the GPS coordinates?"

He doesn't look me in the eye as he drags the line of dripping wetsuits to the side to make space for more.

"Roger?" I push him.

"You know nothing about this place," he bites through his teeth. "I saw two dhows on the horizon I'd rather avoid, so I did."

Several seconds of silence bounces between us as he glares at me, waiting for me to crap him out.

"Why?"

"People I don't want to be associated with. People that we," he says as he waves a hand between us, "don't want to be associated with."

"What do you mean? Illegal fishing? Smuggling?" The coastguard is out and about all the time. We've spotted them at least three times since I arrived here.

"Something like that."

"What the fuck is that supposed to mean?"

"There're people making thousands of dollars out there doing illegal shit and I—" He breaks off, but his gaze burns with anger he's trying to subdue. "It's nothing."

To say I despise illegal fishing would put it mildly, but this is about so much more than him avoiding those two boats he spotted. I huff out a breath, softening. It's probably about money.

"For your information, I'm not doing another dive like that." It's an idle threat, but honestly, Mike can come out with us if Roger's going to be like a teenager, Tarzan-ing around on his mood swings. "If you're pissed at something or someone, I'd like to know what or who it is before we head out, understand?"

Roger leans over the big plastic barrel, gripping the edge so tightly that his dark skin pops veins. "You've got it so easy, you know? You come here, do your time, go back to wherever you came from as if this means nothing to you. As if this place means nothing to you. *Nothing*." He looks like he wants to flip the barrel, water and all, he's so riled up.

"I don't know what to say to that. This three-month stint is actually my salvation."

"How? You have a good job in America; you have education; you can go work and dive anywhere around the world. You come in here, take over, and leave for the next place once you're done. Ne'emba and its people can hardly matter to you."

I stop what I'm doing to stare at him. "Do I *work* as if Ne'emba doesn't matter to me?" If Roger knew what's at stake for me, he wouldn't be so flippant.

He doesn't answer, and it's just as I thought. He's pissed at me, but I'm only the tip of his iceberg. He's now dragging wetsuits out with such fury that I want to hoist the white flag and assure him I come in peace.

"Hold on a second," I say, hands raised. "Let's get to the bottom of this. Do you hate your job?"

He shoots me a glance. "No... Yes."

"I see." I take a deep breath. "Which part do you like, and which part do you hate?"

Roger is quiet for a moment, and I give him time to arrange his thoughts. I'm almost done with the masks and fins when he speaks up.

"I love the sea. I grew up on Pemba, and there's salt water in my veins. But I want more. I want to do more." He stalls, and it's as if he's gathering courage. "Last night you dismissed me as if I had no place here, but I didn't go. I listened to your conversation with the guests, and I should have been there. To learn. What do I even know about these nudibranchs these guests want to see?"

Jeez. The multiple implications of his words hit me at once, and I'll have to come back and work through all of them one by one. But the biggest surprise is that we're getting somewhere. "Okay. I'm sorry. Last night it was late, and I thought you'd like to get home to be with—" *Fuck me*. I don't know her name. Instead of making an ass of myself, I rake my hands through my wet hair with a groan. "Let's have some real talk. You hold the fort. I'm getting us some beers."

I take a blitz shower in the washroom and dress in shorts and a T-shirt. When I come out, he's still busy packing things away, so I rush to the nearest bar and get two cold beers from the barman. I bet there's a no-drinking rule for staff on the job, but this is bro time, and I'm not going to mess this up by talking to Roger without a drink in hand.

When I get back, I point to the beach. "Let's go."

We walk some twenty yards away from the dive center to a cluster of palm trees and sit down, our backs against the trunks. "Do you dive?" I ask him after we've each had a deep pull.

"Yes and no."

"Right." Lots of those coming my way. "Why yes and why no?"

"I've gone down many times, never deep, but I'm also not qualified so—"

"Why aren't you qualified?"

Roger shakes his head and takes another drink. "I was learning with Peter—he was here two guys ago, before Setiawan and now you—but it's always so busy, and we didn't finish, and then he left."

Weird. Basic scuba training can be done in a week. "Okay, that we'll sort out within the next couple of days. I'm qualified to sign off on your training. We can even take you beyond the basic level while I'm here, if you want."

Roger studies me, his gaze no longer angry, but more curious. "Why would you do that?"

Isn't it obvious? "I want to help you, and this place can't have only one dive master. It's insane."

He laughs, if a bit bitter. "People aren't usually so keen to teach us new things."

"Why's that?"

"Once we know something, we leave. Go to better places, like you."

I nod, finally seeing how the current flows here. This young man is frustrated and stuck in a job at a place that won't get him anywhere beyond being the boat guy. If he ups his skills, he will also earn more money and I bet that girl has something to do with half of what goes on here. I have zero scruples in helping him out. If he wants to up his skills, I'll make it happen. This is what's needed to have Roger all-in during dives with guests. He must know what it's like down there, but he hasn't experienced it fully. "I'll teach you everything I know in the time we have. No problem."

"What about all those cameras you dive with?"

"What about them?"

"Show me how they work?"

He's giving me the perfect excuse to go out and film and work on my series without it seeming dodgy. "Sure. Let's get some lunch, and we'll start this afternoon."

Roger shakes his head. "You for real?"

"Yeah, why not? Do you have any other plans?"

"No. But I don't know. Mike might not like it."

"Who's the boss here? Me or Mike?" Technically the correct answer is probably Lexi, for all I know, but when it comes to diving, this is my show, and I'll direct Mike off the stage if he wants to interfere.

Roger shakes his head and flashes me a shy smile.

"So what's up with you and the girl from the spa?" Now that I have him here and the words are flowing, I can find out how deep Roger's frustrations run.

"Deshni? She's the *one*, man. She's the *one* for me but—" He shakes his head, and now the poor guy looks like he's about to cry.

"Hey. It's okay. This is why you need to up your game? I totally get that."

"I'm trying, but it's a lost cause."

"Why?"

"Just look at us. She's Indian, and I'm African. Her parents want her to marry into an established Indian family in Dar es Salaam. I understand why. They've got money." He wipes his face with both hands. "But I can't stop feeling about her the way I do. The heart walks its own path. Alone."

Fuck. I now feel like an ass. I'm faking an engagement while this poor guy can't live his life with the woman he's clearly besotted with.

For a moment we both sit and digest the situation, and then he turns to me. "Tell me what's going on with you and Lexi."

"With me and Lexi? We're good. Eventually we're going to get married." I've vowed to never get married, but Roger doesn't need to know that.

"Are you?" Roger asks. "When you arrived, it looked like you were here to try to patch things up."

What? Really? "No. What made you think that?"

"*Pfft,*" Roger harrumphs. "I see a lot of couples come and go on this island and—" He breaks off with a shrug.

"What?" I feel stripped naked. This guy has a level of intuition I didn't anticipate. "We're good. We're really good." *Jesus Christ. Did I have to repeat myself there?* Defending my fake relationship with Lexi is my only choice, but if Roger has already smelled a rat, how many other staff are looking at us with narrowed eyes, studying our every move?

"Whatever. When you arrived, you were awkward. Something's not right." Roger meets my gaze. "I hope you didn't cheat on her, because—"

"Hell, no!" I'm not sure when this conversation slipped off this slope but—"I'll never cheat on her, or on any woman, for that matter." I've lived through enough of that shit and its repercussions to last me a lifetime. Love is destructive. I've been in the eye of that storm. If you love someone, really love them, you keep your fucking distance. The best way to do that is avoid committed relationships in the first place, like I've managed to do for years. Except now I'm *engaged*—to Lexi, of all people. How did that happen again?

"Good, I'm glad to hear it." Roger stands, and I get up too, a bit shaken. "I hope you're going to go through with what that ring she wears means. You're lucky to have the right to even ask her. That's a blessing I'll never have."

Chapter Twenty-Two

LEXI

After talking to Deshni for over an hour, I barely had time for a bite to eat. I wanted to take a breather after lunch, but I've had zero luck with that. All I managed was to race back to our cottage for a sanitary check-in and a five-minute crawl under the bed to locate my MIA wand. I found it in my bedside drawer, battery dead and charger misplaced.

I'm trying not to be embarrassed by the whole situation. Housekeeping now knows about my toy. So what? During my student days as a cleaner, I came across enough situations to write a book. But still… I'm supposed to be freshly engaged, in love, and in no need of help in that department.

With a shrug, I head out to the beach to meet Matthias de Foch, some rich tech guy from Amsterdam, who comes to Ne'emba at least three times a year. The fact that he's single this time is apparently noteworthy, and for his sister's wedding of all things.

I can spot trouble a mile away, and in the case of Matthias de Foch, red lights and sirens erupt in my head as soon as he clambers out of the floatplane. I know his type: rich and not necessarily by his own efforts. Often generational wealth serves as a springboard to greater wealth. And with that comes a sense of entitlement and arrogance that nothing can peg down a notch.

Inwardly I groan, even as I plaster on a smile. "Welcome to Ne'emba Island. We're so glad you're back—"

"You're new! Thank God. Where's that wilted old couple who ran the show a couple of months ago?" Matthias's eyes travel over my face and lower to my breasts as if I came with the room he's booked.

"Miriam and Don left at the beginning of January. I'm Lexi O'Reilly, the new manager here." I reluctantly hold my hand out, and he engulfs it in his own big, strong, beautifully manicured hand. Of course Matthias de Foch is nothing but tall and gorgeous, with blond hair streaked with sunlight and blue eyes so piercing, it's like staring into the heart of a glacier. His smile is perfect, but those über-whites glint in the sun like a wolf's fangs.

Yep, in my experience, he's the type who would ask for two room keys when checking in, even if he's staying as a single, only to hand one key back to the dumbstruck receptionist with five hundred dollars folded around it. The first time someone solicited sex from me like that, it took several minutes to sink in—and several more after that to recover.

"Great," he says. "I could use some company until the others arrive."

Keeping you company isn't in my job description. "Eh…" Oh, God. *Help. Miles*, I tell myself. *I have miles on me now.* I can deal with this.

"Do you dive?" he asks.

"No, I run the hotel." I pull my hand free from a hold that has become all too long and insinuating. "My *fiancé* manages the dive center." *There. Eat that, you swine.*

At this, Matthias's eyebrow hitches up. "Great. I look forward to meeting him."

I bet you do. I lead the way to the general guest area and fake-smile at him. "I suppose I don't need to show you around, since you've been here so many times."

"Yes, I have." He leans closer, so close chills sprout down my spine as he whispers in my ear, "Send someone over with the good stuff, will you. Even better, bring it yourself and we can get to know each other better." He salutes as the steps away.

What the hell? *The good stuff?* He just flew in from Amsterdam where you can get pot and whatnot on every street corner. He should have sorted himself out before coming here. Nobody on this island is growing their own weed...not under Jem's watch.

I curse quietly as I watch him walk off. *What an asshole.* I should have said something immediately once he suggested we hang out, but I was too stumped for words. And I hate that Jem was right. I might have miles on me, but she has more—and earned them working on this small island for thirty years. Just goes to show, size doesn't always matter.

I don't accompany Matthias to his room, as the porter already has his luggage and knows the drill. At St Chalamet there was always a person one level up who could deal with creepy guests, but here, I'm the one in charge. What do I do when someone comes on to *me*?

Back in my office, I distract myself by working on Deshni's proposal, but by five o'clock I'm tired, I have period cramps in full force, and I only want to call it a day. Some guests are going on a sunset cruise, though, and I need to see them off. Other guests will stay and have drinks on the beach, and I need to be present for them until dinner. Without a doubt, Matthias de Foch will be there, trying to rope in his fun for the night.

I could tell him it's that time of the month. He probably wouldn't care. And then he'd probably come on to other staff. I look over at Jem's desk, which is empty. No help is coming from that side. She's gone home for the night, as it isn't her role to look after guests after five in the afternoon. My thumb slides over my engagement ring's white-gold band, and for some reason, I find the courage to deal with the next couple of hours.

Ten minutes later I'm in conversation with a honeymooning couple from France who arrived two days ago, when I see Tristan coming up from the dive center. He looks deep in thought, but as he sees me, his gaze softens and he smiles. In a second, the whole fiasco from this morning flashes in my mind's eye—as it has throughout the day at the most inappropriate of times, making me hot and bothered, as if the weather wasn't enough. I blush so profusely, I drop my gaze.

I don't usually see Tristan at this time of day. In fact, the only times we see each other are early mornings and late at night, and somehow, until this morning, we'd managed it in such a way that one of us was always asleep—or faking being asleep.

He reaches my side and takes my hand. "Mind if I steal Lexi for a second here?" he asks the guests, who raise their cocktails to him as a go-ahead.

Tristan tugs me out of earshot but doesn't let go of my

hand. "Are you okay?" he asks. He's so close I can smell the post-dive shower on him.

"I'm good." I don't feel great, though, and if I had a choice, I'd go for the lie down I've needed since lunch. Somehow, with the heat, this period is hitting me harder.

He reaches up and brushes his thumb over my cheek. I'm not sure if it's for show, but I lean into his touch. "Are you sure?" he asks. "You look tired."

My body tingles with the delicious warmth of his skin, so welcome after every other warped thing today. I quietly hate myself for being weak, female, and practically obsessed with the part of Tristan Martinelli I can never have.

"I am, and—" My hand moves to my lower belly, right where the Advil I took earlier is making a sub-par difference.

Tristan's fingers slide to the nape of my neck as he leans closer to murmur in my ear. "Babes? Do you need a warm water bottle and a rest?" He pulls his face just far enough away to peer into my eyes.

I blink. How does he know that's exactly what I want? "The guests—"

"I'm here. All those eager night divers cancelled on me for tonight, so I'll look after the guests. No problem."

It's not in his job description, but... I look over his shoulder as Matthias de Foch steps closer to us, just out of Tristan's peripheral vision.

"So this is your fiancé?" Matthias asks. "The dive master?"

Tristan drops his hand from my cheek, and the comfort of his touch is gone. He turns towards Matthias. I knew Tristan was tall, but seeing him next to Matthias, measuring probably an inch taller, makes my heart skip a beat.

"Yes, hi. Tristan Martinelli." Tristan has his hand out to

shake, and Matthias returns the gesture, but his eyes are on me.

"You're quite the couple, aren't you?" Matthias says, and my pulse stutters as his eyes move over my body, this time lower—to the hem of my mini skirt, which suddenly seems indecently short. "Don't mind if I do."

"Excuse me?" Tristan shrugs off Matthias's hand and takes mine in his again, this time with a protective squeeze.

Matthias still doesn't meet Tristan's gaze but keeps staring at me. "The decision usually lies with the lady, so... You talk it through, and...well, you know which room I'm in. We can have a fun time together before the rest of the wedding party arrives."

With that, he gives Tristan's biceps an encouraging pat and turns away. He walks straight up to the waiter with a tray of colorful cocktails, picks one, and continues to the boat where guests are being helped on board by Mike and another staff member.

Tristan's hand is stiff and squeezes mine hard. "What the actual fuck was that?"

"A proposition, Tristan." I close my eyes and cling to his hand. "It was a proposition for a threesome. His place. Tonight."

Tristan shudders. "What the fuck? Does this really happen?"

"Evidently it does here, too." I gulp, suddenly overwhelmed as I glance around the now emptying beach. The guests are almost all gone. "Now I know why they only employ couples. *This. This* is why."

"I've never come across anything—"

"Of course you've never come across something like this. You don't work in the hospitality industry."

"Wait—*what*?" Tristan turns sharply toward me, his eyes peering into mine like they did minutes ago, though this time they're stern, concerned...*angry*. "This has happened to you before?"

"Obviously. When I worked as a guest services agent, at least once every two weeks."

His big hands cup my shoulders, and he's overpowering, dangerous in his masculinity...except this is *Tristan*. In this moment I realize I've never trusted a man like I trust him, and there's a reason for that. I trust him with my body, because he said *no*. I trust him with my soul, because he is solid, sincere, and unwavering in the way he approaches life, friendships, people, and how he chooses to live. As for trusting him with my heart... It can't break twice, can it?

"Tristan?"

He searches my eyes, looking desperate. "Jesus Christ, Lexi. Are you okay? Did anybody ever—"

"I'm fine. And no, nothing's ever happened, but I've got a couple of colorful stories to tell, if you have time."

Tristan drops his forehead to mine. "Babes..." He hugs me, and this feels so warm, so right, full of such a promise of *us*, that I almost cave in to my desire to weep for everything lost in our years apart. Instead, I lean into him.

"I swear, I'll kill him if he *looks* at you again," he whispers, his words making my heart gloat.

Oh yes, this is Tristan, protector to the core. My hands sneak up his chest as I chuckle. "Please don't off any of our guests. That's the quickest way to get fired, and then we're both screwed."

There's a smile on his lips as he runs them up the shell of my ear, setting my skin on fire. I sink deeper into his arms. "It will be worth it," he murmurs.

He isn't doing anything but moving his lips slowly across to my temple, but every lady bit of mine chants, *Yes, please. More, please.*

"You have to admit it's kind of funny."

"What?" he murmurs.

This could so easily devolve into something I've wanted since the day I walked in on him at Evan's house. Seems Tristan can keep his kidneys—we've gotten ourselves here, so no sacrifice necessary—but I still want his cock. I giggle against his neck, where my lips are hovering, hesitant to make the first move. "We've been invited to a threesome, but...we're not even a twosome."

"Hmm..." Tristan hums, laughter shallow in his throat, but he cuts it off. He lifts his head and looks at me, his brown eyes all-consuming. His gaze melts away my willpower. It looks as if he wants to kiss me, as if he's going to kiss me, and I want him to kiss me so badly.

"I'm dealing with this dickhead." Tristan presses the softest, warmest, and sweetest kiss possible to my forehead. "You call it a day." His palms run down my arms, and with a last squeeze of my hands, he turns me toward our cottage and gives me a pat on the ass to send me on my way. "See you later, babes."

Chapter Twenty-Three

TRISTAN

That was a layered mindfuck if ever there was one. The feel of Lexi's body against mine is still hot on my skin, her sweet scent freshly stamped in my memory. When she said, *"We're not even a twosome,"* I wanted to tease, *"We're working on that."* But then I froze, because *what am I doing?* I've been out of control since this morning, but I still know this fake engagement of ours has never included that plan. But I'm fooling nobody here. Plans change. Plus, I let that wand of hers run out of battery and calmly packed it away in her bedside drawer.

Then that skunk came up to us. This guy arrives on this island and thinks the women are here for his taking? Jesus Christ, it never crossed my mind that a guest would so callously suggest a threesome. My mind short-circuits at the idea. *Sharing Lexi?* Watching someone else *touch* her? I fist my hands as my stomach takes a plunge like I just dropped forty stories in an elevator.

I can't afford to be more riled up by the situation than I

already am, but I'm sticking around until that jerk is back from his cruise. I drag my hands through my hair and go scout around for guests to make sure everybody is happy. That's what Lexi would do at this hour.

I head out to the beach, where the ocean breeze is cooling off the early evening and ensuring that the bugs keep inland. Staff has set up inviting circles of bean bags and short-legged tables with snacks where couples can sit and enjoy the sunset, drinks in hand. They do pull out all the stops here. I walk past a few couples, and one guy, who has been diving every day, motions for me to join them. We talk diving and sightings for a full hour, until the boat returns with the other guests. I excuse myself and walk up to where that blond dickhead is wading out of the shallow water.

It's almost dark, but I can see he recognizes me. "That was a nice cruise," he says pleasantly.

"Yeah? Good. What's your name?" I ask as I step with him out of earshot of other guests.

"Matthias de Foch."

He has a slight Dutch accent, and his tone suggests I should have known his name. "Foch?" I repeat. "That's two letters away from *fuck*."

Matthias laughs. "Never thought of it like that."

"Yeah, what De Fuck?" I smile back, but it's a snarl. "Here's the thing, De Foch. If you so much as *fuck* with Lexi or any of the other staff here, female or male, in single format or multiples, whatever, rest assured that a diving accident will come your way."

His smile turns like a jug of milk: sour. "And who do you think you are?"

"I'm the guy who's going to make sure you get off this

island in one piece, in a body bag or in a seat on that floatplane. Your choice."

Matthias gives an incredulous chuckle. "You wouldn't dare."

"You'd be too dead to be surprised," I counter.

He shakes his head with a smirk. "This is a first."

You're telling me. Has nobody ever said *no* to this guy? "I don't like repeating myself, so don't make it necessary to prove a point."

Matthias stuffs his fists in his shorts' pockets, still smiling as if we have this type of conversation every day. "I wonder what Nathan Beaumont will say when he hears about this?"

"He's a friend of yours, is he?"

Matthias shrugs. That gesture could mean anything. It could be a shot in the dark, but I grew up in lawyer families and am used to people twisting words and tossing names around with the aim of intimidating others.

"Nathan Beaumont will blacklist you from his hotels," I inform him, not taking the bait. "So do feel free to entertain him with the details of our conversation."

When Matthias doesn't respond, but only grinds his jaw, I give him the same dismissive pat on the arm he gave me earlier. "Rejection sucks, but you'll get over it." And with that, I walk off to greet some other guests who've been trying to catch my attention.

Once the guests are having dinner and I can officially call it a night, I return to the office to check my email. I'm on a hard-negotiated sabbatical from Miami University, but there are still emails from my research colleagues, and I send them quick responses. I'm halfway through the list when I still. An email from the junior lawyer at Dad's firm has arrived in my inbox.

I've been copied, along with Evan, but the email is addressed to Lexi. I glance through it once, speed reading, then slow down and read it again to decipher all the legalese.

Bottom line: Mia Reed won't be paying off the hackers, and they are free to do what they want with the video footage.

I cover my face with my hands and groan. I haven't seen the video, so for me this is all unreal. For Lexi it's very real, and it pains me to think that something so obscene featuring her will go out into the world. The last thing she wants is to have her name and face connected with a scandal. I need to be with her, next to her, right there to comfort her and tell her it's going to be okay. We'll weather this storm together, and hopefully it will be only in a teacup.

I send a reply, asking the lawyer if they know when the hackers will release the content and if we have any other legal recourse to take. Then I log out and lock up the office for the night. I head to the canteen to see if Lexi has eaten dinner, and when it's a *no* from the sous-chef, I take two prepared poké bowls for us and return to our cottage. It's not that late, and I bet she's still awake.

"Lexi?" I call as I kick off my flip-flops and dip my feet in the foot basin. The windows are shut with their rolls of woven grass mats, and the door is closed. This is the first time I've seen our place like this, and it's considerably more private than having everything open for the breeze. I elbow the door open and smile as I see her sitting on the bed, reading.

"Hey." She closes her book and tosses it aside. "Oh, nice. You brought dinner. I thought I'd missed it."

"Can't let you go hungry, and it's still early. Come eat in the living room?"

She hops off the bed and goes to the minibar. "We've

haven't had a breather since we got here. I can't believe this small island hotel can produce so much work." She holds out a bottle of chilled white wine. "You want some?"

"Sure." I put the bowls with our cling-wrapped food on the coffee table and take the wine from her. She hands me the corkscrew and turns to reach for the glasses. I need my hands busy so I can keep my eyes on something other than her legs. She's wearing those shorty shorts and a tank top, like she did in Miami, and my heart melts a little, my fingers itching to touch her skin, right there where her thigh curves into butt. "You feeling any better?"

"Yep," she says, her back to me. "Thanks for standing in for me."

"Any time." I pop the cork, and she holds out two glasses.

"At least I managed to have a chat with Tessa. I had to talk her off the ledge."

"Why?" I ask as I pour. "Filming has started, hasn't it?"

"Yeah, but she's not feeling it as much as she thought she would. I think it's just nerves. She's worked so hard to get there and now...the moment's too big."

"She'll be all right. It's always at its worst when you start out."

Lexi sighs as she holds the other glass out for me. "The next couple of days are going be crazy with the wedding. I'm glad I got a little break."

"Good." I pour and feel her gaze on me. I look up, catching her in the act. Instead of looking away, she keeps staring, blue eyes wide, a soft smile on her lips. If she knew what that does to my heart, she wouldn't do it.

"So..." She pauses to lick her bottom lip. "Were you able to do anything about Matthias de Foch?"

I put the bottle of wine down and reach for one of the filled glasses. Our fingers brush against each other, and she doesn't let go immediately. We're caught in a few sensual seconds where my need to stand between her and the rest of the world only deepens.

"I told him he'd have an unfortunate diving accident if he so much as looks at you—or any other staff member here—during his stay."

Lexi bursts out laughing. "You did not!"

I reach for her hand and guide her to the sofa, where we both sit down. She doesn't pull away, and it seems like a small victory to have our fingers intertwined and resting on the seat between us. "I did. Let's see if he comes diving while he's here."

"Thank you," Lexi says with a squeeze to my hand before she lets go. "I would have told him off, but coming from you... I bet he won't push me now. If it were me, he would have kept trying his luck until the day he left, or even worse, moved on to the other women on the staff."

"Asshole."

"Yep. Maybe there'll be a bridesmaid to mend his lonely heart." Lexi puts her wine down and pulls the cling wrap off our bowls. She hands me mine, and we dig in. I'm ravenous, having done three dives today—two with the guests and then a longer session with Roger. It was only a walk-in dive to assess his skills, but starting tomorrow, we're going to take a structured approach to his training.

"I had an interesting conversation with Deshni today," Lexi says between bites.

"Yes?"

"She and Sarika want to make changes at the spa, and I had

a look at their proposal. It's a solid plan, but for some reason they've never had a chance to push it with management."

I take a sip of wine, the gears in my head shifting. "It's the same for Roger. He's stuck and wants more from life, but it seems hard to get ahead here."

"How weird," Lexi says. "You'd think Beaumont would encourage their staff to grow."

"I don't know. Roger said people who learn too much tend to leave. So maybe that's not Beaumont's preferred approach. We're lucky. We've had different experiences, and when we go home, we have options. Our time here is limited. But when our three months are done, all these local folks will still be here, as Beaumont needs them to be, carrying on with no practical access to learning."

"Yep," Lexi says, sipping her wine. "That sucks, but I guess it makes sense."

"I'm going to train Roger over the next few weeks and have him dive with me to get his hours. By the time I leave, he could be a master diver."

"What? That fast?"

"If we push it, yes."

"What about your filming and editing and all that?"

I shrug. "He can come with me. He wants to learn the ropes, so two birds with one stone. If I can help him while I'm here, I will." I take a last bite. "The rest can happen in between. I know what I'm doing and where I'm going with it, so it'll work out."

"That would be awesome for him." Lexi stirs the bits and bobs of salad and beans around in her bowl. "I was planning to run Deshni and Sarika's proposal by the head office in France first, but why wait? They've been sitting on the idea so long and to stall while we wait for them to make up their minds is a waste of time."

"So just start implementing it," I say with a nod. "You wanted to show off your skills... You can deal with any backlash after the fact."

"That's one way to bypass Jem." She smirks. "Can't ask for a better opportunity, for all of us."

"Exactly. Did you know Roger and Deshni are a couple and not supposed to be?"

Lexi looks up. "What do you mean?"

"They're in love, but can't be together because of... I don't know." I shake my head. "Cultural differences. Parental expectations. It sounds complicated."

"Oh, God," Lexi whispers as she puts her bowl on the coffee table. "That's who she meant."

"With what?"

"She said she had to see how things work out with—ugh, she didn't say his name, but she must have been referring to Roger."

"What did she say?"

"She was all in tears and told me she'll have an arranged marriage, but it was clear she was already in love with someone else, someone she can't have." Lexi groans as she drops her head back against the sofa and looks over at me. "She made me feel horrible about faking this engagement. She said we're so lucky to be here, together, not even married, and with our *parents' blessing*."

Our parents' blessing is so far off the radar that we didn't bother to tell anybody about our arrangement. But I understand Deshni's sentiment. I put my empty bowl down and sigh into my cupped hands as I lean back too, sinking into the sofa. *What are we playing at here?* Beyond being a means to an end, I'm not sure what I'm doing here with Lexi, or why I agreed to this impulsive idea of Evan's. But I think some part of me knew. This girl has been trying to crawl out of my heart for years, but I've kept her tethered in a secret chamber where only I knew she still existed. And I've waited. For *this*.

We've both been waiting for this. They say people change, but they don't—not that much. Not in the fundamental things that matter. And this is *Lexi*. I've never cared for another girl like I care for her. And now this grown woman is jerking that chain in my heart, making me fall for her again, slowly and then so fast it's like freefalling from the sky.

"Babes," I groan into my hands, needing to divert my thoughts.

"Hmm?"

"We got an email from the lawyer about the Mia Reed video. It's in your inbox."

"And?" Lexi doesn't move, doesn't tense up or sit straight. She only stares at me, relaxed and seemingly unfazed. Must be the wine.

"Reed's not paying the hackers. They don't know when, but that video is going to go out into the world."

There's a beat of silence between us, where the dimmed night songs of the bugs and birds rise above the far-off waves.

"Okay." She swallows hard. "Jeez. What a fuckup."

"I know." I reach for her hand, sliding my thumb over her fingers. "It sucks."

For a long moment, she struggles to keep her emotions contained. "There's nothing I can do about it. Absolutely nothing." She hitches her shoulders with a sigh. "That world is so far away from here. I mean—"

"Yep. Seems kinda dumb."

"I know, right? There's important work to do here for other people. This is Mia Reed's problem. She has her own agenda, over which I have zero say. I was so busy with Deshni's proposal that I didn't check social media today. It's liberating."

"Yeah, going offline is liberating." I reach for her hair where it's piled on the sofa's back and play with a few strands. "You know I'm your person here, right? Whatever happens, we'll weather it together."

"Yes. I know. Just as I'm yours."

Those words... *She's mine.* And I'm fucked.

"I'm going to rinse these out," I say, letting go of her hair and picking up the dirty bowls. I need to get physically away from her, because all I want to do is pull her onto my lap, have her straddle me, and kiss her senseless—just like I wanted to do earlier when I had her in my arms.

"I'm going to read," she says. "The library here is stocked with loads of books I've always wanted to get to but never had the time."

"Good." I stand and take the last sip of my wine. "I'm going to work on the footage I shot today."

"You getting anywhere?"

"Yep. A few things are coming together that can make a story. I'll see where it goes over the next few weeks."

"Great."

I scoot past her, but at the last second she blocks me by putting her foot on the coffee table. "To think, we could be having a threesome right now."

"Yeah?" I look down at her, surprised by the teasing smile on her lips. "You're into that type of thing?"

"No. I never have been..." Lexi trails off as a blush invades her sweet face. "You?"

I shake my head with a chuckle. Might as well address what happened this morning. "Nope. As you've seen, I've been sailing solo for some time now, so going from one to three is skipping an important number for me."

"Yeah? Two. You do two?"

She's poking at me now like I poked at her, and I'm game to see where this goes. "Two max." I sit on the coffee table and put the bowls down. Her foot is right there, snuggled against my hip. *Fuck.* I'm going to have to keep things in check here.

"Does that make us dull?" She puts her other foot on the coffee table too, effectively trapping me right where I want to be, between her legs.

"Dull?" I rest my hands on her feet and gaze into her eyes, making sure she's on board with my touch.

She doesn't shy away from staring right back at me. "What are you doing?"

"I don't know," I confess. "What're you doing?"

Lexi chuckles. "I'm flirting with my fake fiancé."

"I see." *Two can play that game.* This will be such torturous fun. I slide my fingers around her ankles and higher, to her calves and the folds of her knees. Goosebumps speckle her skin, and I smile. "Babes, to get back to your question of being dull—I don't know who you've been having sex with, but two is definitely not dull."

I smooth my hands up to her thighs, letting my thumbs caress the inner slopes that lead to her sex. A shudder runs through her body, and with a soft moan, she seems to sink deeper into the sofa, her legs opening a barely perceptible inch. She's going to drive me nuts, but instead of running my thumbs along the hem of her shorts and over her pussy, I circle my hands to her hips, pulling her toward me and making her drop her feet to the floor. I lean closer, and her chest rises and falls in anticipation of what I'm going to do next.

"What do you want, Lexi?" I ask softly. "Because I know what I want. What I've always wanted but you weren't ready for five years ago." My gaze dips to her lips, and the answer is there, but I still ask to make sure we want the same thing.

Her hands join mine, her palms soft and warm as our thumbs lock, and I'm ready to be guided to where she wants me to touch her. "I want that kiss you've owed me since putting this ring on my finger at Heathrow," she whispers.

My heart hammers so hard in my chest, I swear she can hear it.

Everything within me surges forward, so eager. This won't be our first kiss, but unlike the last time we crossed the line, which tore us apart, one simple kiss could start healing the hurt between us.

Chapter Twenty-Four
LEXI

Somewhere inside me, there's an echo of the vulnerability I felt five years ago, when I asked him to kiss me the first time. I'm not sure if I heard him right. *"Because I know what I want. What I've always wanted but you weren't ready for five years ago."*

This is pure lust, and I bet it's the same for Tristan. But as for five years ago...what if he felt the same but didn't—*couldn't or wouldn't*—act on it because *I* wasn't ready? I pause, trying to be rational as my heart pounds wildly with the notion that maybe, just maybe, he'd wanted me too but did the gentlemanly thing—

Fact is, I'm no longer a teenager in the throes of an infatuation, albeit one that's stood the test of time. I'm a woman who knows what I want, and three months is a long time to stare at the goods locked out of reach in a glass cabinet.

This might be lust, but Tristan's eyes don't shine like those of a guy who's just gotten the green light to fuck his one-night stand. *That* look I know well.

Instead, Tristan's gaze is soft and tender as his fingers find my hips, nudging me closer. I can't think straight. All I can do is follow my body blindly. I slide my hands up his arms, mimicking what he did to my legs minutes ago. I trace over the roadmap of his veins, over the hills of wrist bones, the collection of leather and twisted metal on his left wrist, up his forearms to his elbows, drawing him closer. Somehow he has slipped to the floor on his knees in the space between the sofa and the coffee table, but even like this, he is taller than me. And he's so close, I can see the amber flecks in his warm brown eyes.

"What games are you playing, Lexi?" His lips ghost over my hairline. His stubbled cheek grazes mine and reminds me that he's a man who probably fumbles less with sex and love than I do. Tristan is, after all, a scientist; he'll have a hypothesis, method, and conclusion at the end of this.

"One that needs two players only," I breathe as his lips caress a spot beneath my ear that makes me shift and cling to his shoulders, all hard and muscled.

"And what are the rules?" His mouth covers the short stretch to my jaw, and a galaxy of tingles runs over my skin. His hands move up my sides, firming their hold on my body. My nipples are hard and jutting out, seeking attention from his fingers, his lips.

The Lexi O'Reilly Short Compendium of Happy Work Rules flits through my mind, and somehow none of them apply here. *Male co-workers are off the menu?* I'm engaged to one.

Stick to company policy and obey the rules? To be honest, since landing on this island, I've been confused. Small places like this come with their own challenges, and what works here will never work in New York and vice versa. To be honest, I'm a bit befuddled. Must be the heat.

As for bending the rules with caution, it's the breaking part that comes with hazards...

"Rules don't apply in paradise," I murmur as he trails kisses down my neck. I lean my head to the side, opening up for him. "Except that it's game over when we leave here. No regrets. No expectations." *And no falling irreparably in love.*

I need to keep this light and easy. It's just lust. Just sex. Nothing more. Tristan isn't the commitment kind, and I don't blame him. Being with someone for three months can never change a lifetime's exposure to infidelity and indifference.

He follows a hot lick of his tongue with a slow and sensual chain of kisses that starts at the dip of my collarbone and proceeds all the way to the corner of my mouth. *Oh. My. God.* I can't hold back. I open my legs wider and press my body flush with his, my sex snug against his erection—*holy fuck, he* does *want me*—as my fingers desperately rake into his hair to keep him close.

Tristan's thumb brushes a soft sweep against the underside of my breast. "I'm in," he murmurs.

Then his lips close over mine, and I open for him, our tongues connecting in a languid twist that soon turns passionate and deep. As we kiss, Tristan strokes my breast, shifting from the underside and homing in on my nipple. I moan and reach for his hand to pause him.

His hand stills, and our breathing is haggard as we break away.

"I'm a bit tender," I whisper as his somewhat drugged gaze searches mine. "Kind of all over...places."

The gears seem to shift in his mind, and he drops his hands

to my hips. They hold me anchored, and I want to rub my pussy against his erection in a very wanton way.

"Sorry, angel, it slipped my mind for a moment there."

Angel. I love that.

With a groan and a deprecating chuckle, he moves a few inches backwards, breaking our physical connection as my period puts a pause on proceedings. Which is maybe a good thing. Only fools rush in...

"So there *are* rules." Tristan's tone is teasing as he cups my cheek.

"Only this one," I say on a sigh. His whisper-soft touch is not helping me put a stop to things.

"Fine by me. That kiss was, in any case, not one for the public eye."

"No." I smile. "I suspect we might've been tossed out of Heathrow Terminal Five if we'd carried on like that."

"Good thing I have work to do," he says.

"Good thing I have a book to read." As if anything could distract me from him. *Holy Mother of God and all the saints in a row...* I've been trying so freaking hard to keep that wall between us since that day he arrived in Miami. But my defenses have weakened. The sight of him, of his cock straining in his fist, was the final breach.

"Why is it so hot in here?" he groans, placing an innocent kiss on my forehead.

"I closed the windows against the bugs since I kept the lights on?"

"You know what I mean. Airflow has nothing to do with it."

He stands and reaches for my hands to pull me up, and the gesture is so sweet and so Tristan, my arousal-weakened legs almost refuse to straighten. Any other man would have pushed me to blow him by now, disrespecting my body and need for space.

As soon as I'm up, he hugs me close, his chest hard against my breasts, the warm cotton of his Beaumont-branded T-shirt soft against my hands as I circle my arms around his neck. He cups my butt and pulls me up against him, and with a chuckle I perch my feet on his. "What are you doing?"

"Tucking you in. To bed with you," he says as he walks us across the room. "And no Great Wall of Goose Down tonight, okay?"

"Great Wall of Goose Down?"

"That pillow you thought would ward me off."

"It was more to ward me off." I've been ready to climb over and ride him cowgirl style for the past few nights, and I've had a few dreams that were too real with him so close.

"I see..." He nods with a dry chuckle. "Evan would skin me alive if he knew I so much as looked at any part of you lower than your forehead."

We've reached the bed, and the backs of my thighs are pressing against the high mattress.

"Really?" I remember again that Evan asked me if Tristan was behaving. I'm still waiting for a response to my *define behaving* question.

"Uh-huh."

"Good thing he's on the other side of the world and doesn't need to know what's happening here." Are you really breaking rules if no one is watching?

He searches my face for what feels like a very hot minute. "Goddammit, Lexi."

"What?"

"This wasn't the plan. I—"

"I know," I interrupt him. The plan was a three-month stint in paradise without getting into each other's hair—never mind pants—but we've been in deep waters since arriving at this cottage. Still, I don't want him to go into any explanations. I *know* Tristan. I've *seen* Tristan for years via his social media profiles. I'm familiar with his modus operandi, and it's a risk I'm willing to take. "I can change my plans." *For better or worse.*

For a moment he stares at me, then shakes his head. "I don't want anybody to get hurt."

"Been there, done that." Didn't exactly get the T-shirt, but who would want to brag about being rejected by Tristan? Not me. But we can move on from that now. I've moved on. I mean, I'm a liberated twenty-four-year-old woman with needs. When it comes to sex, he's clearly feeling differently about me too these days. We can have a fling and walk away.

His hands drop away from my body, and he takes a step backward, digging his fingers into his hair. "Fuck, Lexi. You were barely nineteen and tipsy at my fraternity's farewell for me. I wasn't even staying there anymore and leaving for Hawaii—" He breaks off, clinching his hair tight in his fists. "It was nothing but a fucking dirty frat piss-up, something I've totally outgrown, and seeing *you* there—"

I swallow against the sudden tightening in my throat and sink my butt into the mattress, not trusting my legs. I still went there with the hope of seeing him one last time, before he left forever. "I came for you, Tris—"

"But you were one of only a handful of girls there and... Jesus Christ, Lexi." Tristan pulls in a ragged breath and groans. "Do you know what type of guys those frat boys were? Who they probably still are? People don't change. I was going to fucking kill someone if they even looked at you, never mind touched you."

"And yet all I wanted was for *you* to look at me...*see* me." *Differently.* No longer as the gangly girl who hung out with him and Evan, making jokes, fooling around, part of a lopsided bunch of kids treading the waters of adolescence as best we could, but as the girl who wanted to be *his* in every way possible.

Tristan drops his head back, palms hiding his face. "And I did. I watched you grow up, Lexi. Ever since I became friends with Evan, I watched every single transformation, but—" He lowers his face, and drags his hands down his cheeks with a frustrated grunt.

"I get it. I was like your little sister. The one you always wished for." So he wouldn't have to be so alone and forgotten by that mishmash family of his who all seemed to have time for everything but him.

"No! You were *never* like a sister to me. You were always Evan's sister and *off limits.*"

Oh.

That didn't stop us though.

That night he bundled me up in his car and drove me home, walked me to the front porch. Mom wasn't there; she was in New Orleans. Evan was still at the frat party, oblivious. And then, when Tris pulled me in his arms for a final goodbye hug, I asked him to kiss me. And he did. And then—

"Things went too far, Lexi."

I can still see it. *Feel* it. Us stumbling through the front door, kissing, tugging at each other's clothes, me dragging him upstairs to my room between kisses that were so hungry, you'd think we were starved for each other. My single bed, in my childhood bedroom, Taylor Swift posters on the wall. So fucking juvenile. So teenager.

Tristan's hands on me as he helped me rip off my cocktease black dress, his hot kisses on my skin, his hands on my naked breasts, his thumbs on my nipples, his tongue flicking at them and my body contracting at the novelty, the sensations his touch released, the wet and sticky heat between my thighs. His fingers as they slipped into my panties, how I nearly came as he circled my clit and fingered me.

Until he froze. Pulled back. Sat up. Heaved as he dropped his head into his hands.

"Fuck, Lexi," he groans. "Never mind that I was twenty-five and way too old for you. Being with you—taking your virginity, as I knew you wanted me to that night—would have been a fucking dick move. And cruel. Don't you see that?"

I shake my head, every moment of that night, every sensation hurtling back as if it happened minutes ago. "What you did was much crueler."

"Jesus Christ!" He drags his fingers through his hair. "*I* was hurting at the thought of leaving you behind. How would you have felt if we..." He takes me by the shoulders and lowers his face to mine, searching my eyes. "Lexi, when it comes to pussy, the male bar is disgustingly low. Any one of those guys at that frat party would have fucked you, anywhere. Drunk or not. High on whatever drugs were making the rounds or not. Virgin or not. Against a wall, on a vomit-baptized mattress, who the fuck knows. You would've gotten hurt so badly, angel. I rescued you from that frat house as if I was a fucking hero, saving you from being preyed upon, and then I went and used you just like any other prick who's only interested in a one-night stand."

It felt more as if I was using him, desperate for his attention, his love. Clearly none of that was coming from his side. He walked out and never looked back once. Five long years of silence stretching to snapping point. And here we are, going on since December as if that night never happened.

The rejection and abandonment of that moment cast a shadow over my life for years after. Me, men, and idiocy. The perfect trifecta.

Why is it that I'm still not over him? That I keep getting attracted to guys who only use me like Brent Fisherman did? You'd think I would have learned a thing or two, but no, I like to wallow in heartache.

I wipe my cheeks, wishing I could hide. On this stupid island there is no place to run and hide, to digest the truth I've suspected deep down but hearing it from Tristan finally makes it real. He only wanted me safe that night. He never wanted to hurt me, and he had to walk away to ensure that. The thing is, if he hadn't walked away then, he would have walked away a couple of months later because that's how he rolls.

Bottom line: he didn't want me enough. I know that now. I know how he operates. At twenty-five a man is fully formed, apparently, brain and all, and Tristan hasn't veered off his usual path. His track record holds. He is the ultimate playboy and who could blame him. So actually, he *spared* me.

"You know how to kill a guy slowly, don't you, babes?" Tristan whispers as he pulls me to stand again and hugs me to his chest. "Come here."

We stand like that for a moment, me stiff in his arms, trying not to break down into a sobbing mess like I did five years ago when he walked out.

"With the wedding, the next week is going to be mayhem,"

he murmurs. "Maybe that's a good thing...simply because I don't think this is a good idea."

All I can do is nod. We need to let this tension between us cool off. Thank God for periods. At last they make total sense.

Eventually he pulls away and takes my hand, only to lead me to the bathroom. "You do what you need to do. I need some fresh air."

Chapter Twenty-Five

TRISTAN

When I wake the next morning, it's still dark outside. Lexi is curled up on her side of the bed with her back to me. There's no Great Wall of Goose Down, but it isn't necessary. I fucked up last night.

I drag my hands over my face with a slow exhale. I hurt her by walking away five years ago, but if I'd given in to what we both wanted, the hurt would have been so much worse. I wouldn't have been able to live with myself. I was older, more mature. I had to be the one to draw the line.

But last night...I should've stayed. I should've taken her in my arms and held her close until she fell asleep. That would have ironed out the last of our past's creases, but instead, I walked away. Again. By the time I got back—two hours later because I had to be sure Lexi was asleep—I could avoid any further intimacy.

My original scruples no longer stand in our way. I can let Lexi enjoy her game and play by her rules. Based on the way she phrased it, it seems this is only about sex for her. I like a good hook-up as much as any other guy, because there are no expectations of it ever being more than I can give: a good time with some hot-as-fuck memories when we're done.

Except, for me, Lexi will never be hook-up material. I care too much about her. And with her, it will always be much more than mere physical intimacy. Plus, there's another layer to the problem: this isn't exactly a hook-up situation. Last night we cleared the air about what happened years ago, but somehow it only twisted the tension between us tighter.

Lexi thinks she'll be calling the shots, with things being *game over*, no regrets or expectations when we're done here. But I wasn't being flippant when I said I don't want anybody to get hurt.

That *anybody* would be me.

For a long, painful minute, I focus on her breathing. At least she got a good night's rest. With the wedding on her doorstep, she's going to need it.

As quietly as possible, I slip from the bed and get myself ready. When I head out for my run, I pause to make sure I'm hearing right. Lexi is snoring. It's soft and so cute. She's like a kitten, all sweet and cozy. I want to stare a moment longer, but I leave her be, as staying only eats at my resolve to keep away from her. After last night, Lexi would probably be feral if I woke her with an unsolicited morning kiss.

When I return, she's gone like every other morning.

After a quick shower and breakfast at the staff canteen, I don't head straight to the dive center but instead make my way to the office to check on her.

"Tristan." Jem quirks an eyebrow as I walk inside.

Lexi looks up, frowning to see me here, so off script. We're back on stage, and with Jem's eyes on us, I'm going to have to play my role, which seems even more duplicitous and complicated than before.

"Jem," I say in greeting as I walk over to where Lexi's sitting behind her desk. "Babes." I lean in as she swivels in her office chair and looks up, surprise widening her eyes. I block any further movement with my hand on the back of her chair. "Feeling better than yesterday?" I ask, keeping her trapped so we can have this private word.

"You don't need to ask—"

"But I want to know, so I can look out for you."

"I'm fine," Lexi says. And there it is, that sweet blush she has zero control over. "That's a one-day thing."

"Good." I pull away, but don't let go of the chair, crowding her with my body for Jem's sake.

Lexi clears her throat, searching my face. "Good run?"

"Yeah." I smile at her and straighten, but watch as she crosses her legs. *Dammit, Lexi.* "I want to check Mike's schedule for the week ahead. I need him to man the boat when I go out with Roger."

"Roger is your boat boy. What do you need Mike for?" Jem eyes me over the rims of her glasses. "He's going to be busy enough with transporting things from Pemba and with the wedding guests and their whims."

"I'm training Roger up to master-diver level," I say, not fazed by Jem's authoritarian tone. "We'll start with walk-in dives, but later this week we'll need to go out to deeper waters. We need a skipper. It's a standard safety procedure."

"Huh," Jem grunts. "Deeper waters, huh. Diving. Huh."

"Yes, Jem, surely you won't stop Roger from learning how to dive? He wants to up his skills, and Tristan is here to help him out," Lexi says. "If they need a boat and Mike is available, I don't see why they can't go out in the afternoons."

Total annihilation. Awkward doesn't begin to describe it. Jem glares at Lexi. Lexi glares back. I squeeze the back of Lexi's chair. *Attagirl.*

Eventually Jem drops her gaze, and you could hear a pin fall in the room.

Lexi shifts in her chair, her shoulders stiff. "I'll check for you."

My eyes move to her screen, where she has some random gossip page open.

She minimizes it, but it's too late. I know what she's doing. She's checking up on Mia Reed and the bomb that's officially airborne.

"You shouldn't." I squeeze her shoulder, and she tenses under my touch. Now there's one way to give us away. Jem's eyes are on us again, brooding, clinging to us like sand to suntan-lotioned skin. So instead of pulling away, I keep my hand on her shoulder, tracing a line on the delicate column of Lexi's neck with my thumb. She shudders, as if on cue.

I shouldn't play with her like this, but I can't stop myself from touching her. I don't like Jem's scrutiny, and I also need to comfort Lexi somehow and get the message through that she should stop tormenting herself by scouring the internet. When the Mia Reed story breaks, it will be plastered front-page everywhere.

"I know I shouldn't," Lexi murmurs as she types away. "Mike is out on Wednesday and Friday afternoon for now. For the rest, he seems available. Today and tomorrow are madness."

"Great. I'll speak to him." With a soft brush down her arm,

I lean in and kiss her temple. "Good luck. Call me if there's anything I can do to help."

"The first delivery arrives in an hour, and then the guests are coming in three batches," Lexi says. She seems to force herself to relax under Jem's continuing watch. "It's going to be busy."

"You keep Matthias de Foch out of our hair and out of our girls' panties," Jem says on a huff. "He's at his best a couple of meters under water."

Jesus Christ. De Foch has a reputation. "Will do."

I'm hardly out of the office when Jem's voice follows me. "When are you two going to kiss and make up, huh? Properly?"

What? Jem is poking her finger in every single pie here. Lexi responds, but I can't hear what she says. Hopefully she puts Jem in her place. That might be a tough one, though. Jem and Mike are older and have been here forever. Neither of them likes to be told what to do by younger outsiders who are only here to fill a gap.

"Well, there's nothing worse for the vibes in this place than when management is having a personal tiff." Jem's last words float to me through the open office door. "And it's been clear from day one that you two need to patch something up."

Fuck's sakes. And it doesn't help if there's tension between Jem and Lexi either. Things in that office didn't exactly feel convivial. If there's a reason to make this fake engagement real on at least one score, it's the sixth sense of the people working here. The last thing we need is the locals suspecting we're up to no good.

I'm still chewing on this thought when I arrive at the dive center. Roger is already there, for the first time early and literally bouncing on the balls of his feet. At least someone is happy with the changes coming.

Matthias de Fuck-Off-Already arrives in time for the morning's dives, and I'm neither surprised nor pleased. I nod at him in acknowledgement, and he shoots me a grimace. He's an experienced diver, having been at Ne'emba nine times in the past few years if the records hold true. I still want to pummel his face, but I'm on the job and know when to behave. As long as he toes the line, I can toe the line.

When we get back from the morning's outing, some wedding guests have arrived, ready to book their dives, and I can see Lexi already wishing the next week was over. At least there's some arm candy for De Foch now, and with a slow exhale, I thank God that Lexi will be out of his line of fire.

After a quick lunch, I spend some time with Roger, working through the beginner's manual on dive theory, and then we head out for some practical instruction. He is sharp and eager, which makes teaching fun, and he knows a lot of things already. He just didn't know he knew them. At this rate, I'll be able to leave him with more knowledge than the diving. He wants to learn everything about underwater photography too, and during our shallow dive, I hand him my camera to try out. Let him play.

As we wrap up for the day, he comes to stand next to me where I'm taking my camera out of its waterproof case.

"Do you think I took any good photos?" he asks.

"Yeah, definitely." If he wants to get a grip on the art, I'll need to invite him into my closet and show him the apps I use to produce social-media-worthy content. This is the moment to cross that bridge. "Do you want to have a look?"

"Please."

"Come with me. But first dinner." I lock up the dive center, and Roger has a skip in his step as we walk together to the canteen. I smile, praying that there'll be at least one good image to stoke his enthusiasm. "Do you have social media?"

"Of course. Do you think I live under a rock here?"

I laugh. "No, only on an island in the middle of nowhere."

"I'm connected to the office's internet, and then when I go to home to Pemba, it's not a problem at all."

Guests are on the beach for their sundowners, and we don't encounter anybody except the waiters who are scurrying around with hefty cocktails.

We eat quickly, and then I lead the way into our cottage, which has already had its room turndown. It's spotless as always, the mosquito net closed around the bed. "This way."

Roger follows and seems surprised when I open the door to the walk-in closet. "You hide in here?"

"It's the most bug-proof room and comes with lights. So I can work at night without disturbing Lexi." I switch my laptop on. "Go fetch an extra chair? There's one in the bathroom."

He comes back a second later, and I'm already typing away. I take the disk out of my camera and slot it into the laptop. "Let's see what you got."

"You don't need the internet to do this?" he asks as I download our images in my editing app.

"Nope. This I do offline. As for my social media, I schedule posts to go out. I post three images or reels a day, even though I'm here."

Roger nods. "Cool. I want to do the same. Can you show me how?"

"Do you have a computer? Or a laptop?" I ask, already knowing the answer.

"Nope. All I have is this." He holds his phone up, and it's vintage. Everything Roger knows, he's gathered from scraps or learned online from the apps that still work on his dated phone. Not that it's stopping him—this man is ready to climb an exponential wall of learning—but he needs a new device to practice and refine his skills.

I glance at my own latest-edition phone. I can let that go when I leave here and get a new one at home. It's not as if I use it much right now. Maybe I can arrange for a new phone from Dar es Salaam and have it shipped to Ne'emba. That would give Roger a head start. With the floatplane coming in so regularly, that has to be an option. I'm not sure how Roger will feel about handouts, though.

"Here we go." I only took about two shots. The rest are all Roger's. At first there're a lot of duds, but then the moment when something clicked becomes clear. Roger's images are crisp, the colors bright, a split second of paradise captured for eternity. "Look at this one. It's freaking awesome."

I glance over at Roger when he says nothing, only to see his bottom lip trembling, his eyes welling up.

My throat tightens too, but I am well acquainted with this feeling. I have it every time I capture something that seems bigger than life itself, even if it's the tiniest of creatures. "That's talent, man. Pure, undiluted talent. And we're going to hone it over the next weeks."

Roger swallows, his Adam's apple rising in his throat. "I didn't think this was possible."

"Well, now you know. Everything is possible."

He shakes his head. "I need to show Deshni. Can I?"

"Sure. She's welcome to come have a look. It's fantastic on

this big screen. See? This is why I told you not to judge the images while you're still in the water."

For the next three hours, we go through the photos, selecting the best ones. I show him some basic edits, and we're so engrossed that we both startle when Lexi leans into the closet.

"Oh, I thought you were here alone," she says in greeting.

"Hey, babes." At least that sounds natural.

She comes closer, and for a split second I hesitate, but then Jem's words from this morning ring through my mind. We need to keep up pretenses, so I wrap my arm around her butt and pull her toward me. She doesn't object, so I hold on.

"Wow," Lexi says as she leans closer to the screen. "You took that photo?"

I nod in Roger's direction. "He did. The way he captured the light beaming through those fins is spectacular."

"I think it's beginner's luck," Roger says, eyes downcast and shy.

"I think it's talent," I say.

"Whatever it is, don't stop." Lexi looks at us. "In fact, you two can probably help us out with taking some professional photos."

"Of what?" I ask.

"I've been thinking of Deshni and Sarika's plans on and off today. We'll need new brochures to put in the rooms and some new spa menus, the type of thing I can have printed in Dar es Salaam. It would be nice to use our own onsite photos."

"Desh told you about their plans?" Roger says, eyeing Lexi.

"She did, and I think they're brilliant."

Roger's lips curl in a small but pleased smile.

"That's not usually in my wheelhouse, but we can give it a

shot. When do you need us?" I ask, making sure Roger gets that we're a team here.

"Let's see how we can fit it in," Lexi says. "The sooner the better. I don't want it to drag. I'd love to have this up and running before we leave—see if we can increase the spa's profits before the lodge closes for the rainy season." She yawns and rests her hand on my back.

Increasing the spa's profits would be a feather in her cap, for sure. "We'll be there," I say, relishing her touch. "How was your day?"

"I'm whacked," Lexi says with a grimace. "This wedding can be over already."

Roger chuckles. "They just arrived."

"The amount of stuff they flew in is insane. I've been on my feet the whole day. We have the rehearsal dinner too, as if every dinner isn't a rehearsal in some way. Couldn't they have done that in Paris? Chef is great at keeping his cool, but even he rolled his eyes at me today."

"I wonder if they'll even taste the food," I say. "The cocktails they had earlier were loaded."

"The champagne was flowing at dinner," Lexi agrees. "Followed by red wine. Sounds like a headache in the making."

"We'll see if any of them comes for a dive tomorrow. I'll do a sobriety test before we go out." I run my knuckles down her naked leg and trace a slow circle with my thumb on the back of her knee. Her fingers slide down my back, and a second later, her touch is gone.

"Sounds like a plan." She stifles another yawn. "I'm off to bed. You're going to work late tonight?"

I still. I'm not going to go to bed until she's asleep. I retract my hand from the back of her leg. *What the actual fuck am I doing touching her like this?* "I have to catch up. If I don't, I'm going to run into trouble."

Several beats of silence follow. *Fuck.* I might have said too much.

"Catch up with what?" Roger asks.

I drag my fingers through my hair, at a crossroads. Lexi squeezes my shoulder—in warning? Who knows. For me, there's trust between all of us in this small room, and with a shrug, I share. "I'm working on a side project while we're here. When I told you these three months are my salvation, I wasn't joking. You want to see?"

Roger's eyes jump between mine and Lexi's, probably sensing that he's been let into the inner circle. "Of course."

"Hmm..." Lexi hums. "It's Tristan's love letter to the ocean."

My love letter to the ocean.

Nobody has ever seen my project in that light, not even me. But it's exactly that: a love letter. It's more than proving to Dad that I'm worthy, that I can excel in my life away from his expectations, in something totally independent of him. It's a visual manifestation of my love for the place where I found inner peace after my family made my life hell. It captures a love that will stand the test of time, again and again.

I reach for Lexi's fingers where they still rest warm on my shoulder and give them a squeeze. She leans over and kisses the top of my head. My heart stalls at this sweet gesture. Was it for Roger's sake, for keeping up the show, or was it an honest-to-goodness beautiful kiss straight from the heart?

I don't know.

But Lexi's ability to sum me up in so few words shows how well she knows me.

And that is scary as fuck.

Chapter Twenty-Six

LEXI

"The next one will be easier," Jem assures me.

"I surely hope so," I say, forcing my shoulders to relax. "But you breezed through it."

"We've done this so many times, but you stressed about everything." Jem looks around at almost all the staff gathered discreetly under the dining room awning, enjoying the live entertainment.

This wedding has been a challenge for me. I've never orchestrated something so special and intimate on an island in the middle of nowhere before. But now that I'm stepping back and seeing it all come together under Jem's gentle hand, I can relax. There were some tense moments in that office, but everything is perfect. I could have gone for a tan on the beach yesterday, and it wouldn't have mattered.

Deshni sidles up to me with a shy smile. "What do you think?" she asks.

"You and Sarika are amazing." I squeeze her hand. I saw the

bride for her pre-ceremony photoshoot, and she looked striking after Deshni and Sarika's hair and makeup. The sisters' talents are on full display with the entourage too, and those two women are worth their weight in gold, given everything they manage for the spa and for the bridal parties at this wedding destination.

The sun is setting, and the ceremony is finally about to begin. Two more nights to go. After the wedding, some guests have a day of recovery before flying back to Europe. Some are leaving tomorrow. This wedding party is a small group, more friends than family. The various parents keep to themselves, but the bride and groom's friends are a handful. I've seen Tristan only in passing as he's been busy with the diving and afternoon whale-shark outings they asked him to guide. The guests are maxing their experience, and that's totally understandable. If I got an all-inclusive trip to a wedding on Ne'emba Island, I'd make the most of it too.

Enter the ever-generous Matthias de Foch, who is walking his sister down the aisle—on a Persian carpet no less. Her flowing strapless dress flutters in the wind, catching against his leg and almost tripping him. They laugh together, and it's a sweet moment. There's no dad, and the mom isn't exactly mingling. There's a story there, but after my first encounter with Matthias, he's kept his distance. Thank God for Tristan.

I look over to where Roger has stepped up next to Deshni, his fingers brushing hers. Everybody else watches the bride and groom, and I'm probably the only one to notice how Roger and Deshni first withdraw from the line of staff and then disappear into the foliage.

They might not be destined to be together, which breaks my heart, but at least they're making the most of the time they have. At the thought, I close my eyes and battle the knot in my throat.

Where is my fiancé exactly?

Tristan is probably working. It's as if he's on a countdown that has put its foot on the accelerator. At night he works on his TV series, whereas I am dead asleep as soon as my head touches the pillow. So many things to be grateful for right now.

Jem put us on the spot the other day when she said Tristan and I have looked like we had a tiff since we arrived. Are we that awkward with each other? Surely not. We've been trying to play our parts, but it's becoming harder to believe there's nothing more behind them. I love his gestures of affection, even if they're for show. Even if they make my heart beat at an unhealthy rate, and even if they stoke that need in me that's only been building since the night we scraped our past clean.

I mean, Tristan started this sexual thing between us with an invitation to shower with him on that morning that now feels like eons ago. He might have been teasing, but surely if it's just about sex for him, and it's just about sex for me, there's no harm, no foul? I thought I made that clear when I said we'd be done when we say our goodbyes to Ne'emba.

I wipe a rogue tear that runs down my cheek. At least anybody watching me will think I'm moved by this intimate wedding.

That *kiss*…

I knew it would be like that—explosive. I can't stop thinking about it. We might have cleared the air, but as we did, we filled it with something worse: desire, need, and a wish for something I can never have. I'll always fantasize about being Tristan's endgame, but he is the last guy on Earth to tie himself down.

An arm slips around my waist and pulls me back against a hard male chest. I close my eyes, the feel of him so familiar now, that fresh-shower smell when he comes from the dive center intoxicating.

"It looks amazing," Tristan murmurs in my ear.

I wrap my arms over his as he hugs me close. "It does," I whisper back, overly conscious of Jem and Mike, who are watching us as much as they're watching the wedding proceedings.

"Well done." Tristan's lips tease my earlobe and chills break out over my skin, pebbling my nipples.

"Honestly, I don't think I've done much except stress. Jem's an old hand at this, and the team is fantastic."

"Good to know." Tristan makes as if to pull away, but I stop him with some pressure on his arms. "I need to go work on my—"

"I know. But stay for this; it's the important part."

"Lexi—"

"Sssshhhh..." Jem hisses, which is totally unnecessary. We are far enough away from the proceedings, and with the waves rushing up to shore, nobody can hear our whispers—nobody except Jem and Mike.

I close my eyes. I don't need to hear the vows. Who doesn't know them? *From this day forward, for better or worse, for richer or for poorer, in sickness and in health, I promise to love and cherish you.*

I can feel Tristan tense as the pastor's voice carries toward us on the breeze.

The kiss-the-bride part follows, and finally I let Tristan pull away. Cheers rise from the guests, and Jem and Mike turn to us with smiles.

"That never gets old," Mike says. "So when's your big day?"

"I—"

"We—"

Tristan and I speak at the same time and then chuckle awkwardly.

"We haven't set a date yet," I tell them, trapped.

"Huh," Jem huffs. "Couples had to be married in my day, but I suppose nowadays it's hire first, fire later."

What?

"Modern times," Tristan says, putting a stop to the conversation. "I'll see you later, babes."

A last squeeze to my hip, and I watch him walk off, suddenly chilly in the cooler twilight air.

"What's he going to work on now?" Jem asks. "Why doesn't he stay for a glass of champagne? Don and Miriam never hesitated, you know, given that it's the real stuff."

"He's probably tired," I say, sidestepping the truth.

"Aren't we all?" Jem's tone raises not only my hackles, but also the fine hairs on my back.

That wasn't a ghost passing: I would swear Jem is on to us, and I don't know how the hell that happened. What did she mean—*hire first, fire later*? Is she going to send us packing if she stumbles on our secret? Jem could be jerking my chain for the fun of it. I don't know her well enough to decipher that statement yet.

Chapter Twenty-Seven
TRISTAN

I'm so deep into edits, listening to music through my headphones, that I don't hear the knock on the door. I startle when Lexi walks into my closet and rips me out of my underwater world.

"Sorry," she says on a laugh as she leans against the door jamb. "I see you still have it in you to concentrate at this hour."

"When you love what you do, you'll never work a day in your life. Or so they say."

"That much fun, uh?" She steps in and looks at my screen. "Show me?"

I press play on the clip I'm working on. It's an octopus playing with a few cowrie shells. "First he has dinner; then he entertains himself with the leftovers. It would seem he has a collection of shells." I watch with her for a half a minute, still equally enchanted. "It's quite close up... I was lucky. Now you need to imagine it with some music and a voice-over and so on."

"He's so cute. And he really is *playing*?"

"Yep." The octopus gathers all the cowrie shells and drops them, repeatedly. "They're intelligent creatures."

"It's amazing," she says. "You have such talent, and your love really shows."

"It does?" Weird that she would say that. Her praise has me swallowing hard, as it's good to hear from someone who knows me. "Roger and I have been seeing this same octopus for a few days now. He's quite the star, and it's as if he put on this act for us—"

"If you say so, but I like to think you're part of the magic too." She sinks into Roger's seat. "Do you think you'll have enough footage to finish your project?"

"Yes, and some more."

"Good."

"The wedding's over?"

"Dinner's done, and now it's only the bar flowing and some very loud music. It's kind of weird, given how quiet it usually is around here."

"I can imagine." Our cottage is situated far from the general guest area and with the wind carrying the sound away, I wasn't aware of the music at all. "You're off to bed?" *Please be off to bed.* Up close and personal like this is doing nothing for my resolve.

"Tris..." Lexi breaks off, and I look down at where she's working her hands.

"What's wrong?"

"I think Jem knows we're faking our engagement."

I lean back in my chair. "Why? We've been fine." I've been making a hell of an effort, though it's slowly suffocating my heart. The more I act, the more it feels real. The more I *want* it to be real. Wait—*what*? That thought zapped through my head so fast I feel somewhat whiplashed.

"I don't know. The way she watches my every move and the things she says... They're making me uncomfortable, and we still have quite a bit of time to kill on this island."

"Babes—"

"What if she knows? What if she reports to Beaumont? It could end us."

I take a deep breath and rush my fingers through my hair, trying to lean deeper into my chair. But it's as stiff as a plank and not conducive to relaxing. "Here's the thing, Lexi. Nobody ever knows what goes on between two people and in their relationship. Trust me. It could be all golden on the outside, while it's rotting on the inside. It could be a shredded shit show on the outside, but solid gold on the inside. For Jem to speculate—"

"I'm scared of the consequences if someone finds out."

Fuck me. "You're a real worrier, aren't you? As if you didn't have enough on your plate with Mia Reed and doing a good job around here. Have a little faith."

"I know." She shakes her head and sighs. "God, I know. I'm extra."

"I love your extra, but you need to relax, okay? We're doing our jobs, aren't we? Dives are going great, and that wedding was fantastic. We're not sleeping with the guests or other staff, and faking an engagement is hardly illegal." I reach for her hands where she's fidgeting with them in her lap. Every time I touch her, there's this flow of energy. Even now, as she stills, my bigger hand cupping hers, there's an undeniable need buzzing between us. "I told you we needed to make this easy on ourselves. Stressing about every last thing isn't going to help. Jem's just being Jem. She likes getting up people's asses, having her fingers on every last pulse point, so don't feed the control freak inside her by falling for her little traps."

Lexi chuckles. "True."

I let go of her hands, and she stands. "Nighty night then."

"Sleep tight." I wait for her to close the door before I lean back with a groan.

There's only one way this is going to end. As Lexi said, we still have time to kill, but nothing is killing this tension between us. Fuck it. Maybe just once… *Maybe just the tip.* I break out in a dry chuckle. Who the hell am I trying to fool? And to be honest, I've been mean, toying with her. Hot and cold, off and on. She's going to drive me nuts, and I likely deserve it. The need to taste her has only built since our recent, intense kiss. And it's only made worse because she seems open to the idea. At least temporarily.

I force myself to focus on work for another forty minutes, so Lexi has time to fall asleep. When I emerge into our bedroom, it's as I expected: she's out. I quietly get ready for bed. All the windows are open, allowing that blessed breeze to cool us off, so I make sure the mosquito net's slit is overlapping and enclosing us. As I get into bed, I glance in her direction, only to find her eyes glinting in the dark.

"Sorry. Shit. Did I wake you up?"

"Can't sleep."

There's trouble. And then there's *this*. Us. Together. Awake. In bed. Best I divert to known territory. "Still worried about Jem and her jabs?"

"No..." she starts and then chuckles. "I've been doing some bedtime sleuthing."

I lean up onto my elbow. "Bedtime sleuthing? What's that?"

Lexi scoots a bit closer, and the massive bed suddenly feels very small. "You know...working through events, eliminating suspects, and coming to conclusions," she whispers, as if we're on to some conspiracy.

"I see." My hand itches to reach for her hip and pull her closer. "I wasn't aware of any crimes..." *Ah. Actually I am.*

She smiles, and I freeze as her hand settles on mine for a second before she slides her fingers up my arm, my biceps, to my shoulder and down a pec, where she circles my hardened nipple with a fingertip.

Holy fuck. She plays dirty. Soon I'll be straining against my underwear, but instead of stopping her, I do nothing.

"You haven't seen a black charger, by any chance?" Her fingertip still turns idle circles around my nipple, and the least I can do is return the favor, but—

"A black charger?" *I'm so busted.*

"It's got a long shaft and rounded tip. You know, to insert into..."

Jesus Christ. This is a losing battle if there ever was one. This is what abstinence around the hottest woman on the planet does to a guy. I'm a fucking goner. I tug her closer and shift into her so we're flush against each other. She hitches her leg onto my thigh, and my cock goes *fuuuuckkk*. I can feel pre-cum drooling from the tip in anticipation as I grip the back of her thigh and make sure we connect for some mutual pressure.

"Into...?" I ask as I lower my mouth to her hairline and run my lips in soft kisses toward her ear. I grin as I suck her earlobe, and I'm rewarded with a soft moan and a hip roll against my cock.

"You know...my vibrator you put in the bedside drawer? With a battery that was definitely not dead when I used it the last time?" Her breathing is shallow as we continue the slow-dance version of a dry hump, grinding against each other.

"Hmm..." Not going to answer that. Not yet. I clasp her hand and shift it above her head as I lean into her, my thigh pushing hers up, forcing her open for me. I run my nose along hers, tempting her lips with mine as I brush over them. "A vibrator? And when last did you come with your toy, angel?"

"Tristan," she breathes.

"Come on, we're *engaged*, Lexi. No secrets here."

She chuckles against my lips. "So long ago I'm basically going nuts."

Uh-huh. You and me both, babes. The hand has become decidedly dull lately with her and her cute ass and perky tits in my face all the time. "So, you're missing your toy?" I perch up on a fist, making sure I deepen the pressure on her mound and clit. She moans, clearly into this.

"Oh God, Tris... I miss the charger more right now, to be honest. The vibrator is pretty useless in its current state."

I smile, knowing I'm going against every bit of logic my brain has provided since she walked in on me at Evan's house. When it comes to this girl, I'm a lost cause. "Do you want me to help you out instead?"

As answer I get a wanton rub of her pussy against my cock, and she pulls me down for a kiss. I sink into her, wrapping her tongue with mine, and this—*this*—is what I should have known. Lexi is a needy and greedy little siren, and I've been made to please.

We deepen the kiss, seeming in mutual awe of what's happening at long last. My pulse is all over the place, and I need to slow us down. I take hold of her hand and guide it to join the other above her head. Once she gets the hint that I want her to stay like that, and she's not getting out of my trap, I loosen my hold, lean up on one hand, and with the other push her thigh higher, opening her as wide as she can go. "Good girl."

She arches her back and pushes her pelvis up again, riding the pressure of my cock where she needs it. Never mind a good girl, Lexi might just be a *very good* girl. I groan as I thrust against the layer of her silky shorts and slide my hand underneath her cami so my fingertips can caress a hard little nipple. She's pure perfection, and fuck, I need more.

I pause, having to take a breath before I break away from her.

"Don't stop," she murmurs. "I'm so close."

"You are?" *Jeez, I've hardly started.*

"Tristan—"

"Soon, angel." I get up on my knees. "Sit up." I hold out a hand for her.

Lexi moans in protest, but she does as I ask, and as soon as she's upright, I strip her cami off, leaving her beautiful breasts in full view at last. Even more beautiful than the first time—

"Fuck it, babes, you're going to destroy me." I pull her in for a kiss that gets hot with lips and tongue, a sensual mimic of what we've both wanted for ages. She's out of breath when I lean her back and languidly work my way to her breast, licking and sucking at that seductive tip until she drives her fingers into my hair.

"Make me come, Tristan. I can't wait anymore."

But I'm in no hurry and make sure her other nipple enjoys the same attention before I settle back, my desperate cock pressed against her sex, eager to ride her to orgasm. "We're going to do it like this?"

"Don't you have condoms?" she asks.

"Didn't exactly plan to have sex...so no." *Idiot.* There could be some in my diving bag, but I don't want to go dig now. That would give me time to think, and that's the last thing I want.

"They sell some in the boutique."

"We can put it on our tab tomorrow."

Lexi giggles, and I kiss down her neck, ready with some alternative plans. "This little set of yours has been driving me wild since you burst into Evan's bathroom." I roll on my side and tug at the waist of her silk bottoms. She wriggles so I can pull them down.

"It has?" she whispers as she kicks them off, keeping one leg bent and the other straightened out.

She's naked now and my eyes are thirsty to take in every inch of her. "Totally." In the moonlight coming from outside, her skin is creamy and smooth, and I want to run my tongue and lips over all of it. I brush my hand up her thigh and my fingers trace the line of her sex. She's wet, and I groan as I dip my finger into her flesh, into that sweet, tight opening of hers.

She opens her legs wider, and it's like pouring a fucking tank of gasoline on an open fire. I watch her face as I fuck her with my fingers, hard and aching to be inside of her.

"Oh my God." Her hand is in my hair, her breath a warm flow over my skin. "This is going to be so quick."

Damn. I want everything but quick. I want days and hours. Weeks and months. I add a finger and up the pace. She's eager, her hips an echo of my every move. I caress her cheek with my lips and run my tongue along her bottom lip. "Come for me, angel. I promise that as soon as we're good to go, I'll fuck you and make you come on my cock so many times you'll forget what day it is."

"Tris..." She inhales sharply and then seems to hold her breath. "Oh my God—"

Chapter Twenty-Eight

LEXI

I'm coming hard, and Tristan's words are only feeding my body's orgasmic frenzy of fireworks and the shivers chasing though me. He stares into my eyes as he holds his fingers steady, pressing down with his palm right where I need it. I dig my nails into his biceps, having to hold onto something as I breathe through this moment.

"Tris..." If this is what he does to me with a simple finger fuck, I might lose track of months and years once things escalate.

He dips his head, and his mouth consumes mine in a slow, ardent kiss that keeps me floating on that high a moment longer.

His cock is so freaking hard as he presses into me, and I run my hand up his arm to cup his face as he gently retracts his hand.

"That was a pleasure if ever there was one," he murmurs against my lips, as if I just said *thank you*.

"A pleasure I should return," I whisper back. *But first...*

"Out with the truth, Tristan Martinelli. You let my vibrator run down and then hid the charger."

"Guilty as charged."

"It's not charged at all!"

He chuckles against my cheek as he brushes his lips to my temple. "What are you going to do with me now?"

"Sounds like you want to be handcuffed. That can be arranged, you know."

"Now there's a thought." He laughs, keeping me on my back with that magic hand on my stomach as he presses an innocent—*innocent my ass! More like guilty*—kiss to my shoulder.

"Oh, I have so much torture coming your way," I mutter as I roll onto my side and run my hand down his chest. "You have the right to remain silent." I nibble a path down his pec, straight to his nipple, which is clearly a hot spot on his body, given his reaction to my touch earlier. I lick and kiss and suck it, and then, when he moans for more, I give him a little bite.

"Agh! Fuck, Lexi—"

"That's for being so despicable as to hide my charger, knowing we're in the middle of nowhere, and I can't get a new one, and for letting my toy go dead." I chuckle against his abs as I ghost my hand over his cock where it's straining against his boxer briefs. He twitches in anticipation. There's nothing small about Tristan, but I knew this. In some aspects, he isn't exactly full of surprises. My fingers find their way into his underwear, and I lift the fabric over his cock, making sure I don't touch him where his body is begging for it.

Until I shift and lick down the length of his shaft. He gasps, his abs flexing as he clutches my hair. "And this," I whisper, "is for being such an auspicious replacement."

"Babes, I solemnly promise to be at the ready whenever and as often as you need me."

"Good." *And oh gawd*. If the size of his cock and the evident ease with which he makes me come are any indication of the pleasure heading my way, I might never want to let him go. With my need to please him overriding every red flag, I grip his cock firmly and sink my mouth onto him, humming my own pleasure at finally tasting his essence.

I know what I'm doing and get into a rhythm that soon has him breathing heavily, but once as I sense he's on the brink, I pull back and take a moment, forcing him away from the ledge. He grunts his displeasure, and I give him a naughty smile. "More?"

"God, yes." His fingers drive into my hair, and he guides my head back down. This time I take him so deep, I feel consumed. "Fuck, Lexi," he grunts as I slide up and roll my tongue around the head. "I know you said you've got torture in store for me, but…"

I go down again, this time soft and slow but so deep that his body flexes with pent-up tension. When I come up, he wraps his hand over mine at the base and traces the line of my lips with a forefinger. The sensation of his fingertip and the connection to his cock and my lips is so erotic, it pulses straight to my clit. I blink at him, amazed at the way he's turned me on with a simple slide of his fingers.

"You like that, don't you, my angel?" he whispers, holding my head in place. "We'll explore that some more later."

This time when I go down, my control has slipped away and into his hands. Tristan is in charge, and as much as he allows me to play and have my fun, he's leading this dance. He doesn't apply much pressure, but the guidance is there, and as

I give it my all, I know this time he won't allow me to pull away at the crucial moment.

"Are you going to swallow for me, angel?" he asks softly.

The endearment only makes me want this more. There's no way to answer except with an acquiescent hum, knowing I want this as much he does. I'll be ready to come again if he keeps talking dirty in that husky pillow-talk voice of his. When the moment comes, Tristan's hold on my head falls away, giving me the option to pull back, but I'm too deep into his pleasure, too consumed by this act to release him, and too thrilled by the feeling of his climax spilling into my throat to let go, knowing I have the power to do this to him.

His body shudders under my palms, and I look up at his beautiful face in the dark, the pleasure of his release evident in his jaw, which goes slack as he grinds his head deep into the pillow.

After a moment I swallow, and when he looks down at me, I end our game with a kiss to the tip of his cock. "I need a minute."

I slip from the bed and go to deal with the aftermath in the bathroom, rinsing and brushing my teeth then managing the wet mess down south. My release has dunked my body in a post-coital high. Thank God we finally crossed that bridge tonight.

When I come out, Tristan is standing in the alcove that connects the bathroom to the main part of the cottage, back in his boxer briefs—*dammit*—hands on his hips, working his jaw. Neither of us has switched on the lights, overly bug-conscious, but with the moonlight streaming in from outside, I can see his eyes glint as they travel down my breasts to my sex.

"Are you okay?" he asks, taking a hesitant step forward.

"Yes, never better."

He seems to let go of a pent-up breath. "Lexi... You're so delicate...so fucking beautiful." He swallows heavily and takes another step closer. "You blew my mind just now," he murmurs as he slips his hands around my waist. "I'm worried I was too much—"

I glow with pleasure at the compliment, but also because he's checking on me. "Never too much—one round's maybe not enough, but never too much." I want more of what we did, more of what we had out there, and I'm going enjoy every minute of being fucked senseless by Tristan until we're done here.

He chuckles as he kisses my temple, cupping a breast and circling my nipple with his thumb. "So you're up for this wild ride?"

"Yes." *This is what I've wanted for a very long time.* I laugh. "And maybe, just maybe...you can charge my vibrator and bring it to the party."

"Always knew you were a planner."

"Failing to plan, you're planning to fail."

"Rest assured, angel, I don't plan to fail you at all."

Chapter Twenty-Nine

TRISTAN

It's after lunch, and Lexi and Jem are not in the office. They're seeing guests off as they leave for Dar es Salaam on the floatplane. Yesterday I had only half a batch of divers before the wedding, and today there were none, as you can't fly within twenty-four hours of diving. Roger and I jumped on the opportunity to dive this morning, which leaves me the afternoon for my editing work and my night free for Lexi. If only I could wangle it like this every day.

Just thinking of her and last night makes my cock twitch in anticipation. Watching her come apart under my hand is a visual I don't plan to file away—ever. To wake up next to her and pull her warm, naked body into my arms was life-affirming. We overslept, and Lexi had to get going for her morning meeting, but every promise was there in that moment. Thinking about anything else is…um, hard.

I force myself to do so as I sit down at Lexi's desk and make quick work of logging in to my email and social media feeds. I quickly check what's plotting on the platforms where I have my biggest following and reply to some comments, making mental notes about questions to come back to.

When I open my inbox, there's the usual flood of messages. Among all those from colleagues, the one from Dad stands out like a sore thumb. I glance through it. Hmm... Wife number three is pregnant, but they've already decided to call it quits and are getting divorced.

"Luckily this one was so short that the prenup isn't stripping me naked."

I chuckle dryly, feeling no joy at his news either way. But there's something in it for wife number three with the child support. My dad might be a dick, but he pays his dues. Kids are pawns that force people to make moves they don't necessarily want to make. After my arrival, Mom forced Dad to choose between his first family and his second. We all know how that ended—with me being cornered one day by wife number one, when I was six, and told I'd destroyed her marriage. That I was the reason her sons were growing up in a broken home, and she pretty much wished I were dead. I never told anybody about that, because nobody listened to me in the first place. But the notion of being a destructive force when it comes to love has stood the test of time.

Dad doesn't seem heartbroken. He's probably moved on already. Some people love the high of falling in love and making vows, and they'll take the crash that follows any day for those few months of bliss. I'll have yet another half-brother or sister I'll never get to know. Kids are mere collateral damage, encouraged to repeat this fucked-up cycle ad infinitum. I won't buy into it. Listening to those vows at the wedding yesterday had me all clenched up. *For better or worse, for richer or for poorer, in sickness and in health.* The idea of lifelong love is the biggest lie sold to the world in yet another moneymaking scam.

I'll share my life with the sea: the one thing that isn't going anywhere and has never failed me. The one thing I can't destroy by being in it—the one thing I can save by being there and documenting life. This series I'm making *is* my love letter to the ocean.

Dad doesn't ask how I'm doing or how things are, nor does he mention Lexi or her case his firm is working on. I'm still thinking about how to reply to him when Evan pops into my chat box.

EVAN
Bro! You're online!

I laugh.

ME
Yeah. Have the afternoon open for once.

It's morning on that side of the world, and I bet Evan just got back from his run.

EVAN
How are things going with your filming?

ME
Great. Will be able to wrap up before we leave.

EVAN
And Lexi?

ME
She's fine. No complaints.

Evan doesn't need to know I'm planning to make her moan for all the right reasons this evening.

> **EVAN**
> You two aren't butting heads?

> **ME**
> Nope. All's good.

We might be up to other things, but I'll just leave it at that.

> **EVAN**
> Heads up. Word is out that Mia Reed's video has dropped on several porn sites. I'll track it down and let you know where to look.

Fuck.

> **ME**
> You haven't seen it?

> **EVAN**
> Nope. It'll do the rounds soon enough. They might have edited Lexi out. Or not. Either way, look out for her, will you? She's going to be upset.

> **ME**
> Always. If it's only on porn sites, though, she won't have access from here.

> **EVAN**
> Is that so? You been trying to watch something or what? Got flagged by Beaumont in Paris? You should know better, dude.

I smirk. Here sits a man who needs no porn. Trust me, Evan

won't get it, because Lexi is his sister, but I'm one hell of a lucky guy right now.

ME
> You sound kinda desperate there, bro. You do you. Don't worry about me.

Lexi and Jem's voices drift over, and I glance to the open door. My time is up, and I send a last quick word to Evan.

ME
> Gotta run. Keep me posted.

I rush to log off as Lexi and Jem walk into the office. My pulse spikes with adrenaline now that I know for sure the Mia Reed bomb has finally dropped. For weeks I've watched Lexi agonize over it, and it's been eating at me too.

She smiles as they enter the office, but as she comes closer, that surge of protectiveness I always feel around her clamps tight around my heart. I want to protect her, at all costs, from every possible onslaught, whatever form it might take.

That night five years ago, this feeling dictated my every move, my every decision, even the one of walking away. I had to protect her from myself, from the man I saw myself becoming. I wasn't proud. I didn't like what I saw in the mirror. I was becoming like *him*. And here we are, going around this sex-business as if it's a bit of fun on the side. Only this time, I won't be able to walk away from her.

"Oh, here you are. We've been looking for you," Lexi says as I get up from her desk, feeling somewhat unsteady with the force of this feeling and the realization that hit me square between the eyes. *Fuck*. And how the hell do I protect her from this shitshow of a tornado coming her way?

With a hard swallow, I focus on Jem, who seems to have a permanent scowl on her face. "I was just catching up on some emails."

"You're done?" Lexi says.

"Yep."

"A couple of guests want to go for a last snorkel," she tells me as I scoot to the side. "Can you go with them? Roger is already kitting them out."

"They've mentioned whale sharks," Jem says, still studying me as if I'm a bug under her microscope. "Hope you're up for it."

"Of course." *Why wouldn't I be?* As I shoulder past Lexi, I capture her fingers in mine, and she smiles. Seeing her hurt is going to break me, and there's no stopping this freight train. Lexi needs to know about the video, but not in front of Jem, of all people. Maybe I can save her the distress until another day. If the video has only dropped on porn sites, it could take some time for it to reach a wider audience. "The first batch of guests are gone?"

"Phew. Yes. Just waved Matthias de Foch off."

"Good." For all the ways De Foch pissed me off, I have him to thank for pushing us to address our past. Without his invitation to a threesome, Lexi might never have been so bold as to flirt with me, which led to other things... I want to wrap her in my arms and whisper that I'm here, whatever comes her way, and I'll always be here if she needs me, but Jem sits down at her desk with an exaggerated sigh.

"We have a bit of a breather," Lexi says as she squeezes my fingers again. "New guests are arriving tomorrow." She leans in and whispers into my ear, "Maybe you have time for a few spa photos in the morning? Like, really early?"

I nod, but follow her lead in not discussing the spa's future in front of Jem. "That's hardly a breather." It's all on the whiteboard that covers half the wall, and by the look of it, things aren't slowing down yet. "Any arrivals we need to look out for?" I turn to Jem with a hitched eyebrow. She knows everything, doesn't she? And the best way to deal with her type is to soothe the ego.

"No repeaters," Jem says. "The guests are all first-timers tomorrow."

Lexi lets go of my hand as she sits. "The remaining guests are partied out, and we'll have an early night tonight."

"I'm planning on it, babes." At my words, Lexi opens the middle drawer of her desk to reveal a box of condoms that seem to have been tossed in in such a rush that it slipped half out of the boutique's paper tote. She looks up at me with that sweet blush and bites her lip.

I break out in a happy chuckle. "Not messing around now, are we?" I murmur, for her ears only.

"I plan to mess around a lot," Lexi whispers back.

Lexi likes to take charge, that's for sure, right up until the moment she hands it all over. *Noted*.

I drop my gaze to her lips. "I'm looking forward to it."

I want to kiss her senseless right now, but Jem's ever-watchful gaze is on us. We're having a private conversation, and she can't be bothered to pretend to be busy on her computer. No wonder Lexi feels Jem is on to us, or on to *something*. But why? What makes her the relationship police?

Regardless, a kiss would be the perfect move to prove we're engaged. Never mind that I *want* to kiss Lexi. I *need* to kiss her. I brush my knuckles along her arm and reach for her chin, tilting her face to cover her lips with mine. It's a short but intense kiss, laden with promises of things to come. And it leaves Lexi speechless.

As I walk off, Jem forces a funny laugh that doesn't sound natural. "So many private jokes, so many secrets. What are you two planning?" she says, loud enough to make sure I hear her.

Fuck. All I plan is to get it on with my fiancée. So why the hell does Jem make me feel like a criminal?

Chapter Thirty

LEXI

I have some time to kill before tonight, and it would be useful to think about something else anyway. Now that the wedding is over, I can refocus on Deshni's proposal. Sitting at my desk in the office, I open up the proposal file.

Deshni and Sarika are always responsible for the bride and her entourage's hair and makeup, and I can't understand why Beaumont isn't proudly displaying their talents somewhere on the internet. Between everything else these last weeks, I've sourced wedding photos directly from some of the couples who've been married on Ne'emba. If Beaumont doesn't care to showcase these women's talents, I do, and I will. Nothing like an Instagram or TikTok profile with reels and shorts and some breathtaking photos from brides on the beach to upsell what they have here. Hashtags everywhere. When these sisters eventually leave Ne'emba, which they will, this social proof of their skills could be a great springboard for them.

During the quieter times these past few days, I've tweaked Deshni and Sarika's proposal. We're shaking things up, but I'll still let the head office know. I've inserted some of the best bridal photos I've gathered, suggesting that the Beaumont Ne'emba Island website have a separate page for weddings. The destination is doing well enough that nobody has bothered to include this marketing strategy, but that doesn't do the sisters any favors.

I'm nervous, though. This needs to be perfect because I want to do Deshni and Sarika's work justice. They trusted me with this, and I don't want to let them down. I exhale a slow breath, wishing for a moment alone. Usually Jem calls it a day at this hour, but instead of giving me space, today she's working on her whiteboard, updating random stuff. I'll bet she's hanging around to keep an eye on me. It's a feeling I've had for a few days now, and I don't like it. I've noticed that my screen reflects on the glass panel of the cupboard behind me. Jem's gaze often latches to that spot beside my head. I'm *so* being watched.

Screw it. I open my private email, wanting to check in with Tessa as I do every day. She needs support, and this is the least I can do. If I message her now, I might get her before she goes to bed.

I open up Instagram because that's where Tessa hangs most of the time and a little thrill runs through me as I spot the green dot telling me she's online.

ME
What are you up to? Good day?

A message pops back seconds later.

TESSA

> Found my stride! Only had to do three re-takes today. It's a miracle really.

She follows the text up with a photo of her and another actress also playing in the film. They are pulling faces and I laugh. She hasn't only found her stride; she's found her tribe. My heart pangs a little, not being able to be there, but also happy that Tessa has found a friend who gets what she's going through.

"What are you laughing about?" Jem asks as she puts down the whiteboard marker.

"Nothing." I quickly type a *Gotta go* and close the app. I'm basically here to keep an eye on Jem, but the tables have turned. I had no reason to distrust Jem at the beginning, but her recent behavior has me pulling back. I should run this proposal past her—if anybody can give decent input, it would be Jem—but there's a reason Deshni sidestepped her in this process. Deshni knows Jem better than I ever will. Trust only runs so far for anybody, and once it's got a crack, well, it's not so easy to patch things up. Plus, it doesn't take much for that crack to become a crevice.

"Are you going to check in with the guests tonight before dinner?" Jem asks.

That's the last thing I have energy for. "Yes," I assure her.

"I can do that if you want to take an early night," she offers. "You've been going full-on for weeks now, and you've got your first wedding behind you, so why don't you take a break tonight? I'm sure Tristan would be happy too." At these last words, she turns to me, a smile playing on her lips.

I sink back in my chair. Jem is up to something, but an early night would be wonderful. This work isn't hard, but it's constant, and I'm running on fumes—fumes I'd rather save for Tristan. "You don't mind?" I ask, wishing I could read her mind.

"No. When Don and Miriam were here, I was doing it every second night."

"You were?"

She shrugs. "They were only here to keep the boat afloat. You're doing more than that."

I'm battling for my career here—something Jem doesn't need to know. I'm here to impress and more. But one night won't hurt. "If you don't mind, that would be great." I sit up and shake my mouse to bring the screen back to life. If this is an option, I have better things to do than sit here in my petri dish. "Let me send this last email, and I'll call it a day."

It's now or never. Ne'emba falls under the Beaumont Tropical Island portfolio, and I address my email to the corporate manager. Then I add Nathan Beaumont for some clout. At least he knows who the hell I am. Now that my mind's made up, I'm fast. I write the email, attach the proposal, and send it off in a flash.

I switch off my computer and grab my boutique purchase. "I'll see you tomorrow then."

"Enjoy, dear," Jem says, but her tone isn't warm at all.

Instead of going to the cottage, I make my way to the spa. It's quiet in the late afternoon as I walk inside, but Deshni and Sarika are both there, prepping for the next day.

"Ladies," I say in greeting. "Things have calmed down here too?"

"Yes," Sarika says with a smile. "The run-up to a wedding

is always insane, and afterwards we're dead quiet until the next batch of guests arrives."

"So you have zero bookings for tomorrow?"

Both women laugh. "Not a single one."

"Well, that's good news." I cast a glance over the tranquil space. "I've sent your proposal off to France, but we're not going to wait for them."

"No?" Sarika frowns.

"We're not making drastic changes. Tristan and Roger are available first thing tomorrow morning, so we can meet and take photos for a new brochure. We should also discuss price points and see how we can load the new treatments into the system." Everything here works on paper—beautiful, elegant, Beaumont-embossed paper—but it gets captured on the system at the office for invoicing. "Do you think you'll have everything ready? We can do some photos with the sunrise in the sala and here later on."

"Yes," Deshni says, her eyes shining with excitement. "We've been practicing and have the basics ready. We can set everything up for tomorrow morning first thing."

"Fantastic. Let's say at six? That's before the morning briefing, and Tristan will work his magic before anybody is even aware of what's happening here." I give them a wink, feeling totally in cahoots.

They nod, and the meeting is set. I wave goodbye and take the trail that eventually leads to our cottage. The sun is dipping, but Tristan might still be a while. At last I can enjoy the romantic bathtub in our cottage and pamper myself a bit, getting into a spa frame of mind.

Two hours later, Tristan is still not home. Funny that I've

started thinking of it like that. Us. Here. At *home* in the middle of nowhere.

I slip on a wrap dress and head down to the beach. In the dark, I walk along the water to the guest area, the waves licking at my feet. From afar, I can see torches flickering in a line on the sand, but there's also a bigger fire, which is a first. As I come closer, I hear a guitar playing and then notice the half-circle of people sitting around the fire, drinks in hand, cigarette smoke afloat. *Yikes...* that's not *only* cigarette smoke. Someone brought the *good stuff*, as Matthias de Foch asked for. Thank God he didn't get it from someone on the island.

A man is playing the guitar, but it's a woman's soft, melancholy voice that fills the night air and gives me chills. Tristan looks up to me, his gaze like a moth to a flame. The firelight flickers on his face as I approach the group from the side. He holds his hand out, and the rest of the group looks up, their lazy smiles welcoming as I sink down onto the sand next to him.

"I would have been home already," he whispers as he brushes his lips along my temple, "but I've been lured in, and it's too early to pull out."

I chuckle. "They're good."

"Apparently they're famous on the French music scene." Tristan wraps an arm around my shoulders and offers his drink to me. "You want to stay a bit?"

"Hell yes." I take the glass of red from him. This is exactly what I need to relax the build-up of nerves I had while waiting. I'd entered my worrier state, questioning *everything*. I take a drink of the wine. "Yum."

Tristan chuckles. "It's a Châteauneuf du Pape, and it's going to change your life. Apparently."

"I can totally see that happening." I take another sip and lean back into the warmth of his body, resting my head on his shoulder.

Tristan presses his lips to my head as he plays with loose strands of my hair. I feel myself go loose, my body molding to his. We share the wine as we listen to the music, which only amplifies the undercurrent of longing and promises made in hushed whispers.

The woman's voice is soft, but because we're sitting so close, the haunting timbres of her song come across clearly, full of vulnerability. I can't understand all the words, but the song is about love and hurt and loss, and the sincerity and simplicity of her delivery make me think this woman has seen and felt it all.

When Tristan runs his nose along my hairline and temple, I lift my head so he can work a lazy path to that spot below my ear. Nobody is paying attention to us, too high on whatever they've been smoking or sniffing. My breathing stalls as he nibbles and sucks at my earlobe, goosebumps popping up on my skin as if I'm champagne finally escaping my confines. He doesn't stop there. He buries his fingers in my hair and tilts my head until our lips meet in a slow, drugging French kiss.

It's dreamy. The heat of the flames; the wine, sensual and intoxicating in my veins; and Tristan's mouth, his tongue dancing languid and erotic around mine. His fingers trace along my upper arm, and his hand slips to my rib cage as his thumb runs along the underside of my breast... I feel weak with desire. We need to get a room.

I smooth my hand up his chest, somewhat out of breath as I pull away an inch. "We can go?"

"We *should* go," he murmurs. "Staying any longer—"

He breaks off, letting my mind run away with the visual of us having sex on the beach.

Tristan stands and holds out his hand to me. The woman keeps singing, and although I can feel eyes on us, nobody says anything. It's as if we're slipping off the stage as extras, but a few people raise their glasses in silent goodbyes.

We walk into the night, quietly back to our cottage, hand in hand.

Chapter Thirty-One

LEXI

"You're so quiet," I murmur as Tristan leads the way along the water's edge. *And it doesn't help.*

He smirks as he tightens his hold on my hand. "Babes, I'm trying my best to focus on getting you home without getting distracted." He lengthens his steps, and I follow suit up the beach's gentle incline.

"What could possibly distract you here?" It's dark. Soon we'll end up on the path that leads to our cottage. The only feasible thing we can stumble across now is a turtle laying eggs. Imagine that.

"Cute and clueless," he huffs. "My favorite combo."

"What?"

Tristan stops abruptly and turns to me, so I collide with his body, a pillar of muscle. He steadies me, his eyes searching mine in the moonlight. "All I want is to rip this dress off and fuck you right now, on this beach with its soft sand."

My pulse takes off in a sprint. "Oh." If only he knew how easy that would be. "Why don't you then?"

His hands are roaming now, down my waist and over my hips to my butt. I wrap my arms around his neck as he squeezes my ass. He starts to scrunch up the fabric in his fists as he kisses a blazing path down my neck to my shoulder. "Why don't I?" he whispers, and shivers chase over my skin to my breasts. "Sandy sex is a no-go for me."

Dang it. "Makes for a fun shower afterwards?"

"So she says," Tristan teases, his fingers finally connecting with my naked flesh. He draws in a sharp breath. "Jesus Christ, Lexi." He holds up my dress and strokes lazy lines down my naked butt, making me quiver. "You're not a good girl at all, are you?" He gives my neck a little nibble and a suck. "You're a *very, very* good girl, aren't you?"

With a wanton moan, I press my body into his, rising on my toes as he devours my mouth. He firms his grip and heaves me up against his hard length. "This no-panties situation is calling for immediate fucking action."

I giggle into his neck as he strides up the beach and into the short forest walk to our place. No lights are on, but with his eyes adjusted to the dark, he finds his way easily to our front door, kicks it shut, and lowers me to my feet at the side of our bed.

His hands ride up over my hips to the bow that keeps my dress together. He tugs at it in an agonizingly slow manner that only builds anticipation. When at last the knot is loose, he slides it off my shoulders and it falls to the floor with a soft rustle.

"The feel of you, Lexi…" Tristan's thumbs slide under my breasts, then slowly higher as my nipples, already painfully in tune with his every move, harden even more, begging.

He continues this intoxicating exploration as he searches my eyes. "You're still good with this?"

"God, yes." It's more a groan than actual words. I'm mush as he finally brushes over my nipples. I moan at the sensual rush that chases down to my sex. He skims over my chest and cups my face, drawing me closer.

"You smell so good. I could devour you."

"That was the plan." I fumble with the folds of mosquito net behind me, find the gap and step backward, not breaking eye contact with him.

"I see," he says with a nod as he crowds me into our veiled nest, closing the net behind us. His hands ghost over my naked shoulders and down my arms, sending ripples of desire to my already wet sex. "You're such a little planner."

For a long moment I'm only conscious of our shallow breathing as he moves his hands over my body, his fingertips electric where they brush my skin. It's slowly sinking in that, even though I've longed for this, waited for this, Tristan is taking his time and is a master at foreplay. I'm achingly ready to come, and he hasn't even touched me properly yet.

"Tris…" I whisper, swallowing my desperation as I hold on to his biceps.

"Great minds think alike, you know," he says as he pivots me with a firm push to my hip. "Up with you." He helps me along with a gentle shove to my butt, but as soon as I'm kneeling on the bed, his fingers dig into my hips, urging me down. "Spread wide for me, angel," he whispers as his hands move around my ribcage. I do as he asks, splitting on my knees as his hands cup my breasts. I lean back to his chest, into his kisses that land hot and unhurried over the column of my neck as he fondles and squeezes my nipples. Somewhat drugged, I run my fingers into his hair for support. Soon one hand trails lower, with fingertips so deliberate and sure as they slide over my sex that I gasp.

"Tristan." *God.* I'm going to come if he keeps up with this soft, slow circling of my clit.

"Not yet, angel." But he doesn't stop. He'll keep edging me until I lose my mind.

"I—"

He extracts his hand and pushes me down on all fours, butt in the air, exposed. I'm still finding my bearings when a warm, hard slap reverberates from my butt through my body. I yelp in surprise, but fuck, it's a turn-on.

"That's for walking around without panties and not telling me." He grunts as his fingers slide down the length of my slit. "Because this is mine, and a man needs to know what level of coverage his pussy has in order to protect it, you understand?"

I arch my back, pushing said naughty pussy deeper into his touch. "Yes...sir?"

"Good. To think any one of those guys at the bonfire could have caught a glimpse of this—" His fingers glide into me, repeatedly hitting that spot that will make me crest in one minute flat.

"Please, Tris—"

"I'm not done."

"God, I hope not."

He chuckles, and there's a tenderness to it that makes my heart swell. "Well then. *This*, my angel..."

Already I miss his fingers as he extracts them from my sex, and to my surprise, I rather eagerly anticipate another slap to the butt cheek.

"*This* is also for walking around without panties and not

telling me." There follows no burning handprint. Instead, Tristan's hot tongue runs down my spine, down my crack. I snatch in a sharp breath. The sensation is too intense, too erotic, and too novel. I want to crawl away, but his hands snake around my thighs, holding me in place and spreading me open as he licks me deeper.

Even if I wanted to move away, I can't. I'm stunned in place by this new, erotic sensation, spasms promising release already building as his tongue circles—

Oh. My. God.

It's a short stretch from *there* to my clit, and I fist the bedsheets as my orgasm rushes in from all sides, unstoppable. I come apart with a muffled cry as Tristan closes his lips over my clit and sucks, pure pleasure raking through my body.

It's only when he loosens his grip that I breathe fully, dragging in heavy breaths.

He squeezes my ass with a contented sigh. "So fucking sweet."

Oh boy, Tristan definitely doesn't do *dull*. I collapse on the bed, not sure I'm ready to look him in the eye yet. One thing's for sure: *this* wasn't what *I* had planned.

Not that I'm objecting.

Nope. Not at all. I can change my plans any time.

For this, I can even make our first house rule: *No more panties, babes.*

Chapter Thirty-Two

TRISTAN

I give Lexi a moment to gather herself where she's collapsed on the bed, watching her as I slowly straighten and wipe my mouth. *Fuck.* The taste of her...

This woman is something else. The way she comes only feeds my need to make her fall apart again and again. I run my fingers over her smooth calves and circle her ankles in a tender grip, pressing my thumbs down the arches of her feet in a deep massage.

She shudders with a soft moan, and I gently let go. She's naked, and I'm still fully clothed, so I strip and stretch out next to her. I stroke a hand up her back to where her hair hides her face and gather it away gently. "Lexi? You good?"

Her eyes shine in the dark, and a shy smile forms on her lips as she leans up on her elbows. "Better than you, for sure."

I chuckle. I love that she's light and easy like this, making jokes while being vulnerable. "Come here," I say, needing to kiss her, to taste another part of her and to be physically connected again. I hold her hair from her face as she leans into me, and our lips meld together as if we've been made for each other. My fingers weave into her hair as her hand presses to my neck. Our kiss turns slow and deeply erotic. Her touch travels, first over my shoulder and then to my chest, exploring. I quiver under her caress, wanting more of it, everywhere. She obliges by trailing her fingers over my pecs and abdomen, down my happy trail, and when she finally slides her fingers over the flesh of my rigid cock, I groan into her. "Babes…"

"I want this," she murmurs against my lips as she fists my length. More pre-cum wets the tip. "So badly."

As she circles her thumb over the crown of my cock, I'm ready to combust. "Oh yeah? Think you can handle it?" I joke, trying to keep ahead of her.

"There's only one way of finding out…"

With a chuckle I flip her onto her back and hook the fold of her knee with my thumb. I push her legs wide open, and she arches her back as I ease my bigger body between her thighs. She is dainty, and I'll smother her if I release my full weight onto her. I press my cock against her sex and give her a taste with a few slow thrusts of my length along her slit.

For a moment she has my butt firmly clasped with both hands, encouraging me. "Fuck, Tristan," she hisses as she lets go. "The condoms are on your nightstand."

"Yes, ma'am." Already we're playing in the danger zone, as from what I've gathered, Lexi isn't on any contraception, which is a novel situation for me. I get busy, but my thoughts are running away, and my hands can't keep up. *What the fuck would I actually do if I got my girl pregnant? My fake fiancée, to be precise?*

This notion would have wilted me in five seconds flat with any other woman, yet the thought of getting Lexi pregnant sends a foreign emotion pulsing through parts of my brain I didn't know existed. And it makes me fucking harder.

Fuck.

Dude. Get a grip. Focus.

My fingers tremble as I roll on the condom, knowing something inside me has shifted, and my feelings and thoughts for Lexi are no longer under my exact control. When the hell did that happen? And how did I not see it coming? I should be freaked out—I've never had out-of-the-blue brain warp happen to me during sex before…but that's just it, isn't it?

This isn't just sex. Not for me.

"Tristan…" Lexi's soft voice breaks through my wayward thoughts. "You're making me wait." She pokes my thigh with a finger, and I smirk, although it feels forced.

"Giving you a moment there, babes, to mentally prepare." I lean over her again, and this time she circles her arms around my neck and pulls me in for a kiss as she hooks her feet over my legs and rides them up my thighs.

"Looked like *you* needed a moment to mentally prepare," she says, and I bury my face in her neck, kissing her collarbone and lowering to her breast to distract myself with the easy lure of her beautiful body.

She might be kidding with me, but my heart talks back. *Nothing* could prepare me for this. *For us.* For the idiocy of entering into this intimate game with her while she peels off my armor as if it's mere paper.

I reach between us and, for a moment, savor her body's resistance. Then I thrust into her warm, wet heat with a grunt. Lexi digs her nails into my hair as I let her have it all in a few hard thrusts.

She gasps, but it's with pure pleasure and I don't hold back.

I let her feel how I feel—let her know she's mine, even though I can never tell her that, because she laid the ground rules for this game and there will be nothing more when we leave here. We'll be *done*.

I fuck her hard, and when I sense her orgasm gathering in her core, it's enough to slow me down. I want to draw this out, make it last forever, but that's impossible. I'll settle for the next best thing, though, having us tilt slowly over the edge together. I shift my head to find her lips, kissing her savagely for a moment, then leaning up and gripping her chin. "Look at me when you come, Alexandra O'Reilly." *And let your eyes tell me you don't care.*

Her hands slip from my hair, her touch so gentle, soft and unexpected as she rests her fingertips on my cheeks, her thumbs caressing my lips. I'm caught off guard, and I come so fucking hard that I drop my head back with a caveman grunt, heaving as her orgasm milks me for every last drop while her heels dig into my butt.

Jesus Christ.

Breathe. Just breathe.

It's just sex. You've done this countless times.

With this thought flitting through my mind—unwelcome, mind you, because all those other times haven't been with Lexi —I descend from that roaring high and lower my face to hers, eyes closed. I can't—*I can't*.

I can't let her see how much she—*this*, *us*—affects me.

We're breathing in sync, our chests pressed together, and I need to get off her. I roll to the side and gather her in my arms, staying connected for a few seconds longer. She snuggles her head under my chin, and I hug her close, clinging to her.

This is the woman I was never supposed to have. Evan's sister. Anita's daughter. As close as a real family I'll ever get.

This is the woman I've vowed to never hurt.

There are rules because they stop people from fucking things up. And this is a fuckup. These feelings for Lexi aren't exactly uncharted, but I've learned to bury them in a bunker where nobody knows they exist. They're the feelings of a teenage boy and have aged like an excellent wine, long forgotten in a cellar. Now, to have them surface into stark sunlight is a fuckup I've never had to deal with. And even worse? They are no longer the simple emotions of a boy. They've become complex and layered, those of a man.

Lexi deserves better than me. She deserves someone who can commit and give her the world. Not some messed-up cynic who can't—who won't, who doesn't care to even *try to*—keep things straight when it comes to a relationship. When things get real, I leave. For that, I've made sure I have the best job in the world. Out at sea I can face my demons alone, deep cleanse, head back to shore, and hook up. Wash, rinse, repeat.

As I told her, I'm the last guy who should ever put a ring on a woman's finger. And yet, in that moment when I did so at Heathrow, nothing had ever felt more *right*.

Lexi shifts, and her lips press against my throat. I swallow hard, still trying to get a grip.

"You're thinking so hard, Tris. I can hear the cogs turning." She pulls up to my mouth and presses a gentle kiss to my lips as I slip from her body. "No thinking allowed."

"No?"

"When it comes to this, to our time here, no. Let's just have fun, okay?"

Let's have fun. That sums me up perfectly—or *summed* me

up, to be precise. I don't know who the hell I am right now. But is this who Lexi is? I don't know parts of her at all. Five years is a big gap to fill with all those missing pieces of lost time. Evan and Anita kept me up to date with Lexi's life in a casual way, and the past weeks have shown me more. But is she capable of having *just fun* and walking away?

Am I? With *her*?

I'm too scared to answer the question, so I deal with the condom and reach for the tissues on the bedside table. "Fun, hmm?"

"Yes."

I chuckle, desperately needing to get out of my head. I ask the first question that comes to mind, because it's been bothering me. "So, tell me… Who was your first then?"

She drops back to her pillow and watches me intently. "Oh, you want to know now? Regret not giving it a go?"

Giving it a go? As if trying and the resulting failure was an option. And what a way to phrase a rather momentous if clusterfucky moment in every person's life. "No regrets." We've had that conversation. I did the right thing.

"Some random guy I did a group project with during my final year at hotel school." She drags her fingernails across my chest, gentle and yet so sensual that my skin prickles in goosebumps. "Patrick something or another."

Clearly not memorable. And she'd waited at least another year. Why does *that* make me so freaking happy?

"Well then, Lexi. Here's the truth of the matter. I'd rather be the guy you remember for the three orgasms he gave you on night one, than Patrick something or another who took your virginity."

"I see." She leans closer, her nails stroking across my chest to my shoulder. "Sounds like you've got some big plans here. I've already had two...but three? *Only?*"

I laugh outright as I buckle up to please my babes. Fun sex is one thing I know how to have. "How many did you have in mind, my angel?"

"Four. At least. Maybe five?" she whispers, her thigh already sliding over my hip as she presses up.

"Happy to oblige." I help her up to straddle me with a happy grin, pressing pause on all my wayward thoughts. "No rest for the wicked, is there?"

Chapter Thirty-Three

LEXI

Tristan and I are bleary-eyed after an epic night of more sex than I thought humanly possible, but we're up and heading to the spa at ten to six in the morning. There's a comfortable quiet between us as we walk along the dark forest trail, with only shards of metal gray sky visible through the stir of leaves high above. The salty-sweet scent of the sea combined with the earthy mix of tropical forest permeates the air and will always hold the memory of this moment for me as we steal a kiss along the way.

We offer each other glances that speak more than a thousand words. *That was fun... Why haven't we rolled around in the sheets before?* And the one that gives me the most pause: *Were we made for each other?*

Everything came so easy with him, me most of all. Just thinking of it sends sweet tingles of anticipation rushing down my spine, because we're not done. We're still here a while and have basically just started.

"You're good, angel?" Tristan says as he brushes his elbow

against my arm. Our hands are full of his camera equipment and a tripod he whipped out of a crate.

"Yep, you?"

"Very good," he says with a devilish grin. "So how're we going to do this shoot?"

I think for a few paces. "I've been involved in a few room shoots over the years—you know, getting everything perfect for the photographers and models. Plus I've been on stand-by during shoots to plump that odd pillow and rearrange the grapes on a fruit platter." Tristan laughs softly, and I giggle too. "Sounds rather silly, doesn't it?" I whisper, not wanting to disrupt the quiet magic of this romantic moment.

"No, sounds like you know how to do this, and the bar is going to be high," he whispers back. It's as if neither of us wants to let anybody know we're sneaking off to the spa, although people are already up and about and Tristan usually goes for a morning run, which he'll miss today. "I hope my photos will be up to scratch."

"Sure they will. It's not that hard. We'll need some product-style photos and some action shots. You know, the usual spa fare."

"Yes, because I hang out at spas all the time."

I laugh. The closest Tristan gets to any beauty treatments is a sea-sand scrub. "Let's see what Deshni and Sarika want. They have an eye for this type of thing and will know what they want highlighted."

We arrive at the spa to find Roger already there, and it's clear why: the spa isn't the way I left it yesterday afternoon. The furniture and massage beds have been rearranged, and a skylight, which I'd been totally unaware off, is opened in the roof, sending a glow of natural sunlight over the interior.

"This lighting is going to be great once the sun is a bit higher," Tristan says as he takes a look around the space, smiling at Roger. "Well done, man."

"This is what Desh wanted." *And anything for my girl* goes without saying.

"They had this all on hand?" I ask with a smile, pointing to a display of glass cylinders filled with raw spices the women have put together as props, as well as some dried spices and oils.

Roger looks away. "Don't tell anybody, but I might have made a trip to Pemba last night."

Tristan's eyes grow wide. "For real?"

"Nothing I haven't done before," Roger says with a shrug. "I have my contacts."

"Of course you do," Tristan says with a knowing smile as we set his equipment on the spa's counter.

"Where are Deshni and Sarika?" I ask, eager to see what else they've come up with since we spoke yesterday afternoon.

"They're just fixing their saris," Roger says. He follows this with a hand gesture I loosely translate as *I have no words for the beauty you are about to behold*.

My breath catches as Deshni, followed by Sarika, come out of the guest washroom a second later. They're dressed in traditional Indian saris. Deshni's fabric is a honeyed bronze with a gold pattern printed on the hem and throw. Her hair is woven in a complicated plait and coiled into a knot at the nape of her neck. Sarika's sari is a dark green, with a similar gold pattern, and her hair is in an up-do, her face open, her smile warm and kind. Both women have captured the elegance of their heritage, and somehow also of this Beaumont destination, just by standing there.

"Here we are," Deshni says, her eyes shy, clearly waiting for our approval.

"You look breathtaking. This is so much more than I expected," I say, catching a look of pure love and unguarded infatuation from Roger as his gaze runs over Deshni's face. "And this opens up so many more photo ideas. I don't—crap, I don't know where to start. Plus I have to be at the morning meeting at seven with Sarika. Are you going to go dressed like that?" It might give everything away.

"We're thinking of taking a few photos like this, and then Sarika can be my client," Deshni says. "We can do some of those before the meeting. So she'll be back in her uniform by then."

"Excellent," Tristan says, taking visual measurement of the spa. "Let's start at the sala. The sun's almost up, so if you want soft natural light, now's the time."

"Good plan," I say. "We can do these prop shots later. There's a lot to work with."

We grab the props and rush to the sala where we can shoot behind the white muslin curtains that hang around the square, thatched structure. Clearly Roger or the two women have already been here as well, because the light curtains, which are usually wrapped away at night, billow softly in the early morning ocean breeze, and the massage beds are ready for clients.

Tristan puts his tripod down, and I walk around the sala. "From this side, Tris?" I ask, noting how the gentle sun rays reflect the pink dawn on the white muslin. "Maybe with Sarika and Deshni inside? Pretending to do a treatment?"

He comes up next to me, a camera already in his hands.

"That looks good. We'll need bodies on the massage tables though."

I look at Roger; Roger looks at me. "That's us, buddy," I say with a chuckle.

Roger smirks but is already shaking the sand off his bare feet. I'm in my uniform, but I can cover up, or strip to my bra behind the sheets.

"Take your shirt off," Deshni says softly as she shows Roger where to lie down. He complies, and she keeps her eyes downcast, but I spot her sneaky glance and admiration as her eyes trail the ridges of his six-pack. Roger is built, but I suppose that's what you get hauling scuba tanks around for guests all day.

Sarika sends me a look, and there's no disapproval in the pull of her mouth, just a weariness over what stands between two people who are clearly madly in love.

I follow Deshni's directions, and soon Roger and I are in position, fluffy white towels over our bodies. "Keep it vague, Tris," I call to our cameraman. He is already snapping photos from outside the sala. "I have no makeup on, so close-ups will be a no-go."

"You look radiant this morning. You don't need makeup," Deshni says.

I bite my lip to hide a smile. I might have a certain glow.

"I'm keeping it vague, angel, and focusing on Deshni and Sarika," he assures me. "It's looking good."

His words melt my heart, and I relax into the bed, Sarika's oiled hands working my feet. I know we're all faking it right now, but it feels so good. So perfect. I close my eyes, listening to the waves, relishing the soft breeze that steals a touch over my hair as the rhythmic click of Tristan's camera comes closer and closer. When I open my eyes, I find him mere feet from me, a soft smile on his face as he looks at the camera's screen.

"You're winning?" I ask, conscious of how relaxed I've become in minutes, but also knowing I need to be at that morning brief with Sarika.

"Yep. I'll show you later. I think you two need to go if you want to be on time. I know what you want, and with Deshni and Roger's help, I'll take enough photos that some of them are bound to be good enough for your brochure."

"Thank you." I reluctantly sit up. "Can we finish this massage some other time?"

Sarika laughs. "Any time. You just let me know when."

Chapter Thirty-Four

LEXI

I stare at my computer screen and steel myself. It's after six in the evening, and the only thing left to do is to check in with guests during their sundowners. I can finally say we've found our stride. Weeks in, I have my finger on every pulse in this place and know how everything works.

Jem and I are cordial, sort of, and she's been a big help as I got up and running. But now I'm not sure what the hell is up with her. Ever since I became aware of the handy reflection of the glass door behind me, which allows her to see what I'm doing on my computer when she's sitting at hers, I've become even more cautious around her.

My fingers hover over the keys. All I want to do is type *Mia Reed sex tape* in the search bar, but Jem's still at her desk, shoveling papers. For fuck's sake.

Our eyes connect over the short expanse of the office, and she hitches her brow at me.

"What are you waiting for?" she asks, as her gaze drops to

my fingers where they rest featherlight on the keypad before looking up at me again.

"What do you mean?"

"You know what I mean."

No, I don't. It's a bit late in the day to be adding riddles.

"You've had no response from Nathan Beaumont or anybody in corporate as regards the spa's changes, have you? I know because Nathan or corporate would've copied me in."

My shoulders sag. No, I haven't. Deshni and Sarika's spa changes have been in full swing for a few weeks now, and although Jem didn't say a thing, her square shoulders and thin-pressed lips when she realized we went over her head said everything.

"Well, now that they're up and running, I might pull the numbers and we'll see that the spa is already making more money week on week."

"You still didn't follow procedure," Jem says. "Never mind head office, Nathan won't like that."

More like you don't like it I want to huff out, but I bite my tongue for a second. "I'm sure the spa on Ne'emba Island is the least of Nathan Beaumont's concerns. Honestly, I think as CEO he has better things to do with his time."

Jem harrumphs. "Don't for one second think Nathan doesn't care about Ne'emba and what happens here. He'll fly over in a wink if he thinks anything remotely dodgy is happening on our spot of paradise." She stands, switches off her computer and gets ready to leave.

Anything remotely dodgy? What the hell? This is why I can't relax around this woman. It's like she's watching me for the tiniest misstep so she can bask and glow in her own glorious superiority. I'm fuming, but not a whiff of smoke bellows out of my ears as I keep my poker face in place.

"Aren't you going to meet the guests for sundowners?"

"No. I'll go later," I bite out. "I'm going to take half an hour to check my private email and send messages to my family and friends. I do have a life beyond this place, you know."

Dang it, that was mean, but she keeps on pushing my buttons. Ne'emba is Jem and Mike's life and it's nothing to scoff at. She doesn't respond, and when she walks out, I call out after her, half in apology, "Have a good evening!"

I lean back in my chair, close my eyes, and take a few calming breaths. I'm not in the right mental space for this shit, but I can't stop myself either. I type *Mia Reed Sex Tape* into the search bar and wait for a good minute until the screen fills with links.

Since she refused to pay the hackers, Mia Reed's video has made the rounds on porn sites, and now it has finally slipped into mainstream social media. For real. Not just a little bit. More like, in an apocalyptic bang. And probably not the way anybody intended.

Rumors of it being a deep-fake ran thick as molasses, but then there's *me*. Who'd bother to deep-fake that idiot in the video?

I scroll through the search engine, being selective in picking my poison. There's so many to choose from. Seems the world isn't exactly enamored with Mia Reed's performance during cunnilingus. Neither do they care for the suckerfish between her legs. It's *me* who's making my way down the highway to social media hell or heaven—also known as fame—whichever way you look at it.

I'm the woman who walks in on Mia, eyes going like saucers as I freeze on the spot, then retreat like a freaking weirdo, hands in the air, horrified. I'm caught in perfect profile, my head tilted just enough that most of my face shows. It's creepy as I don't blink once, but the rest of the world thinks it's funny as all fuck.

I feel like a complete idiot. I'm pretty much a laughingstock in the States as the current trending meme overlay: *That moment when I...* Add your own video and fill in the blanks. I'm the face of fake human horror and surprise, and people are having a field day.

The fact that I'm shrugging my jacket's arm sleeve back up and that my hand, which for a millisecond rests so close to my breast, drops away in a second, has gone over the world's head. Nobody seems to interpret the video for what it really is. Me walking in on my ex servicing a movie star. No, all they see is a woman, reversing out in horrified shock, beep-beep-beeping like a truck would.

It works in my favor, but still, I'm a freaking wreck. I open one social media site and type in the hashtag most people use. Short videos pop up. *God*. Some of them have been watched over a million times since I looked yesterday. Now I want to puke.

At least in this sleepy corner of the world, I'm still incognito, and I thank God for that. Not that anybody out there seems to know who I am, or actually care. Or if they do, they have no easy way to reveal my identity. Since doing that social-media liposuction session with Evan when this whole shit show started in November, I'm kind of hard to find and tag. No posts, to my knowledge, have included my name.

Dammit. I don't know if I want to laugh or cry.

All I know is that I'm grateful to be here on Ne'emba

Island, where life goes on with dubious WiFi in a different time zone, everybody ignorant of my current status as joke du jour. I couldn't have planned this better. We're not in the eye of the storm yet—I mean, this could still swing way more out of control—but at least I'm far away and so thoroughly distracted by Tristan that I can bear my brief stint of ludicrous internet fame. And it will be brief. I know that. Soon there will be another meme or trending sound or video to distract and amuse the hordes. This *will* blow over, and I will weather the storm.

"Lexi?" Tristan's shadow falls in the door. "What are you still doing—ah, *babes*."

There's a slight reprimand in his tone, but it's sweet and caring. I lean back in my chair and wait for him to round my desk. *Fuck*, he's hot—tanned, tousled hair, five o'clock shadow. I want to lick him.

And yes. I'm in trouble. Big, fat, hairy trouble.

When he left for Hawaii after that frat-party night, I convinced myself Tristan was a stupid teenage crush. Turns out there was more to it than a crush, because it didn't take much for my feelings to resurface. And this time, they're so much stronger.

I don't want to think the words because they will manifest my emotions in a way I can't backtrack from. So much for all my little rules. Yes, I got into bed with Tristan with my eyes wide open, on my own terms, but I underestimated my heart's capacity to fall in love again. I'm going to hurt so badly when our time here is done. The mere thought makes me feel as if I were about to skydive out of an airplane without a parachute.

"It's getting out of hand," I tell him, reminding myself to focus.

"Really?" Tristan comes to stand next to me and drops a kiss on my head. "Show me."

I've been clutching my mouse as if it will run off if I let go. I indulge my masochistic streak and click so the short starts to play.

It doesn't take long for Tristan to break out in a deep guffaw. "Babes...I'm sorry, but you have to admit, that's goddamn funny."

I bite my lip, wanting to laugh but sulk too, and glare up at him. "It's totally cringe."

"I know, and I'm sorry." He shakes his head. "I told you, when I first saw the original video I almost pissed myself laughing." His hand slips over my back to my shoulder for a soft squeeze. "Come on, Lex, have a good laugh too. It's the only way forward."

I sink my head to my desk with a chuckle of despair. He's right. "There's nothing I can do."

"So don't torture yourself." He touches my hand, and I already know what that means—that's how much we've gotten to know each other over the past weeks. He takes control of the mouse, and with a few clicks, he closes all the sites. "Feeding this beast isn't good for your mental health. We came here to escape exactly this, and by sitting here doomscrolling, you're bringing it home."

"I know." Being me sucks. I've never been happier in my life, and it's all because of Tristan. He gets me. The intimacy is next level. *He* is next level. At the same time, my whole life seems to be unraveling into a pile of shreds even I don't care to salvage.

"You're done here?" Tristan asks.

"No. There's another wedding next week, and I need to go

over a few details." I shrug. Jem won't let me touch the wedding plans, but I'm committed to learning everything I can while I'm here, even if it's on the sly. "And I want to run the spa's numbers. Sarika mentioned this morning that they've been fully booked with the new changes. We've had no word from head office, but we've had two five-star guest reviews recently that mentioned the spa and their excellent services."

When I showed the reviews to Deshni and Sharika, they glowed with happiness. If I've achieved nothing else here in my time, at least I've done that for them.

"I'll fetch my laptop," Tristan says. "I have files to send to my production team, and I want to see how I can set Roger up with his own website."

"What did Nick say about your updates?" I ask. He showed me a few edited clips he'd sent to his agent two days ago, and they were fantastic. Tristan's work is coming along. This man has such focus. It's admirable.

"Nick's happy. I'm finally back on track to meet our deadline."

"Great." At least one of us will meet our goals. Tristan will finish his series on time and likely go on to fame and glory. As for me, with my face all over social media, I might have to cut and color my hair black to get a job in the States again. Thank God I've got a foot in the door with Beaumont and their vast portfolio outside of the US. Hopefully the spa's performance will throw that door wide open.

Tristan squeezes my shoulder. "See you in a minute."

I watch as he walks out of the office and disappears only to pop his head back a split second later. "Don't do it, babes!"

I laugh. Tristan is looking out for me. I would be

completely derailed by now if he weren't here to be my anchor and keep me level-headed.

That thought makes me hurt even more.

With brutal determination, I ignore the internet and open the hotel's accounting system to run the numbers for the spa. *Wow...* My eyes do a double take. In just a couple of weeks, the profits have gone up three hundred percent. *Put that in your pipe and smoke it, Jem.*

It's the pick-me-up I need, and on a whim, I download the report, attach it to an email and address it to Nathan Beaumont. He might not have responded to my initial proposal email, but maybe he'll respond to numbers. I keep my email to the point and professional, knowing this is Deshni and Sarika's future in my hands, and send it off.

Tristan walks back into the office. "She won't mind, will she?" he asks as he goes over to Jem's desk to take a seat.

"I don't think so. What she doesn't know and all that..."

Tristan sits and moves Jem's keyboard and computer screen to the side to plug in his laptop. That thing really isn't small. It's heavy too. *Ah hell...* Bad word selection given the direction my mind goes in every time he's around. I watch him from beneath my lashes, heat spreading over my skin as memories of last night's sex replay too vividly in my mind's eye. I bite my lip. *What is he going to do to me tonight?*

Clearly Tristan hasn't thought that far yet. Soon he's typing away and doesn't look up once.

For a moment we're both submerged in our work, but then it becomes weirdly quiet.

"Jesus Christ," Tristan says, and I meet his eyes across the room.

"What?"

"Have you checked your personal email yet today?"

"Still on my to-do list. Jem's eagle-eyeing everything I do, so I haven't. What's up?"

Tristan shakes his head. "No new emails from Sharon at St Chalamet?"

"What's going on?" I ask as I toggle to the internet and open my private email account. Tristan sits frozen at the desk. "You're freaking me out. What is it?"

"I got an email from my dad."

Oh hell. Indirectly *my* lawyer if I could afford him. "What does he say?"

Tristan's gaze returns to his screen. "Mia Reed has signed my dad's firm as her attorneys in New York. She's planning to sue St Chalamet for twenty million dollars."

"*What?*" I feel the blood drain straight out of my body as a rush of chills travels up my arms.

"For having the video leaked." Tristan runs his fingers through his hair. "Wow… Nobody's supposed to know she's planning to sue. This is insider info. Obviously."

Obviously. So far nobody knows about St Chalamet's involvement, and NDAs have been flying around like pollen in spring. The backdrop of Mia Reed's video is still a secret, even though the St Chalamet hacking is out in the open. The hotel group had to let their guests know. Somehow they've managed that whole clusterfuck without too much backlash. But this? *This* is ludicrous. "*Twenty million dollars?*"

Tristan shakes his head. "St Chalamet will be idiots to pay such hush money."

"But their reputation is at stake."

For a long moment we stare at each other, and I'm not sure what he's thinking about, but the lengths to which I've gone to get away from this mess—even faking an engagement—flicker through my mind. People get desperate. People do stupid things. People get chunks bitten straight from their asses in the process.

"You know why Mia Reed never paid those hackers in the first place, Lexi?"

Yes. Deep down I know. "Because they would have dropped the video even if she did?"

"Exactly. She had no guarantee that there weren't other copies floating around. Even if Reed had paid the ransom, someone else could have posted it, and she would've been out a bunch of cash." Tristan leans his elbows on the desk and drops his chin to his steepled fingers. "You have to admit, it's a gutsy move on her part. They don't pay up, she exposes them. The damage to her has been done, and now she's got them cornered."

"Instead of being out the ransom money, she'll be making millions." Mia Reed is clever and conniving. I wouldn't have it in me to pull this off.

"Either way, St Chalamet is screwed."

"They have been from the start."

"Which is what happens if you go slack on your security."

My fingers tremble as I reach for my mouse again. Slowly I close all my tabs and shut down for the night. I can feel Tristan's eyes on me.

This is a shock. Just as I thought the video had done its worst, we're now headed for legal mayhem. What if I'm asked to testify in court? What if I have to face Brent Fisherman again? I just can't. I can't sit here under Tristan's caring gaze and deal with this. I need to get out of here.

"I'm going to do the sunset rounds," I say, needing the

fresh sea breeze on my face, away from this cesspit my computer opens up.

"You want me to come with?"

"I'm good." Doing the rounds alone will force me to focus on the guests and put on a happy face.

"I'll wrap up here quickly." Tristan stands as I walk to the door, but right now, I can't meet his gaze. "Lexi."

"Yes?" I stop and look at him, Jem's desk a barrier between us. I will him to come around and take me in his arms. *Hug me.*

A thick rumble sounds from afar, and we both blink. *Was that thunder?*

"This will be over soon," he assures me. "They'll settle out of court. Trust me, this case will never see the light of day."

"Hopefully." I turn and walk away, surprised to find it so much darker outside than usual. A heaviness hangs in the air, and when I look up, the sky is blackened with thick clouds. For weeks they've been in the distance, providing spectacular sunsets, but now they've reached our little island. It's the first promise of the rainy season to come.

I walk quickly to the guest area, and raindrops fall here and there. Maybe there won't be sunset drinks tonight. I've been so immersed in my head, in Tristan, and in this stupid mess, that I didn't notice the change in the weather.

It's easy for Tristan to say this will be over soon. It's not his face plastered all over the internet. It's not his name that will be trashed in the headlines. My anonymity's hanging from the thin thread of Mia Reed's twenty-million-dollar lawsuit. Settled in or out of court, it doesn't matter. Once it comes out that the video's backdrop is some obscure banquet room in the St Chalamet Manhattan, it's a hop, skip, and a jump to my name becoming another trending but trashy hashtag.

Chapter Thirty-Five
TRISTAN

I go back through Dad's email, reading the one line I didn't share with Lexi again and again:

You've always cared about Alexandra O'Reilly, so I thought I'd give you a heads-up.

That he's bothered to email me about this case is weirdly gratifying. He *trusts* me. But... *You've always cared about Alexandra O'Reilly.*

How does he know? And what the actual fuck am I doing here, reading emails from Dad? Lexi needs me right now. She's so good at pasting a smile on her face and being professional, and the only thing that ever gives her away is that blush she just can't help. When she walked out ten minutes ago, she was emotionally shattered. Yet she was still going to do her job.

I close my laptop and unplug it as lightning brightens the office for a split second. The ensuing thunder rolls in two seconds later. *Shit.* Not good. It's too close. Lexi isn't going to like that at all.

I lock up everything and speed toward the guest area as fat

drops of rain kamikaze from the heavy clouds. When I get to the bar and dining area, the place is quiet. A few guests are sitting around having drinks, and waiters are going about their job as if a storm is par for the course. But the dining room is all set with the roll-down shutters, which I notice for the first time, and hundreds of candles flickering. Jeez, so romantic. And extra as always.

"Have you seen Lexi?" I ask the bartender when I don't spot her.

"She was here a couple minutes ago, jumping at the weather. Maybe in the office?"

"Nope. I just came from there. Maybe she went to grab dinner." I go to the staff mess, but there's no Lexi there either. Jem and Mike are eating with several others, and I avoid eye contact with them, not wanting to get into a long conversation right now.

I'm halfway out of the canteen when I hear Jem's voice, coming loud and clear over a lull in conversation. "Those two are only trouble," she declares. "And that in our spot of paradise."

What the actual...? Not that I have time to dissect her comment now. All I can think of is Lexi and how she looked earlier—and that was before this weather came crashing down. I rush along the decked pathway, unable to dodge the rain despite the thick tree canopy overhead. A full-on deluge is pouring from the sky and to protect my laptop, I push it underneath my T-shirt. By the time I get home, I'm soaked, and a chill spreads over my back with the wind that whips through the vegetation.

The shutters are down, and dim light comes through their fine slats. I kick off my flip flops, heading to the closed door.

Another crackle of lightning flashes, and thunder sounds seconds later. At least they have lightning rods everywhere on the island to protect their rather rustic wood-and-palm-leaf structures.

"Lexi?" I walk inside and spot her curled up on the bed. "Are you okay?"

A pained grunt is all I hear over the rain that pelts the roof.

I drop my laptop to the sofa, shake my wet hair, strip off my soaked clothes, and find my way through the mosquito net. I clamber up on the bed and pull her into my arms. "It's okay. It's going to be fine." She pushes into my chest, and I fold her tense frame against me as she quivers.

"I didn't think about this when I signed up for this gig."

We didn't think about a lot of things, babes... I press a kiss to her hair. "It's not a hurricane. They would have told us, if it were. It will be over soon."

She sobs.

Oof. I didn't realize she was crying.

"I've been better about this, honestly—" she starts, her voice breaking. "It's so long ago now."

"I know." But when you have too much on your plate, even the fears you've overcome bubble up out of nowhere. Lexi is strong. She did, after all, spend a night on a random rooftop when that hurricane drowned her childhood home and swept her family's life away with it. "I'm glad I'm not out on a boat right now."

She sniffs and looks at me. "What happened last year?"

I tense at the memory of it. I haven't really spoken about this to anyone. Even the other crew who were with me on the boat have been side-stepping me as I've been side-stepping them. We filed the reports and other necessary paperwork and scattered. It's still too recent and raw. "We capsized in a storm. In the moment, all you can think of is surviving... It's afterwards that the fear comes. We were lucky. Got a mayday out and a bigger vessel came just in time to pick us up."

"God...and you still go out to sea?"

"I'll never stop."

She brushes at the wet strands of hair that cling to my forehead. "Why do you love the sea so much? For a New York kid, it's kind of weird."

Talking takes her attention off the storm, and although Lexi knows a lot, she doesn't know everything. "It's quiet down there."

"Quiet?" she asks, seeming to relax under my slow strokes down her side and over her hip.

"Yeah." I don't let people in like this, but Lexi is different. She's always been different. "Being on top of the water is somehow riskier. Being under the sea is a safe zone for me." I hesitate for a split second, but then, this is *Lexi*. "Before my parents' divorce, we had one last vacation together as a family in the Cayman Islands. It was tense, as my parents were constantly at each other's throats... I thought they were going to kill each other."

Her eyes go wide as she reaches up to caress my cheek. "Oh my God, really? That bad?"

"I was right in the middle of it. Even out on a catamaran for a snorkeling excursion, they didn't stop. It was hell, and...so awkward. The skipper, the stewards, jeez, my parents went at it as if they didn't exist. Only once we were in the water they were forced to shut up. That moment made quite an impression on me—the sudden stillness with the surprise of the world down there."

"I can imagine."

For a moment we're quiet, and a low rumble of thunder sounds. It's farther away now.

"How old were you?" Lexi asks.

"Nine." I shudder. "After the snorkeling, I got my dad to sign me up for every other water activity that week so I could stay out of their hair. My parents didn't care. They were glad to be rid of me. I think the resort staff took pity on me, a single kid in the middle of all that—so much so that I had my first scuba dive with one of the dive masters. It was only two meters down, but I was hooked on a world without humans, and I've never looked back."

"A world without humans?" Lexi brushes a finger along my jaw. "My world is all about humans."

"It is." I hug her closer. "Where I go, you can feel part of the world even though you're an outsider."

She dips her head under my chin again, and her soft breath soothes over my chest. "I'm sorry," she whispers. "Our house was filled with so much love, until my dad panicked and messed it all up."

I lost everything on that boat, and workwise it set me back months, but the whole ordeal crushed my morale more than anything else. "Losing everything in the hurricane must have been hard for him. He was unable to care for his family as he wanted to—"

"It made him desperate." Lexi swallows hard. "What he went through was so much worse than this, but I think I finally understand his side of the story."

Desperate. Here we are, hacking out our own path in desperation. Ever since I saw Lexi's video with Mia Reed, it's been eating at me. Yes, it's funny, but there's more to her dread of having it out in the world than just being an innocent bystander in a sex tape going viral. "Babes..." I start.

"Hmm?"

"What's really happening in that video? Why did you walk in on Mia Reed?" She looks like she's just at work, but I know Lexi. Ever since that first morning at Evan's house, she's been in my space, and we've gotten so close and intimate with each other, I know there's more to this video than what everybody's picked up on.

The sob that tears through her rips through me, straight to my heart.

"Oof, babes," I whisper as I perch onto an elbow, hugging her close, letting her hide her face in my armpit. "Lexi." I try to soothe her with slow circles over her back, but she seems to curl into herself, pressing as close to me as she can as she cries.

I let her, giving her space to let go of all these bottled-up emotions.

"I was such an idiot, Tris. I thought I needed to go up there...to keep his interest. I went up there with the intention of doing something that I knew was wrong," she whispers eventually. "I thought he *cared* for me, that I meant something to him, because we'd been seeing each other on the sly for months—" she gulps in a breath between two sobs "—and then he asked me to meet him in that banquet room, only for me to—to—" Her body trembles as she weeps, and her pain vibrates into my own. "I never felt so cheap in my life."

I drop back on my shoulder, rage battling on her behalf. The last time I saw her crying like this was when I walked out that night five years ago. Fuck. Of all the hurt I caused that night, did I make her feel cheap too?

I'm a total dick to wrench this out of her. But what a

fucking wanker. My fists clench where I pause for a moment from rubbing her back, wanting to beat the asshole up. Wanting to beat *myself* up.

Lexi, so loving, always gives someone her all, only to be used by men. I might have drawn the line, but I used to be no better in my day-to-day dealings with the women I used to have on quick dial. And then I had the audacity to tell her that *she wasn't ready* five years ago where it was really me. These lies we tell ourselves because we're not ready to face our true selves in the mirror... At the time I hadn't been ready for this woman and everything she gives when loving a person.

Nobody is worthy of her. Least of all me.

"It's okay, babes. Nobody would guess that from watching the video," I whisper my weak platitudes because I can't offer her anything more. "Is this why you got restructured?"

"No. Maybe? Probably? We never discussed it at all. Not even Sharon knows the full story," she mutters, her voice muffled against my chest. Then she perches up, blinks at me with red-rimmed eyes, her nose all snotty, but a smile teasing her lips. "You have to admit it is funny. At St Chalamet I got fired for sleeping with management, and with Beaumont it is a freaking requirement."

I smile back but now I get it. It all makes sense now, why she's been freaked out by this whole fake engagement situation.

She drops her head to my chest with a deprecating chuckle, wipes her nose on my T-shirt, and clings to me. "I need to be octopused."

"Yes, you do," I say with a silly grin as I wrap her in my arms, weave her legs with mine, trapping her so close that we're one body with eight limbs.

Eventually her breathing evens out as she calms, and I loosen my hug so I can play with her hair.

Rain dances on the roof and the fresh scent of wet earth and the cool shift of air that comes with it are so welcome after weeks of solid, humid heat. It's only when Lexi's hand slips from where she'd been resting it against my chest that I realize she's fallen asleep. *Sweet angel.* It's way too early to go to bed, but I'm not surprised. She's emotionally exhausted. She tries to be brave and upbeat, but the past few days have been a wringer.

Even sweeter though is that she was relaxed and comfortable enough with me to fall asleep like this. We do this every night now, but this time it's different. She felt safe in my arms. I blink, my Adam's apple scraping as I swallow. That feeling of safety goes both ways. I've never told anybody about that week in the Caymans. *Is this what being married is like when it's done right?*

I close my eyes, savoring the moment of being this close to her as the rain gradually tapers off. When she stirs with a deep inhale and soft snore, I smile into her hair. Her hand snakes to my side as her head lolls over my arm.

"Did I fall asleep?" she murmurs in a bit of a daze.

"Mm-hmm. Just a catnap."

Lexi snuggles in, and my heart breaks into a thousand pieces. This is a moment in time I'll never have again.

"The rain's almost stopped," she murmurs as she trails a foot over my calf and down to my ankle. "And you have sandy feet."

"So do you," I say with a chuckle.

"All that rain splatter as I rushed home along the beach." Her lips brush up my neck, and I suppress the neediness in my groin as I splay my fingers over her ass and tug her close, wanting the pressure of her pussy against my budding erection.

Lexi trails her fingers through my hair and pulls me down for a kiss, soft and slow.

"Do you think I should go check in on the guests?" she asks as she pulls away for a breath. "Dinner is probably almost done, and it would be a good time."

"No." My fingers find their way underneath her shirt to her breast. "I think you should be a good little honeymooner for once, like all our guests, and stay right here in bed."

"Honeymoon, hmm?" she hums. "Tristan Martinelli, I'll let you know that I fake only one thing at a time with you."

I smile and dip my head to kiss her. Yes, Lexi is as honest and true as it gets. Nothing between us has been fake—except our engagement, and that is starting to freak me out. Not because of the engagement lie, but because lately I've been wondering what it would take to make it all real.

Chapter Thirty-Six

LEXI

Something is different between Tristan and me. Things have been shifting over the weeks, but the way he holds me now, kisses me gently—with some reverence, as if I could break—is new. Maybe it's all in my head, but even now, after telling him the full nasty business that's The Head and Mia Reed, he seems to be even more caring than before.

I don't know if I'll survive tearing myself away from this side of him. Finding him irresistible and consequently having a fun time is one thing. But experiencing this deeper side of him is only bringing us closer. Tristan has always been reserved when it comes to his past. I get that. I don't like people to know that Dad served a sentence for fraud, and that our relationship never found its footing again. Tristan clearly doesn't want people to know he was the emotional punching bag that stood between his parents' verbal abuse for years. As a mere kid.

My heart aches for him. I comb my fingers through his hair as he makes his way down my neck. He's pushing up my shirt, and already the heat of arousal gathers between my legs. I arch my back into his touch, stroking his skin and relishing that he is bare-chested while I'm still dressed. He is quiet as he perches on an elbow and works my shirt's buttons, and in the dim light of the bedside lamp I watch his face. The softness of his gaze and the tender fiddling of his fingers ever lower down my body fill me with hope that maybe he'll say something—something like *he'd like to have more than this*. That he doesn't want this to be over when we're done. That everything has somehow come together exactly as it should be.

But he says nothing. Usually it's jokes and teasing and a lot of breathless heaving between us as we have sex, but now, as his gaze travels over my body, his eyes are doing the talking as if he's lost his voice. I sit up so he can slip the unbuttoned shirt off, and when he brushes his knuckles over my begging nipples, a shudder of pleasure rushes through me. I want to reach for his cock, but he catches my hand and brings it to his lips. "Let me make you feel good, Lexi," he murmurs between kisses to my wrist. "Let me be everything I can be for you."

I close my eyes as my emotions well up. Those words are everything. This is all we can ever be, lovers caught in a time-warped place so far removed from our everyday that it's become a dream we had once, together, in our subconscious, where everything always makes sense in the moment.

He nudges me onto my knees, and I acquiesce, letting him unclasp my bra and strip down my skirt as I tilt my face away, giving him access to my neck so he can't see how this moment is affecting me. I wish the lights were off, because in the quiet of his reverence and touch, it's as if he can see straight into my every last wish and the longing in my heart.

When I'm naked, he rises onto his knees and I caress his

sides as we kiss and touch as if every moment is gift. My fingers find their way into his boxers and push them down. As he kisses me, a desperation washes over us. But instead of becoming more frantic, we slow, both seeming to want this to last forever. When I'm on my back and he's finally reaching for the condoms, I take his wrist. "Leave it."

"What?" Tristan stills, his eyes searching mine.

"I want you bare." Once. Just once. Us, with nothing between us, flayed open and honest. Faking nothing.

"Lexi, I—"

"My period is due in a day. There's no chance." And this is probably why I'm an emotional wreck and feeling everything twice as deep. This will be the first time I do this with someone, and the craving is real.

Tristan sinks down on me with a groan that reflects my every need and want and so much desire. If I could press pause and stay in this cocoon forever, I would. I gather him in my arms, trap him between my legs, and when he kisses me next, his hand cupping my face, it's with such intensity that I cling to him. He rocks into me, and the sweet pressure is already building in my core.

When he finally pushes in, it's measured and slow, as if he could make this last forever too.

"You feel so good, Lexi," he murmurs as he peers into my eyes.

I feel a little drugged by our mutual sensuality, because he feels more than good: Tristan feels right. And not only like this. In every possible way. I hug him closer, my heels pressing on the backs of his thighs, his mouth an inch from mine. "I'm going to come."

"Yes." His thrusts seem to slow, but grow harder at the

same time, keeping me on that precipice for seconds that feel like an eternity of pleasure.

"Tristan." It's half moan, half whimper, because when did this man learn to love my body so well? I'm coming, and it's sweet and intense, like the golden glow of the sun is sweeping through my whole body in a rush of glitter that settles on each nerve path I have.

He presses his nose to my cheek, his breathing ragged as his hips thrust one last time. He spills into me, rippling and pulsing in my core.

For a long moment we're still, coming down from our high. And then he kisses me, and it's as if he wanted to pour his soul into my body too.

And I let him.

But...I'm going to cry. Tears well up, clogging my throat. I push at his shoulders, not wanting him to see how he's affected me. "This is messy," I murmur while I still have an iota of control over myself, before my voice can break.

"Sorry, angel," he whispers and pulls out. He reaches for some tissues on the nightstand and hands them to me. I sit up too, with my back to him, to deal with the mess.

And it is a *mess*. My heart is a sloppy heap of unfulfilled longing and love that has hit a brick wall. He strokes down my back, and I push hard against my emotions. I can't screw this up by showing him how I feel. I made the rules, and I will stick to them, because Tristan has made it clear where he stands.

"Lexi."

"I'm good." I crunch the tissues in my hand. "I'm going to take a shower." At least there my tears can disappear without anybody knowing they existed.

I fumble with the mosquito net and head to the bathroom

without looking back. It's cooled off considerably with the rain, and under the outdoor shower, drops still drip from the overhanging trees, so cold on my heated body that goosebumps spread over my skin and pebble my nipples. I open the faucet wide, step under the warm waterfall, and close my eyes.

Finally, I let go. In his arms earlier, I broke down because of everything that got us here. Now I'm breaking down because I don't want to let go of what we have—of what we've become. I turn my face into the steam and let my silent tears run their course. I startle when the glass-beaded shower curtain rattles. Tristan's hands circle my waist, and he presses his chest to my back. "You know desalination takes time, don't you?" he asks as he runs his lips along the column of my neck.

I chuckle and blink fast. At least he gave me a few minutes alone, but now—"You always shower at the dive center."

"Hmm... Now I see what I missed out on." He pumps some liquid soap from the dispenser and gently turns me around. It's dark, but his eyes search mine as he lathers me up. I have no choice but to close my eyes. Giving in to the moment with him is one thing, but I refuse to let him see inside of me. I know he's taking care of me because I ran off, and Tristan is nothing if not considerate, but he says nothing.

Sometimes the only thing that works, the only thing I need, is words. Not many, just a few choice ones.

Talking may not be in the cards, but I should have known he had plans when he stepped into the shower. Tristan is, after all, not one to stop after one round. No, he is about as insatiable as I am—another thing that only grinds against my determination to get him back at arm's length.

When he drops to his knees, I let him raise my foot to his

shoulder and let go, because once he's made me come this way, he'll fuck me hard, and we'll have gone full circle. And hopefully then I'll be emotionally back in my box.

By the time we're done, the water has turned tepid. He turns off the faucets and hands me a towel.

"You're hungry?" he asks as we dry off. "I skipped dinner."

"Same here." Maybe I also need a drink—a tall, stiff one to drown my feelings in.

"We could go raid the kitchen."

This makes me laugh; he smiles back, and the tense atmosphere between us cracks and disintegrates. "You won't dare touch a thing in Chef's immaculate fridge or pantry."

"He won't know because we won't leave a trace."

"I see. Lead the way, oh reckless one."

Ten minutes later, we hit the path. It's dark and quiet as it seems everybody has gone to bed already. Guests have fully stocked bars in their rooms and rarely hang around after dinner, so none of this is unusual. The lights are switched off everywhere. As we come around the corner to the staff canteen, though, soft voices come from the open seating area, which seems to have one light on in a far corner.

"We're not alone with our midnight munchies," Tristan whispers as he takes my hand.

As the seating area comes into view, my heart skips a beat. Roger and Deshni are sitting at one of the tables, holding hands. Deshni is quietly sobbing.

Tristan squeezes my hand, but it's too late to back off. "Hey, guys."

They both look up, stunned for a second. Roger clears his throat. Deshni drops her gaze and sniffs desperately, trying to hide those tears.

"Sorry to interrupt," I say, tugging at Tristan's hand. These two need some privacy, and we can go to bed without dinner.

But Tristan ignores my signal and walks closer. "What's wrong?"

"Nothing," Deshni says, but she breaks out into a fresh sob.

That's not nothing.

Roger shakes his head. "We're in trouble."

Oh, God. My stomach turns. *That* type of trouble?

"What is it? How can we help?" Tristan pulls out a chair for me.

I sink down into it, flabbergasted that he can't read the room. I *mean*…it's so freaking obvious.

Maybe that's a male thing. It does, after all, not affect them in remotely the same way…and maybe I've been a bit reckless tonight too with giving him free rein to my body. Regardless of what my cycle says, just look what it did to my head!

"My love?" Roger asks, then waits for Deshni's signal. She shrugs, and it's neither a yes nor a no. Roger's gaze jogs between me and Tristan where we sit opposite them. "Deshni's pregnant."

Chapter Thirty-Seven
TRISTAN

It's a good thing we're sitting down. I'm not shocked, but I am kind of horrified. Hopefully this wasn't because of a one-time encounter. It has to be a slip-up. Like me with Lexi tonight. That scares the living daylights out of me.

I swallow at the memory of just a bit ago when—if I'm being honest—I made love to a woman for the first time. I blink. *Did I? Jesus Christ.* That thought came out of nowhere... I'm going to digest that when I have time, and *this* is definitely not the moment.

"How're you feeling?" Lexi's voice is filled with concern.

Deshni shrugs again, rolling a shredded paper napkin between her fingers. Roger wraps his arm around her shoulders and kisses her temple. He whispers in Swahili to her, and I don't understand a word, but I don't need to. The love Roger has for Deshni is evident in his voice, which is gentle, firm, and reassuring.

It strikes me that I know Roger rather well. That's what happens in a situation of mutual trust. You open up. Over the weeks we've spoken a lot, more and more as we got comfortable with each other. I remind myself that he cares deeply for Deshni, and he'll do the right thing, if he's allowed to.

"What are you going to do?" I ask.

Roger looks up. "I need to take time off. Go see her parents and make my case with her dad—with her *mom*. I want to marry Deshni, but I don't want her to be estranged from her family either."

I nod. *Good*. Fight for what you want. Deshni looks into Roger's eyes and although tears are still streaming, she kisses him, and he hugs her close.

"Does Sarika know?" Lexi asks.

"No." Deshni shakes her head. "It's early. But she probably won't be surprised. She's warned me—" She breaks off on a strained sob.

"You'll work it out," I tell her, not knowing what else to say.

"Roger's had such plans since he's been working with you." Deshni shakes her head as our eyes meet across the table, then starts to sob again. "*I* had such plans."

I exchange glances with Lexi. We both probably think the same thing here. We've become instrumental to these plans, but now these two have a new reality they didn't account for. Hopefully it won't derail the whole thing. It shouldn't have to...

"I looked at the spa's numbers earlier," Lexi says. "There's a three hundred percent profit increase since you made the changes. I forwarded it to head office. That's amazing... A great start."

Deshni picks another paper napkin from the dispenser on the table. "They won't want me here."

"You don't know that," Lexi says. "Surely there are provisions for maternity leave and all that?"

"This island is no place for kids," Roger says.

I find it rather perfect, I want to say, but this isn't my life. "You just need a few more dive hours to finish your master-diver qualification. Soon you can work anywhere. You won't need to stay here."

Roger nods, and Deshni bites her lip.

"And with your experience and ideas, Deshni, you can work anywhere too." Lexi lets the thought hang, and then reaches over the table for Deshni's hand. "Once you've put your feelers out, you'll see there'll be many options. There're countless opportunities all the way up and down the coast here, and then Mauritius, the Seychelles, the Maldives."

"We still have time to set things up for you," I add, working with this positive vibe. There's a lot more I can teach Roger. Soon we'll be on the downward slope of our stint here, but we can max the time together.

Roger nods but then his gaze jumps over my shoulder. Deshni stills too. She drops her gaze as she pulls away from him. Feet shuffle behind me, and I turn to find Jem standing in the dark. It's creepy as fuck. When did she arrive? And how much did she hear?

"Jem," Lexi says, also turning. "What are you doing here?"

"I'm coming to check on the movement here. I saw the lights were on."

Fuck me. She pushes something into her pocket, but I can't see what it is.

"I want to know what *you* lot are doing here." Jem's gaze

travels from Roger to Deshni, and then she leans on the table and gives us the same inspection.

"We came for dinner," Lexi says.

"And then we had some team building," I add as I stand. This woman is playing some power game, and I'm not buying it. Roger and Deshni are younger and might be intimidated by her authority, but I don't give a fuck. "Do you want to join us for a midnight snack?"

Jem peels away from the table as I tower over her and stare her down. "No. I had dinner, and I've seen what I needed to see."

Well, bugger off then. We're not done talking Roger and Deshni off the ledge here. "We'll see you in the morning."

"Yes, that you will."

We watch as Jem walks away and disappears into the night. We're all quiet, listening like a bunch of kids almost caught smoking pot. We can't wait to take a drag as soon as it's safe. Jem didn't seem to have heard the beginning of our conversation, but I don't trust her. She's the type that would hide and eavesdrop, and Roger and Deshni have the right to share their news when they're ready.

"Right," I say as I head for the fridge. "Let's see what's for dinner."

It's a whole hour later when we finally call it a night and go our separate ways. I take Lexi's hand as we return to the path, and she links her fingers with mine. It's weirdly comforting to belong to her like this, and for a stretch we walk in silence.

"My problems seem so insignificant now and somewhat immature—even childish," Lexi says.

"Your problems?" I rehash the whole Mia Reed mess. Being thrown headfirst into someone else's troubles does give you perspective on your own. "I wouldn't call them insignificant and immature, just different," I tell her.

"Maybe. But I mean, they're going to bring a human into the world, and they don't even know if they'll have her parents' blessing. It's so important to them."

I stop in the path and force her to do the same. My heart is in my throat. Tonight wants to kill me on so many levels. The mere idea of Lexi... I cup her face in my hands. "Babes, if ever there are repercussions from our time here, please, you tell me, okay?"

Lexi blinks, then takes hold of my wrists and slowly pulls my hands away. "There will be no repercussions." She turns and walks off, and for a second my heart feels like it's frozen over.

I catch up with her. "That's not what I asked, Lexi."

She glances at me. "Yeah, whatever. Obviously."

Fuck me. Her answer is cold, noncommittal, and so disinterested about something this important that it riles me up. "I'm serious, Lexi."

"So am I, Tristan. I know my body, okay? When I tell you there's no chance, there's no chance. You're off the hook, even though you've never been on it."

I don't want to be off the hook. That stops me cold for a moment. This is a first. Which means maybe I want to be caught—hook, line, and sinker—by *her*. But this... We're not fighting, but the tension is as thick and cold as a block of ice.

Too many things have happened tonight, and for some reason, everything seems to have slipped out of my control. "Lexi—"

"Tristan, I'm freaking exhausted. I need to go to bed."

"Okay." I back off. When it comes to us, my timing is never right.

We've reached our cottage, and Lexi walks in, not bothering to wash her feet, which is unlike her. She doesn't mind a bit of a mess, as long as it's a clean mess. I give her space to get ready for bed, and I could hide in my office closet, but instead I sit in one of the occasional chairs in the small living room so I can watch her surreptitiously.

As she slips beneath the sheets, she sighs. "I don't know why you're so freaked out about Roger and Deshni. They love each other to bits. They've got, by simple math calculation, more than seven months to win her parents over. He's a great guy. He's solid. Roger will look after her and their baby come hell or high water for the rest of his life."

"True." But *ouch*. That's just it, right? When we leave here, Lexi and I are supposed to be going our separate ways, as if Ne'emba never happened. I can't do that, nor do I want that anymore. *"They love each other to bits."* That phrase echoes in my mind.

Lexi switches off her bedside light, and I sit in the dark, my past playing out in my head like a reel. A past that predicts a future I don't want. Everything Lexi said is true, but this has nothing to do with Roger and Deshni—this has everything to do with *us*. Everything to do with those three simple words I'm too petrified to say, too stuck in my rut of always keeping an easy way out.

Lexi has played along with my usual game plan from the

start, but it could be a façade, because she's scared of me walking away again and hurting her. She's protecting herself. But what if she wants more? I want more, yet I don't know how to get there. Nothing has ever forced me to dissect my feelings like this—and then I'll have to act on them.

Bottom line? Only *I* can change my ways.

Chapter Thirty-Eight

LEXI

When I wake up, it's still dark. From afar, the sound of waves rolls in, but the birds aren't up yet. I've slept fitfully, my mind too busy with everything going on. *Roger and Deshni. Mia Fucking Reed. Tristan.*

I cover my face with my hands and groan, glancing over at where he's sprawled on his stomach. At some point Tristan came to bed, but I fell asleep without him by my side. It was lonely, and he didn't pull me close as he normally would have done. Probably because I was already asleep.

Probably because last night was too intense. Things felt so right that they were wrong—for me—as clearly Tristan didn't feel the same vibes. *"Let me be everything I can be for you."* Essentially a fun time while we're here. I knew by the end of the evening, when Tristan freaked out about a baby, that we could never have more than these three months. And even the time that remains might be too much for my heart.

I quietly slip from the bed and tiptoe to the bathroom.

I showered mere hours ago, so I dress in a fresh uniform and go to the office. Tristan will wake up alone, but it's not as if I can go anywhere. He knows where to find me.

I falter in my steps as I approach the office. The double glass doors are closed, but the lights are on, and Jem is already at her desk. What the hell? Doesn't she sleep? After last night's verbal sparring match in the canteen, she's up to something. But *what*?

At least we're not the only ones on the job already. Birds are announcing the start of another scorcher, and I can hear soft voices from the kitchen, the clang of a pot or pan. It doesn't matter what's going on in your life; the show must go on.

I open the door and Jem looks up, startled. "Why are you early?"

Lately we've been forgoing all pleasantries.

"Couldn't sleep," I tell her.

"Why's that?" she prods.

I roll my eyes. *Wouldn't you want to know.* Despite everything else happening, my masochistic side needs to see if there are any emails from the lawyer or Evan, guiding me through this shitstorm. Has St Chalamet cracked? Sharon's updates have dwindled to zero. Maybe she's realized that her own employment at St Chalamet is at risk if she keeps playing informant.

I sink down at my desk, suddenly exhausted. This day is going to be a motherfucker. "What are *you* doing here so early?" I ask Jem as I switch my computer on. *Dammit.* With her here, I won't be at liberty to scour the internet for news or do anything private.

"Just doing some prep work."

"The upcoming wedding?" I ask. She might get on my nerves, but Jem is a fantastic manager.

"Among other things."

I hate it when people sidestep and talk in circles. "I'm going to get coffee. You want some?"

"I'm good, thanks."

Fine. Be good.

By the time I've had the obligatory chit-chat with the people in the staff canteen and kitchen, the sun's up, and its heat caresses my cheek as I head down to the beach with my coffee in hand. I can't stomach sitting with Jem in that office right now. I'm still digesting Deshni's news and have no clue how we're going to sort out the spa without her losing her stride. I glance along the beach and spot a fellow human or two, guests who walked out when they woke to the relative cool of the morning.

This place is so peaceful, in total contrast to the hooting traffic jam in my head. Everything and everybody aside, my mind keeps spiraling back to Tristan. I sit down on the sand, wanting to cry. *Yep.* Of all the bad moves of the past six months, he's maybe the worst and will leave me with scars. I take a long drink of coffee, hoping to swallow my tears down with it.

"Lexi."

I look up. Tristan is in his running gear and has approached me without a sound. I would have seen him if I hadn't been so preoccupied with my heartache and the fact that I might have found him, but I'm going to lose him too, and without him ever knowing. I mutter a terse hello into my cup and take another sip.

He drops down next to me. "You're up early. I was—"

"I couldn't sleep. This whole thing with Desh—"

"Why didn't you wake me up?" He puts a hand on my knee. "We can talk it through."

I wish he wouldn't touch me like this, as if we belong to each other. I should keep things light and step away from this as soon as possible. Tristan isn't that guy. "Honestly, I just need to get through today."

"Lexi..." he starts, but he stalls as he looks to the sea.

My ears prick up, and my eyes try to find the source of the sound too. *There*. A speedboat heading straight in our direction.

"Who's that?" I'm so tired I don't know if I'm seeing straight. "At this time of the morning?"

Tristan stands, and I follow suit. "Looks like the coastguard."

"Jeez, they make a lot of noise." We've never had the coastguard come to the island like this before. A slow coil turns my stomach. "Why are they even here?"

"Who knows, but they're patrolling these waters as if they're waiting for something."

I glance back toward the guest area. Waiters have paused their work to look. Along the beach, the odd guest is also staring at the boat plowing through the waves. "Tristan..."

I have a bad feeling. Jem at her desk so early. Jem telling me squat. *Oh my God*. That fist that keeps churning in my stomach gives me a punch from the inside out. "Jem's done something. Last night—"

"Something's definitely up. Something must have gone down during the night." He reaches for my hand, but I pull away.

"This isn't a joke." I rush up the beach to the office. I'm halfway there when Jem appears on the path.

"What's going on?" I ask, noting her stiff demeanor.

"I'm on to you," she says. "That's what's going on. And there's no place to run, no place to hide."

Chills streak down my spine. "What do you mean?" I turn to see Tristan still standing on the beach. The speedboat has anchored, and two uniformed coastguards are wading through the shallow waves. With them are two policemen in black uniform—holstered guns, batons, the works.

My throat squeezes as panic invades me, just like it did all those years ago. I have double vision of sorts. One image is that of the cops as they raided our house, arresting Dad at ten o'clock at night. This one is a fresh overlay, the tropical version. I'm going to be sick.

"Best we go to your cottage, Alexandra O'Reilly. We don't want the guests to witness." Jem has me by the elbow and tugs.

Tristan is walking up to the troop of law enforcement. *Clueless*.

"Tris!" I yell, but my voice croaks and gets lost in the distance between us.

"Don't make a scene. They've got your *fiancé*," Jem hisses. "Come with me. That's Officer Odinga, the tall one. The fat one is Officer Mwamba. Between them, they'll dig down to the root of this."

"The root of what?" I tug, but Jem is pinching my arm painfully. Now Tristan is surrounded by the four men who don't bother to shake his hand. Instead, one of the coastguards slaps a handcuff around his wrists.

Adrenaline spikes my blood, and I want to break free and

sprint to him, but Jem's nails dig into my arm, her other hand circling my wrist. "We're all going to your cottage to see what's going on there."

What the actual...? The two police officers are hurrying along the beach in the direction of our cottage. Tristan stands tall, but the coastguards have him firmly by the shoulder, steering him along.

I sway on my feet, dizzy and sick to my stomach, and so shocked that I let Jem drag me into the forest, losing sight of Tristan. *What if they hurt him?*

We get to the cottage first, and Jem lets go of me by shoving me to a sofa. "Sit."

I sink down onto the seat and watch in horror as the two police officers raid our room. They rip at the bed and open drawers, tossing the contents to the floor. One takes the other side of the room, and the other disappears into the closet.

"What's going on?" I'm rattling like a leaf. "I don't understand!"

"Uh," Jem grunts. "What isn't going on? All this pretending! You think I can't see right through you?"

The coastguard walks up, Tristan in a firm hold between them. He is pale but his gaze immediately finds mine. "You're okay, babes?" he asks.

"*Babes.*" Jem snorts. "As if you can fool me!"

I'm too stunned to speak, only gaping at her. "How?"

"How? How what? How did I know?" Jem's voice pitches.

"Jem," Tristan says, his voice calm as he speaks over her budding triumph. "What's happening?"

"Here!" One of the policemen comes out of the closet, white powder on his fingers. "I've also found this. There's a whole secret workstation here." He holds several memory banks in his hands. "We'll find everything we want on these."

Tristan drops his head with a frown, then he starts to chuckle. "Seriously?"

Jem steps closer. "Officer Odinga, what is that powder?"

Now Tristan looks at me, a brow cocked, that sparkle back in his eye. "This is a bit dramatic for a spot of cornstarch."

Officer Odinga lifts his finger to his nose, smells, and then taps his finger on his tongue, tasting. "Hmm... I'm not sure, but this isn't—"

"Officer, you need to be one hundred percent sure," Jem hisses. "Remember what happened last time."

Last time? All those red flags wave at me, that whiff of something smelling off hitting me in the face, and then there was Matthias de Foch asking for the *good stuff*.

Holy Mother of God—I thought he only wanted weed, but *this*, this is a cocaine raid.

Officer Odinga takes a deep breath and gives Jem a resigned stare. "We'll take this as evidence for the laboratory in Dar es Salaam."

"Don't get high now," Tristan murmurs.

His little joke has no effect on the rest of the crowd, but I lose it, completely. How can Tristan be so blasé? We're being raided by the police for *drugs*! Here, as foreigners! Doesn't he know what happens to drug smugglers in foreign countries? "For fuck's sake, Jem. Honestly. You—"

"Lexi." Tristan's tone is harsh. "Don't."

Don't say a thing. The authority and threat in his voice cut sharply, and everybody jumps. We're all looking at each other, waiting to see what happens next, and in those few seconds, the slow hum of the floatplane circles above.

"That would be the rest of the party," Jem announces. The chill in her tone freezes me over.

I'm shivering. For the first time since arriving at Ne'emba, my fingers are white with cold. It's the shock. First getting fired from St Chalamet. Then the Mia Reed disaster. Now my little stint with Tristan. Third time wasn't the charm. And this is a million times worse than I ever imagined.

Chapter Thirty-Nine
TRISTAN

"Bring the evidence," Jem says. "We'll go to the office now. I have everything prepared."

One half of me is shocked, but there's that other half that's been taking stock of all the signs, if subconsciously. Mike telling us the Pemba harbor isn't a good place to hang out, Roger avoiding certain dhows on dives and being bitter about other people making a quick buck. Why did nobody mention this to us?

I watch in horror as the two officers stack my laptop and all my other electronics into one of my travel crates. "Be careful," I hiss. "I have a lot of important—" *irreplaceable* "—data on there."

"That's what I thought." Jem runs me down with her gaze, matriarch to the core.

I knew she was on to something, plotting, spying, but this is so out left field I want to laugh. Except it's no laughing matter.

Lexi just stands there, looking like she's seen a ghost. I bet this is a rerun of what happened when her dad got arrested all those years ago. It took three years of hanging out with Evan before he opened up to me about what had gone down in New Orleans, just a year after the family lost their home in the hurricane.

After that, I dug around. Who wouldn't, once you realized your best friend's dad was a convicted felon? Not only did Alexander O'Reilly steal from donors, he stole money allocated to the Hurricane Relief Fund. The vitriol was so toxic, Anita left New Orleans for a new life in Miami with the kids. But in the middle of all of it, there was little Lexi, soaking the anger and hatred towards her dad up like a sponge. The family used to call her Alexa, but her name was too close to *Alex* O'Reilly, which was plastered all over the news. So she started asking people to call her Lexi instead, burying Alexa and that past forever. I bet she would have changed her surname if she could.

Even more reason for this fake engagement to have her in a pretzel. For her, this has been fraud from day one. And now this.

"It's going to be fine, Lexi," I call to her, but she doesn't even look in my direction. *They've got nothing on us.* I keep quiet. Saying that won't help, not when we've been living a partial lie here from the beginning. Well, the truth's going to come out now, whether we want it to or not.

A coastguard has me by the arm, and I roll my eyes. The handcuffs are unnecessary, given our location, but I play along, keeping my eye on Lexi, as she's holding it together by a thread.

We make our way along the beach, and the floatplane skids over the water and stops close to shore. Our little group comes to a standstill, and I want to reach for Lexi's hand, but I can't. She's crossed her arms over her chest, protective. Now she blinks in the sunlight, tears brimming.

"Babes," I whisper.

She shakes her head, not looking at me. "No. No... No more lies."

I bite down, wishing I could rewind to...I don't know how far back. Five years probably. I'd start the do-over right there.

The floatplane's door pops open, and all eyes are glued to the man who steps out. Nathan Beaumont emerges in a white short-sleeved shirt and cargo shorts, carrying leather flip-flops in one hand. He salutes the pilot and strides through the water toward us.

Jem splits from our group and meets Nathan halfway. As she holds out her hand to him, he pulls her close for a hug. *A hug?*

I look over at Lexi, and she's blinking. "Oh my God," she whispers. "Of course."

"Of course what?" I ask, leaning closer.

"She started as a nanny here. *His* nanny. Oh, God. I've seen this so many times. Rich people, just dumping their kids with their nannies at the hotel. That bond...nothing breaks it."

Nathan walks up with Jem by his side as they laugh at some joke. The other men stand taller, grappling for their diminishing authority in a *Beaumont's* presence. Jem and Nathan walk past us, so deep in conversation that he doesn't even acknowledge us.

Lexi shudders, and her bottom lip trembles. I look up the beach. The few guests on this side of the hotel shoot us curious glances, but it's mostly the staff who are hovering, waiting to see what happens next.

"Follow them to the office," I tell her. "We're not putting on a show for anybody."

"Is that so?" Lexi whispers. "Tris, we've put on a show from the start, and I can't anymore."

"Keep your cool, babes. Who knows what's really going on. We're only seeing one half of the coin here."

We make our way to the office, the coastguard and police muttering to themselves in Swahili. As we pile inside, we find Jem and Nathan standing at her whiteboard.

They both look in our direction, and suddenly the office seems very small.

Nathan homes in on Lexi and holds out his hand. "Alexandra O'Reilly." He studies her face as they shake. "Nathan Beaumont. I can see why you made a beeline for the middle of nowhere." He lets go, and Lexi drops her limp hand to her side. "That video isn't going to do you any favors in this industry."

Lexi seems to sway on the spot, and I swear under my breath. She looks like she's about to faint.

"The video?" she repeats, eyes like saucers.

Nathan's lips arch up in a wry, dry smile, and he shakes his head. "Your meme is trending everywhere. If we wait long enough, it will reach this last outpost too."

"Nathan," I say, feeling useless. If only I could reach out and hold her. Touch her. Anything.

He turns to me, and our gazes clash. He looks down at my handcuffs. "Hmm... A bit extra, don't you think?"

"Sir," Officer Odinga interjects as he takes a step forward. "We've discovered some evidence." He nods toward the crate of my things the other officer is holding.

"I see." Nathan sighs. "That's not necessary, Officer.

Please." He waves at me, and Officer Odinga unlocks the handcuffs, muttering under his breath. I shake my hands as I reach for Lexi. She flinches under my touch and steps away.

"Please," she murmurs, but doesn't look me in the eye.

Nathan clears his throat. "Here's the thing I've learned, Ms. O'Reilly, Dr. Martinelli: if it sounds too good to be true, it's too good to be true. Finding the perfect couple for a position that is notoriously hard to fill at the last minute? Too good to be true. Dodgy stuff starts to happen? Well, as you might have learned from the incident at St Chalamet, we can leave nothing to chance."

"St Chalamet?" Lexi says, breathless. "What do you know about St Chalamet?"

"Everything," Nathan says. "I know everything." He crosses his arms and leans against Lexi's desk. "I totally understand why you had to skip town and come hide it out, Ms. O'Reilly. But I don't understand what your fiancé is doing here."

Chapter Forty

LEXI

I'm done. I'm finished. I don't care what Nathan Beaumont has on me or not. If he knows *everything* that happened at St Chalamet, I've put up with this lie for nothing. And even worse? I'm taking Tristan down with me.

He's going to be collateral damage, and I know how that feels. It hits me so hard in this moment that I love him—that I've always loved him and never stopped—that I gasp. I can't hurt him like my dad hurt me.

"Mr. Beaumont," I say, raking my courage together. "Just so you know, this was my idea. Tristan had nothing to do with it. I suggested the fake engagement to get the job. Please—"

"I knew it!" Jem says. "I knew something was off from day one! Her! What with her dad spending time in prison for stealing—"

"What?" Blood rushes to my head as it drains to my feet at the same time. How did she know? I sway and prop a hand up on the wall to keep me steady.

"Lexi—" Tristan says, taking a step towards me.

I hold my hand up to stop him from getting any closer. Jem dug until she found treasure.

"Say that again?" Nathan says, his eyes narrowing.

"Her dad is a convicted—" Jem starts.

"Let her talk, Jem," Nathan cuts in.

I pull in a deep breath. My dad did his time; this is my crime. "I said our engagement is fake and—" My voice breaks. Tristan reaches for my hand, but I jerk away. "Please. I—" Inside I'm rattling like a bird trying to take flight in a cage.

"Can we have this conversation in private?" Tristan interrupts.

"Gentleman," Nathan says, addressing the coastguard and police. "Please excuse us. I think we have an in-house issue we need to deal with first."

"Yes," Jem says. "Officer Odinga, you and the men go check out the dive center. Who knows where they've been stockpiling the drugs. And watch out for Roger, that boat boy. He's been doing night trips on the sly to Pemba. That's how it always starts. I don't trust him either."

"Roger has nothing to do with anything!" I beg, wishing I could go back in time. My legs give out, but Tristan's there, helping me to a seat at the round meeting table in the corner.

"Lexi," he whispers urgently in my ear. "Just don't—"

"I have you on record," Jem announces as the police file out. "Nathan, I'll show you all my evidence."

What evidence can she have? I'm not sure why Jem keeps yammering about drugs, because that's ridiculous. But nonetheless, everything in this moment reminds me of my last meeting at St Chalamet, where my integrity, self-worth, and reputation were ground to a pulp. And even that pales against my current horror, now that other people are being dragged into my mess. Roger, of all people. And Deshni without a doubt too.

Nathan sits down next to me, and Tristan squeezes my shoulder before he takes another empty chair.

Jem has her phone out, searching for something and muttering incoherently.

Nathan looks at Tristan. "Dr. Martinelli," he begins, and Jem clamps her mouth shut. At least when he speaks, she doesn't interrupt. "I have to ask you again, now that the police are gone, what are you doing here?"

"I'm the dive master," Tristan deadpans.

"I don't think so," Jem says. "Ever since you arrived, I've been suspicious of your dubious dealings. You're in cahoots with Deshni," she says as she points a rude finger to me. "And you're training Roger, going out by boat, teaching him things. And then you confirmed *this* last night in your own words." She's flicked open some app on her phone, and next thing, my voice fills the room from a hazy recording.

"Once you've put your feelers out, you'll see there'll be many options. There are countless opportunities all the way up and down the coast here, and then Mauritius, the Seychelles, the Maldives."

"We still have time to set things up for you," Tristan's voice says.

The recording cuts, and I'm at a loss. *What the hell?*

"Worst of all," Jem says, pointing that finger at Tristan, "you had the audacity to call your midnight meeting *team building*."

"Are you suggesting we're setting up a drug-trafficking ring? In the three months we have on the island?" Tristan asks. "Because we're not. There's a serious misunderstanding here."

"There's *no* misunderstanding," Jem contradicts, her tone

heavy with accusation. "You're busy with some serious illegal things here, and I aim to get to the bottom of it."

I glance at Tristan, and he's grinding his jaw. "Jem," he says. "You're a real gem, but you've got it all wrong."

"Explain then, Dr. Martinelli, because from where we stand," Nathan says, "it's not so ludicrous at all. The last couple who managed the resort had connections with the drug mafia in the Seychelles, who'd set up a trafficking route from the coast inland. They took the job at Ne'emba with the sole purpose of establishing a network connecting the lodges along the east coast and using Ne'emba as a midway cache. This might come as a surprise to you, but I'd rather believe the worst and be proven wrong than wait until things get out of hand and we're forced to shut down completely."

"Drug trafficking?" I repeat, dazed. "As in a whole ring?"

"Yes, a *whole ring*," Jem repeats. "And now that you've said this engagement is fake, there's all the more reason for us to wonder why you're here." Jem's cold stare eats at me like a fungus. "Now, would you care to show us what work you're doing on your laptop, Dr. Martinelli?" She makes quotation marks around the word *work*. "What you're doing in such secrecy that you set up shop in your *closet*? With all your gadgets and what not." She looks at Nathan. "For all I know, they have their own ways to get internet. Plus, when he arrived, there was white powder everywhere. I swear they had stock that got damaged. What with the endless trunks and boxes of gear he brought in, nobody would suspect—"

"Let's not jump to conclusions when it comes to white powder, Jem. As for the internet, I'm not sure they're that advanced," Nathan cuts in. "We keep on top of the latest technology."

"At least someone talks sense," Tristan grumbles under his breath.

A knock sounds on the closed office door, and Mike walks in. "Nathan, welcome back," he says in greeting. "Sorry to interrupt, but we have nine guests gearing up to go diving. They're all asking for Tristan. Roger is orchestrating. He even told the coastguard and the police to bugger off. Apparently, they can raid the place while they're diving, so…"

"That's my man," Tristan says with a small smile.

I shake my head. Now Tristan needs to lead the dives, despite being a drug trafficker in the making.

"Well then, Dr. Martinelli," Nathan says as he stands. "As you know, the show goes on. Best you get on with the job. Mike will go with you, though. Jem, we'll need to delay all other activities until Mike is back. We're not done here."

Tristan stands too, and for a moment our eyes meet. "I'll see you later, babes. Just—"

"It's fine," I say. "Please go. I'll be fine."

I watch as Tristan files out with Mike on his heels. Nathan takes a deep breath and sighs. "What does one do to get a cup of coffee here? And some breakfast? I only flew in from the Seychelles, but we left too early—"

Jem is a jack-in-the-box. "I'm sorry, Nathan. It's been so busy. I'll get someone—"

"Please, Jem, I'd love to have some of those banana fritters you used to make. And make sure the toast is just so."

Her gaze softens. "You always loved those bananas. Let me see what I can get Chef to do. And I'll let the guests know about the delay in activities until Mike is back."

Jem rushes out, and I collapse in my seat. If that's the last I see of her, it will be too soon. Nathan leans over with his hands on the table for a second and studies me. I don't have the courage to look him in the eye. I just wait for his scorn.

"It's Lexi, right?"

I nod. "Mr. Beaumont—"

"Just Nathan," he says with a soft smile. "Good job on the spa. I got your email last night and saw the numbers. I'm impressed."

My jaw drops. "You never responded to anything."

"As you see, I only do when things go wrong," he says as he sits. "Now that we are finally alone, why don't you tell me what's going on?"

I have one chance. *One*. No more lies. From now on, I'm not bending the truth one bit. "How much do you know about what happened at St Chalamet?"

"Well...St Chalamet is a competitor we're in bed with," Nathan says, smiling.

God. I can read between the lines. *He's* in bed with someone who works at St Chalamet, someone fairly high up by the sound of it.

"And when something like the Mia Reed situation happens," he continues, "our first response is always 'Thank God that wasn't a Beaumont hotel.'" He smirks. "The whole thing backfired a bit, though, don't you think? I'm not sure *you* going viral was Mia Reed's intention. I bet she was rather hoping *she* would go viral."

I drop my face to my hands. "It's been horrible. I'm slowly dying of embarrassment. And to think The Head is walking away without a blemish to anything, least of all his reputation!"

"And who is The Head?"

"Brent Fisherman," I choke out. "To think I fell for—

I actually fell for..." I stall, fire invading my cheeks. Did I just blurt out his name and almost give away that I slept with my superior? To Nathan Beaumont, of all people? The man I want to impress most in the world?

Dying right now would be divine intervention. I need divine intervention.

"Right," Nathan says as he shifts in his seat. "I see how it was. He was your senior, was he? How high up?"

"General manager in training," I whisper. "God, I was so dumb. He used me to—to... I don't know. He *used* me."

"Yes. I'm sorry this happened to you. What he did was the ultimate fuck-you to St Chalamet's management, and he knows it. Dragging a hotel you work for into scandal is a quick way to damage a reputation without taking any hits yourself."

Nathan's sympathy is so out of left field that I choke up again, and for a long moment, he lets me do just that. I take a few shaky breaths to get a grip.

"You see, Lexi, a company's culture is spread from the top down. Brent Fisherman should have known better than to prey on younger members of his staff." Nathan leans back, and I wipe my face, the truth of the situation only hitting me now. I never expected to feel this level of relief at finally admitting the truth. To be *seen* like this. "I'll put Fisherman on our blacklist. Trust me, he'll never work at any of the big hotel chains in the world again."

I want to burst into tears again, but instead I give him a shaky smile. "Thank you. For understanding."

"The worst for you has come to pass, with the video going viral as it did." He studies me for a few long seconds. "Given how things have turned out, I'd reconsider my position, if I were you."

"What do you mean?" I ask.

"I believe Mia Reed is suing St Chalamet for damages, but honestly, that's a long shot. If I were you, I'd request payment from St Chalamet to keep quiet."

My eyes widen. *Did he just suggest I blackmail St Chalamet?* "You can't be serious?"

"They threw you under the bus, Lexi, without blinking. It will serve them right."

My throat tightens. I'd never thought of that angle. "I'm not the type to... I don't know."

Nathan leans closer. "Think it over, sleep on it, and see how this pans out. Postscript, you never got the idea from me."

I bite my lip, dropping my gaze. *Who is this guy?*

"Now, that's your story. Want to tell me what Tristan Martinelli is up to in his spare time?"

This is Day One of No More Lies, not even tiny white ones. *Sorry, Tris. I'm doing this for you.* "He's working on his love letter to the ocean," I say. If Nathan understood me, maybe he'll understand Tristan too.

"A love letter? To the ocean?"

"Yes. He's been working on a TV series about symbiosis in the oceans for years. He's trying to wrap it up, but he has a deadline and..." I trail off. "You should ask him, really. Even better, you need him to show you."

"I see. Okay." Nathan glances at the crate where the police dumped Tristan's electronics earlier. "That explains a lot."

"It's amazing. *He's* amazing. Please, I know he hasn't said anything because it was all so rushed, and that's my fault, but he needs to finish it."

"Well, we don't just allow people to film at Ne'emba. There's a reason these reefs are so well preserved. We don't allow hordes of divers to go through here. People care, but they are negligent too, and they can damage delicate corals without even trying."

I nod. I know nothing of diving. But I do know the past few months have been enough. I can't anymore. I need a break. Like, a proper break. And I need to get away from Tristan while I can still keep myself together and my last shred of dignity intact. "You don't really need me here," I start, trying to find the words for what I need. "Between Jem and Mike—"

"I know. They have everything under control. They are the custodians of the land here, and as you can see, they take it very seriously. The thing is, they've never wanted the responsibility of being the managers. I don't know why, but we've always had a Beaumont face from Europe as front of house here."

"Yes, I see." Jem and Mike might not like ultimate responsibility, but the final moment to take responsibility for all my actions is now. Even if Nathan has been kind and understanding, I need to go. I want to go. After last night with Tristan, this is the moment to rip off the Band-Aid. "That's perfect, though, that they have everything in hand, because I'm going home. I honestly can't pretend anymore. This fake engagement is too much. I can't work for Beaumont with a clear conscience...and I can't be around Tristan."

At this he hitches his brow. "Really? He hasn't—"

"No, no. Nothing like that. I just need space." I don't want to stick it out here with him until April, making roadkill of my heart.

"Hmm..." Nathan steeples his fingers together. "I can't stop you, as you well know. If you want to go, the floatplane is here. We can arrange flights for you back to Miami. No problem."

"Thank you." I stand and straighten my clothes, and Nathan follows suit. "This was a great opportunity, and I'm sorry. I didn't want to disappoint you like this."

"I think you didn't want to disappoint yourself. St Chalamet hasn't done right by you. I can understand that you'd want a break."

Jem chooses this moment to walk back into the office, a tray in her hands. "Nathan, we've put together some of your favorites. The bananas are almost done."

Nathan picks up a croissant and chugs back a glass of orange juice. "Keep them warm, Jem. I have a dive to catch. Help Lexi arrange flights home for today. She'll take the floatplane to Dar. We'll catch up later."

I watch, jaw slack, as Nathan walks out, leaving me alone with my nemesis.

Chapter Forty-One

LEXI

I hasten out of the office, mumbling as I shoulder past Jem. "Excuse me. I need to pack my things."

"Where're you going?" she calls after me, but I just shake my head, my heels hitting the wooden boardwalk as I almost slip into a run. Now that my mind is made up, nothing is stopping me. The need to leave is almost overwhelming. If I stay here a minute longer than necessary, I won't be able to breathe.

When I get to our cottage, I groan into my hands. The police have wrecked it. Who knew you could create such havoc in so little time. Our things are strewn on the floor, bedding twisted in a lump, my vibrator lying lonely on the bed, partially covered by the mosquito net they tossed up to check for drugs under the bed.

To think you can reach your lowest low and highest high on the same day. Being accused of being a drug-smuggler on this side of the planet—it can't get lower than that. But then, with every passing minute, I'm floating higher on the relief of having wiped my slate clean. I'll never work for St Chalamet—or probably even Beaumont—again, but that's fine. I'm starting to think this five-star environment isn't for me. It's just too much. I can hack out a career at a small boutique hotel or a motel chain and feel right at home.

For a short second, my training pleads to kick in, but there's no chance in hell I'll plump a pillow now. I head straight for the bathroom and start packing. I'm almost done when someone calls my name. *Jem.* I lean against the vanity for a second, taking a deep breath. I can't avoid her now.

I walk out of the bathroom and meet her gaze where she's standing, eyes wide and bosom heaving, in the middle of the living area. "What's happened?" she asks.

For real? *You happened, Jem.* Serves her right to be clueless. "I'm leaving. I need a flight from Dar es Salaam—"

"Yes, but Nathan…the police…the coastguard…"

None of them jumped to conclusions. That volcano in me, the one that's been building pressure for weeks when it comes to her, erupts. "None of them found anything!" I say, throwing my hands in the air. "There's nothing to find. You have no clue what's going on here. And with your wild assumptions, you're going to ruin Deshni and Roger's lives!"

"Wild assumptions? Nobody has proven me wrong yet," she bites back.

"Nathan didn't buy this drug-smuggling fantasy you've sketched. He just went diving, with Tristan. When they come back, Tristan will show him what he's been working on." *And once Nathan has seen Tristan's work, he might be able to negotiate a way to keep on filming,* I can't stop myself from thinking.

I give Jem a cold stare, childishly gratified that she'll have to sit with her mess until lunchtime. By then, I'll be gone. I turn my back on her as I head into our closet and force myself to take a deep, calming breath. Losing my head with Jem isn't going to help anybody here.

I sort through our two rails of clothing and slip my clothes from the hangers. The Beaumont uniforms they can keep. "You have all the evidence you need," I tell her as I palm my phone and passport, where they've been snuggled between my underwear. "Deshni was only putting forward plans to improve the spa. If Roger has sailed out in the middle of the night to Pemba, it was to get fresh spices from Pemba for the spa, not to haul drugs! Deshni and Sarika have fantastic ideas, but I see why they never wanted to share them with you." I shove my valuables into my purse, which I haven't used for weeks, and poke my head out of the closet. "I bet the reason nobody ever gets ahead in this place is *you*!"

I stare at her, unflinching, and she's the one to drop her gaze first. Jem's broken pieces finally fall into place. "You don't trust yourself, do you?" I ask, my voice softer now. "With the ultimate responsibility of this place? With actually dealing with difficult guests and being that last line of defense?" I can relate to that. Even with Matthias de Foch, I was like a gaping fish out of water, and Tristan had to step in. Next time, I'll deal with De Foch's type myself.

"What do you know about it? You had all the training! One big hotel after the other," Jem says, defensive, but there's a vulnerability in her tone I've never picked up on before. "Ne'emba is my life. I've grown into my job."

I swallow a snarky comment. Despite everything, I've had privileges this woman has never had. "Maybe," I say. "But Jem, you're holding other people back too, whether it's consciously or subconsciously. You love Ne'emba, but just because you don't have the guts to run this place by yourself doesn't mean you can't give others the opportunities they need and crave."

Jem wipes her face and drops down to pick up a pillow. "Where do you want to fly? I need to book you a ticket."

I bite my lip. "Miami. Please."

She nods. "Okay. I'll book it now. You can get to London on the same day if you leave here by noon. From London, there'll be many options."

"Thank you…" I hesitate for one last second. "You need to advocate for yourself, Jem. Tell Nathan what you want. I promise he'll make it happen."

"Maybe."

I watch, clutching my arrival-day jeans in my hand, as she walks out of the cottage. I toss them into my gaping suitcase as all the fight drains out of me. I look back at the closet, where I've emptied my side. Tristan's disconnected chargers sprout from the plugs like alien seedlings. His airport engagement ring catches the overhead light, and I close my eyes as I run my thumb over the diamond one last time. This is going to hurt.

With a fist squeezing my heart, I try to take it off. On a good day it fits perfectly, but now, just like when we arrived, it won't budge. I rush to the bathroom sink, soap up, and eventually wrench it from my finger. Back in the closet, I put it down where Tristan's laptop has made a dust-free rectangle. Clearly housekeeping needs a talking to. I reach for the Beaumont-embossed writing pad he's pushed to the side and pick up a pen.

Dear Tristan,

I told Nathan about your project. I knew it would be better coming from you, but he had me in a corner, and I didn't want to lie. I'm done doing that. This was an adventure, wasn't it? I loved every minute we spent on this island, but they don't need me here. Leaving now makes things so much easier. We had a hard cut-off date from the start, and now we don't need to have that godawful awkward flight all the way home where we both try to get out of a sticky situation.

I hope you can negotiate something with Nathan to finish your series. He's one of the good ones.

And so are you.

Love,
Lexi

I drop the pen and leave the letter there, putting the ring on top so Tristan can't miss it. I kneel to squeeze and zip my suitcase closed. For a moment, all I want is to collapse on top of it and weep, but there'll be loads of time for that later. I am, after all, freshly unemployed.

"Lexi?"

The surge of tears I've been holding back surfaces afresh, and I push my fist to my mouth. "Hmm?" I manage.

"Where are you?" Deshni asks.

"In here." Time to face the music. I walk out of the closet with my suitcase in tow, my purse over my shoulder.

Deshni looks pale. "Lexi? What's going on?" She holds out a piece of paper. "Jem asked me to give you this reference number for a flight to Miami. She's emailing you the full itinerary. I—"

I pull her close, hugging her so tightly I squeeze the air out of both our lungs. "I've got to go. I'm so sorry. Jem can fill you in on everything."

"But why?" Deshni pushes me to arm's length and searches my gaze, her eyes shiny with tears. "Is it true? About Tristan and you not being engaged? How can that even be?"

It seems rock bottom has a secret trapdoor through which I just fell into a pit of despair. *This. This part of the lie is the worst.* "Yes. I'm so sorry we deceived you. W-When we made the stupid decision to do this, we didn't think." We had no idea what we were walking into. No idea how this would affect other people's perception of us. It feels as if I've shattered all the trust Deshni put in me with one blow.

"But..." Deshni shakes her head, clearly stumped. "I thought you were in love."

I force down every feeling that wants to surface, and instead give her a peevish smile. "Seems we fooled quite a few people, but not Jem."

And of all the fools, I was the biggest one. Such a stupid idiot to think this could end any way besides total annihilation of my heart and soul. "Listen, Nathan Beaumont is happy with the spa's numbers. I'd bet he'll come see you now that he's here, if he has time. Be strong. Roger loves you so much, and you're going to be such amazing parents..." I choke up and take a deep breath. "Everything is going to be fine." I give her arm a last squeeze. "We'll keep in touch, okay?"

Before Deshni can say anything else, and before I can explode with tears, I pick up my suitcase again. From the corner of my eye, I spot my vibrator, still half-concealed on the bed. I can't bring myself to reach for it. I'll leave it for Tristan, as a memento.

I walk out of the cottage, down to the beach, and straight for the floatplane. A waiter rushes over to help me and takes my suitcase. "Thank you." I give him a weak smile as I slip my shoes off.

The pilot pops the door open, and I wade through the water. Several hands help me up and into the plane, but my eyes are glazed with tears, and I just murmur *thank you* over and over, not able to look anybody in the eye.

I slump down in an empty seat, and the pilot leans back to look at me. "Not a nervous flyer, are you? This ride can get a bit bumpy."

"No, no," I say on a swallow. "I'm good, thank you." So good, in fact, that if we crash into the ocean, with the way this day's been going, it will feel like I've met my final destination: fish fodder at the bottom of the sea.

"Excellent. Buckle up. Barf bag is in the seat pocket in front of you."

Fantastic. I'd love to have a deep cleanse, and my guts have just been waiting for the go-ahead for the past hour.

Chapter Forty-Two

TRISTAN

As I walk up to the dive center, I spot the two police officers and two coastguards loitering outside. "Just so you know," I say in passing, pinning Officer Odinga with a cutting glare, "if you damage anything in this dive center during your raid, I'll make you pay for it."

Roger did me proud, telling them to take a hike until we're out with the guests. Now my student is coming up to me, concern in his eyes. *Fuck*. My head can't get around Jem's accusation. To think she was blindly dragging Roger and Deshni into this mess too. And Lexi... *Shit*.

Roger pulls me to the side for a second, away from the few guests who are still in the dive center. "Stupid police raid. As if this type of thing would happen again so soon—"

"Why did nobody tell us?" I say, baffled and annoyed to be caught off guard.

"Bro, you should see the pile of papers we had to sign. Every one of us not allowed to say a word," Roger says as he shakes his head. "Can't let Beaumont be part of the drug problem on the coast, see? Ne'emba and Beaumont have a reputation to uphold... Imagine getting tagged as Drug Island! Love Island? Any day, but drugs!" He huffs. "In the end it was only management and two maintenance guys who were caught. It was a big hush job."

Fuck me. Lexi. *This* is what she went through with St Chalamet. All I want is to go back to that office and drag her into a hug, reassure her, but I have no choice but to do my job. I rake my hands through my hair, forcing myself to focus on the dives ahead as I step in the direction of the dive center.

Roger's hand on my arm stops me. "What's going on, Tristan?" he asks, and cold fingers squeeze my heart at his edgy tone.

"What do you mean? We've got nothing to do—"

"I know, but rumors are going around that you aren't really engaged to Lexi? You've been *pretending*?"

I don't know how to answer him, so I just nod. I can't even look the guy in the eye.

"How?" Roger sounds stunned.

This. This is one thing we never imagined. Having to deal with questions from people who trust and respect us. "Because we're idiots?" I mutter under my breath. "We were both desperate. Lexi for a new job, and I to finish my TV series." I look up at Roger, but he now averts his gaze. "Roger."

"I thought you loved her." He says this as if nothing else matters. "Like I love Deshni. Now I see you're not the man I thought you were."

No. I'm not the man he thought I was. I swallow as I drag my hands through my hair. "Let's just get through this morning, okay? We can talk after the dives. It's all more complicated than that."

"Is it?" Roger's frank stare only magnifies the truth in those two words.

I'm punched straight in the chest. It isn't complicated at all, is it? *I do love her.* I love Lexi like Roger loves Deshni. I'm still reeling from that truth when Nathan Beaumont walks into the dive center, ripping me out of my haze.

"Care if I join you?" he asks.

Every brain cell seems to malfunction at once, but I have to get a grip. Filming my TV series won't be in the cards anymore, but that's not the primary reason I'm here. Not now, anyway. I need to keep it together, not only for the guests' safety, but for Roger's future too.

"Sir." Roger nods at Nathan. "I'll see you on the dinghy." He files out with the last of the guests, leaving me with the man on whom my whole future suddenly hinges.

"No problem. You're qualified?" I know the answer. Nathan, after all, interviewed me.

"I'm a dive master," he says. "I've been coming to Ne'emba for more than thirty years. Started with snorkeling as a kid and got qualified as a dive master when I turned eighteen. This place is magic."

"I know." Here's someone who gets it, and I hate that I wasn't open about my real work off the bat with this guy. "Do you need help—"

"I'm good. Just the oxygen tanks." Nathan walks toward the wetsuits.

I prep his scuba gear while he suits up. The air around us is charged with a thousand unsaid things. Might as well put a dent in them now and advocate for Roger's future. "I've been teaching Roger to dive," I tell him as I connect the regulator to the oxygen tank. "He's qualified for Open Water Two now and is logging hours toward master diver."

"I never knew he was interested."

Neither of us has to play dumb here. "We both know you need a local to run the show. You good to go?"

"Yes." Nathan heaves his scuba kit over his shoulders as I gather my camera and fins. "That's a pretty impressive setup you have there," he says as we head out. He's eyeing my underwater camera and lighting equipment. "Care to tell me more?"

It's time to put my cards on the table. "I have a deadline for television series I sold to a streaming service. I've been filming on the side since I arrived here," I confess. "I've been working on it for so long, but as karma has it, as soon as you have a deadline, things start going wrong. When this opportunity came up...well, Lexi and I thought we could kill two birds with one stone."

Nathan shoots me a look, but we've reached the dinghy. "I see," he says as he lifts his scuba gear into Roger's outstretched hands. "We'll discuss this later."

Roger is clearly on edge with Mike on the boat, and the guests I've gotten to know over the past few days are looking on, likely sensing the awkward tension between us. Yep. I've crashed straight into a dead end, but I need to get through these dives.

With Nathan's last-minute addition, Mike is taking up a seat we can't spare. It's cramped. "It's fine, Mike," Nathan says. "We're good."

Mike reads between the lines, gives me a curt nod, and jumps out of the boat. *Well, thank fuck for that.* The last thing I need is Jem's husband's eyes on me the whole morning as he wonders where I hid the cocaine.

I settle in next to Nathan, and we hit the waves. Luckily the site for our first dive isn't too far from the island. It's when the floatplane flies overhead that the tense grip in my stomach twists. "You're staying a few days?" I ask Nathan over the noise of the dinghy's engine. To my knowledge, no new guests are arriving today, and the pilot is probably heading home.

"That would be Lexi flying out," Nathan says.

My heart stalls. "Lexi? On the plane? Did you fire her?"

He shakes his head. "She wanted to go."

She's gone?

I'm winded, not wanting to believe Nathan, but the coil in my gut tells me it's true. We've reached the dive site, so there's no stopping the process now. I plunge in with my back to the water, letting the oxygen tank take the hit. I signal to Roger that I'm okay and wait for the guests to drop back. Once everybody is in the water and next to their diving buddies, I give the signal, and we descend.

It's quiet. Only the sounds of my breathing and the rhythmic rise of air bubbles to the surface intercept this strange silence I love so much. There are other noises, but they're subdued. I usually find this calming, and my body relaxes into this familiar world where I feel so at home, but today my heart is a jackhammer in my chest and my wetsuit feels too tight.

Nathan is my dive buddy, and as we descend, I try to focus on him. My mind is going into overdrive, and it's dangerous territory.

I wait for my training to kick in and shift my mind into the right gear, but everything in me refuses. All I can think of is

Lexi. *Of us.* How it felt to be with her. *Easy.* I could just be with her—no expectations, no judgment, just love.

Love.

She's gone. Fear rises in me, so strong that for a minute I need to concentrate on my breathing. As the emotion swells, I realize my love for her is like oxygen that's gotten stuck deep in the ocean. It's at last breaking free and surfacing, catching the light as it dances and balloons toward the sky and freedom.

And this feeling isn't new. I've loved her since forever, but we were trapped. Because of her age. Because of time. Because of *me*.

She's left me. At this thought, I can hardly breathe at all.

Beaumont shakes my arm. He signs with his hands, asking if I'm okay and holds out his spare regulator. I inhale deeply and exhale such a rush of air it curtains the space between us. When the air bubbles clear, my gaze connects with his. His eyes are wide with concern, but I nod and return his okay signal.

We're doing a drift dive and herding everybody together in the same general direction is important. The current isn't strong, but divers on the edges can lag and we could lose them. I turn around to watch and count the others. I need these dives done and everybody back at shore safely—myself included.

With steel determination, I force myself to focus on what I need to do. Then Nathan indicates my camera, asking that I show him how I film and take photos.

Between filming and keeping the dive going, forty minutes pass quickly, but nothing keeps my mind away from Lexi and the recurring thought that *this* is no longer what I want.

I want Lexi, and everything else can wait—maybe forever.

When we resurface after the dive, Roger helps the guests back onto the boat, one by one. As soon as everybody is settled in the dinghy, I clamber in and strip out of my wetsuit. "Since you're a dive master," I say to Nathan, "could you lead the next dive with Roger?"

I turn to Roger as his jaw goes slack. I lean closer to where he sits by the rudder. "With everything that happened this morning, my head isn't in the game. And this is your chance to prove yourself."

"Sure," Nathan says, his gaze jumping between me and Roger. "Where's the next dive?"

"The Pinnacle." It's a shallow and easy dive as you circle a coral mound a few times at different depths.

"That's fine," Nathan says with a nod.

I peel off the last of my wetsuit and hand it to Roger. "Your turn."

Roger says nothing, but strips to his swimsuit, and we scoot around and swap places. As soon as he's wrangled the wetsuit on, I set the GPS directions and steer the dinghy in the direction of the next site.

While everybody else dives, I have the open ocean and the waves slapping at the dinghy's side as white noise as I work through the mess in my head—and my life.

By the time the second dive is done and we're on the way back to Ne'emba, my mind's made up. It's amazing how easy it is to make decisions when there's only one thing you really care about—one *person* whose wants and needs you put way above your own.

The divers are tired and quiet on our way back. At full

speed, the dinghy is noisy and bouncing, and people cling to the side straps. As soon as we hit the shore, I jump out. "Roger, see to the guests. I need to go check—"

Nathan's eyes are on me, sizing me up. "Meet me and Roger for lunch," he says. "I'll help here, but we need to talk."

"Sure." So we're still going to bang heads today. I don't care. I sprint down the beach, take the shortcut through the guest area, and head straight to our cottage. I dig my fingers into my hair as I walk through the much-loved space. It's still a mess, and for once, nobody from housekeeping has been here.

None of Lexi's things are in the bathroom. I head to the walk-in closet, blinded by emotion at seeing her side empty. She's gone. Lexi has left for real. My chest tightens. My eyes find the piece of paper and the engagement ring left on top of it.

I pick it up, and the paper quivers in my hand as I read the lines. She loved her time here with me, but *we had a hard cut-off date from the start, and now we don't need to have that godawful awkward flight all the way home where we both try to get out of a sticky situation.*

Fuck. *Godawful awkward flight? Sticky situation?* Lexi's one-upped me, using my own age-old strategy of running away before things get too serious.

I lower the letter to the desk and pick up the ring. It looked so perfect on her hand, and I loved seeing it on her finger. I'd subconsciously claimed her as mine before I even understood what she meant to me.

The only reason Lexi ran is because she has no clue how I feel about her. She would never have gone if I'd told her I love her. And she has to love me too, because why else would she flee like this?

This isn't it. We're not done. No. We've just started. Only one thing is going to happen once I've dealt with Nathan Beaumont and set things straight with Roger: I'm going to get my girl.

I take a quick shower and make my way to the guest area. I spot Roger where he sits, clearly ill at ease, with Nathan at a table. They're having beers, and I signal a waiter to bring me one too. I give Roger a look as I sit down. *This is it, bud. Drinks with the big boss only comes around once in a lifetime.*

"How was the dive, Roger?" I ask.

"It went fine," he says, not looking me in the eye. "The coastguard and police have left. They found nothing."

"Of course they found nothing," I huff. "That was a messed-up situation. Jem jumped to conclusions."

Roger may have lost all respect for me, but I will negotiate to my last breath to get him the life he wants, the life he deserves with Deshni and their baby.

"So…" Nathan begins before I can say anything else. "We have a half-qualified dive-master-in-the-making and a rogue oceanographer trying to make a buck on the side."

I almost spit my beer out. "It's not about the money. It's never been about the money." Hell, if only he knew what a money-drain this project ended up being.

"No?" Nathan raises his eyebrows.

"This TV series is Tristan's love letter to the sea," Roger says with a frown. "Like me, he has salt water in his veins. When he says it isn't about the money, it isn't about the money."

Thank you, Roger. I can't believe the man is standing up for me.

Nathan smiles and raises his beer in salute. "Duly put in my place."

"And Tristan has taken time to teach me, which nobody else has," Roger elaborates.

An uninvited heat spreads over my cheeks. Must be too much sun from sitting on that boat for an hour.

"I see." Nathan turns to me. "For now, I can't let you film here, not without the legal paperwork in place. But even if we give this the green light, it could ruin Ne'emba Island's exclusivity. The last thing we've wanted, from the start, is for the island and the reefs to be overrun by careless tourists. Plus, if there's money involved, the proceeds—"

"I had sponsorships for most of the other parts we filmed," I cut in. "Nobody asked for proceeds. This is a nonprofit venture."

"And yet you must be gaining something from it," Nathan says. "Even if it's something personal."

I stall as my thoughts tumble over each other, falling flat. Yes. This is personal. It's always been personal. I'll gain my father's acknowledgement. His pride in me. His attention and time. His *love*. I've been working, waiting, *begging* for years for love from the one person who doesn't know or care to give it. That's wasted time I'm never getting back. "Honestly, the TV series is no longer important. I don't care if I finish it. What I do care about is Roger and his family. I will make sure he gets his qualifications, even if I have to fly him over to Miami to do it." I take a deep breath and stand. "Nathan," I say as I hold out my hand to him. "It's been a privilege."

Nathan stands too, and we shake. He chuckles drily as he cocks his brow, but he says nothing. It riles me up that this man can read between all our lines. Lines Lexi and I had written but didn't even grasp the full meaning of until someone like him spelled it out for us. I bet he knows I'm going to chase my fake fiancée. "Walk with me, Roger. You two can talk later."

"Excuse me for a moment, sir," Roger says to Nathan.

"Sure, but do come back, Roger. We've a lot to discuss."

For a minute, Roger and I walk in silence to the managers' cottage, and the stress seeps out of me. This is the beauty of making the right decision. "I need to get all my equipment together and pack. I'm going to back up my phone and leave it for you. I'll see how I can get a laptop to you so you can start using it. As for my cameras…" I take a mental tally of what I have, what I deem replaceable, and what are the absolute essentials Roger won't be able to carry on without. "In fact, I can leave my laptop and my second camera with you as a kickstarter. And I've backed everything up on my external hard drives, so I don't need to have my laptop. I want you to keep taking pictures right along with diving."

"You can't do this," Roger says, his eyes wide. "You're crazy!"

"Sure I can." Maybe I am a bit crazy, or maybe I've finally come to my senses. I've found the perfect solution for my untapped trust fund. "You, *sir*, are the first to receive a *prestigious* scholarship. I'll set things up as soon as I have time."

Money can't buy you love, but it sure as shit can make things happen for other people.

Roger shakes his head, befuddled.

"This is me," I say as we reach the cottage. "Please can you check with Mike to see if he's available to take me to Pemba Island? I have to catch up with Lexi, stop being an idiot, and finally tell her how much I love her."

"For real?" Roger says, a smile in his voice.

"For real. And once I've caught up with her, I'm never letting her go."

Chapter Forty-Three

LEXI

I stare at the ceiling, listening to Mom getting ready for her day. She's an early riser, and even though I'm still exhausted, the jet lag is real. I've been lying awake for two hours already, replaying everything that happened my last morning on Ne'emba Island.

I haven't told Mom yet. When I arrived late yesterday afternoon, I was *done*. Flying from one outpost in the world to the next, changing flights four times, isn't something I would recommend.

"Lexi!" Mom had said when she opened the door. She ushered me into the apartment—as it was freaking snowing outside, which happens in Alaska—and gave me the longest hug. God knows I needed that hug, and when she wanted to pull away, I clung to her and burst into tears. When she said something about me and being in a pickle, I cried even harder.

"This sounds like more than a mere pickle," she'd finally added.

"I don't want to be called a pickle or be in one ever again," I'd sobbed between hiccups, and that was the end of it.

We didn't talk any more, but she'd made me sweet tea while I took a warm shower and then gave me some soft fleece pjs to sleep in. I don't have any winter clothing with me—I never planned a detour to Anchorage, but once I flew into Heathrow and memories of Tristan putting that ring on my finger hit me, I couldn't go back to Miami and Evan's place. Not with the pile of questions he'd ask and everything *Tristan* still in his house. And Tessa's in LA wasn't appealing either. I didn't want to go anywhere but home—and right now home is wherever Mom is.

When Mom passed me one of her menopause sleeping pills with instructions to *"just take half"* as it would *"help with the jet lag,"* I didn't protest. I was out by seven last night, but now…I can't avoid this reality any longer.

I get up, pull on one of the shawls Mom seems to accumulate during her travels, and head out to face the music.

Her two-bedroom apartment is open-concept, and as soon as I step into the living area, the scent of brewing coffee hits me.

Mom looks up from the kitchen counter. "Hey. You're feeling better?"

I nod and bite my lip. This is going to suck.

"Want some coffee?"

"Please." I scuffle over to the counter and settle on a barstool. "Sorry to descend on you like this."

Mom isn't exactly private, but I'd be stupid to think she doesn't have her own life here. For all I know, I could've knocked on her door while she had a friend over. A *boyfriend*. Not that I've ever met anybody. Not that I've ever asked. I mean, how do you dig into your Mom's love life without it being awkward, especially since she never says anything in the first place.

Mom gets busy with the coffee and also pops some bread in the toaster. She sets out a jar of Nutella. She knows me so well. And she's waiting, very patiently, for me to open up.

I take a deep breath and huff it out on a long *Soooo...* "Ne'emba Island and Beaumont didn't work out."

"Ah, sweetie..." Mom shakes her head. "Why?"

"I quit." *I might have to put that in writing at some point...*

"Why?"

I bite the bullet. "Because I lied about being engaged to get the job, and I couldn't do that anymore."

"Engaged?" Her eyes are wide as she puts the coffee pot back on its stand. "To whom?"

I'm going to have to explain everything from the start, but Mom will need to fill in the gaps. I plan to leave many. "Tristan went with me with Ne'emba Island. The jobs were for a couple, so we faked an engagement to get the gig. He needed somewhere fabulous to finish his TV series, and I...I wanted to get out of the country and away from this whole Mia Reed mess..." I trail off, remembering I have an NDA.

"By the Mia Reed mess you mean the video."

"You know about that?" I ask, not encouraged by the look on Mom's face.

"Evan filled me in once I made the connection between those trending videos and you. I'm your mom, Lexi; I'd know my daughter's face anywhere." She reaches over and pats me on the hand. "St Chalamet never deserved you."

"I couldn't tell you. I'm not supposed to talk about it at all."

"I know. But that's water under the bridge now. What's this thing with Tristan?"

God. She's going to drag it out of me. "I'm sorry. I should have told you over Christmas... Only I couldn't."

"Lexi, I don't think I understand."

Yep. She's using *that* tone. "I *lied*, Mom, to Beaumont during my interview. About being engaged to Tristan Martinelli in order to get the job. We went together to Ne'emba and, and, a-and..." I can't finish. I'm so choked up I can hardly breathe.

"Oh lordy-lord," Mom says as she circles the counter and puts her arm around my shoulders. "How could you lie about being engaged? To Tristan, of all people?"

"It's easier than you think," I say between sobs. "Especially when you're far from home and nobody knows you." Except that Jem felt something was off and started digging so deep she managed to find out about Dad... It hardly matters now. "But then the office assistant accused us of setting up a drug trafficking ring!"

"What?" Mom's arm drops, and she sinks down on the stool next to me. "Where's Tristan now?"

"Still on Ne'emba. I spoke to the resort owner, and he didn't buy into the drug-trafficking story, thank God, but I couldn't stay." The moment the police handcuffed Tristan hit too close to home, and that was the domino that toppled the rest. "I just hope they'll give Tristan a chance to finish what he's started."

"Oh my goodness, Lexi," Mom says. "What about you?"

I pull my sleeves over my palms and wipe my tears. "I don't know. Maybe Motel Sixty-Nine by the dive bar down the road is looking for a night manager?"

"Oh, honey." Mom's hand draws slow, soothing circles on my back. "This too shall pass."

Yes. Mia Reed will grow old and ugly. Deep fake will rule the internet as AI takes over. This work crisis will fade. I will find something else. Somewhere. Somehow. At least this Ne'emba Island disaster struck while I'm still financially supported by St Chalamet. Even if I could go back and work at Beaumont Hotels, I'm not sure I could look Nathan Beaumont in the eye. And I'm certainly not interested in groveling. But the world is big and wide, and I might have to take a pay cut, but I'll find a job eventually. Summer and tourist season are coming, and I haven't tried Alaska yet.

The thing that shall *not* pass—not today, not tomorrow, probably *never*—is the feelings I have for Tristan. At the thought, a heaving sob rips through me, and Mom hugs me close.

"What really happened, sweetheart?" she asks softly. "With Tristan?"

"I was so stupid. I-I…" The words are stuck.

"As an engaged couple, you had to share a place, didn't you?" she asks. "A room or a studio or something?"

A cottage. The most romantic place in the world. "A bed! There were mosquitoes, and we had to be behind the net as they feasted at night, so we ended up…"

"Sleeping together?" Mom asks. "But not in a platonic way."

"Mm-hmm." There. The truth is out. My face is still pressed to my palms and my cheeks burn.

"You always loved Tristan," Mom says softly. "And if ever there was a boy who needed love, it was him." She shifts in her chair, and it scrapes over the floor. "Sometimes the timing isn't right, sweetheart. And sometimes timing is everything."

"What do you mean?"

"Time will tell." Mom stands, and I look up at her. A faint smile plays on her lips. "Sometimes things happen for a reason."

No more wisdom, please. "Mom, I lied, and look where it got me."

"Hmm..." She moves to the other side of the counter and pushes the toaster's lever down. "Life isn't black and white, Lexi. It's a shape-shifting splash of all the colors, showing you only what you want to see in the moment." She leans over with her arms on the counter. "Maybe now you'll understand why Dad did what he did. Desperation makes people do weird things—wrong things. I don't agree with what you did, or say your problems justified your actions in any way, but if you can find it in yourself to forgive Dad after all these years, it will be great. I've forgiven him, and..." She clears her throat, and that little smile is back. "We've been seeing each other."

Wait. *"What?"*

Mom laughs. "We started by chatting online. We're sort of dating, and he was here for two weeks while you were at Ne'emba."

Holy Mother of God and all the saints in a row. My pulse races. My mouth is dry. This is coming from left field, and nobody peeped a word to me. "How? Why?"

"When you know, you know. I've always loved Dad, and he's done his time. He's sorted himself out with a new business, restoring furniture. He's doing great, and well...life is for living. I don't want to grow old with anybody else."

"Does Evan know?"

"We've been speaking about it." Mom drops her gaze for a second and hitches her shoulders. "Evan doesn't have the baggage you have. It helps that he was older when that whole mess happened. I didn't want to say anything... Not until—" She breaks off and looks up at me. "Not until the timing was right."

I might have lost the love of my life, but Mom reconnecting with hers sends joy through my veins. I can see she's happy, truly happy—for the first time in a very long time. "I'm so glad for you. For you both."

"Thank you." The toast pops, and she puts it on a plate for me. "What are your plans for today?"

Cry all the tears I have? Mope. Sleep. Scroll my phone watching videos featuring me as the face of mock horror and then sink into the Earth's core? "I don't know. Try not make stupid, hasty decisions?"

Mom chuckles. "Good plan. You're welcome to stay for as long as you like, but know that I'm moving back south over the summer."

So much for my Alaska plans. Maybe it's for the better. "These winters getting to you?" I tease.

"They're killing me." She pours two coffees as I spread Nutella over my hot toast. Comfort food at its best. "I'm looking for a position back in New Orleans and will spend spring break over there."

"You are?" *With Dad.* My heart expands at the thought. Mom's right. Forgive and forget. It's time, and who am I to hold a grudge? With what I've done, I'm a chip off the old block. "Can I come with and see him?"

"Of course, sweetheart. He'd love nothing more in the world, and neither would I." She raises her coffee cup in toast. "It's time for us to go home."

Chapter Forty-Four

TRISTAN

The taxi pulls up to Evan's house. It's just like that day months ago now when I came to Miami and Lexi was here. I pull in a deep, cleansing breath of relief. Just through that door and I'll see her again. The thought is enough to propel me out of the taxi and up to Evan's house.

I'm exhausted but traveling for forty-eight hours straight without a phone or a laptop does things to you. I had a lot of time to think, and I had to arrange my thoughts one way or another, as I couldn't shop for a new phone or laptop while traveling. Every airport duty-free has endless booze and jewelry, but if you want to shop electronics, you're mad. I ended up asking for paper at the Heathrow business lounge. That was a novel experience on both ends, but the receptionist finally handed me some sheets of printer paper.

At least I could write, and the process was eye-opening. Honestly, it was cathartic.

I ring the doorbell and start digging for the house key, but I can't find it. The taxi driver carries the rest of my luggage to the door, and I hand him a tip with a quiet thanks.

My heart sinks. What if nobody's here? It's nine in the morning on a Saturday. Surely they'd be here? I finally get hold of the house key, squashed in my carry-on bag's side pocket.

The door jerks open. Evan blinks, confused, giving me a split second to take him in—boxer shorts, hair disheveled, and a wonky line of hickeys leading the eyes south.

"Bro!" Evan's eyes go wide. "What the hell? What're you doing here?"

"Lexi's here?" I've been worried about her, but now the anxiety fists my stomach with a nasty twist.

"No." Evan shakes his head as he steps closer to look outside. "She's supposed to be with you."

"She left Ne'emba four days ago."

"What the actual…? Dude! Have you lost my sister?" Evan's tone rises with a flash of panic. "What do you mean she's left Ne'emba?" He steps aside to let me in and rakes his hands through his hair, his eyes wild.

"Things went down, man, and she left." My hands curl into fists. "I don't have a phone, and—"

"Jesus Christ. You don't have a fucking phone? You got mugged or what?"

I shake my head. "No, someone else needed it more."

"Fuck me." He rushes away and up the stairs.

Yep. I'm an idiot, that's what I am. When I was so generous with Roger before I left, I didn't think very far. My head was too full of *Lexi* and getting back to her. I didn't for one moment consider she wouldn't make it home. Jem confirmed that she'd booked her a plane ticket straight through to Miami with all the easiest flight connections. Lexi was hopping from one airport to the next. But now...

I drag my things into the house and close the door. Evan comes down the stairs, his face flushed and his phone glued to his ear. "Fuck. Her phone is off." He glares at me. "I'm going to have to phone my mom. Tristan, if something happened to Lexi, it will kill her."

And *he* will kill *me*.

"Maybe she went to Anchorage?" I'm praying so hard now, the words shake my core. Where else could she be? In LA with her old roommate?

"I'm sending Mom a message. Testing the fucking waters. She may actually be up already. You're dead fucking meat."

I walk to the living room and collapse onto the sofa, broken. How can I lose her when I haven't even told her I love her yet?

Evan sends his message and paces the room while I stare at him, nuked with worry. After a few minutes his phone pings, and as he reads, he physically deflates. "She's in Anchorage. Has been there for two days already. What the fuck, dude? And why the hell does nobody let me know!"

Our gazes clash across the room, and I drop back into the sofa as tears sprout behind my eyes, my throat squeezing tight. I put my hands over my face. *God.* I never want to feel this anxiety again. The relief is slow to seep into my muscles—this was too real, too close a call, too *everything*.

"Things didn't pan out as we expected," I begin, dragging my hands down my face. I'm so tired, but I owe Evan an explanation.

By the time I'm done reliving the whole clusterfuck that was our last day on Ne'emba Island, we've had coffee, and now he's pouring me a stiff whiskey. It's a bit early in the day, but who the hell cares. My body isn't on any clock right now.

"But that's not the whole story, is it?" Evan hands me the tumbler with raised eyebrows.

There's no being skittish about it now—not after he prodded into details that probably gave everything away. "I'm a goner, Ev. I'm in love with her. I've never thought—knew or imagined... Godammit, Evan, she's the only thing I can think of, and it aches, it *aches* not to be with her."

"Excellent," he says, clinking his glass with mine. "Things panned out exactly as I expected."

Jesus Christ. "You're a real asshole sometimes, you know that?" But I'm not complaining.

"You can thank me later. Let me book you a flight to Anchorage."

Right on cue, something scrapes upstairs, and I look up to the ceiling. "Entertaining, are you?" Evan is the most private guy I've ever known. He likes his business to be his business only.

"If you want to call it that," he says with smirk. He's back on his phone, typing away. "You're good to keep going? You made it all the way from Ne'emba to here. Why stop now?"

"Yep. I'm good to go. I need... I just need to get to her. You get it?" I want to laugh now that the adrenaline spike is fading.

"Nope. I don't." He doesn't look up, confirming that whatever is going on upstairs is a hook-up. "Anyway. Via Denver in two hours? Shortest layover, and with the four-hour time difference, hell, you might be able to tuck her in tonight."

The notion is so sweet, but things may not be smooth sailing. Still, I smile. "Best get cracking."

"I'll drive you."

"No need to—"

"She'll be here when I get back." With that, he disappears up the stairs again.

I take a blitz shower and toss some clothes into a carry-on bag. I grab my warmest jacket, and by the time I'm done, Evan is showered too and ready to go.

"Thanks, bro," I say as we get into his car. "I owe you."

"Yep. Big time."

I laugh. "Mind if I check my email on your phone while we drive?"

"Sure. You're such a fucking Neanderthal." Evan hands me his phone. "Jeez, no phone for how many days now?"

"Four and counting. I'll sort it out in Anchorage. It's weird. I got weaned while on Ne'emba. You should try it."

"Uh…nope. Thanks."

I open the internet and log on to my email, scrolling for anything important. Nothing from Lexi. More than one email from my agent, Nick Mallet. He's going to be pissed. Too bad, so sad.

Then there's an email from Dad. I open it and scan. Bottom line, it will take time, probably months, but after initial contact with St Chalamet, the hotel group has agreed to settle out of court. At issue is the amount they'll pay Mia Reed, and that's something the lawyers will negotiate. Reed would like to sue them for every last bedsheet, but this case is never going to see the light of day if St Chalamet has a say in it.

I lean back with a groan and close my eyes. *Idiots*. The truth will come out, sooner or later. It's sitting there like a time bomb, except nobody knows when it's going to explode. Paying Mia Reed won't stop anything, but St Chalamet will probably settle as soon as possible, hoping it will all go away.

"All good?" Evan asks.

"Mostly." I look over at him. "What's your take on Lexi's part in that video that's trending?"

"Old news already." Evan shrugs. "I've seen fewer of those popping up, and in six months it will be buried under all the new crap that keeps being piled on."

"Yeah. Probably."

And until then, until *forever*, I plan to help her not give a damn and just live her life. And I'll love her all the way.

Chapter Forty-Five

LEXI

Today was better. Totally.
Probably.
Nope. Who the hell am I trying to fool? The only thing that made today better was that Mom wasn't at work and we went to shop for my own pjs and other essentials. I had a long call with Tessa and basically bawled my eyes out. Nothing helped. Not even Tessa's dry remark *that for once I'm the one doing the ditching.* Now I'm in freshly washed and still-warm-from-the-dryer fleece pjs and pulling on new sleeping socks too. Everything is soft and cuddly, but nothing is going to distract me from my broken heart.

I choke down my tears. Day five of being torn from Tristan, and there hasn't even been an email from him. *Nothing.* My heart isn't just broken, it's splintered into a thousand pieces.

I'm a mess. I'm not good company and want to stay in bed, but Mom will only allow me to wallow so much. She is, after all, one to turn that frown upside down and has already popped the popcorn for some Hallmark movie we're going to watch. As if I needed romance right now. My sleeping cycle is still so messed up, but better to watch some mind-numbing TV than doomscroll my phone for hours.

As I finally scrape my scattered courage together to emerge from the bedroom, the doorbell rings. Mom didn't say anything about ordering takeout, but I'll take it. I'm in a stuff-my-face mood, and that isn't going away anytime soon either.

I wipe my eyes, and as I walk into the living room, Mom calls, "I'll get it."

She opens the front door, and snow drifts into the doorway. On cue, a laser of cold slices through the apartment. The weather here is a bad motherfucker and not doing anything for my state of mind.

"Perfect timing," Mom says. A man's tall frame fills the door, his face obscured by a fur-trimmed hoodie. Mom wraps her arms around him in a hug, and my heart falters. For a long second, my mind plays with me, making me think it's Dad. He's here... Of course it's Dad—who else would Mom hug so close?

But then he pushes the hoodie back, and his gaze meets mine over the length of the room. My pulse falters, and my stomach drops. "Tristan?" I mutter, convinced this is an optical illusion.

Mom steps away to let him in.

"Babes."

Time stands still. I want to tell him to not call me that, but in the same breath I want to tell him how much I missed hearing him call me that. Beyond it all, I want to touch him and make sure he's real. That Tristan Martinelli is actually standing in the doorway of Mom's small apartment, snow dusting his broad shoulders.

"Come inside," Mom says as she reaches for her coat and scarf. "I'm going for a drink at Elsie and Joe's." She turns to me with a wink and a sly smile. Heat and chills somehow manage to spread over my skin at the same time. "See, sweetheart? It's all about timing."

With that, she's out the door, and Tristan closes it behind her. He drops his bag and stares at me as he shrugs off his thick jacket and toes off his shoes. He's not ready for this weather either.

"What?" I say, folding my arms over my chest as he hangs his jacket on one of the hooks on the wall. "Why are you here?"

"I—" He takes a step closer but falters. "Lexi, I—" He breaks off again and drags his fingers through his hair, streaking the snowflakes through. "Babes—"

"What happened? Did Beaumont fire you?"

"No. I left." He swallows hard, and I blink. His fingers are trembling.

"Left? How did you just leave? What about your project? Your deadline?"

Tristan shrugs. "It can wait. You forgot a few things on Ne'emba Island, and it was important that I brought them to you in person, if you know what I mean." He licks his bottom lip, trying to disguise the smile that makes my heart go weak. "I brought the charger too."

I choke on a laugh as I roll my eyes, heat invading my face. "You shouldn't have." I wish I had it in me to run up and jump him, forcing him to catch me as I hug him with all my life, but I'm aflutter with fear and hope and a desperation I never knew existed. All I manage is a measly step in his direction. "I left it for you as a reminder of…fun times."

"Lexi—" he starts again as he takes another step closer.

Then he chuckles drily when I remain in my spot. "Not going to make this easy, are you?"

"I don't understand. What is there to make easy? Ne'emba was a mistake and a fuckup, to say the least."

"Don't say that." He shoves a hand into his jeans pocket and pulls out a clunky fold of white paper. "I also knew I was going to mess this up, so..." He looks down and then meets my gaze, a flush on his cheeks. "I wrote you a letter."

"A letter? Why on Earth would you do that?" I eye the paper he's carefully unfolding, my pulse going wild as I inch forward.

"Because I've never done this before, and I don't want to mess it up." Something slips from the paper's fold, and he catches it in his palm, out of view.

A long beat of silence hangs in the air. "Doesn't look like you planned to mail it, now did you?"

Tristan fiddles with the paper with those fingers, those perfect, manly fingers that know just how to touch me. "No. They didn't have envelopes at Heathrow Terminal Five. I opted for hand delivery."

My heart skips a beat. *Heathrow Terminal Five, where all this started.* "I see."

He takes a few more steps and closes the gap between us, forcing me to look up at him. "Here. Read it, please."

I'm too scared to unwrap my arms from my body. This grip I have on myself is the only thing keeping me standing. "No... Since you're here, *you* read it."

"Don't let me mess this up, Lexi. I don't plan to ever do this again."

"Go break a leg then." If he wants to apologize for

everything that happened, I won't stop him, but I was the fool to rush in.

"Okay, this is the rough draft," he says softly. "I don't think I can do more than a rough draft...with my handwriting and all."

"Good thing you're reading it," I tell him as I gauge the unruly pen scribbles that lean askew on the page. "I don't want to misread here."

"Yep." He clears his throat. "Dear Lexi."

"An auspicious start," I tease, nodding encouragement.

He smiles, his gaze shy, and I want to hug him so hard, it almost consumes me. "Okay, shush now. Otherwise I'm going to chicken out."

"Okay. Please don't chicken out." I suck in my lip and dig my nails into my ribs, trying to stay calm. Something is up, and Tristan has flown all this way. That says something, doesn't it?

"Dear Lexi, Growing up I didn't have the best example of relationships, of love or how any of this works," he reads. "Flying here from Ne'emba, I had a lot of time to dig through everything going on in my mind, and I've realized that—that I'm scared." He pauses. "I'm scared that I'm going to turn out like my dad: flippant, dismissive, and emotionally unavailable. I'm scared that eventually I'll hurt you." He takes a deep breath. "The last thing I want to do is hurt anybody, least of all you." He meets my gaze, and his eyes are shining with tears. "And then I realized I was already hurting you, like I hurt you five years ago, by not being truthful with you in the moments where the truth matters the most." He lowers the page but keeps talking, even as his voice breaks. "And this isn't the man I want to be. When I told you *you* weren't ready, I was only lying to protect myself. *I* wasn't ready. And by not being truthful, I'm more like him than I ever care to be. So here's the truth. The feelings I've always had for you have changed. They've evolved so much that I can no longer deny that I'm in love with you, that I *love* you, that I love you so much it hurts when I'm not with you. All I can think about is you. I need you with me. I need you to be happy and cared for, for me to be happy." He swallows hard and wipes roughly at his face. "To be one hundred percent clear," he says as he tilts my chin up with a fingertip, "you're the only person I want to be with, for better or worse, for richer or for poorer, in sickness and in health. I want to promise to love and cherish you, forever."

Tears run down my cheeks, and I close my eyes as his thumb brushes them away.

Tristan has written a love letter—to *me*.

"So you see, angel, when at Heathrow I bought this ring and said I was the last man to ever put a ring on a woman's finger, what I should have said is this: This beautiful hand, this perfect finger is the *only* finger I ever want to put a ring on." He turns his hand palm up, and there rests the airport Tiffany. "Can we try again, and this time make it real?"

I'm sobbing now, wondering how I can cry so much when I'm sad, and cry just as much when I'm happy.

"Say something, Lexi," he whispers. "Anything."

My throat is too tight. My heart is beating too fast as I sniff and look at the ring. "I missed it."

He lifts my hand to his mouth, kisses the heel of my palm, and slips the engagement ring back on. It slides on without a hitch. In this moment, it's as if the whole world rights, and there can never be any more wrong.

Tristan doesn't let go of my hand, and I squeeze his fingers.

"I know the people who were supposed to love you the most also hurt you the most, Tris, but you don't have to make it so hard for the rest of us to love you."

"Yes." His expression tells me I've basically summed it all up. "Please, Lexi. I don't know how else—"

"I love you, Tristan Martinelli. Always have." I fling my arms around his neck, sending his letter flying, and as if he senses everything I need, he cups my butt and lifts me so I can wrap my legs around his hips. "I missed you so much. What took you so long?"

His chest heaves and shudders against mine, and we draw in shaky, emotional breaths as we cling to each other. I bury my face in the warmth of his neck, inhaling his scent, still thinking I've slipped into a heavenly dream.

"Ne'emba Island is very far away," he informs me.

I laugh. "It is."

He walks us to the sofa, and I slide down, but as soon as he sits, he pulls me to his lap to straddle him. "And then I thought you went to Miami, so I made a little detour and got yelled at by Evan, who probably still wants my blood."

"Oh hell."

"Hell indeed," he whispers as he pulls me closer. Our lips aren't even an inch apart. "But this...this is heaven." He kisses me softly, and I sink into him—the warmth of his embrace, of his heart and soul. He pulls away and brushes his thumb over my lips. "What say you, my angel?" His gaze searches mine. "Please say yes."

"Yes, babes," I say, smoothing my hand up his chest. "It's always been yes."

Epilogue

TRISTAN

Lexi and I are in Miami. After spending a couple of days with Anita, we headed back. For now, we're staying with Evan, but as soon as we've figured life out, we'll get our own place. Evan had to travel for work this week, so we are blissfully by ourselves.

And it is bliss. I watch as Lexi putters around the kitchen, making breakfast. She stifles a yawn, and when she catches me staring at her, she blushes. Babes might not be getting enough sleep, but she doesn't seem to mind.

"You know, if you keep on looking at me like that, nothing else is going to happen today," she says, offering me a mug of coffee.

"And what's the problem with that?" We're both still a bit jet-lagged, and having an outrageous amount of sex is probably not helping in that department. My gaze dips to her cleavage as she leans on the counter with her elbows. Her blue silk cami strap slides from her shoulder, and I bet she made that happen on purpose.

Lexi straightens and gathers the strap back to her shoulder with a smirk. "Nothing's wrong with that." She turns to the fridge, giving me the perfect view of her sweet ass in those little shorts.

I grin into my mug as I pull my new laptop closer. One thing I can't put off anymore is the email to my agent. I don't know how he's going to get us out of the contract with the streaming service, but that's his problem. I've got a scholarship program to set up, and I need to get back in contact with Roger. Plus, I want to dig into Miami University's programs to see if Roger can sign up for online courses.

I open my inbox and look through the list of new emails. My gaze stops on one from Nathan Beaumont. The subject line reads: *It was fun, but Ne'emba needs you back.*

My hand hovers, my fingers suddenly quivering as I hesitate. Finally I double click, my heart in my throat.

> Tristan,
>
> I hope you managed to resolve your family issues during your personal leave. As much as I've enjoyed managing the dive center, I have a corporate job I need to get back to. You haven't officially resigned, so my expectation is that you will be back, and soon.
>
> We also never discussed your project. Roger showed me a completed episode he found on your laptop. I'm open to hearing how you'd like to continue your filming at Ne'emba. Beaumont can sponsor part of this project, provided we get the right exposure in the final product. Let's discuss.
>
> Roger needs to complete his training, and we've been

talking about bringing in some other recruits. I'd like your advice on an exchange program with students from Rosenstiel to see how we can enhance the guest experience here at Ne'emba, with ongoing research on the reefs etc.

Jem and Mike will be leaving for training in France and the UK as soon as we have you back on board. We'll be doing a staff restructure here going forward in June when the lodge reopens after the rainy season. I'll be emailing Lexi separately, as she'll be needed here as well.

Let's set up a call to discuss.

Nathan Beaumont

I'm going to fall off my chair. "Babes."

"What?" Lexi turns back to me, egg carton in hand.

"You're not going to believe this."

"Lately I'm ready to believe anything. I mean, look at us, setting up a drug smug—"

"They want us back," I interrupt, not able to keep this news to myself for a second longer. "Nathan Beaumont's emailed me. He wants us to go back to Ne'emba—"

"You can't be serious." Lexi puts the eggs down as she circles the kitchen island to come to my side.

As soon as she's within arm's reach, I pull her close. "It's here, in black and white." I point with my free hand to my laptop screen as I brush her warm, soft skin with my thumb. "Pinch me, because this isn't real."

Lexi sags against me as she leans in to read the email again...and again. "This must be a scam," she says. "Surely nobody—*surely*..."

"Check your email," I say, squeezing her hip. Her skin has

sprouted a carpet of goosebumps. My heart is beating all over the place.

Lexi steps away from my embrace and heads to our room. I stand and pace, rubbing my face with my hands, adrenaline spiking my blood. I can't believe this either. She comes back seconds later with her phone. She's not been on it much lately, what with us spending so much quality time together. The time at Ne'emba weaned her too. Hell, I'd go back to someplace similar just to be so disconnected again.

She sinks down on the sofa and swipes at her phone. I walk over and slump down next to her, watching her face.

"Oh my God. Nathan emailed me too." She glances up at me. *"Lexi,"* she reads, *"'I hope you managed to resolve your family issues during your personal leave.'"*

"He just copied that line from my mail."

"He sure did," she says with a chuckle. *"'Jem and I have been talking, and she'd like to do some managerial training at our head office in Paris and at our hotels in London. Mike will join her, and although we can source staff to manage the activities at Ne'emba, finding an excellent and passionate resort manager, who has fresh ideas and who has worked at Ne'emba and knows the drill, is hard.'"*

Lexi lowers her phone. Her voice cracked a little on those last words.

"Babes?" *Oof.* She's got tears in her eyes. "Hey, hey... babes... That's *you*. Excellent and passionate. Fresh ideas. Knows the drill." I kiss her on the forehead and then her temple and lower, catching her tears.

"Why must he be so freaking nice?" she murmurs as she turns in to my arms. I hug her close.

Here at last is someone from the industry who gives Lexi

what she wants and needs to hear. "Nathan's one of the good ones. You called it first."

Now she's laughing in my neck, and God help me, this woman. She's my everything. "Come on, read on. That wasn't all of it."

"No, it wasn't." She sits straight again and reads from her phone screen. "'*As we haven't received your resignation*'—God, I didn't officially resign, I just thought it was a given—'*I'm assuming you'll be back once you've had time to recover from recent events, which include being falsely accused of drug trafficking. My sincerest apologies for that. We hope you'll reconsider and return to Ne'emba. We, the Beaumont team, would love to have you (as soon as possible, preferably with Tristan in tow). Let's schedule a call to discuss. Nathan.*'"

Lexi tosses her phone on the sofa, and it skids over the edge to drop to the floor. She's on me in a second, straddling my lap. "What's happening?" she says, her eyes wide as she grips my shoulders and gives me a little shake. "Babes?" she says. "What is this crazy?" Her fingers run over my shoulders to caress my neck. She cups my face, and I have my hands on her ass, tugging her closer.

"I don't know. Left-field type of crazy stuff. It's been crazy from the start... Maybe they're just tapping into... I dunno? Our crazy?"

She kisses me, and when she pulls away, she whispers, "Imagine going there with a clear conscience, living and working as we want to, without anything hanging over us..."

No unresolved tension between us, no fake engagement...*no Jem*. I can't wait to watch my girl shine. "So, are we doing it?" I ask. I know what I want. I can only hope—

"Doing it?" she murmurs, her lips cruising down my neck. "Of course we're doing it."

I chuckle as I maneuver her onto her back, the sofa a very receptive surface for what we've been doing most recently.

"Of course we're doing it," I mumble as I run a string of kisses to her lips. "We're *doing it* right now, and afterwards, we'll schedule that call."

And just for the record? I plan to never stop doing this with her by my side.

Acknowledgments

This book was born out of so many small things—just like all my other books, to be honest. It only takes one little pebble in my shoe to spark a story idea. Somehow, it seems to make itself happen and I'm not always sure how it did when I look back on it. I spend a lot of time at my computer, staring blankly into space, and sometimes I have no idea where a story will go and then a character will make the decision for me. Those are really the best of times.

Trouble In Paradise had its first pebble moment years ago when I worked in the safari industry. The company I worked for owned an off-grid (at that point in time) island off the coast of Zanzibar. I've never been there but have stared at Mnemba Island's website many a time in longing. Then I moved to Tanzania for work, and it was even closer than before. Still totally unaffordable, but I learned how to dive while living on the east coast of Africa, and it was simply magical. Tristan's love for it "being so quiet down there" is a reason a lot of people love diving. It is a very introspective activity; just you, the fish, the scenery down there which is so different from everything we see on land. I'll always love the sea, but to be honest, I'm a fair-weather diver and have no ambition to go deep. I'm here for the pretty fish.

The second pebble is also rooted in my life before writing, from when I was working in the tourism industry. Off-grid places, or small lodges like this one, often only employ couples because of the isolated nature of the job. How much truth is there in my fabrications? Probably more than you can ever imagine.

The third little pebble is, of course, the romance writer in me, who had to go: what if you put two people together on an island, faking an engagement to get the job, and then ending up sharing accommodation just like in this book? As they say, the rest is history.

No work of fiction is written alone—yes, there are endless hours by yourself where you just chip away at the story, hoping something will take shape, but after the first draft there is a tribe of people who makes a book shine. I would like to thank Cecilia and Michael Gibbons, Merjane Schoueri, Jenny Hwang, Amanda Holly, Meg Chronis, and my sister Mathilda, who all helped shape this book. All my love and thanks to my husband Richard, who has been a pillar of support with every book I've written, and my kids, who are starting to ask, "When can I read your books, Mom?" Haha. Soon, but not too soon. And if you do, I don't want to know about it!

I'd like to thank Bonnie Macleod from One More Chapter who gave this book the green light, and Jennie Rothwell for all her and the One More Chapter team's hard work to make this book shine.

And then, lastly but always firstly, thank you to my lovely readers. I hope this book transported you to another place and gave you the escape you needed. *Trouble In Paradise* is the book I've wanted to write for a very long time. I hope you've enjoyed the journey just as much as I did.

The author and One More Chapter would like to thank everyone who contributed to the publication of this story…

Analytics
Imogen Wolstencroft

Audio
Fionnuala Barrett
Ciara Briggs

Contracts
Laura Amos
Inigo Vyvyan

Design
Lucy Bennett
Fiona Greenway
Liane Payne
Dean Russell

Digital Sales
Laura Daley
Lydia Grainge
Hannah Lismore

eCommerce
Laura Carpenter
Madeline ODonovan
Charlotte Stevens
Christina Storey
Jo Surman
Rachel Ward

Editorial
Rosie Best
Kara Daniel
Charlotte Ledger
Federica Leonardis
Jennie Rothwell
Tony Russell
Sofia Salazar Studer
Emily Thomas
Helen Williams

Harper360
Emily Gerbner
Ariana Juarez
Jean Marie Kelly
emma sullivan
Sophia Wilhelm

International Sales
Peter Borcsok
Ruth Burrow
Bethan Moore
Colleen Simpson

Inventory
Sarah Callaghan
Kirsty Norman

Marketing & Publicity
Chloe Cummings
Grace Edwards
Katie Sadler

Operations
Melissa Okusanya
Hannah Stamp

Production
Denis Manson
Simon Moore
Francesca Tuzzeo

Rights
Ashton Mucha
Alisah Saghir
Zoe Shine
Aisling Smyth
Lucy Vanderbilt

Trade Marketing
Ben Hurd
Eleanor Slater

The HarperCollins Distribution Team

The HarperCollins Finance & Royalties Team

The HarperCollins Legal Team

The HarperCollins Technology Team

UK Sales
Isabel Coburn
Jay Cochrane
Sabina Lewis
Holly Martin
Harriet Williams
Leah Woods

And every other essential link in the chain from delivery drivers to booksellers to librarians and beyond!

ONE MORE CHAPTER

One More Chapter is an award-winning global division of HarperCollins.

Subscribe to our newsletter to get our latest eBook deals and stay up to date with all our new releases!

<u>signup.harpercollins.co.uk/
join/signup-omc</u>

Meet the team at
<u>www.onemorechapter.com</u>

Follow us!

@onemorechapterhc

Do you write unputdownable fiction?
We love to hear from new voices.
Find out how to submit your novel at
<u>www.onemorechapter.com/submissions</u>